BallShark

Book One in the

BallShark™ Select Baseball Series

Randy Floyd

BallShark Books • **BALLSHARK** • BallShark, LLC.

Florida

For Baylee, Brock, and Maddox

It's all for you, and for my love of the greatest of games.

He niuhi ʻai holopapa o ka moku.

The niuhi shark that devours all on the island.

A powerful warrior. The niuhi shark was dreaded because of its ferociousness. It was believed that a chief or warrior who captured this vicious denizen of the deep would acquire something of its nature.

(Pukui: 841-91)

Part I

Prologue to Part I

Eleven-year-old boys don't tell stories.

Well, I guess that isn't really true. Lots of my friends tell stories, but they don't write any of them down. I think it's probably because nobody wants to take the time to do it, or maybe nobody knows how to do it. I'm not sure that I really know how to do it either, but I have a story. It's a good one, and it's definitely one that needed to be written down. So I'm going to try to tell it, and my dad is going to help me. Neither of us knows exactly how it's going to work out, but we're going to do it together, and it's usually fun when we do things together.

My name is Ryne and the story is about my baseball team, the Intimidators. We picked the name because we thought it made us sound tough, but I guess we all learned during the season that there is a difference between sounding tough and actually being tough. That's because of the one guy on our team who this story is really about.

His name is Mano.

Mano is from Hawai'i. It was a big mystery to all of us why Mano and his father came all the way from Hawai'i to Texas, but I'll get to that later. All that matters is that one day, Mano paddled onto the Intimidators like a surfer waiting to catch a great wave. Then he caught that wave, and took the rest of us up on top of it with him for the ride of our lives.

Yeah, my dad helped write that last part. He's going to start writing some of his part of the story now, too. But before he does, I just wanted to write one more thing. It's about the first time I saw Mano.

He was standing by the bleachers, all by himself. He had an old, dirty bat bag on his shoulder, and he was wearing his cap so low that you could barely see his eyes. He wasn't wearing baseball pants, just some board shorts and a neon yellow t-shirt that was ripped under both arms.

I remember thinking that he looked sort of poor and sloppy, and I hoped that he wasn't going to be on our team.

I'm ashamed to write that down, but I guess that's part of the deal when you write stories. You have to be honest, or you won't really be telling the whole story, even if you have to tell the bad stuff about yourself.

* * *

Ryne's Father, Shaun

My name is Shaun Dunston. I'm Ryne's father. I'm glad that Ryne told the truth about how he felt the first time he saw Mano. This may surprise him because my son probably thinks his father is a fair man, but the first time I saw Mano? Well, I didn't want him on the team, either.

It's embarrassing as a parent to admit that, especially now when I realize how completely wrong I was about Mano. It's a terrible thing to judge someone by the way they look, and from the way Mano dressed, I didn't think he looked like a baseball player should look. The simple truth is that I didn't want to give the young man a chance. None of the other parents did, either. The Intimidators' coaches and players felt the same way. We all did.

We were all wrong.

We were wrong before Mano ever stepped on the field, before he ever picked up his bat or put on his glove and proved that he was not only a one-of-a-kind baseball player, he was something much more than that. Maybe I should feel some comfort in knowing that everyone felt the same way about Mano, but I don't. Mano and his father were new to our town. I should have jumped down out of my seat on the bleachers, gone over to them and introduced myself, but I didn't. Instead, I just sat there in the stands and judged an eleven-year-old kid based on nothing more than the clothes he was wearing and the bag he was carrying. I remember the ripped neon yellow shirt and the ragged board shorts. I remember the old, dirty bat bag tucked tightly to his back. I also remember over-hearing his first conversation with Coach Ramirez from the bleachers behind home plate.

Mano stood near the on-deck circle, his head up, his fraying cap low, looking directly at Coach. The Intimidators were warming in the outfield, stretching their arms out, and getting ready for another hot, early summer practice. Coach Ramirez was already chomping on his gum like he was mad at it.

"Where do you play, son?" Ramirez asked him, his jaws grinding hard on his chew.

Mano spoke quietly, just loud enough for the parents in the stands to hear. "It doesn't matter, Coach. I'll play wherever you say."

It was the perfect response from a new player to his coach, but Coach Ramirez was accustomed to working with players who knew their positions well. A player who was willing to play any position? It probably meant he wasn't really good at any of them.

Ramirez grunted. "Alright. Drop your bag in the dugout over there, get your glove, and go warm up with the others." Mano headed to the dugout quickly, but not quickly enough for his new Coach. Ramirez added a sharp "Hustle!" and it startled Mano so that he stumbled a bit and nearly fell. Coach Ramirez wagged his head and you could almost see him thinking, "Great. He can't even run without almost falling down." Of course, I don't know if Coach was actually thinking that or not, but I was.

Like my son, I'm ashamed of the things I thought the first day the new boy from Hawai'i showed up at practice. I guess if there's one thing I've learned in life, it's that I'm wrong an awful lot.

And I was very, very wrong about Mano.

Ryne

It was our last practice before our first game of the summer season.

We were warming up our arms with some short throws when Mano came over to us. He just stood there with his glove on his left hand and a ball in his right hand. I guess he was waiting for someone to be polite and ask him to throw, but no one did. Finally, our shortstop Miggy glanced over at him.

"Who are you?" Miggy said, in a not very friendly voice.

Mano turned to him. His hat sat perfectly straight on his head and the brim was pulled really low, even with his eyebrows, so his eyes were hidden way back in the shadows of his cap. "My name is Mano," he said, kind of shyly.

I should point out that Miggy has always been sort of a hot dog. He's good, but he thinks the Texas Rangers should already be asking him to sign a contract. He throws really hard, is pretty fast, and can hit better than anybody on our team. Plus, his dad is Coach Ramirez.

"You wanna throw?" Miggy asked.

"Sure," Mano replied. Miggy waved him over to the end of the line next to me. Then he walked over next to my throwing partner, Jimmy

Styles, and held his glove up. "Bring it," he ordered, flipping his right hand impatiently.

Mano turned his shoulder and made a soft toss. Miggy caught it and lobbed it back, even softer. He rolled his eyes when Mano tossed him another easy one. He limped one back so gently that it barely made it to Mano's glove. After Mano made another simple warm-up throw, Miggy immediately changed the pace. He threw one about three-quarters speed. It wasn't too fast, but it seemed much faster because they were standing so close. The worst thing was that it went about four feet over Mano's head and deep into the outfield.

"Sorry 'bout that," Miggy snickered. As soon as Mano turned and headed after the ball, he started to laugh more openly. I guess I should also point out that in addition to being a hot dog, Miggy can also be a real jerk.

Mano brought the ball back. He was about thirty yards away when he lobbed it while on the run. The ball sailed through the air and landed perfectly in Miggy's glove. It wasn't hard, but it was on the money. Right then, I guess I should have known that Mano was a ballplayer.

Miggy didn't wait for Mano to return to his spot. Instead, he cut one loose right at him. It wasn't full speed, but it was close. Mano never slowed down. The ball was headed right at his chest. I sucked in my breath, but then Mano put up his glove. There was that great Pop! sound the ball makes whenever it finds good leather. Mano hugged his mitt to his chest until he returned to his spot. He stopped, made another full shoulder turn, and then casually tossed another throw to Miggy, this one with a little more behind it, but not much.

This time Miggy threw one back at him low and hard. It was a sloppy, two-bouncer, the kind that we might field in practice as part of a bad hop drill. In warm-ups however, it's the kind of throw that you just let go so it doesn't clip your shin.

Mano didn't let it go. Instead, he picked the ball easily off the grass on the second hop. His glove hand was fast and soft, and I think if

2

someone had slid a cup full of water across a table at him as fast as Miggy had thrown that ball, he would have caught it and brought it to his mouth without spilling a drop. He was that smooth.

He quickly passed the ball right back toward Miggy. Miggy was ticked. He angrily snatched the ball out of the air. Just as he turned his shoulder and prepared to release his best blazer, we all heard a familiar, loud bullhorn blast coming from the dugout.

"MIGUEL!!" Coach Ramirez yelled. "GET OVER HERE, NOW!"

Miggy dropped his missile in mid-throw, almost like he practiced it all the time. The ball slid out of his hand behind his back, but he still followed through as if he was throwing it as hard as he could. I think he was hoping to make Mano flinch. Mano didn't, though. Instead, he just stood there with his glove dangling at his side. He reached up and pulled his cap a little lower as Miggy turned and ran toward the dugout.

* * *

Sometimes, I get a queasy stomach before our games. I don't know why the feeling is called "butterflies." In my stomach, it feels more like a bunch of bats flapping crazily around in a dark cave.

That first Saturday of the summer season, I had a pretty bad case of the bats. In fact, they were flapping so hard in my stomach that I had to spend time sitting in one of the smelly port-o-lets just beyond the outfield fence before our game started. I was late to the batting cages and I missed being part of our normal pre-game hitting routine. I wasn't the only one who missed his turn, though. Mano missed out, too.

I saw him standing by the cages. He was looking for something and seemed worried. He kept walking back and forth, scanning the area around the cages. Our hitting coach, Coach Weaver, saw me and waved me over. "Hurry up, Ryne. It's game time. Jump in and I'll throw you a few." I dropped my bag, grabbed my helmet and bat, and stepped into the cage. I looked at Mano as he walked past and Coach Weaver called out to him. "Still can't find it?"

Mano looked up. He had his new Intimidators hat pulled down low, the brim even with his eyebrows. He didn't say anything. He just shook his head. That's when I realized what he was trying to find: his old, crummy bat bag.

Coach Weaver threw me about ten pitches and I took my cuts. Then I quickly pitched my bat into my bag and hustled toward the field. When I left, Mano was still wandering around the cages. I remember thinking that the nice thing to do would have been to help him, but it was game time, and I was already running late.

Our dugout was like a bee hive. Everyone was busy stowing away their new gear. Each of us had brand new, matching black and gold bat bags. Our new batting helmets for the season—black with gold trim—hung on pegs on the fence. Our bats were in a neat line in the bat rack. Most of them were brand new, too. I jumped in and added my stuff to the mix. When I looked up again, Mano had come over to join us. He was standing on the outside of the dugout. He had a new uniform like everyone else—black jersey with gold letters on top of white pants—but he still looked out of place.

Coach Weaver walked up to Coach Ramirez, who was standing next to me. He gave him a report on our time in the cage. Coach Weaver told him, "They looked good. I think they're ready."

Coach Ramirez nodded toward Mano. "What about the new kid?"

Coach Weaver sighed. "He didn't hit. He can't find his bat bag."

Coach Ramirez shook his head and snorted. "It doesn't matter. He's only practiced once so he's not going to play today, anyway."

It was finally game time and we were the home team. We grabbed our gloves and charged onto the field. I took my position at second base and fielded some grounders. Our first baseman, Brazos Walker, casually tossed me one and I scooped it and fired it back at his glove. Brazos has tons of hair that he tries to keep stuffed in his cap, but sometimes the hair wins. When it does, his hat pops off his head like one of those party favors with a string. When you pull the string, the end pops off and silly string shoots out. It's exactly the same thing with Brazos' cap.

Of course, Brazos' hat popped off just as I let go of my throw, and his silly string hair came shooting out all over the place. He bent over to grab it and when he did, the ball zoomed over his head and skipped under a section of fence. Coach Ramirez saw it immediately and pointed at me, and then the ball.

Go get it.

It was my overthrow (even though Brazos' stupid hair caused it) so according to Coach's rules, it was my responsibility to fetch it. I hustled through the gate in the fence and chased the ball as it ran away like a scared rabbit. It came to rest next to an equipment shed. I picked it up and turned to run back to the field.

When I did, I saw Mano's crummy, old bat bag. It was sticking out of a garbage barrel next to the shed.

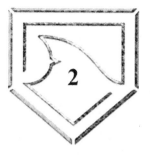

2

Shaun

Mano's father was a large, strong man. I'd been to Hawai'i once when I was a kid and I remembered the smooth, dark skin of the local Polynesians who are native Hawai'ians. Mano's father fit the image I carried in my memory perfectly. His skin was a deep caramel color and his teeth were impossibly white. He kept his black hair pulled straight back where it was gathered into a short, tight ponytail. He wore crisp white, short sleeve Aloha shirts over his khaki shorts and simple sandals. Around his thick neck was a thin, silver chain. A shark's tooth hung from it, pressed flat against the hollow of his dark neck. One look at him and suddenly all I could think of was luaus, coconut shells, fresh pineapple, surf boards, and gigantic waves crashing against empty beaches of perfect sand.

He came to the first game of the season and sat in the far top corner of the bleachers by himself. He spoke to no one, and no one spoke to him. I don't think any of the parents were purposefully being rude, but none of us took the first step to introduce ourselves, either. He was a physically intimidating man, and he seemed to be unaware of the world immediately surrounding him. He sat in that corner perfectly still, staring out into the distance as if he was searching for something way out beyond the horizon.

On the field, the Intimidators had settled into their fielding positions. They looked like a professional team in their snappy black and gold uniforms, nine pistons in a super charged engine that, once started, would roar through their opponents with speed, power, and precision. Then the game started, and the Intimidators engine didn't.

The Raiders, our opponents, were an aggressive team. Their very first batter of the season proved it by swinging at the very first pitch that Jimmy Styles threw. He made solid contact and hit a sharp grounder between short and third. Miggy made a nice backhand play to intercept it, and then turned and launched a wild throw that sailed over Brazos Walker's head at first base and into the Intimidators' dugout. The rocket crashed into a row of new water bottles and shiny batting helmets before exploding into a loud metallic pinball symphony as it rattled around inside the metal cage. Coach Ramirez and Coach Weaver scattered as if they were two soldiers under fire from the enemy. Coach Ramirez popped out of the dugout like a crazed jack-in-the-box and screamed, "ARE YOU KIDDING ME?!" He picked one of the batting helmets off the ground and slammed it furiously on the back of the bench. "KEEP THE STUPID BALL DOWN, MIGGY!"

At shortstop, Miggy threw an angry punch into his glove that would have knocked out a heavyweight boxer. It was not exactly the best start to a season.

The runner was awarded second on Miggy's overthrow. He stole third on the next pitch. On the pitch after that, he scored.

Jimmy Styles wound up and fired a missile of his own over our catcher's head. Chase Girardi, decked out in brilliant black and gold catcher's gear complete with a shiny, midnight black hockey-style mask, leaped high like a bullfrog from his crouch to snatch at it, but it ticked off the top of his glove and careened into the backstop. The leadoff hitter trotted home and it was already 1-0. That was only the beginning of a long, hot afternoon.

I don't remember looking over in the direction of Mano's father again until the fourth inning. It was blazing hot by then, over a hundred degrees. Mano was in the dugout. He was sitting at the far end of the bench, perfectly still, his back ramrod straight against the metal bench. He took turns, first focusing intently at the action on the field, then staring at the scoreboard down the right field line. The crooked numbers for the Raiders added up to 9. The zeros for the Intimidators added up to zero. It was 9-0 after four innings.

I noticed that between every pitch that was thrown to his teammates in the bottom of the fourth inning, Mano would turn his head in the direction of the scoreboard, almost as if he could will it to change, but the zeros remained stubbornly in place. It was then that I remembered his father. I turned and looked up at the furthermost corner of the bleachers. Apparently, the impressive looking Hawai'ian wasn't as strong as he looked. At least he wasn't strong enough to stay faithful to the Intimidators to the end of their embarrassing first game defeat.

Mano's father was already gone.

*   *   *

Ryne

In the top of the fifth inning, two bad things happened. I guess I should say two more bad things happened.

First, Wee Willie Keller, our tiny but super-fast center fielder, yacked about a gallon of Gatorade in the dugout, just as we were about to take the field. It went in as lemon-lime, and came out pretty much the same way, only a lot yellower and a lot faster. His mom came and sat beside him after Coach Weaver waved her over. She took one look at Wee Willie, whose face was tomato red, and decided he'd had enough of the heat for one day.

8

The second bad thing happened with one out and nobody on base. One of the Raiders' outfielders, a huge kid with feet like canoes (I know because he mashed my foot into second base after he hit a double in the second inning) came to the plate and hit a bullet down the third base line. Our third baseman, "Hootie" Gibson, (he has a nose kind of like an owl) stepped in front of it. The ball took three quick hops, but on the last one it jumped up just as Hootie bent to make the play. Hootie took it right on the end of his pointy beak.

There was a crunch, and then there was blood. Hootie dropped his glove and fell to the ground while Miggy ran over to rescue the ball. The umpire called time, and then the coaches ran to Hootie. One of our fans ran out of the stands with a towel. Then somebody from the concession stand ran onto the field with ice for Hootie's new and improved nose. While all of the adults ran around, we just sat on the hot ground and barbequed.

I remember thinking as I slowly went from kneeling to sitting in the dirt next to second base that our black uniforms sure may have looked cool in our team photo, but they didn't feel very cool on the field when it was a hundred degrees (and they were even less cool when we were getting drummed 9-zip.) In fact, I figured we probably looked less like "Intimidators" and more like a bunch of charred burgers on a grill.

Hootie was finally air lifted by the coaches off the field and under a tree next to the Raiders' dugout. I saw his parents over there, waiting anxiously to see if his little, pointy beak was just bent or if it was broken. Everybody clapped and cheered as the coaches carried him away. That's when I realized that Hootie's dramatic exit was going to leave us with a huge hole at third base.

As soon as he deposited Hootie under the tree with his parents, Coach Ramirez walked slowly back onto the field and went to the mound. He waved his hand toward left field. Curtis Weaver, Coach Weaver's son, jogged in. Coach Ramirez handed him the ball. He clapped Jimmy on the back and sent him to third. Then he turned back toward the outfield and waved our right fielder, Sammy Styles (Jimmy's younger brother) over to left. That left one more hole to fill.

Coach Ramirez walked slowly toward the dugout while Curtis started his warm-up tosses. That's when our bat boy, Alfonso, ran out of the dugout. He's Miggy's little brother and he doesn't play baseball. He plays soccer and it drives Coach Ramirez crazy. He's a smart kid, the smartest seven-year old on the planet in my opinion, even if he does play soccer.

Alfonso had two fresh water bottles. He stopped at first and gave one to Brazos and then he motored over to me so fast it was almost as if he was riding a scooter. "Here ya' go, Ryne," he chirped. He's a friendly kid, too.

"Thanks, Alfonso," I said. He started to run back to the dugout, but I stopped him. "Hey, what's going on over there?" I could see that Coach Ramirez and Coach Weaver were talking.

Alfonso leaned in close to me and whispered. "Dad's mad. I don't think he wants to put Mano in the game."

I couldn't believe it. "That makes no sense," I said. "We only have eight players." Coach Ramirez had already been forced to bring Jacob Dickey off the bench to play center when Wee Willie erupted like a volcano. Alfonso wiped sweat off his forehead with the back of his tiny hand. "He lost his bat bag and so he doesn't have his glove. Dad thinks he's not responsible."

Something twisted in my stomach. It felt worse than the bad case of the bats I'd had before the game. I looked over to the dugout. Coach Ramirez had his hands on his hips while Coach Weaver dug around in his coach's bag. He pulled out a glove.

Coach Ramirez flipped his hand at Mano and Mano instantly jumped off the bench. Coach Weaver handed the glove to Coach Ramirez. He held it folded between his huge arms, wrapping it against his chest in a bear hug. Mano stood in front of him with his head up, his hat still pulled as low it could go. Coach Ramirez is tall, probably six-four, and when you're standing in front of him and he begins to lecture you, it seems like he's eight-four. I wondered if that's how he looked to

Mano, because I could tell he was getting one heck of a lecture. Every time Coach Ramirez snapped his head down at Mano to make his point, the bats rolled in my stomach.

Coach Ramirez finally handed Mano the glove and he headed off in a trot to right field. Curtis had just finished his last warm-up throw and we were finally ready to play. Canoe-foot was at first and the Raiders' lead-off hitter was up again. This time, he didn't swing at the first pitch. He let it go, but only so he could get a close up look at what kind of heat Curtis could bring. He let the next two pass as well, for good reason. Curtis wasn't fully warm and both pitches were high, just beneath the top of his helmet. Then Curtis settled down and threw two good ones in a row. The count was full at three balls and two strikes. That's when everything around me suddenly seemed to change, going from full-speed to slow-motion.

Curtis threw the next pitch straight down the middle. The Raiders' lead-off batter was ready for it. He hit it in almost exactly the same place he hit the first pitch of the game, right between third and short, only this time he hit it a lot harder. In fact, he scorched it.

Jimmy was playing the line and dove at it, although it was kind of stupid to dive because the ball was already past him. It was *moving*. However, Coach Ramirez had positioned Miggy deeper in the grass, toward third base. He'd moved him to exactly the same place both times the Raiders' lead-off hitter came up after that first inning, when Miggy had launched the grounder he'd hit into our dugout. This time, the shift worked. Miggy shuffled to his right as the ball took two quick, smokin' hops and snapped his glove down. It landed right in the center of the pocket. Then things seemed to slow down even more.

I was already moving toward second base. I remember that I was pretty motivated because it was one of those times that I was positive we were going to get a double play, even though the lead-off hitter was Bugatti-fast. Miggy never even looked in my direction. Later, I figured what he really wanted was to get revenge for his error in the first inning. He wanted to shoot down the lead-off hitter with his big gun all by himself, instead of wiping him out with the double play. Of course, it was the wrong play.

The throw was a long one, about the longest throw a shortstop can ever make. Miggy can make it and a lot of times, he can even make it look easy. His arm whipped around, and the ball jumped out of his hand like a rocket that leaves a vapor trail. I watched as the ball headed toward Brazos. His eyes got big. Then he jumped, launching off the first base bag. When he did, his hat popped off again, and all of that silly string hair shot straight up in the air, almost like it was reaching for the ball, too. Even if he'd had extra extensions, it wouldn't have been enough. The ball was gone. It passed over Brazos, hit the top of the fence hard, and shot down the right field line toward the far corner of the outfield.

Canoe-foot was coming hard from first. He was thinking double play too, and so he'd already dropped into his slide, but when I kept going across the bag without the ball, he immediately popped back up. The third base coach waved at him crazily and he took off again. The Raiders' first base coach was going crazy, too. His right arm was whirling like a helicopter blade. Their Bugatti-fast leadoff hitter never slowed down. He hit the corner of the first base bag with a smooth turn and headed right for me. That's when things slowed down so much they seemed to stop, like that crazy, super slow-mo they have on ESPN.

I remember hearing my name. Someone was screaming it, but it sounded like it was coming from far way, like I was in a dream. So I turned my head and looked up.

The ball was coming at me.

It was instinct, nothing but pure instinct that made me put my glove up. Then there was a sound. It was a sound I've never heard before on a baseball field. It was like the air was splitting apart. The ball ripped into the webbing of my glove. I felt my wrist bend and my whole hand was yanked backward as the ball tried to take my glove with it and just keep going. But just as quickly, it seemed to let go of its bite, surprising me by leaving my glove and my hand still attached to my body.

The Bugatti-fast kid ran straight into my tag. He didn't slide. He didn't even slow down. In fact, he was on his way to third. I stuck my glove out and it punched his shoulder just before he reached second base. I don't think he could believe I had the ball. I know I couldn't, but before either of us had time to think about what had just happened, someone was yelling my name again. This time it was Jimmy Styles at third.

"RYNE, HOME! GOOO HOOOMMME!"

Instinct took over again. I've made that relay so many times I could do it in my sleep. Canoe-foot had rounded third. He wasn't super-fast, but he was paddling hard. My arm isn't the strongest either, but I have always been able to put a baseball exactly where I want it. My mom told me once that when I was a baby the very first toy I ever picked up was a ball and that I've been throwing one ever since. I guess eleven years of throwing practice has paid off.

I turned and threw the ball as hard as I could, about a foot to the third base side of home. Chase was already standing in front of the plate, his hockey mask off. The ball came in about belt-high which was right where he wanted it. Canoe-foot didn't slide, either. I guess he was as sure as everybody else that he would score easily. Chase slapped the tag into his ribs as he ran past him and stepped on the plate. The umpire pointed to Chase's glove and then his fist came up immediately.

"YOU'RE OUT!!"

It wasn't exactly the double play I thought we would get, but it was still a double play. Suddenly, everything jumped from slow motion back to regular speed. We ran off the field. The parents were whooping and cheering for us. Coach Weaver was banging his hands together too, excitedly waving us into the dugout. Coach Ramirez, as usual, had his eyes locked on Miggy. He wasn't clapping or cheering.

He wasn't doing anything except staring at our shortstop as Miggy walked slowly toward the dugout.

I looked over at Mano as I ran. His head was up, his hat still low. The glove Coach Ramirez had given him was tucked under his left arm. He was cruising back in with the same effortless speed he'd gone out, coming toward the dugout from the far corner of right field, the spot where Miggy's latest misfired rocket had ended up.

Curtis ran over from the pitcher's mound and popped the bill of my hat, knocking it down over my eyes. "Sweet throw!" he said. "Thanks for getting me out of that."

I remember thinking in that moment my hat was almost positioned exactly like Mano's, low over my eyes. For some reason, that embarrassed me. I pushed it back up immediately.

* * *

We were down to our final out in the bottom of the fifth inning. It took just three pitches to get us there, too. The Raiders' starting pitcher threw hard and he never missed the plate by much, if he missed at all, and he hadn't missed much the whole game.

Chase took the first pitch of the inning down the middle for a strike. He swung at the next one and hit what we call a "baby stroller" to second because it's strolling along so slowly your mom could make the play. He was tossed out easily.

Sammy followed him, and didn't bother wasting any time watching pitches. He swung at the first one he saw. Unfortunately, he did exactly what Coach Weaver hates. He hurried his swing and his big barreled bat came around too soon so that the ball hit off the end of his bat. It made an odd THOK! sound and the ball flopped up into the air like a wounded bird. The pitcher didn't even have to move off the mound. The sorry creature dropped straight into his glove and died. We were quickly down to our final out and it was Miggy's turn to bat. If he managed to get on base, Hootie's spot was next. Except Hootie was out of the game, which meant Mano would bat in his place in the lineup.

Coach Weaver pulled the lineup card out of his pocket. He was coaching first base and Coach Ramirez was at third. He shouted over to Mano in the dugout. "Mano, you're on deck!" He pointed to the row of bats lined up in the rack on the fence. "Borrow a bat and a helmet and let's go!"

Mano stood up and walked over to the rack. When he did, the "bats" in my stomach took off again. I watched him standing there, looking at all of our expensive composites. Every bat in the rack cost between two and three hundred bucks each. Mano didn't look like he wanted to touch any of them. He seemed lost. I felt sick.

I heard a deep voice behind me. The voice only said one word and when I turned around, I suddenly felt even sicker.

"Mano."

Mano's father was standing just outside the gate to the dugout. He blocked out the sun he was so huge. In his big right hand, he held Mano's bat bag.

Mano hustled over to his dad and took the bag. He moved quickly to his place on the bench and unzipped the crummy old canvas, then he pulled out the ugliest batting helmet I've ever seen. It was a navy blue-black color and was beat up and scratched. The thing definitely belonged in a baseball museum, but his bat was even worse. It was old and had a long, thin barrel. It was also made out of wood. I couldn't believe he was actually going to hit with it. If cavemen had played baseball, I'm sure it was exactly the sort of stick they would have used.

Mano slipped the batting helmet on his head, directly over his cap. He pulled it low until it was even with the brim, just like his hat, right above his eyebrows. He grabbed his ancient stick and stepped out onto the on deck circle. I snuck a quick peek over my shoulder at Mano's dad. I was sure he somehow knew that I had seen Mano's bat bag in the trash, and that I had chosen to leave it there, but when I turned around, he was already gone.

At the plate, Miggy dug in. He took the first pitch. He always does. It was high. So were the second and third. I think it might have been the first time all day the Raiders' pitcher was in danger of actually walking a batter.

Miggy stepped out of the box and looked over at his dad. I saw Coach Ramirez flashing him signals. At one point in the middle of all his twitches, he touched his belt. It was the take sign, which made sense since the count was 3-0. Miggy adjusted his black and gold batting gloves and stepped back in.

The Raiders' pitcher was obviously tired. He threw one that wasn't even close to being a strike for ball four up around Miggy's eyes, but Miggy had already made up his mind. He took a huge tomahawk cut at the sorry pitch, even though he was supposed to be standing still with the bat on his shoulder. Honestly, we never know for sure what Miggy is going to do. I'm sure he was still mad about his two horrible throws, plus he probably figured his dad was going to chew him out after the game anyway. We were down 9-zip. There were two outs. Heck, nobody scores ten runs with two outs.

He knocked the ball solidly back over the pitcher's head into centerfield. It was a pretty good rope, the kind Coach Weaver loves. Miggy did a big, dramatic turn around the first base bag. He looked like some kind of jungle cat on the prowl. The Raiders' center fielder came up with the ball quickly, and fired it back in to second. Miggy skipped back to the bag, clapped his hands, and put his fist up to Coach Weaver. Coach Weaver bumped it and immediately pointed Miggy across the field to Coach Ramirez at third so he could get his sign. Miggy turned toward his dad.

Coach Ramirez had his hands up in the air above his head. He had a wild, angry look on his face. He slammed both of his arms down to his side, furiously. Miggy just shook his head and looked down at the ground. In another moment, he lifted his head and stared down the first base line toward home plate. Mano was coming up.

3

Shaun

None of us in the Intimidators section of the bleachers saw "The Throw" except for Jennifer Girardi. Chase's mother always sits in a folding chair in front of the bleachers, just off to the third base side of home plate so she can have an unobstructed view of her son playing catcher. At that moment, it conveniently provided her the best view of the first base line, all the way to the far right corner of the outfield.

When "The Throw" happened, most of the parents were still buzzing back and forth about the unfortunate bounce at third and the grisly damage it had done to our star third baseman. All of us knew that losing Hootie Gibson would be a huge blow to the team. He was a solid fielder, but more importantly, he was a power hitter. Every parent knew that while Miggy was always capable of hitting the ball out of the park, Hootie was truly dangerous. He was a real threat to the fences every time he stepped to the plate. He was big for an eleven-year-old kid. Heck, he was big for a fourteen-year-old kid. He was definitely going to be missed.

When Miggy launched his second wild throw of the game in the top of that fifth inning, it disappeared from the view of the parents sitting in the first base bleachers. Between them, the backstop fence and the high dugout effectively block any good view of right field, so as soon as the ball rocketed over Brazos' head at first base, it vanished momentarily from everyone's eyes.

Everyone except Jennifer Girardi.

Jennifer is a petite woman with short blonde hair and giant bug-eye sunglasses. She is small, but makes up for it with her voice. As the ball mysteriously returned back to the infield and into Ryne's glove, I heard her distinct and powerful yell. It came out in one single, surprised and very loud syllable.

"OHHH!"

Before any of us knew what was happening, Ryne had tagged the runner trying for second and was turning toward home. Jennifer stood up in excited anticipation as Chase expertly removed his mask and stepped confidently in front of the plate. Ryne spun and shot one of his patented BB throws at him. It was headed right for the heart of Chase's catcher's mitt. Jennifer could see it all developing. She leaped to the fence.

"GET HIM, CHASE!"

The Raiders' runner didn't slide. Chase caught Ryne's BB and popped his glove sharply to the left, surprising the runner. He lifted his arms to try and avoid the tag, but Chase put his bare hand over the ball and then shoved both hands squarely into the runner's ribs. He was out and our stands erupted. Jennifer went crazy. "DID YOU SEE THAT?" she screamed. She belted loudly again, "OH, MY GOSH! DID YOU SEE THAT?!" She turned back to the field, bouncing and yelling, "YOU GOT HIM, CHASE! YOU GOT HIM! WHAT A GREAT PLAY! WHOO HOO!!"

It was a great play by Chase, and, of course, it was a great play by Ryne, too. But I don't know that anyone on the field or in the stands understood "The Throw" that had set it all up.

That is—no one but Ryne.

19

Still, even if we had all missed the "The Throw", none of us missed what happened next when Mano came to the plate for the first time.

*   *   *

Ryne

I followed Mano out of the dugout. I was our number six hitter, behind Hootie who was batting fifth. Miggy was in the clean-up spot, although every player on the team thought he should bat fifth and Hootie should hit in the clean-up spot. But Miggy's ego fit better in the fourth spot in our order, and *everybody* agreed on that.

Mano looked down the line at Coach Ramirez before he stepped into the box. It seemed sort of pointless to me since he didn't know our signs yet, but he took a good long look anyway. Coach Ramirez went through his normal series of fidgets, swipes, nose touches, and ear tugs. Mano nodded at him and stepped into the batter's box.

The Raiders' pitcher threw another ball that was way high on the first pitch. It was the fifth straight high one that he'd thrown, and it brought their coach to the opening of their dugout. He grooved the next one though, a fast ball that Mano watched all the way into the catcher's mitt.

I remember thinking that Mano's stance was strange. He stood like a statue, his bat held high, and his elbow cocked at an almost perfect right angle to his body. What really made him look like a statue though, was the fact that he *never* moved. He didn't waggle his bat, tap his front foot, or even wiggle his fingers. He stood perfectly, absolutely still.

The count to Mano was a ball and a strike. The pitcher had looked over at Miggy's lead at first before each of the first two pitches, but after the second one he forgot all about him. Maybe he didn't care because it was 9-0 with two outs in the bottom of the last inning. Whatever the reason, Miggy took off for second base on the third pitch. Mano stood perfectly still again and the pitch went a little wide for ball two. Miggy made it to second without a throw from the Raiders' catcher. Now the count was two balls and one strike.

The Raiders' coach was still standing at the entrance to the third base dugout. I think he wanted to come out, but at the same time he didn't want to come out. Changing pitchers was the last thing he probably wanted to do, and I bet he was hoping Mano would just strike out and the game would be over. The pitcher wound up and threw another one.

Again, Mano stood perfectly still. This pitch missed, but not by much. It was a little high, but to be honest, I thought it was a call that could have gone either way. The ump thought it was a ball, and what he thinks is all that counts. The count moved to three balls and one strike and Mano still hadn't moved. Finally, the Raiders' pitcher managed to throw him a good one, a belt-high fastball on the inside corner of the plate. I watched as "Mano the Statue" suddenly came to life. His launched into the ball with a swing that was smooth and powerful.

When the bat and ball met, there was a loud CRACK! It's a sound I've heard before, but never on one of our fields. I heard it a lot when our team went to a Texas Rangers game last year and we arrived early enough to catch batting practice. The cracks there were amazing, clear and loud. This one was, too.

I watched the ball from where I stood next to the on deck circle. The sign on the fence in the left field corner said 225. The fence was tall too, one of those twenty-footers with the foul pole that goes about another ten feet above it. The ball that Mano hit went over the foul pole. It actually went *way* over the foul pole, and it kept going, too. When it finally came down, it smashed onto the metal roof on the concession stand—the stand was probably another hundred feet away—and it made a loud crashing sound like thunder. I saw several people standing in line jump at the boom it made. The ball took one big bounce and disappeared.

21

Everything got very quiet in an eerie way. I looked over and saw Mano cruising back toward home plate. I expected to see him jogging in a home run trot down the first base line, but he wasn't there. I guess he had been running flat out from the moment he hit the ball and he was already almost to second base when he stopped. I don't know if he even watched the ball after he hit it. He must have just taken off, running as hard as he could. The umpire had both of his hands held high in the air. He pointed dramatically toward the bleachers and cried, "Foul!"

Coach Ramirez stood perfectly still for a moment. He seemed shocked. He had turned and watched the ball with the rest of us. He was in a good position to see it too, right as it passed over the foul pole. When he heard the ump, he turned back around and started toward the plate.

"Are you kidding me?" he said. He repeated it again, but in a different way, and a little louder. "You've got to be kidding me!" He began moving toward home plate. "The ball went over the pole! That's fair. It's fair! You *know* it's fair!" The umpire had removed his mask to make the call. He put it back on and pointed for Coach Ramirez to return to third base. Coach ignored his finger. He kept coming.

"IT WENT OVER THE POLE," he yelled, loudly. "THAT'S A FAIR BALL!"

The umpire took off his mask again and pointed at him. "Go back to third base, Coach," he said, calmly. "Don't make me toss you."

Coach Ramirez stopped in his tracks. He didn't turn around. He just stood there for a moment like he'd run into an invisible wall. "IT WAS FAIR!!" He shouted again. "YOU KNOW IT WAS FAIR!"

This time the umpire pointed and yelled back. "NOT ANOTHER WORD, COACH! ONE MORE AND YOU'RE DONE!!" Coach Ramirez threw up his hands and turned around and steamed back to the coach's box. The umpire moved back behind the Raiders' catcher.

He pointed to Mano and then to the pitcher. Mano stepped back in the box and resumed his statue stance. After that, it was over quickly.

Coach Ramirez was steaming mad. The Raiders' exhausted pitcher wound up and threw another bad pitch. The ball was outside, so much outside that the catcher had to reach way across his body to backhand it. Mano didn't move again. He let it go past because it was clearly ball four. Except the umpire was mad too, I guess. He punched the air and drew his fist back across his chest.

Strike three. Just like that, the game was over.

* * *

There are 108 stitches on a baseball.

One of my coaches told us that little bit of trivia when I was eight years old. He held the ball up at our first practice and told us that every stitch was put in the ball by someone by hand. The leather pieces were sewn together around the guts of the ball, one stitch at a time. He told us that a team had to be put together the same way. One pitch, one hit, one play, one game, one stitch at a time. I've never forgotten that. I've also never forgotten that magic number of 108 stitches.

After the game, Alfonso came up to me. Most of the players had already gone, including Mano. He asked me to follow him. I did, and he took me over to the back side of the concession stand. He pointed up in the air. There was some tangled, rusty chicken wire hanging over the side of the roof. I could see a ball was stuck in it.

"Will you get it for me, please?" he asked. He had a strange look on his face.

I looked around. There was a big trash dumpster that sat near the corner of the building. I went over and climbed up on it. I looked around to make sure no one was watching and quickly scrambled up on the roof. I stayed low and snuck over to the chicken wire. I reached down, pulled the ball out and crab-crawled back as fast as I could. I jumped down on the dumpster. Alfonso came over and held his small hand out.

"Thank you, Ryne," he said, sincerely. Like I said, he's a really good kid.

"You're welcome," I replied.

I guess he wanted the souvenir. It was just a long, long foul ball. Or maybe it was a home run. I guess it depended on whether you thought the umpire was right or not.

"Whoa," Alfonso suddenly blurted. His eyes grew big. "*Look at this.*" He handed the ball back to me.

It's true that every baseball has 108 stitches. But the stitches on this one were a little different. I counted them. One, two, three, four, five, six, seven…eight. Eight. Yes, it was eight.

Eight of the stitches on the ball Mano had hit were broken.

Ryne

It rained. For a week. Every day.

We didn't meet for practice because every baseball field within a hundred miles was wet, so I did some other stuff. I spent most of that week on the Xbox, watching TV, playing some computer games, reading an adventure novel about pirates and a lost treasure, and thinking. There's not much else to do in the summer when it rains. I did think some about baseball. I thought about Mano and his amazing throw. I also thought a lot about the stitches on the ball I'd retrieved for Alfonso, but more than anything else, I thought about Madison McMannis. Her *Midnight in Deep, Dark Outer Space* birthday party was coming up at the bowling alley and she had sent me an invitation. I'd heard that for outer space parties, they turned off all of the normal lighting and used black lights that made the whole place look crazy, like you're floating around in outer space. Then they gave you a special ball that was painted with wild colors and used pins that glowed. It sounded pretty chill.

The party was on Saturday afternoon, the same time as our next game, so I wouldn't have even been able to go if it hadn't rained. When my mom dropped me off at 2:00, the rain was ending and the sun had popped out. It was bright outside for the first time in a week, then I stepped into the bowling alley and it was immediately so dark that I had to stop inside the door and close my eyes for a minute so they could adjust. When I opened them, the place was more fantastic than I'd imagined. Inside, it really was like midnight, only you could see. The floor was covered with fluorescent dots of different sizes with a mix of strange squiggly patterns. The ceiling was covered with stars, meteors, and huge planets that were painted in neon paint: yellow, orange, pink, blue, and green…a bunch of different colors. Giant red meteors and bright white comets with huge, fiery tails occasionally streaked across the sky. The bowling lanes were painted an aqua blue, like the ocean. Some of them had lime-green rails to keep the ball from rolling off into the gutters, for kids who had trouble throwing straight. At the end of each lane, the mechanical arm that set up the pins was a bright tangerine-orange.

Saturday afternoon was reserved for parties so the whole place was crammed with kids. I walked over to the main desk and told the guy who worked there that I was looking for the McMannis party. His face was painted with pink and yellow neon paint and he was wearing a tall, fuzzy wig that glowed in five different shades of purple. Even his eyebrows were painted; one pink, one yellow.

"OVER THERE, LAST FOUR LANES ON THE LEFT," he shouted. It was pretty loud. Almost every lane was full. The sound system was playing some techno-space music, and with kids screaming and the multi-colored balls crashing down forty alleys into four hundred glowing pins, you had to yell to be heard. He asked me what size shoes I needed, gave me a pair of eights, and then pointed me over to several racks of balls. "MIKE WILL HELP YOU PICK OUT A BALL OVER THERE."

I nodded and walked over to where "Mike" was standing. He had on a wig too, but it was a long train of pink, orange, and green curls that went almost all the way to the floor. He had me stick my fingers in the holes of several different balls until we found one that wouldn't yank my knuckles off when I let it go. I thanked him and started toward Madison's group at the end of the alley. When I turned, Chase was standing there in front of me. He screamed at me, "*DUDE!*" His face was painted with four or five different neon colors. In fact, his hands, arms, and the parts of his legs that weren't covered by his shorts were painted, too. On the knobs of his knees were two smiley faces, one yellow and one pink. He looked ridiculous, like he'd opened a box of Lucky Charms and it had exploded all over him. I almost didn't recognize him. In fact, I'm positive I wouldn't have recognized him if he hadn't been wearing his Intimidators jersey. The black shirt was invisible, but you could still easily read the giant gold letters.

"WHAT THE HECK?" I screamed back. "WHAT HAPPENED TO YOU?"

He shook his head and held out his arms. "THE GIRLS DID THIS TO ME! THEY'RE DOING IT TO EVERYBODY!"

Suddenly, we were attacked. Five of Madison's friends ran over and grabbed us. They were shrieking and laughing hysterically. Chase started laughing and I realized that it was an ambush. He'd set me up. The gang of girls grabbed me by the arms and pulled me toward the far four lanes. Madison was waiting for us.

"WE'VE GOT ANOTHER ONE!" one of her friends screamed.

Madison walked over. She was a sight. Her hair looked like the guys who worked at the bowling alley, only it wasn't a wig. She had streaked her long blonde hair with what looked like every color in the neon rainbow. Her face and body were painted too, but it was her clothes that really grabbed your attention. She wore a spangled top and shorts that bounced colors and twinkling lights back at you so fast it was like being attacked by a thousand bags of Skittles.

"HI RYNE," she shouted, smiling. Her teeth glowed. They were a bizarre white under the black lighting. "THANKS FOR COMING!"

"SURE!" I shouted back. "THIS PLACE IS AWESOME!!"

"I KNOW!" She threw her arms dramatically in the air. "DON'T YOU JUST LOVE IT?!!"

Before I could answer, I felt the five girls pulling on me. "COME ON, RYNE! YOU'RE NEXT!!"

I sat my ball down and they led me over to a small table where they kept the paints. I really had no choice, so I just stood there patiently while they decorated me. Four of them each took an arm or leg while the fifth worked on my face. Chase stood close by, laughing at me. They finished in about five minutes and stepped back to admire their work. All five stood in a line and held out their arms and wiggled them up and down like octopus tentacles. Then they all shouted in unison with alien voices.

"YOU...ARE...ONE...OF...US...NOW!!" They screamed again and ran back toward Madison and the lanes.

I held my hands out toward Chase. "WHAT THE HECK? YOU SET ME UP!"

He just laughed. "MY SISTER MADE ME DO IT!" His twin sister Katie was one of Madison's best friends. "C'MON. LET'S GO BOWL!"

* * *

We bowled for about an hour. Chase and I dominated, but that was probably because we were the only two guys invited to the party. Chase had been invited because he was Katie's brother and their family was close friends with Madison's family. Chase had asked them to invite me so he wouldn't be the only guy.

We had fun, though. We demolished a couple of baskets of cheese fries, some pepperoni pizza, and about a gallon of Dr. Pepper while we played. The first game, Chase bowled a 125 and I bowled a 112. Our 227 wasn't great, but it was still over a hundred points higher than the two girls who bowled with us. The second game was even worse.

Chase scored a 132 and I came up to a 130. Together, the girls barely cracked a hundred, but they didn't seem to care. Whenever it was their turn, they stood with the ball between them and walked to the line together. One of them would take the crazy colored globe and try to push it down the lane. It never gained any speed and we spent most of the time watching it inch along like a tired snail toward the glowing pins. When it finally arrived, it would push a pin or two or sometimes more over, and the girls would jump and grab each other like they'd just won an Olympic medal while they ran back toward us squealing.

We drummed them easily.

During one of the frames, while we watched the wildly painted snail crawl down the lane, Chase leaned over. He was close enough to my ear that he didn't have to shout. "Katie told me that Madison likes you."

My face started to get hot. I turned and looked at Chase. He was smiling and his teeth had that odd white glow. I just shrugged and he bumped me with his shoulder. "She's nice," I said. Chase looked at me as if he were confused. I bent closer to his ear so he could hear. "She's *really* nice," I said. I don't know why I added in the "really."

Chase nodded. He leaned in to my ear again. "She's the only one of Katie's friends who doesn't get on my nerves." I bobbed my head in agreement. Most of my sister Samantha's friends get on my nerves too, probably because they are eight years old and squeal even more than Katie's friends. Around our house on the weekends when Sam has her pals over, it sounds like someone is constantly stepping on a puppy's tail.

"Hey, I gotta go to the bathroom," I said in Chase's ear. I was bursting with Dr. Pepper. "I'll be right back."

The bathroom was on the far side of the building. To reach it, you had to go around the corner and down a hallway past the food court. On the opposite side of the food court was an enormous arcade. I didn't notice it on my way to the bathroom because it was behind a glass door that was black as night. Apparently, they kept it shut down to keep kids out until a certain time, but on my way back, someone had opened the double glass doors and turned on the black lights. I stopped to check it out.

You had to walk down two flights of stairs that were covered with the fluorescent dots and squiggly lines to get inside. The room was still as dark as midnight, just like the rest of the bowling alley, and it was huge, almost as big as a football field. Instead of a space theme it was set up so you felt like you were under the ocean. There were neon fish all over the walls which glowed in the same aqua blue, ocean color that colored the bowling lanes. On one wall there was an enormous blue and white whale. It covered almost the entire surface and was surrounded by tropical fish of all different sizes. I couldn't believe how real it looked.

I stood on a landing at the bottom of the first flight of stairs. There was a glowing yellow rope that was strung across the front of it to keep you from going down any further, but you could see across the whole, huge ocean. There were no kids yet, so even though all of the machines were lit and ready to play it was quiet, except for some strange music that sounded like waves rolling on a beach mixed with a mysterious deep, low throbbing sound.

I saw something far out across the ocean. It was white and it stood out brightly under the black lighting, glowing like Madison's teeth when she had smiled at me. It was moving back and forth among the rows of intensely lit games in sort of a wandering pattern, cruising slowly and easily. I don't know how I knew from just watching the movement, but I did. It was Mano.

The white object I could see was his hat. When he turned down one row of machines and headed back toward me, I could see the brim was pulled low. He kept moving, past a row of pin ball machines, made a sharp turn, and then turned around and headed for the back wall. I could see there were several sports-themed machines back there, including a row of six Pop-a-Shots, a basketball game. I looked around, didn't see anyone else, and so I slipped under the glowing rope and headed toward the back of the arcade.

It seemed to take forever, but when I finally got to the back of the room, Mano was standing in front of one of the Pop-a-Shots looking up. He had one of the basketballs in his hands and he was staring at the hoop. He kept staring at it for a long time. I kept expecting him to shoot the ball, but he never did. Then I realized he wasn't looking at the goal. He was fixed instead on the huge wall behind the machines. Rising from its base was a picture of a mammoth shark. It wasn't a cartoon picture, either. This shark looked every bit as real as the whale at the front of the room, only much more serious. Its mouth was open and you could see rows of insanely bright, razor-sharp teeth. The white area around its eyes was bright too, but the eyes were dark and scary. Its fin was cutting through the surface of the water and its tail was whipping around like it was making a fast turn.

Mano stood perfectly still, just like his statute pose at the plate. He never moved, just kept staring upward at the epic-sized shark. Finally, he slowly lifted his hand and flicked his wrist. The basketball arced through the air. It hit the front of the rim and bounced back hard. It bounded over the front of the machine and managed to slip past him and started rolling toward me. We both bent to pick it up and when we did, something slipped out of Mano's shirt. The ball had rolled straight to me and I picked it up before Mano could grab it. He looked up at me. I could only see the white part of his eyes, way back beneath his hat.

"Hi, Mano," I said. I tried to sound friendly. I looked down at the object that had fallen out of his shirt. It was white and it glowed like his hat under the black lighting. It looked like an enormous, very sharp tooth on the end of a thin chain.

"Hi," he said, in a low voice. We stood there for a moment. The silence was awkward. Then I remembered that I was painted up like some sort of carnival freak and he probably didn't recognize me.

"It's me, Ryne," I said, thinking I probably looked like an idiot.

"I know," he said, softly.

"Are you here for a party?" I asked. Mano just shrugged his shoulders.

"No. I'm staying in the apartments across the street. I just walked over." It was the first time I'd noticed he had an unusual tone to his voice. It wasn't really an accent. It just sounded interesting, like the ocean and the beach and places that are far away.

"Oh," I sort of mumbled. I didn't know what to say. I pointed to the large, bright triangle hanging around his neck. "Is that a shark tooth?"

Mano put his hand over the tooth, like he didn't know it was showing. "Uh…yeah," he kind of sputtered. He quickly pulled at the chain and tucked it back into his shirt.

"It's cool," I said. "Where did you get it?"

He looked down at the floor. "Uh, I got it back home."

"In Hawai'i?" I asked.

He nodded fast. "Yes. Molokai. That's where I'm from."

"Did you find it on the beach or something?"

Mano dropped his head and looked at his feet. "No." He stood there and didn't say anything else. He just kept looking down. That's when my confession popped out of my mouth, surprising us both.

"Hey, I'm sorry about your bat bag."

Mano looked up at me. "Why?"

Now it was my turn to look down. "The other day, I saw where it was. I should have told you."

Mano didn't say anything.

"I don't know who put it in there," I told him, truthfully.

Mano stared at me. I could still only see the white part around his eyes. "I left it leaning next to the shed. My dad said somebody probably thought it was trash and threw it away." He even laughed a little. "It doesn't look very new."

I watched him. I couldn't tell if he really believed that story or not. I realized I needed to get back to Madison's party. I'd been gone so long Chase probably thought I was stuck in the bathroom with a bad case of the bats. "Hey, I gotta go," I said, sticking a thumb over my shoulder. "I'm here for a birthday party."

Mano smiled. It was the first time I'd ever seen his teeth. They were super-white underneath the black-lighting, almost blinding.

"Okay," he answered. I started to walk away. Then I stopped and turned back around. "Hey, I was thinking. Maybe, would you...I don't know. Would you like come over to my house one day and hang out?"

Mano's smile circled, becoming smaller. He looked surprised. "Uh, sure," he replied.

I grinned. "We can talk about it at practice. I'll see you on Tuesday, okay?"

Mano smiled again. "Sure. I'll see you on Tuesday."

I turned and began jogging back across the arcade. When I got to the stairs, I sprinted up them, taking two at a time, but when I got to the landing again, I stopped in front of the glowing yellow rope and turned around.

Across the ocean, Mano was standing perfectly still once more. He was looking up. He was staring at the picture of the enormous shark.

* * *

When I returned to Madison's party, Chase came up to me. It was still super loud so he put his mouth to my ear. "Where did you go?"

"I was just checking out the arcade."

"Awesome! Did they already open it? That's where we're going next."

I looked over at Madison. She was standing in the middle of her group of friends, laughing hard. The neon rainbow in her hair was bright and her sparkling outfit was still throwing off its colorful shower of Skittles. Just then, she looked over at me and I quickly turned away. Chase tugged at my elbow and I leaned my ear in to him again.

"Katie said that she and Madison are going to come to our game next Saturday," he said. "Madison told her she wants to see you play."

The bats in my stomach took off again.

"I guess we'll need to play a lot better than we did last week," I said, trying to sound cool. "We don't want to look like idiots."

All I could see were Chase's crazily painted cheeks and his bizarro, white teeth as he grinned. "Yeah, it's probably better if you don't look like an idiot in front of her."

I gave him a push. He pushed back. We pushed and shoved some more, which seemed to help the bats in my stomach.

"C'mon, let's go to the arcade," Chase said.

I suddenly remembered Mano. I started to tell Chase that I had seen him, but I didn't. When we got to the arcade, it was already filling up fast with kids. I looked for him, but he was already gone.

5

Ryne

On Tuesday, it rained again. So Coach Ramirez called a special batting practice at The Hitting Wheel, a giant indoor batting cage facility. The Hitting Wheel is just like it sounds. The spokes of the wheel are thirty-two cages that point back to the center of the wheel, or the hub. The hub catches all of the balls that are hit into it and feeds them into the pitching machines. The machines can be programmed to throw at different speeds, starting as low as thirty-five miles per hour and going as high as eighty-five miles per hour. As far as batting cages go, The Hitting Wheel is awesome.

Right next to The Hitting Wheel, there's a smaller wheel, too. It's called The Whiffle Wheel. It has eight much smaller spokes and it pitches little yellow golf balls, the plastic kind with the holes in them. You hit them with a super-thin bat called a Lightning Stick. The coaches tell us it's supposed to improve our hand-eye coordination and bat speed. Sometimes it feels like you're trying to hit a bee with a broomstick, but it's a lot of fun.

I was one of the first to arrive and when I walked in, Mano was already sitting by himself in one of the folding chairs against the wall about half way around the wheel, watching a couple of high school players bang away in the cages directly in front of him. He had that beat up batting helmet on over his cap and it was pulled down low. He had his

35

dark wooden bat sitting across his lap as he watched. I started toward him, but then I saw Hootie and his father sitting in the short stand of bleachers right by the front door and I changed directions.

"Hey, Mr. Gibson, hey Hootie," I said, as I swung my bat bag onto the bleachers. When Hootie turned to me, I was shocked. He was wearing a mask that covered his entire face. It attached with black straps that ran around his cheeks and connected in the back and over the center of his head. There were three pads, one on his forehead and two on either side of his nose, which was now fat and black. Even though it had been over a week since he had taken the shot to his beak at third base, his eyes were still bloodshot and ringed with black circles. He looked less like an owl now and more like a sad raccoon.

"Wow!" I almost shouted. "That looks painful!"

Hootie nodded. When he spoke, he mumbled. It sounded like he had the world's worst cold. "Uh huh. You got that right."

"How bad is it?" I asked.

Mr. Gibson put his hand on one of Hootie's big shoulders. "His nose is broken and he has an orbital rim fracture." When I screwed up my eyebrows, Mr. Gibson clarified. He pointed high upon his own cheek. "It's the eye socket. There's a bony cup around your eye to protect it and he has a pretty good crack in it."

I asked the most obvious question that I could think of. "Can you play with that mask on?"

Mr. Gibson and Hootie shook their heads together. Mr. Gibson looked sad. "No, he can't play for a while." The way he paused made it seem like 'a while' would be a very long time, maybe the whole season. Hootie's eyes were watery. I couldn't tell if he was starting to cry or if his eyes were just glassy all the time now.

Right about then, Jimmy and Sammy Styles walked in. They were followed by Coach Ramirez, Miggy and Alfonso, Coach Weaver, Curtis, Brazos, and Wee Willie. The coaches went to the front desk

36

and everybody else came over to the bleachers. Wee Willie darted around all of us and jumped up next to Hootie.

"Cool mask!" He said. "Can I touch it?" He put his hand up and Hootie flinched.

"No, you can't touch it!" He honked. "It still hurts!"

Wee Willie moved in for a closer look. He was amazed. "Whoa. How do you breathe?"

Hootie opened his mouth. He took in a deep breath and blew it out into Wee Willie's face, like he was trying to extinguish the candles on his birthday cake. *"Like that,"* he fumed, sounding irritated.

Wee Willie made a face. "Nice, Doritos breath," he gagged.

Coach Ramirez walked over. He had a huge cup of tokens. He started counting heads. "Where's Chase?" he growled. With perfect timing, Chase walked through the door. I pointed to him. "There he is." Chase ran over to us.

"Sorry I'm a little late, Coach. We had to pick up my sister's friend."

I gulped. Katie and Madison were both walking through the door. Chase nodded at me and grinned.

"Okay, that's nine so we have everybody," he said, including Hootie in the count.

"What about Jacob?" Brazos asked. Jacob Dickey wasn't exactly a standout player for us. In fact, Chase had once offered the theory to me that he was probably on the team just to keep the bench from flying away during high winds. Coach Ramirez moved him around from position to position in practice. He was practically homeless on the field because of it. He'd only played in the first game because Wee Willie had hurled a swimming pool of Gatorade in the dugout and Coach had been forced to put him in the outfield.

"He's not on the team," Coach Ramirez said flatly. "His mother called me and said he doesn't want to play baseball anymore. So that leaves us with nine."

Ten, I thought. *It's ten. Coach is forgetting Mano.* That was when Katie and Madison walked over by the bleachers and I suddenly forgot all about Mano, too. Madison looked directly at me. She smiled and lifted her hand with sort of a shy, secret wave. I didn't know what to do, so I just bobbed my head quickly at her and looked down.

"We're in cages five, six, and seven. Let's go," Coach Ramirez ordered. We picked up our bat bags and moved around the wheel to set up camp. Jimmy, Brazos, and Miggy went into the cages first. Miggy always goes first. I got in line behind him. I sat my bag down, knelt and unzipped it. I pulled out my batting gloves and my gold and black Intimidators helmet. Chase came over and sat his bag next to mine.

"*She's here,*" he whispered beneath his breath.

"*I know,*" I whispered back, fiercely. "*You said she was coming to our next game! You didn't say anything about practice!*"

"*Katie invited her.*" He unzipped his bag and pulled out his own helmet and gloves.

"*Since when did Katie start coming to practice?*" Katie never came to our practices. And I knew for a fact she had never set a foot inside The Hitting Wheel. Chase sat down on the turf floor and crossed his legs. He looked up at me like he knew a secret. "*I think she and Madison planned it.*"

The bats in my stomach started to flop.

In the cage, Miggy began making his stretching noises. Nobody makes noises when they stretch, except old people and Miggy. He twists his back and groans. He pulls his arms and grunts. It's like he's winding himself up to pass some serious gas. He picked up his bat and began to rotate it over his head with both arms to loosen his shoulders and neck. Then he began rocking his hips from side to side. Chase looked over at him and snorted, "Look at him. He should be on *Dancing with the Stars*." I laughed. Both of our moms loved *Dancing with the Stars*. Of course, both of our dads hated it. I snuck a quick look over at the girls. They were busy texting on Madison's phone.

Coach Weaver walked over to our cage. "You ready, Miggy?" he asked. He had a token in his hand. Miggy nodded and moved into the batter's box. Coach Weaver dropped the token into the machine and selected forty-five mph on the digital readout for our warm up round. Usually we hit a round at forty-five miles per hour, two at fifty-five miles per hour, and then finish at sixty-five miles per hour, even though there's a lot of whiffing at sixty-five. The coaches want us to try and catch up to faster pitching to improve our bat speed. Coach Weaver tells us that you never know when you are going to run into a pitcher who has a lot of "giddy up" on his fastball. Anyway, each round is twenty pitches, so by the end of practice we each take eighty swings, which are a lot more than we ever take during a live batting practice.

Miggy settled into his stance. At the other end of the cage are two traffic lights, one red and one green. When the light moves from red to green, it means the next pitch is on its way. As the ball leaves the machine, it makes a weird noise, sort of a *PFFFTTHUMP!* sound as it's ejected. Miggy waited for the first pitch and then there was the familiar TINK! sound that echoed loudly as the composite bat made contact with the ball. That TINK! sound is much louder inside the metal building. In fact, when The Hitting Wheel is full, there are so many simultaneous TINKS! it sounds like somebody is pouring coins into a giant jar.

Miggy finished his first round and stepped out of the cage. I stepped in and waited for Coach Weaver to come over with a token. He was chewing Brazos out about an extra bit of waggling he was doing with his bat that Coach thought was "entirely unnecessary." That was when Mr. Blyleven walked up.

Mr. Blyleven is old, probably in his eighties. His son owns The Hitting Wheel. He hangs out during the week, when it's not as crowded. He doesn't work there, but he does stuff to help out, like empty trash barrels. Mainly, he just walks around, picks up lint he finds on the turf, and watches the kids hit. Every now and then, he'll stop by and say something to you. It's usually something nice, unless you're whiffing. Then he always says the same thing in a low, gravelly voice.

"Keep your head on it, son."

Mr. Blyleven is also really tan—like a golfer—and has a cool handlebar mustache. It's white as snow and it matches his hair, which he wears kind of long. I think that's why he always has something to say to Brazos, like they're both part of some secret tribe of long-hairs. He walked up just as Coach Weaver was starting in on Brazos and his new bat waggle. He stood there but didn't say anything. He just nodded along with Coach's speech and then he walked over to our cage. When he saw us waiting, he pulled a token from his pocket.

"Go ahead, Ryne," he motioned to me with his hand. "I've got it. Is this your first round?"

"Yes sir, Mr. Blyleven," I answered. I thought it was pretty cool that Mr. Blyleven always remembered my name, until I remembered one day that it was on the back of my practice jersey. He dropped a coin in the machine and programmed it for our warm-up speed of forty-five miles per hour. I stepped in and waited for the light to change from red to green, wondering the whole time if Madison was watching. The light changed from red to green. The machine whirred. *PFFFTTHUMP!*

I whiffed.

The light went back to red and then to green. The machine spit another one at me. *PFFFTTHUMP!*

I whiffed again.

The light did its Christmas tree flicker once more. The machine coughed out another ball. *PFFFTTHUMP!*

I whiffed for the third time, at forty-five stinkin' miles per hour!

"Keep your head on it son," Mr. Blyleven grumbled. I looked at him quickly over my shoulder and gave him an embarrassed smile.

"Yes, sir."

I managed to foul the next one off, weakly. Slowly, I began making better contact, but my first round of cuts was not good. In fact, I stunk.

When I left the cage, Mr. Blyleven was still standing there, but I looked right past him to the bleachers to where Madison and Katie were sitting. Their heads were still down, looking at Madison's phone. They had probably missed the whole thing.

"Got to keep your head on it, son," Mr. Blyleven reminded me again.

"Yes, sir. I know."

He smiled at me. He has really blue eyes that look even bluer because of his white hair and golfer's tan. That handlebar mustache lifts with his cheeks whenever he smiles really big. He had that big smile now. He lowered his voice, but it was still all gravelly. "Leave the girls at home next time," he advised. "They're just a distraction."

I looked at him and felt my face go instantly red. Just then, we both heard a new sound echo inside The Hitting Wheel. The sound was loud and different. We both turned toward it at the same time.

CRRAAACCK!!

Directly across the hub of the wheel from us was the cage where the two high school kids had been taking batting practice. As we both watched, there was another loud *CRRAAACCK!!* and a ball rifled straight back down the center of the cage and smashed into the hub of the wheel.

"Joltin' Joe," Mr. Blyleven mumbled. "Who is that?"

The two high school players were standing outside the cage. This time, one of them whooped loudly as a third *CRRAAACCK!!* rang out across The Hitting Wheel. Mr. Blyleven started walking slowly around the outside of the giant wheel toward the sound. He looked like he was hypnotized. I sat my bat down on my bag and hurried to catch up with him. The wheel is huge, so it was a long way to the opposite side. Every few steps we took, we could hear another *CRRAAACCK!!* and a ball would zing back through the heart of the cage into the hub of the wheel. The two high school players were slapping high fives and whooping loudly after every hit.

"Rip it, little man!" one of them shouted. "Rip it!!"

Mr. Blyleven walked up behind them. He didn't say anything. He just stood with one hand thrust deeply into his pocket. With the other, he slowly massaged his handlebar mustache. He had a deep, faraway look on his face.

Inside the cage, Mano stood perfectly still in his statue pose. His feet were just wider than his shoulders. His back elbow was cocked in a perfectly straight line. That scratched and beat up batting helmet was pulled low on his head. The light changed from red to green. The machine whirred and whispered. *PFFFTTHUMP!* The ball shot at us like a bullet.

"Mano the Statue" suddenly came to life once again. His hips rotated. His shoulders and arms followed them, smoothly. Suddenly, his bat was a blur. It met the bullet and the *CRRAAACCK!!* seemed even louder. The ball shot back on almost exactly the same line on which it had come in, right down the center of the cage toward the hub of the wheel. The two high school players lifted their hands again. They slapped them together loudly.

"SAA-WEET!" one of them yelled.

When I looked over at him, Mano had already returned to his statue pose. He wasted no time or energy flipping his bat around. He just brought his hands back immediately and returned his elbow to its cocked position as he waited for the next pitch. That's when I looked over at the digital readout on the machine. The two digits were flashing. The two red numbers were blinking their last pitch warning.

The readout said 75 mph.

The light changed from red to green. *PFFFTTHUMP!* The ball rocketed toward us again. I waited for the statue to come to life and destroy it once more. But the ball shot past Mano and blasted into the rubber mat that hung on the back of the net. It fell harmlessly to the ground and rolled back toward his feet. It was the only ball that hadn't been sent back where it came from.

I heard Mr. Blyleven mumble again, softly. "Well, Joltin' Joe," he said, mysteriously. He added even more softly under his breath, "That ball *was* a little high."

"He doesn't swing at pitches out of the strike zone," I heard myself say.

Mr. Blyleven turned to me. "Do you know him?"

I looked up. "Yes sir. His name is Mano. He's on our team."

Mr. Blyleven looked confused. "He's on the Intimidators? Why isn't he over there practicing with you?"

I started to answer but just then I heard one of the two high school players say loudly, "Okay, little man. Get ready. Here it comes!" One of them had dropped a new token in the machine. I looked over at the digital display. It flashed 85 mph.

Suddenly, Mr. Blyleven sprang into action. He reached into his shirt pocket with one hand and pulled out a rubber band. With his other, he swept his long, white hair back into a ponytail and quickly tied it off. He walked up to the two high school players and stuck one of his tan hands between them.

"Excuse me, boys," he said firmly. The two players turned to him, saw that it was Mr. Blyleven, and immediately stepped aside. He pulled a folding chair that was next to the cage's entrance over behind the plate and spun it around so the back of the chair faced the cage. He quickly climbed on it like he was mounting a horse and leaned forward in a classic plate umpire pose.

I walked over to him and whispered, "What are you doing, Mr. Blyleven?"

"These machines have a tendency to get a little wild on the highest setting," he whispered back. "I want to check their accuracy."

Mano never turned around toward us. He kept his eyes straight ahead, watching the red light.

We all waited. I think I was holding my breath. Maybe Mr. Blyleven was, too. Finally, the light turned green.

PFFFTTHUMP!

The ball came at us so fast that I flinched.

But Mr. Blyleven didn't. Neither did Mano. He didn't move. He didn't swing, either. The ball made a sharp THOP! sound as it whacked into the rubber mat on the netting. It dropped to the ground and began rolling back toward Mano's feet. I leaned over to Mr. Blyleven. He whispered. "*High.*"

I looked back down toward the red light. We all waited. The light turned green again.

PFFFTTHUMP!

I had stood behind the cages and watched the high school kids hit before, so I knew how scary-fast the ball came at them. No one I knew had ever stood in the cage when the machine was throwing at the highest speed. Our coaches wouldn't allow it. Like Mr. Blyleven said, the machines could throw a little wild and they were probably afraid we might get hit. I know I was.

The ball shot past Mano again and drilled the rubber mat. I turned to Mr. Blyleven. He just nodded his head and whispered. *"Strike."* He seemed disappointed.

In the cage, Mano did something that surprised me. He brought his hands down and softly tapped the plate with the end of his bat, but quickly brought it back up into its cocked position.

PFFFTTHUMP!

THOP! The ball hit the mat and rolled toward his feet. This time, I didn't need Mr. Blyleven to tell me. I knew.

It was a strike.

Just then, I felt a small presence on the other side of me. I looked to my right.

It was Alfonso. His eyes were big and bright. He didn't say anything. He just stared through the cage at Mano. I heard one of the high school ball players whisper, "C'mon, little man. You can do it. *Just swing.*"

The light changed from red to green.

PFFFTTHUMP!

Mano came to life. His old wooden bat ripped through the zone like lightning. It caught the bottom of the ball and sent it straight back into the net above the rubber mat. It snapped into the net so hard I thought it was going to rip all the way through. All of us, except for Mr. Blyleven, jumped. "That was a strike," Mr. Blyleven said, nodding that he agreed with the machine. By his account, the machine had thrown one ball and three strikes.

"That's it, little man!" one of the high school players yelped. "You're on it. You're on it!"

Mano brought his bat quickly back to his shoulder. He cocked his elbow. He stared down at the red light. Mr. Blyleven leaned forward a little bit on the folding chair. I moved in next to him a little closer.

Alfonso pushed himself even closer to me. The high school players were whispering together.

"C'mon, little man. Stay in there. Stay in there. *Stay in there...*"

The light turned from red to green. This time there was no *PFFFTTHUMP!* sound and no ball came out of the machine.

I turned to Mr. Blyleven. "What happened?"

The light at the end of the cage returned to red and began to flash at us. Mr. Blyleven turned immediately to his right. Coach Ramirez was standing next to the token machine, his hand on the emergency button. He glared at all of us furiously.

"What are you doing?" he seethed. He pointed one of his giant fingers at Alfonso and me and then to the other side of The Hitting Wheel. "Both of you need to get your little rear ends back over there right now!!" He looked into the cage where Mano was standing. "And you," he said, pointing his finger at him. He lowered his voice. He started to say something, but changed his mind. "Why don't you just go back...?" He trailed off. He waved the back of his hand at Mano and said, "Quit trying to show off. Just get your stuff and go over there with the rest of my team."

Mano quickly exited the cage. Both of the high school players clapped hands on his narrow shoulders as he walked by.

"Great job, little man. Just outstanding," one of them said.

Mano walked past Mr. Blyleven, Alfonso and me and went straight to the bleachers where his old, cruddy bat bag was laying. As he passed, Mr. Blyleven studied him like he was an algebra problem. He marveled one more time in a whisper so low that no one else but me could hear it.

"*Joltin' Joe.*"

*   *   *

When we returned to the other side of The Hitting Wheel, Coach Weaver sent Mano, Chase, and me to The Whiffle Wheel. Alfonso followed us.

"What were you guys doing over there?" Chase asked as he handed me a Lightning Stick.

"We were watching Mano hit," I said. He was walking next to me. "Here, Mano," I said, handing him my Lightning Stick. Mano just nodded his head and took it quietly.

No one else was at The Whiffle Wheel so we had it all to ourselves. Chase handed me some tokens. I turned and gave half of them to Mano. We each stepped into one of the small cages. I was in the middle cage, sandwiched between Chase and Mano. Chase dropped his token in and immediately began swinging at those angry yellow bees as they zipped at him. Mano seemed confused. Before I could offer to help, Alfonso stepped up. "Just drop the token in over there. Push the green button and it will start," he said. Mano looked back at him. He smiled a little and nodded his head.

I went over to drop my token in the machine, but stopped for a moment to watch Mano. He dropped in his own token, pushed the green button, and took his place in the batter's box with his Lightning Stick. The first bee popped out. Because the air shoots through the holes in the plastic, they actually do make a noise that sounds like a bee as they come at you.

The first one charged at Mano. He swatted at it and missed. Then he did something I'd hadn't seen him do.

He laughed.

The next bee zipped at him and he swatted and missed again.

He began laughing harder.

By the time the third bee had whizzed by his thin Lightning Stick he was laughing so hard he could hardly swing. I looked over at Alfonso and he was laughing, too. Finally, one of the bees flew right into the bat and Mano smacked it. The little yellow ball shot back toward the machine and dove quickly toward the ground, which only made Mano laugh harder.

Alfonso laughed and clapped his hands. "You got one!" he exclaimed happily.

After that, Mano picked up the game quickly. He whacked the next six yellow balls easily, while still managing to laugh during every swing. I looked over at Alfonso. He was laughing right along with him, cheering every time Mano nailed one of those angry bees with his swatting stick.

"What's so funny?" Chase asked. He was hanging on the net behind me, looking curiously over at Mano and Alfonso. I turned to him. "I don't know," I said, beginning to laugh myself. "But I think this may be the first time Mano has ever swung at bees with a broomstick."

Chase wrinkled his nose. "That kid's like an exotic," he said, smugly. I suddenly felt a little angry, and I hardly ever got angry with Chase.

"An exotic. What is that supposed to mean?"

Chase shrugged his shoulders. "You know, he's just way different. He's like a white deer or something. Just sort of strange and weird." He walked back over to the token box, dropped in another coin and waited for the machine to begin releasing the bees at him again. What was so strange and weird about Mano? Then I remembered that I had thought there was something odd about our new teammate, too. From behind me, I heard Alfonso suddenly say to him, "Hey, do you mind if I try?"

I turned back toward them. Mano responded instantly. He opened the door to his cage and Alfonso bounded in happily. Mano handed him the Lightning Stick and one of the tokens. Alfonso ran over to the token box, dropped it in, pressed the green button and immediately ran back to set up in the batter's box. The Lightning Stick fit his small hands perfectly. I remember thinking it was the first time I'd ever seen him hold anything other than a soccer ball in his hand.

The first bee shot out of the machine and he swung at it and missed, but he laughed. He missed the next ten in a row, too, and his laughter slowly faded into a giggle. As he missed the next nine, the giggle disappeared completely. It was replaced by grunts as he tried to swing harder and harder to swat the bee. When the last bee zipped past his thin bat, he let out a frustrated yell as he swung as hard as he could. He turned back toward Mano. His face was red and I could see his eyes filling up with huge tears. I could tell he was embarrassed.

Mano opened the cage door and stepped inside. He walked over to Alfonso. He was taller, so he bent over at his waist and said something to him that I couldn't hear. Whatever it was, Alfonso nodded quickly. He handed the Lightning Stick back to Mano. Mano showed him how to stand, his feet just wider than his shoulders, his knees bent slightly. He bent over and gently lifted Alfonso's elbow into a cocked position. He said something else that I couldn't hear, but Alfonso let out a little burst of laughter. He handed the stick back to him, walked over and dropped another token in the machine.

Alfonso stepped back into the batter's box. The first bee swarmed out of the machine and headed toward him, but he didn't swing. He just stood perfectly still. He looked almost exactly like Mano at the plate, only smaller.

The next bee flew angrily out of its hive at him and again, he didn't swing. Mano said something to him very softly in his unique accent. It was just one word. I could hear it clearly but it was a word I had never heard before. I had no idea what it meant. It sounded like, "*Nee-you-hi.*"

Alfonso stood perfectly still at the plate. His elbow was cocked. The hive whirred and spit a bee at him. Alfonso swung. It wasn't a text book swing, but the Lightning Stick popped the bee squarely. It shot back toward the machine and quickly dove to the ground.

49

Alfonso turned around gleefully and shouted, "I got one!"

Mano laughed gently. He spoke clearly in his smooth toned voice, "Yes! Get another one!" Alfonso turned quickly back toward the machine. The next yellow ball came at him and he missed it. He missed the next one, too. And the next. Alfonso turned back to Mano. The frustration was back on his face.

Mano simply said, "*Nee-you-hi*." Alfonso nodded. He let the next two pass. On the third, he took a mighty cut. He smashed the bee this time and sent it back so hard it popped off the metal facing above the machine.

"Home Run!" Mano shouted, lifting his hands into the air.

Alfonso dropped the Lightning Stick and threw his hands into the air. He ran to the rear of the cage and threw open the door. The machine spit another bee at his back, but he didn't care. Mano held up his hand and Alfonso slapped it hard. "I did it!" he belted proudly. His face was bright, his eyes shining. "I did it!" he exclaimed again.

Mano laughed. "Yes, you did!" Mano looked over at me. He was smiling. I smiled back at him. Maybe Chase was right and Mano was an exotic.

Maybe he really was one of a kind.

6

Shaun

When Ryne approached his mother and me and asked if Mano could come to our home, I had no idea how significant that simple request would become. Looking back now, it was just the first of a series of seemingly innocent circumstances during the Intimidators' summer season that eventually came together in an unexpected way, at exactly the right time. Life is that way, isn't it? Sometimes important things seem to happen at the perfect moment. I've never given much thought as to why, but that's beginning to change now. In fact, I've begun to wonder if maybe there is a great design for everyone's life and maybe that plan is what's responsible for moving us toward new adventures. If so, even though we may not understand why or how the plan works, we should still follow the course that has been laid out in front of us and see where it takes us.

I don't know where the road to our amazing summer journey actually began, but I do know this - the day that Mano showed up at our home was very important. It began the series of events that would eventually change the way Ryne and other members of the Intimidators treated him. That Friday night was the first time the team began to see there was something truly special about the new kid from Hawai'i. I don't think I'm being overly dramatic when I say that night changed the team's season. It was the beginning of something special for the boys, their families, and so many others who would come in contact with the Intimidators during their magical summer season.

Ryne's invitation to Mano gave his mother a chance to do what she does best, which is to show kindness to everyone. It was Hope's idea to turn the invitation into a sleepover event for the entire Intimidators team. I almost fell on the floor when she suggested having our home invaded by ten eleven-year old boys for a "Friday Night Movie and Popcorn Sleepover Festival" the night before the young season's second game, but Hope has a unique gift. She can drive kids like cattle. I'm convinced she could drive a wagon train of a hundred eleven-year old boys across the Texas Panhandle in a week, cook beans and hotdogs for them every day, and have the entire herd happily mooing and passing gas in unison, all without chipping a nail. Of course, she'd be sure to bring me along to clean up the enormous stinking piles they'd leave behind.

That's why I'm thankful for our twin *Fortresses of Solitude* in the backyard. The Fortresses of Solitude were originally intended to just be a single Fortress of Solitude for Ryne, similar to Superman's secret getaway. Then Ryne's little sister came along and one ultimate tree house just wasn't enough. So we added the second fortress and created a pair of spacious, kid friendly condos in the trees for our children that are more interesting than the home their mother and I live in on the ground. They are connected by a sixty-foot rope bridge that hangs between two giant oak trees in our backyard. Each fortification is identical and is equipped with a refrigerator, a television, two beds, and enough carpeted floor space for 10 sleeping bags. Between them, we could comfortably house two baseball teams, just as long as they stayed outside and kept their stinking piles with them.

When the boys began arriving, we quickly shuttled them outside to the backyard. I had fired up the barbeque and was grilling enough burgers and dogs to feed Washington's starving Revolutionary Army at Valley Forge. The Intimidators swarmed onto the gently rolling staircases that lead from the ground upward to the fortresses to set up their camp. Ryne's little sister, Samantha, stood next to me and pouted.

"I don't want them to stay in my fortress, Daddy," she said over her puckered bottom lip. "They're going to mess it all up."

I bent down to her. "They won't mess it up, Sam," I fibbed. "Actually, of course they'll mess it up. But we'll get Mommy to clean it."

"That's your job, Buster," Hope chirped as she swept past us. She was carrying a tray of cheeses, lettuce, and bright red sliced tomatoes that I knew none of the Intimidators would touch with a ten-foot fork. "You know our deal," she reminded me.

"Yes, ma'am. However, I failed to read the fine print in that marriage contract before I signed it."

She winked at me. "You should have gotten a lawyer."

"But I am a lawyer!" I protested.

"I meant a better lawyer," she joked.

Samantha looked up at me. "Daddy, what's fine print?"

"It's really tiny words that mommies put on the back of marriage contracts. You have to have a microscope to read them."

"What do they say?"

"They say that mommies get to make all the rules," I sighed.

"Yay!" She shouted happily. "I can't wait until I'm a mommy! Because the first rule I'm going to make is that no boys are allowed in my tree house."

"Good rule," I agreed. "Boys are gross."

Hope poked me in the ribs with her finger as she hurried past on her way back to the kitchen. "You got that right, Buster." The doorbell rang again. Hope directed me as she disappeared through the backdoor into the kitchen, "Shaun, will you get that please?" I closed the cover to the grill and slipped through the house to our front door. When I opened it, Mano was standing there with his father. They both appeared unsure of whether they were at the right place.

"Hello," I said, extending my hand. "I'm Shaun. I'm Ryne's dad."

Mano's father smiled warmly. He swallowed my smaller paw with his much larger one and shook it firmly. "*Aloha*. I am *Kekoa*." His voice was calm and smooth with a fascinating Polynesian accent. He placed his other hand on his son's shoulder. "This is *Mano*." He pronounced both of their names very deliberately. *Keh koh' ah* and *Mah-no*.

"Hello, Mano." He grasped my offered hand and shook it every bit as firmly as his father had done. I noticed immediately that his hands and wrists were thick and strong.

"Well, hello!" I heard Hope exclaim from behind me, interrupting us. She whisked in from the kitchen carrying a bowl of freshly sliced fruit. "I'm Ryne's mother. My name is Hope," she twinkled, flashing one of her million watt smiles. She tucked the bowl under her arm and offered her small hand to Mano's father. He took it in his large mitt and held it gently. "*Aloha*, Hope. I am *Kekoa*," he said, introducing himself. He turned to his son once again. "This is my son, *Mano*."

"Hello, Mano. I'm so glad you could come." I think she could tell he was a bit nervous. She offered her hand to him and he took it gently, just like his father. "*Aloha*," he said, shyly. He was dressed in a traditional Hawai'ian shirt, clean board shorts that looked new, and fresh sandals. He looked very different than that first practice. He had left his baseball cap behind this time, too. His hair was neatly combed. His eyes were dark, but they shined brightly.

"Won't you come in?" Hope said to Kekoa.

Mano's father shook his head politely. "I am very sorry, but I have an important appointment. I do hope that we can visit some later," he replied. His face was bright, open, and honest.

"Of course," Hope answered, taking charge. She turned her attention to Mano. "Mano, why don't you come with me? The team is in the backyard." She smiled and ushered him into the house saying, "Would you mind carrying this bowl for me?" She handed him the bowl and placed her hand on his back. As they started to walk away, she turned her head and smiled reassuringly at Mano's father.

"We'll take good care of him," I promised.

The large Hawai'ian smiled graciously. "*Mahalo nui loa*," he said, warmly. He handed me a sleeping bag and a small backpack. Both appeared to be new and unused, as if he had just purchased them. He shook my hand firmly once more and then left.

When I returned to the backyard, the Intimidators were engaged in an improvised game of disc golf using trees as their targets. Our home sits on several acres and the boys had their pick of prominent oaks to serve as flag sticks. There were two foursomes playing. Jimmy, Sammy, Wee Willie, and Hootie made up one group while the second was composed of Curtis, Brazos, Ryne, and Chase. Discs flew crazily around the yard and crashed into tree branches like stray UFOs from outer space. Hope walked out to the edge of the patio and yelled for Ryne. He was about a third of the way through the makeshift golf course and had to sprint a good ways across the yard.

"Hey, Mano," he said, smiling and wheezing a little when he finally arrived.

"Did you take a puff from your inhaler before you started playing?" Hope immediately inquired.

Ryne grinned. He was accustomed to having to account for his asthma, particularly during the scorching hot summer months in Texas. "Yes, ma'am. I took it." He turned to Mano. "Hey, do you like disc golf?"

Mano looked puzzled. "I…I don't know. What is it?"

Hope placed her hand gently on Mano's back again. She smiled at him and then at Ryne. "It's fun," she said, encouragingly. "Ryne will teach you. Do you have enough discs, Ryne?" Ryne smiled at his mother.

"Of course! C'mon, let's go, Mano." They both took off, galloping across the yard like a couple of colts.

Hope leaned in close to me. "You know it's tough to be the new kid," she said. I nodded, feeling a little guilty as I remembered my first impressions of both Mano and his father. "Yes it is," I agreed.

"This will help him get acquainted with the boys," she insisted confidently. I've found it interesting how sometimes people are given names that actually end up reflecting their character. If I was pressed to name the most impressive characteristic about my wife, it would be that no matter what the circumstances, she is always full of genuine hope that things will work out for the best. I lifted the grill cover and turned my attention once more to the dogs and burgers. Hope continued gazing out across the large backyard as one of the foursomes became a five-some. "I wish Miguel had been able to come," she mused, thoughtfully.

I shrugged. "It's probably best that he didn't."

She shot me a stern look. "Why would you say that?"

"The boys act differently when he's not around," I replied, honestly. "Miggy is like an extension of his dad's presence. Ramirez is not exactly what sports people call a "player's coach." He creates tension among his players all the time. Miggy no doubt gets an extra dose at home and he carries that tension around on his back like a gorilla." I gestured toward the boys with my hot dog tongs as one of them whooped loudly after making a good shot. "Those boys are more relaxed and more themselves whenever Miggy isn't around."

Hope didn't argue with me. She simply said, "That needs to change."

I nodded my head in agreement. "Sure it does, but I don't know that it ever will. Of course, they may never become a real team if it doesn't."

Hope walked over and put her arms around my waist and gently shook me. "You should worry less about the team and more about their friendships."

I smiled thinly. "Teammates don't always become friends," I warned her.

Hope never missed a beat. "But they can." Then she added in a firmer voice, "And they should."

I turned and looked to the backyard. Discs were flying. Boys were laughing. Hope squeezed me and nuzzled near my ear. "Have faith," she whispered, confidently.

* * *

Ryne

My Fortress of Solitude is my favorite place in the world. Samantha has one, too. Dad tried to build mine himself, but after three weeks Mom told him it looked like a tornado had blown a bunch of random boards into one of the big oak trees in our backyard. So she convinced him to hire a professional and the guy they hired should have his own show on cable. He did a really good job.

Honestly, I'd rather be in my fortress than in my room. It's decorated with baseball pennants from every major league team, and their minor league affiliates, too. There are four gaming chairs for whenever friends come over to hang out and play video games. Mom keeps my refrigerator stocked with juice, different flavors of Gatorade, bottled water, and a variety of sodas. I also have a small pantry filled with snacks, a microwave for popcorn, and an air conditioner. The air conditioner is one of those window units and it keeps me completely cool, even when it's a billion degrees outside. The best thing is the television. It's the perfect size for gaming and makes my fortress an excellent movie watching cave day or night. Samantha's fortress is pretty much like mine. The only difference is it's decorated like a doll house on the inside. There's also a bridge that connects us. I didn't want the bridge at first, but Mom insisted on it. It's one of those bridges that sways back and forth so it's actually pretty awesome.

Chase, and Brazos put their stuff in my fortress when they arrived and Jimmy, Sammy, Curtis, Wee Willie and Hootie put theirs in Samantha's fortress. When Mano came, Dad put his stuff in with me.

We ended up playing about ten holes of disc golf while my parents made dinner. Dad is pretty good with the grill and the burgers were stellar. The only downer was when Mom tried to get all of us to "try something new." (She does that a lot.) She made us put tomatoes on our burgers because they were good for us, but everyone except Curtis ending up pulling them off. You could put broccoli on a burger though, and Curtis would probably still eat it in three giant bites.

It was already starting to get dark when we finished, so Wee Willie suggested we play flashlight tag. We had fun chasing each other around through the dark for about an hour. When we got tired and sweaty, we all piled into my fortress to watch a movie before we went to bed. Wee Willie snatched the box of Blu-Rays and began scanning the choices while the rest of the guys scrambled for the chairs. Hootie popped open the refrigerator and began taking drink orders.

"Somebody get on the popcorn," he ordered.

"Who died and made you king?" Jimmy asked.

"I'm getting the drinks. Besides, I'm injured," Hootie reminded him. I thought he looked like a deranged hockey player in his mask.

Brazos couldn't resist taking a shot at him. "Dude, it's just a scratch. You need to get tough."

"Oh, let me see you take a smokin' grounder off your nose, Brazos!" Hootie honked back. His broken beak made his voice sound foggy so that whenever he spoke, he sounded like a goose.

"I'll get the popcorn," I volunteered, heading to the microwave.

"You've only got baseball movies in here, Ryne?" Wee Willie suddenly asked me as his fingers ticked through the selections.

"No, there's some other stuff," I replied.

Wee Willie pulled a pink disc jacket out of the box. "What the heck is this? *Hello Kitty Goes Shopping*?"

"That's Samantha's," I explained.

"OH, RIGHT!" The whole team piled on together.

I laughed. "No, really. It's hers."

"Seriously? Who wants to watch a movie about a cat who goes shopping?" Curtis asked. "Cats don't shop. Cats don't do anything. My sister has a cat. You know what it does? It scratches litter all over the floor in our laundry room. And if you go in there barefooted, that stuff sticks to the bottom of your feet."

Sammy curled his lips. "Dude, that's nasty. So you're walking around your house with little rocks the cat whizzed on stuck to your feet?"

"That's disgusting!" Jimmy chimed in.

"Hey Curtis, just keep your socks on while you're over here tonight, okay?" I requested as I plopped the first packet of popcorn onto the microwave dish. "I don't want to find any little wet cat rocks in my carpet after you go home."

"Oh, how about *The Sandlot*?" Wee Willie interrupted excitedly, as he pulled out the case.

"Yeah!" Chase yelled. "I haven't seen that in a couple of years." Everyone immediately agreed, except for Mano. He was sitting lightly on the edge of one of the beds, like he was afraid he might mess it up by leaving an impression of his rear end on it.

"What do you think, Mano?" I asked him. Mano shifted on the bed nervously. "I…uh…I uh…well, I…"

"Do you want to see it or not?" Chase asked, impatiently. Everyone stared at him. I realized he had the same look on his face that he'd had earlier when I'd asked him about disc golf.

"It's about kids who played baseball a long time ago," I offered. "It's a great movie."

"Wait a minute," Curtis chimed in. "He's never seen *The Sandlot?*"

Mano seemed to shrink back from everyone. "No, we don't watch a lot of movies," he said, quietly.

"Wow," Jimmy remarked. "Who hasn't seen *The Sandlot?*"

"Knock it off, Jimmy," I said.

Jimmy lifted his hands up. "What did I do?"

Hootie burped his soda. It rolled out of him low, long and loud. "We're watching it," he announced when the burp finally finished. "Decision's been made."

"Well, I guess we have to watch it, if King Hootie says so," Brazos chided.

"What's your problem, Brazos?" Hootie honked back. "If you were choosing, we'd probably end up watching the stupid shopping cat movie!"

Wee Willie held up the pink case threateningly. "*Hello Kitty* or *Sandlot?*" he teased.

"SANDLOT!" Everyone except Mano screamed in unison. I looked over at him. He was just sitting there on the corner of the bed.

"Put in *The Sandlot*," I told Wee Willie. "Then get over here and help me pass out the popcorn."

60

Wee Willie slipped the disc into the player and Sammy hopped up to turn off the lights. As the movie started, I began dumping popcorn into bowls. I kept reloading the microwave and Wee Willie helped me pass them out until everybody had their own. When I finished the last two, Wee Willie took one and plopped down onto the bed opposite Mano, propping his feet up. I took the other and made my way back to where Mano was sitting. I hopped on the bed and stretched out my feet. He looked over at me. "You can put your feet on the bed. It's okay," I said.

He gave me a short smile and took off his sandals. Then he swiveled around until his feet were on the bed, too.

I hadn't seen *The Sandlot* in a long time, either. It's one of my favorite movies, baseball or otherwise. As it began, I realized that I'd forgotten that Smalls was a new kid, too, just like Mano. Except Smalls had no idea how to play baseball and Mano is a really good player. In fact, he is more like Benny "The Jet" Rodriguez than Smalls.

As the movie played, we all watched and waited for our favorite parts. It's weird, but when you've never seen a movie before, nobody talks. I guess it's because you don't want to miss anything. After you've seen a movie a few times, nobody shuts up. Just like when Benny the Jet hits a ball right into Smalls glove on purpose, so he can get the confidence to play with the rest of the team. Hootie blew out a bunch of air and made a raspberry sound with his tongue. "Nobody could do that!" he said.

"I bet Miggy could," Sammy said confidently. It was the first time someone had mentioned Miggy's name the whole night.

"Yeah, he probably could," Curtis agreed.

"No way," Hootie said. "That's bull. Nobody could do that, not even Miggy."

I looked over at Mano. His eyes were glued to the big screen. His hand moved from the popcorn bowl to his mouth slowly, one kernel at a time.

When all of the Sandlot kids convinced Benny to skip baseball for a day so they could go to the pool, I started to feel uncomfortable. I knew what was coming. On the screen, I watched Squints do his fake drowning act so he could trick a kiss out of the lifeguard, Wendy Peffercorn. And when her bright red lips started moving toward us, I felt my face suddenly get all hot and tingly.

Just as he planted one on her, Brazos belted at the top of his lungs, "THAT KID LOOKS LIKE A FROG! SHE'S KISSING A FROG!"

Everyone busted up laughing, except for Chase. He turned around to look at me and cocked his head to one side. He grinned, like he knew a secret. I knew what he was thinking, so I just waved him away with the back of my hand.

For the rest of movie, the Sandlot kids had to figure out how to get the Babe Ruth autographed baseball that Smalls had swiped from his stepdad's trophy case back from The Beast. We all howled as they failed again and again, even though some of the ideas that came up with to try and get it back were absolutely amazing.

Every now and again, I would sneak a peek over at Mano while everyone was laughing to see if he was enjoying the movie. I never saw him laugh once. At one point, he even put his popcorn bowl down, pulled his knees up under his chin, and hugged them tightly to his chest, almost like he was watching a scary movie. I don't think his eyes ever left the big screen, even for a moment.

When Benny the Jet summoned the courage to finally pickle The Beast, something strange happened. Just as Benny cleared the fence and came face to face with the monster dog, Mano began to slowly rock back and forth. I could see that he was squeezing his legs even tighter, turning himself into a ball. I'd have been willing to bet you couldn't have separated his arms from his legs with a crow bar.

Then Benny took off with the ball, and The Beast took off after Benny. I heard Hootie yell, "YOU'D BETTER RUN, DUDE!"

Benny took off across the neighborhood with The Beast in hot pursuit. Curtis chimed in, "Think you could out run that dog, Wee Willie?"

Wee Willie answered, "Heck yeah! There's no way he would catch me. When I'm scared, I can fly!"

The Beast closed the gap. He was right on Benny's heels. I looked over at Mano. He was rocking back and forth, faster and faster. And it sounded like he was mumbling something to himself. It looked like he was actually afraid. It was almost like he thought the movie was…I don't know…like it was real.

Benny motored around the neighborhood at light speed and The Beast never let up. Just as The Jet finally leapt to the fence and The Beast soared through the air after him, Mano yelled.

"*Nee-you-hi*!!"

We all turned and stared at him. He was sitting on the bed. It looked like he was shaking. Then the lights came on as the door to my fortress suddenly opened. Mom was standing there with one hand on her hip. Wee Willie hit the pause button on the Blu-Ray.

"It's after midnight, boys!" she scolded. "Lights out was thirty minutes ago!"

"But it's almost over!" Sammy whined. "Can we just finish it?"

Everybody joined in with his cry. "Oh, c'mon…pleeease!"

Mom just shook her head. "You've all got a game tomorrow and you need your rest," she lectured. Then she looked at me sternly. "Ryne, you knew what time curfew was tonight. I didn't want to have to come out here. Actually, I wanted to come fifteen minutes ago but your dad convinced me to give you extra time to do what you were supposed to do."

I hung my head. "Sorry, Mom," I said weakly.

She looked over at Mano with a concerned expression on her face. He was slowly beginning to uncurl from his ball, but he was still trembling. "Are you okay, Mano?" She asked.

Mano nodded his head quickly. "Yes, I'm fine," he answered, but I knew he wasn't telling the truth. Mom watched him for a long moment. It was the same look she gives whenever she knows something's off with me or Samantha. It's a look that is usually followed by a thermometer.

"Okay, then," she said. "Let's get to bed, boys. Good night. Sleep tight." She closed the door. Hootie stood up. He stretched and yawned.

"Let's go, guys," he said to Curtis, Wee Willie, Jimmy and Sammy. The five of them headed out the door to Samantha's fortress across the bridge. When they left, Brazos and Chase began rolling out their sleeping bags. I looked over at Mano. He seemed a little better, but he didn't move.

"I guess Mano and I will take the beds," I announced. Chase and Brazos suddenly seemed super tired. They yawned together which made me yawn, too. They both dropped their heads immediately onto their pillows and burrowed in to their sleeping bags. I stepped between them and picked up the remote.

On the big screen, The Beast was frozen in mid-leap. I reached over by the door and turned off the light. The room glowed from the TV and in the dark the screen was even brighter. I took the remote and stepped back between Chase and Brazos.

Mano's eyes shined once again in the darkness of the room. They were fixed on the image on the screen. I sat back down on my bed.

"You okay, Mano?" I whispered. He still didn't look good, but when I spoke he turned toward me.

"Yes," he said. He even smiled a little, but it was one of those sad smiles that kids give when they've been sick for a while.

We both pulled back the covers and laid our heads down on our pillows. I rolled over onto my side and looked over at Mano. He had the blanket pulled up almost to his nose like he was cold, or maybe like he was trying to hide. I thought about asking him again if he was okay, but my eyes felt really heavy.

Then I guess I just fell asleep.

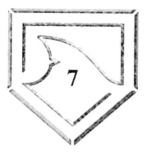

7

Ryne

Dreams are strange. Sometimes my dreams are like awesome movies. In some of them I can fly or maybe I'll even have super-strength so I can lift buildings and stuff. Once I had a dream that I played football for the Dallas Cowboys. Only problem was when the coach sent me into the game, I didn't know any of the plays. I still scored touchdowns though because the defense never covered me and I was open every time I went out for a pass. Those are the kinds of dreams I love.

But then some of my dreams are just stupid. It's like my brain takes all the stuff that happened over the last few days or weeks and makes it into a lousy dream omelet that has ingredients that nobody would ever put together, like peanut butter and brown rice made with turtle eggs. They just don't make any sense.

This was one of those stupid dreams. I was in some sort of concert hall with a huge stage. It was totally packed with kids and it was dark, except you could see everyone because they had that glow in the dark paint on their bodies and in their hair like at the bowling alley. Chase was with me and we were on the front row, waiting for a band to come out and start playing. People kept pushing in on us, mashing us closer and closer to the stage. When I looked at Chase, he was wearing a huge purple wig that had springy curls. He had this crazy look on his face and he was laughing like he was having the time of his life.

But I wasn't.

I was starting to feel like I was drowning. The people were like water. They just kept pouring into the hall. I kept thinking somebody would close the doors and say that the room couldn't hold any more people. But they just kept coming, and coming.

Finally, I couldn't take it anymore. I knew I wasn't supposed to do it, but I crawled up a small set of stairs that led to the stage. It was a dumb thing to do in front of all of those people, but for some reason I thought no one would see me do it. I just had to escape.

I stood up and looked out across the concert hall. From the stage, it now looked like it was a thousand times bigger. It just kept going and going.

That was when I saw Madison. She was standing with a bunch of her girlfriends in the middle of the giant crowd, just laughing and talking. All of them had their smart phones and their fingers were attacking the screens furiously as they texted and giggled.

Suddenly, I wanted to run. I had to run before she saw me. So I started to take off across the stage, only I could barely move. My feet felt like they were stuck in wet cement and every step I took they just moved slower and slower. So I fell down on the floor and used my hands to help pull me along, sort of like a crab. I kept pulling to try and go faster, but no matter how hard I tried, I just couldn't seem to make any progress. The end of the stage seemed like it was waaaayyy over there.

Then I heard my mom's voice. She was standing right there on the stage in front of me. I looked up at her from my crab crawl position. She was reaching down, handing me a lime green hot dog on a bun that was an electric blueberry color. "You didn't eat your dinner," she said to me.

Yes I did, I thought. I remembered eating a hot dog and a hamburger, but I didn't eat one of those green and blue hot dogs. Why would she make me eat one of those? Was it supposed to be good for me?

That's when I realized I needed to go to the bathroom. Bad. Really bad. I sort of panicked, wondering how far the bathrooms were once you got off the stage.

Then the dream instantly changed and magically, I was in the bathroom! It was huge. There must have been a hundred stalls. The doors were shut to each of them as if every single one was occupied. So I dropped down onto my hands and knees and started crawling across the floor, checking for feet until I finally found one that appeared empty. So I jumped up, wiped my hands on my pants (Gross, I realized I had been crawling on the bathroom floor!) and pulled on the handle.

When it opened, Chase was standing there. Only it wasn't a bathroom stall anymore. We were in my room. The purple wig with the springy curls was gone. He was wearing his baseball cap. He reached over and started pulling on my arm.

"C'mon, dude," he said, urgently. "Put on your uniform. We're going to be late."

I just stared at him. I wanted to speak, but words wouldn't come out of my mouth. I remembered that Madison was at the concert. I needed to go back and say something to her, but I couldn't remember how to get to the hall. Chase reached out to me again. He shook my arm. "Wake up, dude! We're going to be late."

That's when I woke up.

Chase was standing next to my bed. He had his hand on my shoulder and was shaking me.

"*Ryne...Ryne...wake up*," he was whispering urgently.

"Wha... Wha... what is it?" I said, groggily. Then reality rushed in and quickly the dream disappeared like a mist. I remembered that we weren't in my room, but in my fortress.

Chase put his finger to his lips signaling me to be quiet. He motioned over toward the other bed.

Mano was lying on his side, facing away from us. He was groaning and mumbling.

"Something's wrong with him," Chase said. "I think he might be sick."

"What time is it?" I asked, trying to wake up. My eyes were foggy with sleep but through the window I could see that it was still very dark outside.

Chase pushed a button on his digital watch and the numbers glowed bright blue. It said 2:32 am. We'd only been in bed a few hours.

Mano moaned again. I thought I heard him say something.

"Is he awake?" I whispered. Chase shrugged. I spun out of my bunk and stood up. I grabbed a small flashlight that I keep on the nightstand between the two beds in case I have to go into the house in the middle of the night to go to the bathroom. I clicked it on but directed the beam at the floor so it wouldn't be so bright. I leaned over Mano. He groaned again and this time I heard him clearly mumble, "*No...no.*"

"He's talking in his sleep," I determined.

"Then he must be having a really bad dream," Chase said. "Because he's been doing that for a while."

I didn't know what to do. "Should I try and wake him up?" I asked.

Chase just looked at me helplessly. "I don't know. Maybe."

I reached out toward him hesitantly. Just then, he let out a louder groan and rolled further onto his side. When he did, the covers pulled up and

69

his t-shirt came with them, exposing his back. What we saw caused both of us to suck in our breath at the same time.

The scar was huge. Against his brown skin it was very white, as if the area had been bleached. It went up from the top of his shorts in a large, uneven half-circle and began to disappear under his arm.

I slowly turned the flashlight from the floor. I brought it up a little higher and the beam grew slightly brighter. We could see that the scar was jagged, similar to a zipper, but with uneven teeth. I heard Chase mutter, *"Holy cow. What the heck happened to him?"*

I shook my head slowly. "I don't know. But it looks like…."

"What is that?" a voice whispered from behind us. Both of us jumped. It was Brazos. His eyes were wide and his long hair was bunched into corkscrews all over his head. It looked like the wig Chase had been wearing in my dream, only it wasn't purple.

Mano suddenly shot straight up in the bed causing all three of us to jump. Chase yelped in surprise and stumbled back into Brazos, who grabbed me, and all three of us fell back toward my bed. Mano glared at us, his eyes filled with terror. He was breathing hard and fast.

"It's okay, Mano," I said, putting up my hands like a defensive back in football. "It's just us."

Mano lifted both of his hands toward his face. His hands dropped quickly to his chest and began patting. He pulled his necklace from beneath his shirt and grasped the big tooth at the end with both hands. He spoke in a low voice, almost a whisper. *"He niuhi 'ai holopapa o ka moku,"* he said. His unique accent was stronger than normal. I figured he must have been speaking in his native Hawai'ian, but I didn't know if he was still talking in his sleep.

"What did you say?" I asked him, carefully.

He didn't answer immediately so we all three sat very quietly, wondering if he was still dreaming. Then his eyes seemed to clear. He looked directly at us. He hesitated, as if he was holding a secret he couldn't share. His breathing began to slow down and I could tell he really was awake. He finally said, "It's nothing. It's just something from an old Hawai'ian legend."

"What kind of legend?" Chase probed immediately.

Mano looked at him uncertainly. "Uh...."

"Yeah, tell us about it," Brazos added. He sat down on the edge of my bed. So did Chase. Even though it was the middle of the night, all three of us were eager to listen.

* * *

I thought Mano still appeared a bit unsteady. "Do you want some water?" I asked him. He nodded. I hopped over to the fridge and grabbed a bottle. I handed it to him and then sat down between Brazos and Chase.

Mano took a sip. He seemed to become much calmer, more like the kid who'd stood fearlessly in the batter's box at our first game and at The Hitting Wheel, taking lightning fast cuts with that old, wooden bat at 85mph fastballs.

"My *kupuna* used to tell me a story," Mano began.

"Your what?" Brazos asked.

"My grandfather," Mano said. "*Kupuna* is Hawai'ian for grandfather."

"Cool name," Brazos said.

Mano continued. "When my *kupuna* was just a boy, there was an old man who lived by himself outside his village on Molokai. It was said he had been a powerful warrior when he was young and that he was much stronger and faster than any other warrior on the island. He was also greatly feared because in battle, he was never seen by his enemy until it was too late. He would appear suddenly and attack, and then disappear almost immediately."

"You mean, like a ghost?" Brazos offered.

Mano shook his head. "No, nothing like that."

"Like a shark," I said. Both Chase and Brazos turned to me immediately. Something strange about the scar on Mano's back was beginning to come together in my mind. I had clicked off the flashlight. Outside, the sky was clear. The moon was bright and a soft light was filtering into the fortress through the window above our beds. Mano's dark eyes were shining like wet, black stones. He touched the tooth hanging around his neck without thinking.

"Yes," he agreed. "He was a *niuhi*."

I could feel Brazos and Chase tense on either side of me.

"What is that?" Chase asked.

"*Niuhi* is the Hawai'ian word for shark," Mano explained. He paused before adding, "Actually, it means man-eating shark."

"You mean like a Great White?" Brazos whispered. Brazos had watched every episode of *Shark Week* on the Discovery Channel the previous summer. Chase and I had pretty much seen them all, too. We thought the shows were cool, but Brazos was completely fascinated. He had a calendar on his refrigerator at home and had the first week in August, Shark Week, already circled in bright red.

"Yes, a white shark, or a tiger shark," Mano added. "There are lots of tiger sharks around the islands." He sat there for a while, almost as if he was trying to decide if he should go any further. "The sharks were hunted. It was believed that anyone who captured the *niuhi* would also capture its spirit."

"They hunted sharks?" Brazos asked. He was fascinated. He knew from the Discovery Channel that catching a shark wasn't something you did with a cane pole and a couple of minnows. "How did they catch them?"

"It was very dangerous, a sport that was only for chiefs," Mano explained. "The old man who lived alone outside my *kupuna's* village was a chief."

"Did he catch a tiger shark?" Chase asked.

Mano nodded slowly. "Yes, only he would not speak of it. My *kupuna* said that everyone knew that it was true."

"How did they know?" I asked.

Mano's eyes seemed to grow darker. "Because he only had one arm. The shark took the other, from his elbow down." He looked at all of us and then said something that chilled us to our bones. "My *kupuna* said the chiefs would sometimes use themselves as bait. Some of them would cut themselves on their forearms until they bled, and then enter the water and wait."

Brazos sucked in his breath. "He used his own arm for bait?" he gasped. He reached for his elbow and began to slowly massage it. I felt my left hand travel to my throwing arm. I imagined what it would be like for it to be gone, ripped away in the jaws of a man-eating shark.

"Hey, Mano," Chase said, breaking our stunned silence. "Those words you said earlier. He noo-something?"

"He niuhi 'ai holopapa o ka moku, " Mano repeated for us.

"Yeah. What does that mean?"

Mano paused. Then he said, "It means the *niuhi shark that devours all on the island.*"

I thought about that word. Devour. It wasn't a word that I really used. Once I'd eaten a whole large pizza after one of my ballgames. I was starving and I had eaten every bite by myself, crust and all. Mom had said, "Well, you certainly devoured that pizza, Ryne!" When I asked her what devour meant, she'd told me to look it up in the dictionary. When I did, I'd found that it meant to destroy something completely.

Mano looked out the window. The moon had moved and now the entire room was bright. We could see his face clearly. The strange feeling I'd had earlier about the scar on his back was suddenly no longer just a feeling. "Was it a tiger shark that attacked you, Mano?" I asked. Chase and Brazos didn't move. They were still and quiet.

Mano kept staring dreamily out the window. After a moment, he calmly said, "Yes. I saw the stripes."

We all wanted to know what happened, but no one had the courage to ask. I swallowed hard. When I spoke, my words came out in a whisper. *"Hey, Mano...it's okay. You don't have to talk about it, if you don't want to."*

He continued looking up out the window at the moon. "I was spearfishing," he said. His voice sounded far away, like he was somewhere else. "I like to spearfish. It is quiet beneath the water. Peaceful."

He stared into the moonlight. "I always floated out on my board to a spot where the water begins to get deep, close to the edge of the reef. There were many fish that day and I caught two of them right away. I was putting them on the cord that was attached to the back of my board."

"You keep them on a cord?" Brazos asked.

"Yes. It is a very long rope, to make sure the fish stay far away from you."

The question was in all of our minds, but Chase asked it. "Why?"

Mano turned to him. "So if the shark comes, it will go after the fish instead of you."

Chase nodded slowly. His eyes grew wide.

Mano turned back toward the window. "All of the sudden, every fish around me disappeared. They knew something bigger was coming."

We held our breath. "It came from the deep water, swimming up right toward me. It was very big and it moved slowly. I was so afraid, I could not move," he said, helplessly. "There was no place for me to hide. Then I remembered the fish. I had not tied them to the cord yet, so I just let them go. When I did, it went for them."

I felt my throat begin to go dry.

"The shark took them and just turned away," Mano said, looking back to us. "When it did, I swam quickly back to my board. I was still very frightened, but I believed I had been fortunate to escape."

Brazos and Chase drew in closer to me.

"I climbed up out of the water, and I did not move. I just lay there and remained very still, floating on my board." His voice had become almost a whisper. "There was no noise. It was perfectly quiet, just like when I had been under the water. That's when I felt it."

Mano closed his eyes and reached under his right arm with his hand to touch his back, the place where the scar had disappeared from our view. "The pain was very sharp at first. That went away quickly and I felt something new. It was like I was being pressed. I was squeezed until I could not breathe, like I had fallen between large stones and they were crushing me. Then it just stopped." Mano closed his eyes. "I do not know why, but the shark let me go."

It was eerily quiet. No one spoke. We realized that Mano had just told us he had actually been caught in the jaws of a tiger shark. None of us had ever had anything like that happen in our boring lives. What could we say?

I stared at the white tooth hanging around Mano's neck. It was large and looked very sharp. I finally summoned the courage to ask him, "How did you get its tooth?"

Mano breathed in deeply and exhaled. His eyes remained closed. "It was stuck in the bottom of my board. My father found it the next day."

"Can I touch it?" Brazos boldly asked.

Mano opened his eyes. He looked different somehow, almost like he felt better after telling us the story. He took the chain from around his neck and handed it to Brazos. Brazos held the tooth in the palm of his hand. Chase reached down and touched the pointed tip. "It's like the t…tip of a knife," he said, his voice cracking.

I glanced up from the tooth at Mano. He was looking out the window again at the moon. There was a sound coming from outside. It was a noise that I knew, one the bridge between our fortresses makes whenever someone is walking across it. We all turned toward the door and it pushed open slightly. It opened a little wider and Wee Willie's head poked in. He looked at us with his eyebrows raised and said in a surprised voice, "You guys are awake?"

"Yeah," I answered. "What's up?"

Wee Willie came toward us. "I'm thirsty and Sam's refrigerator is out of water," he said. Then he added, "Hey, did you know Hootie snores? Holy cow, he snores. And with that mask on his face, he sounds like Darth Vader with a bad cold." He suddenly saw the tooth in Brazos' hand. "What's that?" he asked, curiously.

Brazos didn't answer. We all looked over at Mano. "It is a tiger shark's tooth," Mano answered. He even had a small smile on his face now.

"Awesome!" Wee Willie breathed, excitedly. "Where did you get it?"

I looked at Mano. He smiled a bit.

"Do you want to tell the story?" I asked. Mano nodded. I turned to Chase.

"Chase, go get the guys," I said. He stood up immediately and went to the door. "But be quiet," I told him. I was afraid any noise might wake my parents. Chase nodded and slipped out onto the bridge.

"What's going on?" Wee Willie inquired.

"Just wait," I answered.

Chase was gone for a few minutes and then we heard the bridge creaking as he returned with Hootie, Curtis, Jimmy, and Sammy in tow. Jimmy and Sammy looked as if they were already pretty awake but Hootie and Curtis walked in like a pair of zombies.

"What time is it?" Hootie mumbled. His hair was mashed flat on one side and his mask was crooked.

"Just sit down," I said.

Curtis tugged a gaming chair closer to the bed and flopped wearily into it.

"It's still dark outside," Hootie complained, pointing out the window. "Look, the moon is still out. Seriously. Why did you wake me up?"

"Because Mano has something important to say. He just told Chase, Brazos and me something amazing. I think you guys should hear it, too."

I turned to Mano. He nodded. Then all of us listened as he told the incredible story about how he got his scar once again.

8

Shaun

The ride to the game on Saturday was surprisingly quiet. Hope took Curtis, Hootie, Brazos, Jimmy and Sammy, Wee Willie and Samantha in our Suburban while Ryne, Mano, and Chase rode with me. The three boys sat on the bench seat in the back of my pickup truck in a straight row, staring blankly out the window. They looked exhausted.

"You guys stay up late last night?" I asked, suspiciously. I glanced at Ryne in my rear view mirror. He sat up a little straighter. "We went to bed right after Mom came out," he answered.

"She wasn't very happy about having to come out there," I said, giving him one of my *I told you so and now we're both in trouble* looks in the mirror.

Ryne shrugged his shoulders sheepishly. "Sorry, Dad," he said.

Hope had gotten up early to cook a huge IHOP style breakfast for the team complete with waffles, pancakes, eggs, bacon, sausage, and bowls of neatly diced fruit. Even though Ryne had the entire squad sitting at the huge picnic table in our backyard dressed and ready by 9:00 am, it was obvious to his mother as she looked around the table at their sleepy faces that something extra-curricular had taken place the previous night. She was not pleased.

"They stayed up last night," Hope fumed to me as we took our seats in the stands. I opened her pop-up chair and secured it to the bleachers. She sat down and glared up at me while Samantha bounded over to join her friends on the playground.

"They're eleven and twelve-year old boys," I said, trying to calm her. "It was a sleepover. They probably just stayed up talking and horsing around for a little while."

"I think it was a lot more than just a little while," she continued. Hope rarely gets angry with either of the kids, or with me, but all three of us know that she can be a volcano. Volcanoes are awesome forces of nature. They're beautiful and mysterious. They also lie dormant for years until they decide to erupt unexpectedly and spew boiling hot lava all over an unsuspecting village.

Or a husband.

"Hi Mrs. Dunston," Chase's sister Katie said to Hope as she and one of her friends climbed up the bleachers toward us. Seeing the girls caused Hope immediately to cool down. "Well, hello Katie," she chirped happily.

"Hi, Mr. Dunston," Katie said to me with a little wave of her hand.

"Who is your friend?" Hope asked.

"This is Madison," Katie said. Madison smiled sweetly and gave her own polite wave to both of us.

"Oh, yes!" Hope exclaimed. "So, how was your *Midnight in Deep, Dark Outer Space* party?"

"It was great!" Madison replied. "We had a ball!"

"Ryne said it was a lot of fun," Hope returned. "I don't think he was too crazy about the paint job you gave him, though."

At the mention of Ryne's name, both girls exchanged a look and then giggled. Madison blushed. Katie giggled some more. "We're going to go sit over there," Katie said, pointing in the direction of the stands closest to the Intimidators' dugout. "We'll see you later!"

"It was nice to meet you, Madison," Hope said, waving as the girls left. She turned to me immediately. "That little girl has a crush on Ryne."

I looked at her blankly. "Katie?"

Hope rolled her eyes. "No, Goofy. Madison."

"How do you know that?" I asked, mystified.

"Couldn't you tell?" she asked. She glared at me like I had the intelligence of a doorknob.

"How could I tell?"

Hope wagged her head. "Boys. You never change, do you?"

"Hello, Shaun." I looked up and was greeted by a pair of sparkling blue eyes and a snow white handlebar mustache. "Hey, Mr. Blyleven," I said, standing up. He took my hand in both of his and squeezed it firmly.

"Oh, sit down," he ordered in a gruff voice. "Your back end is blocking that nice lady's view of the field." He winked at Hope as I turned around, embarrassed that I was blocking Gloria Styles' view. Jimmy and Sammy's mother cackled at me as I sat back down.

"What brings you out today?" I asked. Old Mr. Blyleven was a regular at The Hitting Wheel batting cages that his son owned, but he only occasionally attended Saturday games, preferring to spend his weekends at the lake fishing. He'd been fishing a lot in the past year since his wife of forty-four years had passed the previous summer.

"I came out to watch that new boy," he said, cheerfully. His blue eyes brightened. "I saw him at *The Wheel* the other night. The kid is an amazing hitter. I haven't seen anyone hit the ball like that since Joltin' Joe DiMaggio."

Hope and I looked at each other. "Are you talking about Mano?" Hope asked.

Mr. Blyleven nodded enthusiastically. "Yes, I believe that's his name. What's he doing here all the way from Hawai'i, anyway?"

Hope and I both shrugged. "We don't know," I answered.

"He seems to be a very sweet boy," Hope offered.

Mr. Blyleven snorted. "Sweet? No, ma'am. Sweet's for tea. That boy is a salt and vinegar hitter." He turned and started back down the bleachers. Hope nudged me. "Who is Joltin' Joe Dimarjo?" she whispered.

"DiMaggio," I corrected. He played for the Yankees, a long time ago."

"You mean like back in the 80s?"

I chuckled. "No. Back in the 40s."

"Wow," Hope murmured. She watched Mr. Blyleven as he found a seat directly behind home plate. "How old is he, anyway?"

"Mr. Blyleven? Pretty old. He probably should be powering a fossil-fueled engine by now."

Hope elbowed me. "Be nice, Shaun."

On the field, the Intimidators had completed their warm-up and were jogging toward their dugout from the outfield. I saw that Ryne and Mano were trotting in front of the group. Hope leaned in to me.

"Well, it looks like Ryne has adopted Mano," she whispered as they came toward us. She lifted her hand and waved to our son. Normally, Ryne would have returned the wave. Today, he was distracted. Someone else was waving to him from the section of the bleachers closest to the dugout. I watched him nod in the direction of Katie and Madison. Hope elbowed me again.

"Did you see that?" she proclaimed breathlessly. "I'm telling you, there's something going on between those two."

*   *   *

Ryne

The Phoenix is a pretty dumb name for a baseball team. They wore ketchup red jerseys with ketchup red pants. Their socks, belts, and numbers were mustard yellow. Their hats were a mixture of ketchup and mustard, a red brim with a yucky yellow crown. On the front of the cap there was a big splash of mustard with a ketchup P in the middle. The Phoenix was spelled out in fancy, cursive letters on the front of their jersey.

We watched them take their warm-up, fielding grounders and pop-ups in the outfield. Chase and I were leaning on the dugout fence and sizing them up when Wee Willie squeezed between us.

"Who puts 'The' in their team name?" he asked. It was a good question. "Shouldn't they just be called Phoenix, like the city? I mean, we're the Intimidators, but we don't put 'the' on the front of our jersey."

Chase shrugged. "Maybe it's supposed to be like The Hulk or something," he mused.

I thought the uniforms were about the ugliest I'd ever seen. "They should have called themselves The Burger Kings," I joked. Curtis heard me and laughed. He passed it to Jimmy, who repeated it and he broke up, too.

"That team didn't lose a game during the spring season," Coach Weaver said to us. "They won their first summer league game 15 to nothing last week, too." The dugout, which was already quiet, went totally silent. I felt like an idiot for making the comment.

Coach Ramirez finished his meeting at home plate with the umpires and The Phoenix coach and walked over to us. Immediately, everyone took a seat on the bench. "This is a very good team, gentlemen." He suddenly paused from his normal pre-game lecture routine and looked at us. "What's wrong?"

No one said anything.

"Oh, right. You had a little party last night, didn't you?" He looked directly at me. "Well, wake up Intimidators!" His voice climbed quickly into his standard yell. "This team will mow you down in two innings if you're not ready to play, and I can tell by your droopy-eyed, sad puppy faces that all any of you care about is getting home early and taking a nap!" He jerked his cap off his head and rubbed his hand through his thick salt and pepper hair like he was aggravated. "We won the flip so we're the home team," he said. He barked at us. "Now get your gloves and get on the field!"

Everyone filed out of the dugout. Coach Weaver stood at the door and reminded us of our positions as we came out. I was last and Mano was in front of me. Coach Weaver sent him to right field. When he heard his name, Mano took off in a full sprint.

I heard Coach Ramirez mumble underneath his breath. "At least he's figured out how to run." I looked up at him. I suddenly felt angry. I wanted to say something to defend Mano, but I kept my mouth closed.

* * *

Chase has a video game called *Honor Bound*. It's a two player game where a couple of soldiers go on missions around the world helping countries who have crummy armies learn how to fight better. The game is programmed so you can create new ways to fight. Once we got stuck in a bombed out building with soldiers from the crummy army we were helping and all they had was a box of hand grenades.

83

The bad guys were further away than we could throw the grenades, so we had our *Honor Bound* soldiers pick up a couple of boards from the destroyed building and use them as bats to hit them at the bad guys like baseballs. We wiped out about fifty of the enemy soldiers in ten minutes while the crummy army cheered us on. I mention that because the first inning against The Phoenix felt almost *exactly* like that video game. The only difference was this time it felt we were the other army.

Each ball that was hit in the first inning was like one of those grenades. The Phoenix slapped every pitch that came near the plate and the balls exploded past us. The first two batters hit grenades straight over the pitching mound into centerfield. The second one was hit so hard that it bit into the grass in front of Wee Willie and then shot past his glove all the way to the fence where it exploded into the chain link barrier. Before he could get it back to the infield the first runner had scored and the batter took third.

The next hitter swung at the first pitch Jimmy threw. He hit a grenade way over Curtis' head in left field. It bombed into the base of the fence and bounced back near Wee Willie. He was able to get it to Miggy, who cut the throw and then tossed it to me to hold the runner at second, but the runner at third scored and it was 2-0. Then their clean-up hitter stepped up.

He wasn't big, just a normal sized kid with long, skinny arms. He wore a yellow armor shirt underneath his red jersey that made them look even skinnier, like he had a couple of No. 2 pencils poking out of his sleeves. Jimmy threw him two balls that were low. He threw the next one down the middle, and that was the last time anyone saw that baseball. Pencil Arms hit a grenade straight over Wee Willie's head in center. Wee Willie took one step, turned and watched it. It wasn't that high, but it zipped over the fence and took two hops before exploding into a green mist as it bounced into a swampy pond beyond centerfield. It was 4-0 and thoughts of the mercy rule were already starting to creep into my head.

The next two hitters blasted grenades right at Miggy. He couldn't field either one of them. The first one was a hard hit, two-hopper that took a bounce and detonated over his shoulder. The second one wasn't hit as hard, but Miggy peeked up at me a little early as I went to cover the bag and the grenade scooted beneath his leather. The runner from first went to third as Curtis backed up the play and threw the ball to me at second. There were runners at first and third and we still hadn't recorded an out.

The next Phoenix batter was a tall, left-handed kid. He dug into the box and made a big show of holding up his hand to the umpire to call time while he did it. Coach Weaver yelled out to me to pinch back toward first base a bit. Brazos moved over toward the first base line a little, too. All of our positioning was wasted because Big Lefty ripped Jimmy's first pitch over both of our heads into deep right-centerfield.

I turned to hustle into the outfield for the cut-off, hoping this grenade wasn't going to leave the yard, too. Wee Willie was running full speed toward the right centerfield fence, but even though he is the fastest kid I've ever played with, I already knew there was no way he could reach it. That's when I saw Mano.

He was moving in a streak across the grass, churning up pieces of turf with his cleats. His wasn't even looking at the ball. His head was down and his arms and legs were pumping. He was racing toward the same spot that Wee Willie was headed for, only he was coming from further away. I didn't think he would reach the ball before it bounced through to the fence, but he did. He closed the gap and dove. He crash landed onto the grass and the ball took one bounce before jumping into his outstretched glove. He slid a few feet on his belly and instantly, he was back on his feet.

The runner at third had hesitated only briefly to see if the ball might be caught. When it hit the ground, he jogged home. The first base coach had smartly held his runner at first. When he saw the ball skip, he didn't wait any longer. I heard him yell to the base runner from behind me, "GO!"

The runner took off. I moved in position to field the cutoff from Mano. Miggy slid in behind me to cover the second base bag to hopefully hold the hitter at first. I held up my throwing hand and my glove and started yelling, "Cut! Cut! Cut!" Mano threw the ball toward me, but it went over my head like an elevated train riding on a rail. It went over Miggy's head at second too, and stayed on a straight and true path, headed toward third base.

Sammy is a quiet player. He pays attention to everything the coaches say, but he hardly ever says a word - he just does what he is supposed to do. I think that's why the coaches decided to give him the job at third base instead of Jimmy when they realized Hootie would be out for a long time. He was already straddling the bag at third and was in perfect position to receive Mano's incredible throw.

I turned around in time to see the third base coach for The Phoenix screaming at the runner, "DOWN! DOWN! GET DOWN!" The ball skipped once and snapped solidly into the pocket of Sammy's mitt. Sammy swiped at the runner's leg as he slid. Like our new third baseman, the infield umpire was exactly where he was supposed to be, too. He dropped his big fist like Thor's hammer.

"HE'S OUT!"

The third base coach clapped his hands to his head and spun around like he couldn't believe it. Big Lefty rounded first and took off for second when he saw that Mano's throw was going to third. After tagging the runner, Sammy had immediately looked up to check the runner at first. He coolly jumped to his feet and pegged a throw to Miggy at second. Miggy dropped to his knees like a catcher as the throw came in low, perfectly on the bag. He dropped the tag and Big Lefty slid into it. His foot stopped when it hit Miggy's rusty-colored glove and never even reached the base. The field umpire was able to make the call easily. He pointed at the play and dropped his big Thor hammer again.

"HE'S GOT HIM!" He belted loud enough for everyone in the stands to hear.

The Phoenix dugout erupted. The third base coach blew up. The first base coach exploded, too. Their fans began screaming like an angry mob. Then the third base coach yelled a word I can't repeat. When he did, the field umpire looked over at him and immediately punched the sky with his finger. "You are out of here, Coach!"

The Phoenix coach turned as red as his jersey. I think he was mad and embarrassed. He stormed through the dugout and off the field. To his credit, he immediately went to his fans in the bleachers and told them to calm down. Surprisingly, all of them obeyed him and things quickly became normal again.

Miggy tossed the ball back in to Jimmy. Our pitcher was standing just behind the mound, staring into the outfield at Mano. He kept looking as Mano jogged back to his position in right field. Jimmy looked over at me and nodded his head slowly. I wasn't sure what he was thinking, but I felt strange. I could hear our fans still cheering the double play. They were loud like they had been in our first game when Mano had thrown the ball to me and we had doubled the runners at second and home. Something about this play felt different, though. It was as if something had just changed and things were never going to be quite the same.

Jimmy climbed back on the mound to face the next hitter. His next two pitches were beautiful fastballs inside. They were hard pitches to handle and the batter fouled them both straight back. Then Jimmy went into his full wind-up. When his arm came around it looked like he was throwing another fastball, but this pitch came out of his hand super slow. The change-up floated through the air and then dropped like a rock as it crossed the outside corner of the plate. It froze the batter and all he could do was watch as the umpire punched him out. The inning was over and we headed to our dugout, down 5–0.

As the rest of us jogged in, Jimmy walked very slowly off the mound, sort of like pitchers do in the major leagues. He arrived at the dugout but stopped short of going inside. He just stood there and waited.

Mano cruised in from the outfield. When he reached Jimmy, he stopped. They both just stood there for a moment. Jimmy lifted his glove.

Mano's hat was low as always, his eyes tucked way back underneath the brim. He suddenly reached up and took his cap off. He was smiling. He reached up with his glove and lightly bumped it into Jimmy's. Neither of them said a word. They both went inside and started gearing up to bat with the rest of us.

Coach Ramirez walked into the dugout after us. He pointed at Sammy. "Great heads up play, Sammy," he said. He looked over at Miggy. "Good job getting that tag down at second, Miguel." He turned toward Mano. I expected he would say something nice, about how his amazing throw had resulted in a double play for the second consecutive game. Instead he said, "Be sure you hit your cutoff man next time. You have to play the game correctly. We aren't looking for hot dogs out here, understand?"

Mano nodded. The happy smile on his face disappeared instantly. I saw Jimmy look at Coach Ramirez, his eyes wide with disbelief. I guess if you weren't there, it wouldn't seem like that big of a deal, but I don't think Mano smiled much after that anymore.

Ryne

The score was 5-1 when we came up to bat in the bottom of the fourth inning. All of our games have a time limit and Coach Ramirez was checking his watch as Jimmy and Curtis stepped out of the dugout.

"This will be it, gentlemen," he warned us. "There's only five minutes left."

Coach Weaver clapped Curtis on the back. "Go get it started, son," he said, encouragingly. Curtis bobbed his head at his dad, went up to the plate and promptly struck out on three pitches, the last one looking. As he ran back toward the dugout, Coach Weaver shook his head. "We don't go down looking," he said to Curtis from the first base coach's box, "*Ever.*" He turned to the rest of us in the dugout. He was frustrated, probably because we had only managed to score two runs so far in the season. "You've got to swing the bat to score runs, boys!" he snapped.

I don't know if Jimmy heard him as he was walking to the plate or not, but it probably wouldn't have mattered. Jimmy had singled his first time up, had stolen second and third base, and scored our only run on a fielder's choice when Miggy grounded out to second. He'd also become a totally different pitcher, throwing three shutout innings after our first inning nightmare. I noticed that he had been quiet and focused ever since the first inning had ended, too. There was one more thing I'd noticed. Jimmy had made it a point to sit next to Mano on the bench after every inning. They didn't talk or anything. Jimmy just sat there next to him as they both watched the game.

The Phoenix pitcher threw a high one on the first pitch and Jimmy let it go. The next one was low and outside, but he was swinging anyway. He hit the ball hard and it shot down the foul line, just inside the first base bag. The right fielder had to run a long way to get it and by the time he got it back in, Jimmy was standing on third base with a triple. He turned to our dugout across the field, beating his hands together.

"Let's go!" he shouted.

Sammy was up next. Coach Weaver had rearranged the batting order after our first game and moved Sammy into the seventh spot, and dropped me all the way down to eighth (which he probably decided after my miserable performance at The Hitting Wheel.) Mano batted after me, in the ninth and last spot in the order. Sammy stood outside the batter's box and watched Coach Ramirez flash him signs. He stepped in and did exactly what Coach had told him to do.

He bunted.

The ball acted like a mouse. It scurried out in front of home plate toward the pitcher, who looked completely surprised. A bunt was probably the last thing he expected since we were trailing by four runs, so he got sort of a late jump off the mound. He scooped it up and thought about trying to get Jimmy who was already almost home, but he gave up the idea and turned and threw an absolute worm killer toward first base. The ball kicked up dirt as it shot past the glove of The Phoenix first baseman and headed down the fence line toward their right fielder. Coach Weaver immediately waved Sammy to second where Coach Ramirez held him, holding his hands high up in the air. It was 5-2 and our fans were going nuts.

As I walked to the plate slowly swinging my bat, I could see my parents. They were sitting close to Jimmy and Sammy's mom. They were clapping and cheering. Our section of bleachers was almost completely full. I even saw Mr. Blyleven sitting right behind home plate. He had his arms across his chest and he was the only person not clapping. He looked right at me. He unfolded his arms, leaned forward on the bleachers and ran his fingers down his handlebar mustache. He nodded at me and I knew what he was thinking.

"Keep your head on it, son."

I knew that Madison was watching me. She and Katie had both stood up as I'd walked out of the on deck circle by the dugout. "C'mon, Ryne!! You can do it!" I heard Katie yell. I glanced over at both of them quickly. Madison was smiling at me. I noticed she had her blonde hair pulled into a ponytail. It was hanging out of the back of one of our black Intimidators caps. "C'mon, Ryne!" she echoed after Katie. "Go get 'em!"

I wasn't nervous. I don't know that I was feeling anything, really. I had grounded out to shortstop my first time up and this would only be my second time to bat. I remember thinking that I needed to hit one back through the middle, or through the box, as Coach Weaver always says. If I hit it good, it would probably bring Sammy home and we'd be one run closer. I thought, *I just need to put one solidly back up the middle.* That's exactly what I ended up doing, only it didn't quite happen quite the way I thought it would.

The Phoenix pitcher checked over his shoulder at Sammy on second and threw a first pitch fastball to me out over the plate. I was ready. I kept my head on it and smashed one right back up the middle, just like I'd wanted. The pitcher really didn't even have time to react. The ball hit the dirt on the front of the mound between his feet. It shot straight up in the air between his legs like a bottle rocket and…well, I guess there's no gentle way to say this… It *cupped* him.

I heard him burst out, "OOOAAWWW!" as I took off running toward first. He spit out a bunch of air like a balloon going flat and crumpled to the ground, holding himself while the ball sort of dribbled off the mound to his right. The second baseman came in to grab it and Sammy stopped at third. The plate umpire immediately called time and two coaches ran out of The Phoenix dugout.

The Phoenix pitcher was on the ground rolling from side to side. When the coaches got to him, they put him on his back. It was obvious where he'd been hit. I looked over at him and glanced at the stands. Several people had stood up, including Katie and Madison. I could see Katie whispering in Madison's ear and I knew exactly what she was telling her. Madison opened her mouth wide and quickly covered it with her hand. I felt my face begin to burn.

After what seemed like forever, the coaches helped The Phoenix pitcher to his feet. He walked gingerly toward the dugout while everyone in the stands stood up and clapped politely. Coach Weaver came over to me at first base, placed his hand on my shoulder and teased me in a low voice. "Well Ryne, I guess that's a whole new way to knock a pitcher out of a game."

I think I was supposed to laugh, but I didn't. I was too embarrassed. I remembered when Chase had told me Madison was coming to our game at her *Midnight in Deep, Dark Outer Space* party. The only thing I'd worried about was looking like an idiot in front of her. Now it had happened. I'd just knocked the pitcher out of the game. Not by hitting a home run or anything, of course.

I'd just hit the poor guy south of his equator.

* * *

Once my mom told me about a strange feeling she had. She called it déjà vu. She said it meant having this weird sensation that you have already been in the same place or same situation before, but you really haven't.

In two straight games, we had made double plays that started on amazing throws by Mano. Two players had been knocked out of the game by line drives that took wicked bad hops. I don't know if it was just a coincidence, déjà vu, or something else. All I know is that when Mano walked to the plate, I had a strange feeling in my belly. It was like I knew something was going to happen before it actually happened.

Big Lefty for The Phoenix was a pitcher, too. They brought him in to warm up after I knocked out their starter. He was already the tallest kid on the field and he looked like he grew an extra two feet when he stepped onto the mound. The Phoenix coach handed him the ball and hustled back to the dugout as Big Lefty took his warm up tosses. The first one zipped wildly out of his hand, zoomed high over his catcher's head and blasted into the backstop. The second one was just as bad. It went so wide that the catcher didn't even bother to reach for it. He just held his hand up for another ball from the umpire, as if he did this routine with Big Lefty all the time. The third pitch smacked the catcher square in the center of his glove with a loud, leathery POP! After that, the next four pitches did the same thing. Coach Weaver was standing next to me by the first base bag. I heard him mumble to himself, "That kid has got to be hitting about 70 miles per hour on the gun."

Big Lefty finished his warm-up by uncorking another wild pitch over the catcher's head. It hit a green, metal GOOD SPORTSMANSHIP STARTS HERE sign about halfway up the backstop. It rattled the hooks free that held the sign to the fence, causing it to crash to the ground. Their whole team broke up laughing as the umpire went over and picked it up. He chuckled as he carried the bent metal over to The Phoenix dugout and handed it to their first base coach. He was laughing, too. Everybody thought it was funny, even Big Lefty.

Wee Willie was standing on deck. We would be back at the top of our order after Mano's turn, and he would hit next. After watching Big Lefty's wild warm-up, I figured he was probably already shaking like a Chihuahua.

Mano had walked his first time without ever swinging his bat. He was stepping into the box for just the second time in the game. Sammy took his lead at third and I crept slowly off first. Big Lefty looked right at me. I wasn't going to give him a chance to pick me off. I had almost no experience stealing bases off lefties, so my plan was to stay tight to the base. Normally Coach Weaver would have pushed me to get a bigger lead, but he was eyeing the left handed pitcher carefully, too.

Big Lefty lifted his leg with a short kick and fired. The pitch shocked everyone by going *behind* Mano. The ball hit the base of the backstop and shot immediately back toward the plate. It all happened so fast that Sammy didn't even have time to move toward home. The catcher tossed off his mask and found the ricochet quickly. He took a couple of steps down the third base line, holding the baseball near his ear as if he was going to throw. Sammy took one look at the catcher's threatening face and moved back toward the third base bag. I stayed exactly where I was. My feet felt like they were glued to the infield dirt. My heart was thumping in my chest. Several of the parents in the stands had gasped as the ball had screamed behind Mano's back. I had flinched myself because I was positive that it was going to hit him.

Mano, however, didn't seem to be worried at all. He had just stepped out of the batter's box like he was supposed to, on the chance there was a play at home. As he'd watched the ball bound back toward the plate, he'd simply held up his hand calmly, telling Sammy to stay at third. He remained cool through it all.

The catcher returned the ball to Big Lefty. He snatched at it with his glove. He looked angry, probably because he had no idea where the ball was going whenever it left his hand. *Yeah, you might be mad because you don't know where the pitch is going*, I thought. *But guess what, buddy? The rest of us are scared out of our minds.*

Mano stepped back into the box. He lifted his old wood bat back into its cocked position. He was completely still again, just like a statue. I saw Mr. Blyleven. He was standing up behind the fence, bent over slightly at the waist so he could get a good look at the pitch. On the field, the umpire was bending slightly lower, just over the catcher's shoulder. Big Lefty looked over at me. He gave his little leg kick and fired.

Pencil Arms had hit his home run low, but this blast traveled even lower. I don't think the ball ever got more than about a foot or two higher than the centerfield fence as it blew past it on its way to the pond. It hit the center of the green goo that covered the top of the water and blasted a sheet of the nasty gunk high into the air.

I don't even remember my feet moving. I do remember there was a huge roar from our fans. It came at me like a wave from the ocean and seemed to carry me around the bases. I looked out past centerfield toward the slimy pond as I rounded second. I was amazed. That gooey water was a long way beyond the fence, and Mano had managed to hit the ball deep into the middle of it.

Unbelievable, I thought. *Absolutely unbelievable!*

As I reached shortstop, Coach Ramirez waved at me. *Hurry up*, he mouthed. I made the corner of the third base bag and turned toward home. As I did I caught a glimpse of Mano. His head was down and he was moving much faster than I was. In fact, he was right on my heels.

The entire team was waiting for us at the plate, even Hootie, who had an absolutely wild look in his eyes behind his protective mask. Jimmy and Sammy were bouncing together like two squirrels on a trampoline. Brazos had Wee Willie in a playful headlock as they both screamed at the top of their lungs. Curtis and Chase had their arms linked together and were swaying back and forth in a mini-wave. Miggy was there, too. He was clapping, but I could tell he wasn't as excited as everyone else.

I picked up my speed and ran into them, making sure I touched home as they collapsed on me and began beating on my batting helmet. I turned around just in time to see Mano roll in behind me. His head was still down as he came into the middle of the screaming huddle. He stamped his foot deliberately into the center of the white base and looked up at me as we were both swallowed up by our crazed teammates. I expected to see a huge smile on his face. Instead, his lips were tight. I saw his eyes way back beneath his batting helmet. They looked really dark again. Almost black.

Our team wave rolled slowly back toward our dugout as our fans blew it out even louder. It was a moment I will never forget.

We still had two more outs to score the winning run, but Wee Willie and Brazos both struck out. Big Lefty only threw one more wild pitch and thankfully, he saved it for Brazos. The ball just missed his helmet, burning like a meteor right over the top of his head. I think Wee Willie might have fainted if that had happened to him. As it was, Willie never took the bat off of his shoulder when it was his turn at the plate. He went down on five pitches. I honestly think it took all of the courage he could muster just to stand in the batter's box. Brazos wasn't much better, but at least he swung at the third strike. The pitch sizzled into the catcher's mitt. The catcher jumped up and casually rolled the ball out toward the mound as The Phoenix sprinted off the field.

The game was over. We tied, 5–5.

Epilogue to Part One

Shaun

The first two weeks of the summer baseball season went by fast. When I was a kid, I always thought that summer seemed to go by too fast. Now that I have kids of my own, I realize that summer doesn't slow down and wait for you as you get older. Instead, you have to slow down. If you don't, you'll forget to enjoy it.

After the game ended against The Phoenix, I decided to savor the moment. Hope went over to the huddle the coaches have after every game with the players to wait for Ryne, while I headed to the playground to collect Samantha. When I got far enough away from everyone, I stopped for a moment beneath a nice shady tree and looked up at the scoreboard. It hadn't been cleared yet for the next game, so I pulled out my smartphone and snapped a picture of it. Someone once said that a tie is like kissing your sister. I think it was a football coach. Whoever it was, I guess the idea is that there isn't much point in playing a game if it doesn't produce a winner. It's sort of like walking in a circle. If you just end up where you started, why even bother?

I've always thought that something was wrong with that way of thinking because it leaves out all of the things that happen to you on the journey. Heck, baseball is a game that is all about ending up where you start. Batters begin at home, run the bases, and if they make it around to score, they end up right back where they started, at home.

I couldn't begin to imagine a more perfect outcome to the game the Intimidators had just played than a tie. A win might have been too much for them at that moment in the season. Instead, the tie would allow them to focus on what they had learned about each other during the game. For the coaches, families, and fans who had really watched the game, it would allow us to focus, too.

What would we focus on? That something special was happening on this team beyond the score of the games, beyond the wins and losses. If we could all move our focus away from the scoreboard for a minute; if we could really open our eyes; if we could slow the summer down for just a moment, maybe we could see it.

I stood there for a while in the shade checking my phone to make sure that I had a good photo. As I did, I saw a white SUV swing into empty space in the far corner of the parking lot. It parked at an angle to me, but I could see there was something written on one of the doors. Because of the sharp angle I couldn't see all of it, but one of the words and the first letter of the next word stood out.

Texas A…

The driver opened his door and stepped out. He was a tall man with wavy hair. He had the build of an athlete. He peered around as if he was looking for someone. The passenger's door opened and a shorter, stockier man with a military haircut stepped out. He stood in the open frame of the door and joined in the search.

Suddenly, a small rental car entered the lot and drove in the direction of the SUV. It stopped several feet away. A large man dressed in khaki shorts and a flowered shirt stepped out. Even from a distance, I recognized him as Mano's father.

The taller figure stepped away from the SUV and approached him with an extended hand. He was followed by the shorter, stockier man who held out his own hand to greet him. They stood there for a minute talking and then Mano's father went to the trunk of the car and opened it. He pulled out a long tube. He carried it over to them and pulled out a scroll of some sort. He unfurled it and stretched it out across the hood of his car. All three of them stood there between the vehicles studying the document while Mano's father pointed and gestured.

"Daddy?"

I jumped, my heart fluttering. Samantha was standing right next to me. I grabbed my chest.

"You almost gave me a heart attack, Sam!" I wheezed. "Where did you come from?"

"The playground!" she chirped, innocently. "Is the game over?"

"Yes, sweetheart. It just finished."

"Did we win?"

"Actually, we tied."

She stuck out her tongue. "That's no fun," she proclaimed. "But at least we didn't lose again!" Like her mother, Sam is the eternal optimist. I laughed.

"Always looking on the bright side, aren't you sweetie?"

"Can I have a snow cone now?"

I reached down, gathered her up into my arms, and swung her in a flourish up onto my shoulders. She squealed in delight.

"Of course! Let's go get Ryne and Mom and we'll all have one."

I started off in a slow horse trot back toward the field while Sam spurred me on. "Let's go, hossie!" she said. I whinnied for her and broke into a lope as she laughed.

But as we galloped off together, I snuck one more look at the three men hunched over the hood of the car in the parking lot. They were studying the document even more intently. The scene only added to the air of mystery that surrounded Mano and his father. I thought of Mr. Blyleven's question. *What is that boy doing here all the way from Hawai'i?*

I couldn't help but wonder.

Why had they come to Texas?

Part II

Prologue to Part II

Ryne

Things began to change for our team after those first two weeks of the summer. We played a total of eighteen baseball games, one every Saturday plus another one during the week. I don't remember another drop of rain falling from the sky either, so we were able to practice twice a week, too. We also went to the Hitting Wheel every Thursday night. The only days we weren't together as a team were Friday and Sunday.

I guess I should probably mention that our record was 16-1-1. After our first two games, we didn't lose for two whole months. We played so well that Coach Ramirez rarely ever yelled at us. Of course, we didn't give him any reason to yell, either. Each game we played, we seemed to play just a little bit better than the last one.

After we won our sixteenth game in a row, we had a special practice. It was special because we didn't actually practice. Instead, our parents surprised us with a picnic at the water park. Our regular season was over and we were getting ready for the playoffs which began the next weekend. Coach Ramirez brought the stat sheets that Hootie's dad kept during the games. He read some of them to us while our families stood around and clapped like we were being given ESPYs while we ate watermelon and spit the seeds at each other. Our team statistics were impressive: we averaged 11.3 runs per game, we gave up an average of 2.7 runs per game, our team on-base percentage was .632 and our batting average was .503. Our defense made a grand total of 7 errors over the 16 games.

Coach Ramirez went around the table and talked about our individual stats too, but I stopped listening at that point. I really didn't care very much about mine. In fact, I don't think any of us really thought about our individual statistics, except for Miggy, and we already knew his because he tracked them on a chart he kept in his bat bag. He would pull them out on occasion and show them to anyone who was unfortunate enough to sit next to him on the bench.

Actually, the only individual stats I was interested in were Mano's. Since he wasn't with us at the water park, I knew it would give Coach Ramirez an excuse not to read them. He wouldn't say a word about his 10 triples, 16 doubles, or 11 home runs. He wouldn't mention that Mano had hit 40 of the 48 times he went to the plate, giving him a .833 batting average, and that only three of his hits had been singles—and two of those had been bunts! He also wouldn't talk about the fact that the highest he had allowed Mano to bat in the order during those 18 games was sixth, even though his batting average was almost two hundred points higher than Miggy's—who had the second highest average—and he'd hit seven more home runs than our star shortstop. I also knew that he would leave out every single amazing catch, throw, and flat out hustle play that Mano contributed from right field during our amazing run. Most importantly, I knew he would never give him credit for inspiring every single member of our team, except for Miggy, to play better and harder than we had ever played in our baseball lives.

When Coach Ramirez had finished speaking and our parents had finally finished clapping, all of us, except for Miggy, headed over to the lazy river to wash off the sticky watermelon juice that had run down our chins and elbows. We grabbed some tubes, formed ourselves into a loose donut, and floated off with billions of other people into the giant stream that runs like a race track around a couple of huge water slides in the middle of the park. Hootie, whose face was starting to finally look normal again, shouted in my direction.

"Where's Mano?" All eyes turned to me. I shrugged my shoulders. Mano had been over to my house several times after our early season party. He and I had started to become friends.

"I don't know," I said.

"Coach didn't say a word about him," Jimmy noted. He didn't sound surprised.

"He never does," Brazos added as he bobbed on his tube between Chase and Curtis.

"Do you think if he knew what had happened to Mano, he might treat him better?" Wee Willie wondered out loud.

None of us had said a word to anyone about what Mano had told us that night in my 'Fortress of Solitude'. It wasn't like Mano had sworn us to secrecy or anything, but for some reason, we had all decided to keep it to ourselves. A small surge from the river lifted us higher. The sudden swell threatened to rip us apart, but we all grabbed tightly to each other and held on, keeping our donut intact. When we had settled back into the gently flowing current, Chase said what everyone already knew, but no one had ever said out loud.

"It wouldn't make any difference," he said, flatly. "Coach is jealous of Mano."

Sammy nodded his head. He was the youngest of all of us, but whenever he spoke, he seemed much older. Sammy's mom once said that he is an 'old soul', whatever that means. "He thinks everything Mano does makes Miggy look ordinary," Sammy said.

Curtis suddenly spoke up. I figured he knew some stuff about Coach Ramirez because his dad was his assistant, but I also figured that Curtis and Coach Weaver probably had the same "zip it" agreement my dad enforced with me. Dad will tell me private stuff sometimes, but it's strictly between us. "My dad wanted to move Mano to clean up," he confessed. "But Coach Ramirez told him no. He said that Mano probably wouldn't be able to handle the pressure." Everyone was quiet for a moment while that truth soaked into us. It was one of those things about Coach Ramirez I suspected, that he would have no problem making up some junk like that to try and keep the spotlight on Miggy, but actually hearing it was true made me feel horrible.

"You know, before I got hurt, my dad thought I should bat clean up," Hootie added. "But he told me it would probably never happen. Now he says that Mano is the best hitter on the planet and it's ridiculous for him to bat anywhere but fourth." Everyone nodded in agreement.

I looked over at Jimmy. Since our second game, something had happened to Jimmy. He wasn't the same ballplayer anymore. Heck, he wasn't even the same kid anymore. Even though he was our number one pitcher, he had never been very confident. Whenever Chase would call a curve ball with a runner on third, Jimmy would shake him off. He was terrified he would bounce it and allow the runner to score. At the plate, he often took what Coach Weaver called half & half swings. He would go halfway through the strike zone and stop his swing. He got a lot of blooper hits to right field that way, but it drove Coach Weaver crazy. After our second game, something changed. Jimmy stopped shaking off the curve. He threw it whenever Chase called it, and he threw it for strikes. He also stopped the half & half swings and starting cutting squarely through the center of the baseball. His batting average had climbed steadily and whenever he hit the ball, he hit it hard. I'd noticed that whenever we were at The Hitting Wheel, he made sure he was in the same cage with Mano. Between rounds, they sat on the folding chairs behind the cages together. Sometimes Jimmy would ask him questions. During our games, they were always together between innings on the bench, and they watched whatever happened on the field with total concentration. It was like they both entered into some sort of unique baseball "zone" while the rest of us stood around trying to find the secret door that would let us inside.

There was one more thing I'd noticed, too. If Coach Ramirez ever approached Mano to say something to him in the dugout during a game, Jimmy would inch closer to our right fielder until their shoulders touched. It was almost like he was protecting him.

"What do you think, Jimmy?" I asked.

We were coming to the end of the ride. We rode up over another swell in the lazy river and all of us bobbed up and back down quickly. Time was growing short. There was a narrow inlet into a slide right ahead that was only big enough for one tube at a time. Right before we reached it, the gentle stream began to turn into rapids. Our tubes started to shake. Soon it was impossible for us to hold them together anymore. Our larger team donut began to break apart into eight individual donuts. Suddenly, Jimmy spoke. When he did, his jaw was firmly set and his face was absolutely serious.

"I'll tell you what I think,' he said in a loud voice over the sound of the churning water. "Mano is our village chief. Not Miggy." His tube broke away and headed toward the chute. He disappeared over and down the slide.

I looked at Hootie. He was next. His face was every bit as serious as Jimmy's. "He's right." He was swallowed up into the slide chute and shot away from us, too.

One by one, we all took our turns. Brazos and I were last. Our tubes bumped together as they fought to see which one would go next. Brazos looked at me. His long hair was plastered to his shoulders like wet spaghetti. "You know, nobody really understands sharks," he said, mysteriously. I stared at him, not understanding what he meant. His tube started to edge ahead of mine as it was pulled by the churning current. At the last moment, his rubber circle won the fight, but it spun him around backward as he was pulled toward the top of the slide. He smiled at me and just before he was whisked over the edge he said, "They probably never will." In a moment, he was gone.

It was my turn. My tube slid into place, and I was over the edge, too.

10

Ryne

The week leading up to our first playoff series was a long one. We practiced on Monday, Tuesday and Wednesday, and we went to The Hitting Wheel on Thursday. Coach Ramirez gave us an "off day" on Friday to rest and told all of our parents to keep us on lockdown. We were supposed to take it easy, drink lots of water, and stay out of the heat. Our playoff series would be the best two of three, with the first two games played on Saturday and the third game, if neither team swept the Saturday double-header, would be played on Sunday.

The weatherman on TV wore a bowtie and had about twelve hairs that he combed from one side of his bright, bald dome over to the other side. He said the forecast for the weekend was SIZZLING HOT. On the screen, those words were written next to Saturday and Sunday and every day of the following week too, with some animated fire over the triple digits that made them look like they were burning. "It will be like playing baseball in the Sahara desert," Dad groaned.

I knew that none of the coaches or parents would approve another team sleepover, but I asked Mom if Chase and Brazos could spend Friday night at our house. It was *Shark Week* on the *Discovery Channel* and there was an episode premiering on Friday night the three of us had been waiting anxiously to see. I thought she would probably say no, but she surprised me by immediately agreeing. "It will be good for the three of you to spend some time together before your big weekend," she'd said.

It had been a strange week because there was only one thing on everyone's mind. The parents had spent most of the week whispering while they watched us practice. At our Thursday night batting practice at The Hitting Wheel, Mr. Blyleven had pulled me aside. He wanted to know what everyone else wanted to know.

Where was Mano?

*   *   *

Before Chase and Brazos arrived on Friday, I went out to my 'Fortress of Solitude'. I went to one of the beds and slipped my hand between the mattress and the box springs and pulled out the letter that Katie had given me after our practice on Monday. The envelope said *Ryne* in cursive letters across the front. I opened it, pulled out the letter and read it again.

Who writes letters anymore? I wondered. Every girl I knew just sent text messages. Even my grandparents sent emails to Samantha and me, and on my last birthday I had even received a few electronic cards from people, a couple of them with electronic gift certificates. Madison had written me an *actual letter*. It was in purple ink on really fancy notepaper, and it smelled good too, like she might have placed a tiny drop of perfume on it.

I had already read it about a dozen times, but now I needed to write something back to her, so I read it one more time while I thought about what I should say. I didn't have any fancy paper, so I had just planned to use a spiral notebook and a black pen. I pulled out the notebook, opened it and sat there for a minute. I wrote one line and read it. I thought it sounded terrible, and it looked even worse. Compared to her handwriting, mine was pathetic. So I ripped the page out and

107

started over. This time, I wrote one line and tried printing the words, but it looked stupid, almost like I was a kindergartener trying to make my letters the right height by making sure each one touched the lines above and below it. So I ripped it out and started again. Just then, there was a small knock on the door to my fortress. I scrambled to hide the letter from Madison inside my spiral notebook. "Who is it?" I asked, trying to buy some time.

Samantha's tiny voice answered. "It's me. Can I come in?"

"No!" I almost screamed. "I'm busy!"

"Please, Ryne," Sam whined. "I want to show you something."

"I said I'm busy!" I repeated. I didn't want to be bugged and I figured she had a butterfly or a snail or a flower or some other silly thing she had found outside that she wanted me to see.

"Pleeease, Ryne," she pleaded again. "It's important."

I rolled out of the bed and crammed the notebook beneath my pillow. I went over to the door and threw it open. Samantha was standing there with one of her play purses. She has about ten of them, all of them different shades of pink. She usually fills them with Barbie doll clothes.

"What is it?" I demanded.

"Can I come in?" She asked me, sweetly.

I immediately felt bad for being such a jerk. "Sure," I said.

Sam walked in and sat down on the bed opposite mine. I noticed the corner of my notebook was sticking out from beneath my pillow. I casually nudged it back underneath before I sat down.

"I have something I want to show you," she said, formally. Sam can be kind of prissy sometimes, like she's a queen. "But I want you to close your eyes first." I rolled my eyes and sighed. I was sure I was about to be treated to a new Barbie wedding dress she had bought with her allowance.

"Really?" I complained.

"*Close your eyes*," she said, in what my mom calls her "sing-song" voice. "It's a surprise!"

I knew this could go on for a while, so I complied and closed my eyes.

"No peeking," Sam said.

"I'm not peeking, Sam," I said, honestly.

"Hold out your hand," she requested.

I held out my hand. I could hear her fiddling with the clasp to her purse.

"*Keep them closed*," she sang.

I kept my eyes closed as she pulled out whatever 'surprise' she had and placed it in my hand. Immediately, I could tell by the feel that it was a baseball.

"Okay, open your eyes!" She squealed with delight.

I opened my eyes obediently. The ball, which was a faded, brownish-green color, sat in the flat of my palm. It was a lifeless creature that looked like it had been pulled from a sewer. "Holy cow," I said. It was like she had just placed a giant, dead lizard's head in my hand. "Where did you get this disgusting thing?"

"Alfonso gave it to me yesterday," she said proudly. "He told me to give it to you."

"Why would Alfonso tell you to give me this?" I asked. Underneath the dried slime I could see part of the word *Official*. It was one of the league balls we used during our games.

"He said you should keep it, in case Mano doesn't come back."

I looked up at her and suddenly it dawned on me. This was the ball Mano had blasted off of Big Lefty from The Phoenix into the center of that gunky pond two months earlier. It was the first homerun he had hit, not counting the one the umpire had stolen from him in our first game.

"I know it's gross," Sam said, like she was apologizing. "You can't even use it anymore because it's broken." I didn't understand what she meant. I was too busy trying to figure out how in the heck Alfonso had found the ball and how he'd managed to fish it out of the middle of that nasty pond.

"What do you mean 'it's broken'?" I asked her.

"Turn it over," she said, pointing at the ball. "On the other side, it's broken."

I reached down with two fingers and my thumb and picked the ball up carefully. I couldn't get the giant, dead lizard image out of my mind. I rolled the sad creature's head over. Sam was right. It was broken. Just like the first ball Mano had hit and that I'd helped Alfonso pull down from the top of the concession stand. Several of the stitches were split as if they had snapped from the force of the blow Mano and his bat had delivered.

"Hey, did you know Alfonso is adopted?" Sam suddenly asked.

"No, I didn't know that," I replied as I studied the stitches. "How did you find that out?"

"He told me," she said, casually. "He's not even from the United States. He's from a different country that's far away."

"Where?" I asked, interested.

"Domino-can-public," she answered.

"Dominican Republic," I corrected.

"Yeah, that's what I said," she insisted.

"Huh," I mumbled, thinking. "I didn't know you hung out with Alfonso."

"Yeah, we play on the playground together sometimes during your games. He's very nice, but he always leaves when it's time for Mano to bat."

"Really?" I said. Mano had begun to draw somewhat of a crowd wherever we played whenever it was his turn to bat. Word about him had begun to travel. "What about when Miggy bats?"

She shrugged her shoulders. "He never says anything about Miggy, but he talks about Mano a lot. He really likes him. Once he even called him Super-Mano."

I was quiet for a moment. I wondered if Alfonso had ever called our right fielder Super-Mano in front of Coach Ramirez or Miggy. I doubted it. It was obvious to everyone that neither Coach Ramirez nor Miggy liked to hear about Mano. "Did Alfonso say why he thinks Mano may not come back?" I asked. Sam paused, like she was thinking. Honestly, we are really close. I'm not normally sharp with her like I was when she knocked on my door. I like having her around most of the time. She's girly and she does squeal a lot, but she's a really good sister.

"It's a secret," she finally whispered.

I sat up straight on the bed. I could tell she actually knew something and wasn't pulling my leg.

"Can you tell me?" I asked.

"You won't tell anyone, will you Ryne? Alfonso told me I shouldn't tell anyone."

"No, I won't. I promise."

She held up her little finger. I made a hook with mine and curled it around hers. "Pinky swear, double dare, I won't share…promise, promise, promise," she said. It was our way of promising to keep each

111

other's secrets. We had been doing it since she was five and I was eight. Neither of us had ever broken our pact when we did it. I nodded and repeated at the end, "I promise, promise, promise." We dropped our fingers.

"Mano went back to Hawai'i," she announced.

I was floored. "*What?*"

"Alfonso said Mano's daddy called his daddy and told him they were going back to Hawai'i."

"*Forever?*" I asked.

"He doesn't know."

"When did Alfonso tell you this?"

"Yesterday, when he gave me that yucky ball and asked me to give it to you."

My head was spinning. Mano and I had become sort of close. I couldn't believe he was just gone. He hadn't even said goodbye. I looked at the disgusting ball in my hand. Suddenly, I didn't care that it was gross anymore. I closed my fingers over the laces and gripped it tightly. My finger found the busted seam. I stood up and turned and threw the ball as hard as I could against the back wall of my fortress. It hit squarely between the two beds, right in the heart of a Chicago Cubs pennant, with a loud crash. The pins holding the Cubs pennant flew off and it fell to the floor.

Sam jumped up from the bed, holding her hands to her ears because of the loud noise. "*Why did you do that?*" she screeched at me.

I looked at her. I could feel my face burning with anger. "*He just left us?* What kind of garbage is that? You don't just leave your team! What are we supposed to do now?" I could barely control myself. "You don't do that to your teammates! You don't just walk out on them!"

Sam looked at me with sad eyes. "Maybe his dad made him go back to Hawai'i," she offered.

"Of course, he made him!" I spewed at her. "Kids don't get to make choices. We just have to do what we are told to do."

"Then why are you mad at Mano?"

I felt tears stinging my eyes. I looked away from her. "Because he didn't tell anybody. He just...left us." My stomach was bubbling, but not like when I get the bats. It felt like tears were pouring from my eyes, down my throat and directly into the middle of my belly. Sam came over and put her hand on me. I refused to look at her. I didn't want her to see me cry.

"Maybe his dad wouldn't let him tell anybody, either," she said, softly. She put her arms around my back and hugged me. "I'm sorry, Ryne. I know you really liked him. Alfonso was very sad, too."

She let me go and walked across the room and lay down on the floor. She stretched her arm underneath the bed and pulled out that gross baseball. She stood and sat it on the comforter. "Alfonso told me it was really important for you to have this ball."

I looked up at her. "Why?"

Sam smiled. "He said you were Mano's best friend on the team."

Best friend? Some friend, I thought. He didn't even tell me he was leaving. I looked at the dead lizard head on the bed. What could Alfonso possibly think was so important about that stupid ball? I wondered.

"Samantha! Where are you?" It was Mom's voice. I walked over to the window. She was standing in the backyard. Sam ran past me and opened the door.

"I'm up here with Ryne!" she yelled.

"Come on in, honey. I want you to take your bath now so you can help me get the fruit ready for the games tomorrow." Mom always brought sliced oranges, watermelon, and grapes for the whole team for our games. She added, teasingly, "If you hurry, we'll make some caramel apples for the boys."

"Can I have one, too?" Sam pleaded.

Mom laughed. "Of course you can, Sugar. Now come on down and let's get your bath." She could see me standing in the window. "You probably want to shower before Chase and Brazos get here too, Ryne," she said. I looked down at her from the window and nodded. Sam skipped to her down the stairs and then they disappeared into the house together.

I closed the door to my fortress and walked back over to the bed. The ball was laying there, all brownish-green and gross. *It's nothing special*, I thought. Broken laces or not.

It was just another ball, and Mano was just another player, I thought, angrily. There was nothing special about either of them.

* * *

So have you heard from Mano?" Chase asked. They were the first words out of his mouth as he entered the fortress.

I shook my head. "No, I haven't," I answered, honestly.

Chase was mad. I could tell he had been thinking about little else. "Well, he'd better be there tomorrow," he threatened. "I can't believe he missed every practice this week. He didn't even come to the *Wheel*. What I really can't believe is that Coach Ramirez hasn't said a word about it. He hasn't asked us if anyone has seen him or anything."

I shrugged my shoulders and went over to the refrigerator. I wanted to change the subject as fast as I could. "You want something to drink?"

"Yeah, hit me with one of those purple Gatorades."

I picked out Chase's favorite flavor and tossed the plastic bottle to him. He caught it and flopped down onto one of the beds.

"You know Hootie is going to play tomorrow."

I turned around, surprised. "Really? That's great." I tried to sound excited over the news, but I was flat. Chase could tell something was bothering me.

"What's wrong with you?"

I pulled a red Gatorade out of the fridge and twisted off the top. "Nothing, I'm good."

Chase took a sip of his drink and eyed me. "Katie told me about the letter," he confessed.

I swallowed my first sip of Gatorade hard. "She did?"

"Yeah. What did it say?"

I leaned against the refrigerator. "Didn't Katie tell you?" I was fishing, hoping I would catch the right answer.

Chase shook his head. "Nah. She said Madison wouldn't let her read it. She wouldn't even tell her anything that was in it."

I was relieved. It was the answer I'd hoped for. "It's sort of private."

"Seriously? You're not going to tell me?" Chase acted like I was holding out on him. I felt a little guilty. "Maybe later," I stalled.

The door to the fortress popped open. Brazos was standing there in a neon orange tank top, shorts, sandals, and his Intimidators cap. His hair was a little shorter, like he'd just received a fresh trim, but it still reached just above his shoulders.

"Did you lose a fight with a weed-eater?" Chase teased.

Brazos took off his cap and shook what remained of his mane. "I asked my mom to give me a trim," he replied. "It's going to feel like we're standing on the surface of the sun tomorrow and I wanted to get the hair off my shoulders." He put his hat back on, turned to me and immediately asked, "So what's up with Mano?"

"How am I supposed to know?" My answer came out sounding ruder than I'd intended.

"Whoa. Somebody's lost his chill," Brazos observed. "What's up?"

"Nothing," I lied. "Sorry."

"Forget it," he said. "I'm sure everybody has been pestering you about it since you and Mano are friends."

"We're not that close," I insisted. "Heck, he's closer with Jimmy than he is with me." I wanted to change the subject. "Hey, the show comes on in ten minutes," I noted. "You guys want popcorn or anything?" Both of them nodded.

Brazos walked over to the fridge and helped himself to a bottle of water while I slipped the first bag into the microwave. "Hey Chase, who's that cute blonde who's been coming to the games with your sister?"

I snapped my attention to Brazos. "That's Madison," I answered, cutting Chase off before he could answer.

"She's kind of interesting." He grinned mischievously.

Chase quickly jumped into the conversation between us. "She's been coming to see Ryne."

Brazos laughed. "Yeah, I know. It's pretty obvious." He punched my shoulder. "Just messin' with you, Ryne. You can tell she REALLY likes you."

I felt my face redden.

Chase picked up the remote and clicked on the television. He quickly pressed in the digits for the Discovery Channel and instantly a huge Great White shark filled the screen.

"Oh, I saw this one on Monday!" Brazos said, excitedly. "That shark is like twenty feet long. It's one of the biggest they've found so far cruising around that island with all of the seals."

Chase joined in. "That Ring of Death the seals have to swim through to get to the island is crazy!" The Ring of Death surrounds Seal Island. It's where the sharks wait for the cuddly critters to swim to and from the small isle. Watching the great whites tear into them after the innocent creatures swim unknowingly into their path is sort of like watching teddy bears get massacred. "Man, seals must be really stupid," he added.

"Or really brave," I countered.

Chase looked over at me. "Huh. I guess I never thought of it that way."

The show on Great Whites soon ended and immediately the one we had been waiting for began. It was called *Jaws of the Tiger*. It had been advertised as a collection of stories about attacks around the Hawai'ian Islands by tiger sharks. The commercial had also included one interesting scene where a Hawai'ian man made a remark about the *niuhi*. After Brazos had seen the commercial, he'd told Chase and I and we'd decided to seek permission for the sleepover so we could watch the show together.

As it turned out, the Hawai'ian man who had appeared in the advertisement narrated a large portion of the two hour drama. As story after story of swimmers, surfers, body boarders, fisherman and some just plain unlucky people who had been attacked by tiger sharks were told, he spoke about the history of sharks around the islands and the great respect they carried in Hawai'ian culture. He was a smart-looking guy with gold-rimmed glasses, but he spoke without the smooth accent that both Mano and his father had. He sounded like some normal guy from down the street. About halfway through the show, he began to talk about ancient Hawai'i and the niuhi shark legends. He told us some of the same stuff Mano had mentioned about the chiefs hunting them, except he didn't say anything about how they did it. Then he said something shocking. Whenever the chiefs caught a niuhi, they would often eat the shark's eyeballs. They believed it would give them the ability to see into the future.

"Sick, man. That's just gross," Chase practically barfed.

Brazos disagreed. "Nah, that's too cool. Dude, I would definitely eat their eyeballs. Think about it. If you could see into the future? That would be like a super-power!"

Normally, I would have agreed with Chase, that it was gross, and also that it sounded pretty ridiculous. Then I thought about Mano, and I wondered. Was it possible?

The Hawai'ian guy went on to say that the chiefs didn't just believe they would be able to see into the future. They really believed that by catching a niuhi, they would become like him. They would become more aggressive, fast and dangerous. Those traits would make them fierce fighters. He told a story about a Hawai'ian native who had to fight a niuhi to pass his final test before becoming a warrior. He succeeded and one day he became a great warrior teacher for the famous Hawai'ian king named Kamehameha.

His name was Kekūhaupi'o.

Kekūhaupi'o became Kamehameha's teacher when the future king was still very young. One day Kekūhaupi'o found out that his student had quit his training. Instead, he was choosing to play, doing fun stuff like going to the cliffs in Hawai'i and trying to jump off the rocks into the water below without making a splash.

"Cool!" Brazos shouted. "Kids were even penciling way back then!"

We love to pencil. A lot of times we go to the community pool during the summer and jump from the high dive. We have contests to see who can slip into the water perfectly straight without making a splash. It amazed us to find out that a Hawai'ian king from a couple of hundred years ago had spent time doing the exact same thing we did for fun.

Anyway, Kekūhaupi'o told Kamehameha that he would miss his purpose for his life if he didn't stop playing around. The Hawai'ian guy with the gold-rimmed glasses said that Kekūhaupi'o taught Kamehameha that the chief who only wants to please himself instead of caring for his people is not the chief who will become a great ruler.

Kekūhaupi'o's lesson reminded me of the first time Mano had joined us at The Hitting Wheel. It was the day he had helped Alfonso learn how to hit those tiny yellow balls with the Thunder Stick. It had been such a nice thing to do, but what I remembered was that even though Mano didn't know Alfonso at all, he seemed to really care about him. He had stopped what he was doing and had immediately helped him. It was like he was doing exactly what Kekūhaupi'o had taught Kamehameha, to care about others more than he cared about himself. It reminded me of Jimmy's words at the water park. *"Mano is our village chief, not Miggy."*

Chase hit the pause button. He pointed at the screen. A boy actor who was supposed to be Kamehameha was standing on a cliff, staring out across the ocean. A large shark tooth hung on a cord around his neck. "Check it out. That kid reminds me of Mano."

"Me, too," Brazos agreed. "Hey, he's going to show up tomorrow, right?"

"Yeah, he'll be there," Chase pronounced confidently. "I just hope he hasn't been really sick or anything."

I could feel both of them looking at me. "Yeah, me, too," I added, weakly.

"Do you think...?" Chase started. He stopped.

"What?" Brazos pushed.

"Well, you know. The stuff about the niuhi. Do you think it's true?"

Brazos stuffed a handful of popcorn in his mouth. "Yep. I do."

I shot a surprised look at Brazos. "You do?"

"Yeah," he mumbled around his popcorn. "Mano is just like one of those warriors. He's fast. He's strong. He's not scared of anything, and when he's batting, he acts just like a shark."

"What do you mean?" Chase asked.

"Sharks seem pretty harmless when they're just swimming around, right? They just sort of hang out, until they decide to go after something. Then they become total killers. Mano does the same thing. He just stands there at the plate, all still like a statue, until he decides to go after a pitch. Then, WHAM! It's just like when a shark hits its target. You don't know when it's going to happen, but you know that when it does, it's all over."

Chase looked at me. "What do you think, Ryne?"

"I don't know," I said, truthfully. "But I don't think Mano is some sort of niuhi super hero. I mean it's not like he's Peter Parker and got bit by a radio-active shark."

"What do you think it is? Why is he so much better than the rest of us?"

I stared at the screen. I thought about Kamehameha and his teacher Kekūhaupi'o. The legend of the niuhi was interesting, but the story about Kamehameha's teacher wasn't a legend. He just sounded like a completely awesome warrior coach.

"Maybe part of the reason is he's had better coaching than us," I said, thinking out loud.

Brazos and Chase didn't say anything. Maybe they thought I was dissing Coach Ramirez and Coach Weaver, but I wasn't. My mind went back to the coach I'd had when I was eight, the one who had told us about the stitches on the baseball and how a team had to be put together just like a ball, one stitch at a time. He had always been trying to teach us something special about the game. He was my favorite coach. Heck, he was my favorite teacher. He'd said that each of us should know our role on our team and that no matter how big or small we might think our role might be, it was still our responsibility to do our jobs the best we could for our teammates. We were always supposed to put our team before ourselves. He said that when we got older and learned things like how to put down a sacrifice bunt, we would begin to understand what he meant. Now that I thought about it, what he'd said was similar to what Kekūhaupi'o had taught Kamehameha. None of my coaches since then had talked about that sort of stuff. For the most part, they just yelled when we did things wrong.

There was a knock at the door. We all sat up. "Come in," I said.

Dad stuck his head into the fortress. "Hey, boys. It's ten o'clock. Just thought I'd remind you that lights out is in thirty minutes." He grinned. "Big day tomorrow. You guys ready?"

"Yes sir," Chase and Brazos answered together.

"Hey, Mr. Dunston. Do you think Mrs. Dunston might make another IHOP breakfast for us tomorrow?" Brazos pleaded.

Dad grinned. "Don't worry. She's going to make sure you guys are fully fueled for your double-header, Brazos."

Brazos clapped his hands together with a loud pop. "Your mom rocks, Ryne!"

Dad looked over at me with his warning face. "Thirty minutes, Ryne. Got it?"

"Yes sir," I said, knowing what he meant. He wanted lights out so that when Mom checked on us from the kitchen window in thirty-five minutes, he wouldn't get in trouble.

He threw us a wave. "Good night, boys."

There was only about fifteen minutes left in *Jaws of the Tiger*. Chase hit the play button and fast forwarded through the commercials. The last segment of the show was about a shark attack off the island of Molokai. Up until then, the stories had been about attacks near Maui and Oahu.

"Hey, isn't that the island where Mano is from?" Chase asked.

"Yeah," I answered. We all became quiet as the story was told. It was different than the others which had been about swimmers, surfers, fishermen, and even a young couple on their honeymoon who had been attacked. This was a story about a Zodiac boat that had been found washed up on the beach by a boy who lived on the island. From the pictures, the boat looked brand new. It was sparkling white with a small deck on the back that housed an outboard motor and a ski pole. The steering wheel stood behind a small windshield and had a few dials and other gadgets next to it. Up front, there was enough room for a couple of people to stretch out and sunbathe.

"Cool boat," Chase remarked.

"That ride is off the chain, dude. I wish I had one," Brazos chimed in.

The whole story about the boat was a mystery. The boat was registered, but when the police checked it out the guy who it was registered to didn't even exist. The interesting part was that a chunk of the platform on the back of the boat near the motor was gone. What remained of it was splintered and broken. In the busted wood, they had found something that had been left behind. It was a shark's tooth. A big one.

"Whoa," Brazos said. "Look at that. It's huge!"

The tooth had been identified as belonging to a tiger shark. It wasn't just any tiger shark. From the size of the tooth, researchers estimated that the shark may have been over twenty feet long. It would have been almost *double* the average size of a tiger. Maybe the most interesting part of the story to us was that it had just occurred the previous summer and still no one knew the real story behind the mystery Zodiac. The assumption was that whoever had been on the boat had been taken by the shark.

"Wow. That happened last year," Brazos said. "I wonder if Mano knows anything about it."

"I'll bet he does," Chase said. "He was still living in Hawai'i last year, wasn't he?"

Both of them turned to me. "I guess we'll have to ask him," I said. I felt guilt stab me in the gut, but I couldn't break my promise to Sam. Besides, I figured everyone would find out on Saturday anyway when Coach Ramirez would have to tell us that Mano had gone back to Hawai'i.

Just before the show ended, they cut back to the smart-looking Hawai'ian dude with the gold-rimmed glasses. He said, "There is an old Hawai'ian saying. *He niuhi 'ai holopapa o ka moku.*"

"Hey…" Chase started.

I held up my hand for him to be quiet. The Hawai'ian man added, "It means *the niuhi shark will devour all who are on the island.*"

I got goose bumps on my arms. "That's exactly what Mano said," Brazos reminded us.

The last thing we saw was an enormous tiger shark swimming directly at the camera. We all stared as it came right at us, its jaws opened wide. It looked as if it was going to swallow the camera.

It looked as if it was going to swallow us all.

Shaun

When we arrived at the brand new Central Texas baseball complex on Saturday morning at 9:00 am, it was already hot. The air was stagnant and stifling. You could smell the asphalt in the parking lot beginning to heat up like a griddle.

"Ugh," Hope grunted as we stepped out of the car. She tugged at the front of her fresh Intimidators parents' t-shirt and said, "I wonder if they would consider moving the playoffs to Alaska next year?"

"Or maybe they could just build a lazy river around each of these fields? We could float around them in our bathing suits while we watched the games," I suggested.

Hope's face brightened. "You are a genius, Buster! Wait right here and I'll go to Home Depot and get you a shovel and a water hose so you can get started."

All around us, players and their families were piling out of their vehicles. The parking lot seemed to stretch out forever. There were rows and rows of shiny SUVs, minivans, and a growing number of motor homes on the outer edges. It felt like we were arriving at Sea World or Six Flags. Baseball World had been in the planning phase for a decade and it had taken nearly two years to construct. The park sat on five hundred acres and contained thirty baseball fields. Each field was a mini-replica of the home parks for the thirty major league clubs. There were also a couple of small lakes with fountains, several playground and picnic areas, and even a high quality restaurant called *The Hot Corner*. The owners had recently announced a partnership with Major League Baseball to make the park even grander. Plans were in the works to create what one newspaper had dubbed a "Baseball Disneyland." Six hundred acres were scheduled to be added sometime in the near future and the master strategy was to construct a baseball themed amusement/water park that would surround the replica fields. When all was said and done, Baseball World was slated to become one of the largest family theme parks in the world.

Maybe I could convince them to add those lazy rivers around the fields I thought, as I began to unload the Suburban in the sweltering heat. I looked over at Hope who already had Brazos, Chase, Ryne, and Samantha standing in military formation while she slathered them in sunscreen. Sam stood patiently while her mother vigorously rubbed lotion over all of her exposed surfaces, but the boys fidgeted and whined with every powerful stroke. Then my loving wife approached me.

"Give me your nose, mister," she ordered in her best drill sergeant voice.

Now it was my turn to whine. "Ah, c'mon, Hope," I complained. "I'll put some on when we get inside, okay?"

Ignoring my request, she slapped lotion on the end of my snout and began to rub with gusto. "Hush it, Buster. Do you want to have skin like an alligator when you're fifty?" The boys began to heehaw like donkeys.

"No, ma'am," I answered dutifully, grimacing as she worked me over.

When we were all thoroughly basted and ready to broil, we began the long trek across the parking lot. Just before the entrance, Brazos pointed out an ESPN truck and crew unloading equipment. "Check it out. ESPN is here!" When an extremely attractive young woman nartly dressed for television stepped out of a white sedan that was arked next to the truck, I thought the boys would faint.

"That's Kelly Duerson!" Chase practically screamed.

"Aaahh, dude. She is so seriously gorgeous!" Brazos needlessly announced.

I must have nodded in agreement because I suddenly received a fork in my ribs. Hope dug her two fingers into me playfully and then skittered them up my side in a way that only she can do. The tickling sensation made me jump, bark, and howl all at the same time.

"HEY, HEY, HEY!" I yelped, laughing. "What was that for?"

She grabbed my arm and pulled me in close. "Eyes forward, soldier," she commanded with a grin. "There's nothing to see over there."

"Oh, there's plenty to see!" Brazos chirped.

I glanced over at Ryne. He looked sharp and squared away in his Intimidators playoff jersey. It was a deep gold with black letters, essentially the reverse of the ill-advised black jerseys with gold letters they'd worn all season long. His matching bat bag was tucked tightly to his shoulder. He was marching along, lost in thought.

"Help me out here, Ryne?" I begged, trying to get his attention. "Kelly Duerson has nothing on Mom, right? You've heard me say that *at least* a thousand times."

Ryne glanced up. "Sorry, Dad? What did you say?"

If he'd noticed the ESPN truck or Kelly Duerson, he had already forgotten about them and moved on to something else. Hope continued our playful banter. "C'mon, Ryne. You'd better back Dad up here. Does he secretly want to make a trade for Kelly Duerson?"

Ryne smiled, but it was hollow. He was clearly preoccupied.

"I wonder why ESPN is here?" he asked absently.

"Probably to see our team play," Sam piped in. "We're all going to be worldly famous, like celebrities!"

"Worldly famous?" Hope reached over and tweaked Sam's ear. "No more Disney Channel for you, young lady," she teased. "You spend way too much time thinking about being worldly famous."

"Just you wait and see," Sam promised. "We'll all be worldly famous on ESPN today!"

We stood in line to pay our entry fees. A giant baseball hovered above our heads, high in the air over the gates. *Baseball* and *World* were written in enormous iron letters bracketing the ball. After receiving our tickets, we passed through turnstiles whose steel arms were formed into miniature baseball bats. Hope pointed them out to the kids. "Oh, look! Aren't these little bats cute?"

Inside, we were immediately greeted with a gift shop and a large concession stand called the *Press Box*. Several *Press Box* concession stands were scattered strategically across the park. Each of them sold traditional baseball game staples like sodas, water, sports drinks, nachos, hot dogs, hamburgers, sunflower seeds, peanuts, and of course, Cracker Jack. They also sold multi-flavored frozen drinks in over-sized Baseball World cups. The demand for the frozen treats was so great that each *Press Box* operated a separate "Frozen Drinks Line Only" to handle the requests. The line at the first *Press Box* just inside the gate was already twenty people deep.

"Dad! Can I have one of those?" Sam beseeched me. She watched as several kids exited the line with the frozen, wildly colored mountains of ice. The vibrant flavors beckoned through the clear domes that covered the cups.

"Absolutely," Hope answered for me. "But let's wait until we get the boys over to their field." She nudged me sharply with her elbow. "I want one, too!"

Beyond the *Press Box*, there were two large maps detailing the layout of Baseball World and the location of each field. Between the maps was a giant airport-style television screen. Instead of announcing arrivals and departures of planes at various gates, this screen directed park visitors to the day's match-ups and notified them of impending game times at each of the thirty fields. The boys scanned the large board quickly and found their team name.

"There we are!" Chase said, pointing his finger at a location in the middle of the board. It read **Intimidators v. Blasters. 11:00 a.m. PNC Park, Home of the Pittsburgh Pirates.**

We moved to one of the maps to find PNC Park. Baseball World was appropriately platted into a National League and an American League. Each league was further subdivided into an Eastern, Central, and Western division. Within each division, there were five stadiums.

Because there was only a single entrance into the facility, it was quite a haul to reach the various fields. The creators of the facility had planned for the long hikes, and they had done it with style. A vintage train depot waited just beyond the maps. Tracks stretched off into the distance, one set headed toward the National League and the other toward the American League. Two trains operated on each track and left on a prompt fifteen minute, rotating schedule. We arrived just before the next National League train was due at 9:15. As we stood in line, all of us were giddy with anticipation. Then Sam shouted, "Look! Here it comes!"

Steaming in from the distance was a small, but authentic steam locomotive engine. It was tugging three passenger cars and a caboose. Just before it pulled into the station, the conductor blew the whistle. It let out a loud, satisfying blast that thrilled us.

"All aboard!" the conductor shouted. From the waist up, he appeared dressed for the part in a vintage, pinstriped engineer's hat with matching overalls. When he stepped out onto the platform, we could see that the overalls had been hemmed into shorts. His two thick legs poked out of them hilariously, like hairy tree trunks. "All aboard the National League Express!" he belted again. Immediately we began to board the open air passenger cars. The boys and Sam bounded in ahead of us and slid excitedly into one of the bench seats. Hope and I sat down in the row behind them. Sam immediately flipped around on her knees to face us.

"This is awesome, Dad!" She giggled happily. "I love it!"

I leaned forward. "You boys know that years ago all the clubs traveled between cities by train."

Brazos turned to me. "Yeah, I remember that baseball player's ghost talking about it in *Field of Dreams*."

"What ghost?" Hope asked.

"He's talking about Shoeless Joe Jackson," I said.

"Why would a ghost need shoes, Daddy?" Sam asked.

I turned my head patiently between the two women in my life as they waited for an explanation about the plot of one of the best baseball movies of all time. I smiled at Brazos. He rolled his eyes. "Why don't we just rent the movie when we get home?" I suggested.

The train began inching forward and slowly picked up speed. We probably never traveled faster than 15 mph during the journey and in less than five minutes, we had already arrived at the first stop, the Eastern Division. The conductor picked up his microphone and announced, "First stop, National League Eastern Division. Atlanta's SunTrust Park, Philadelphia's Citizens Bank Park, Washington's Nationals Park, New York's Citi Field, and Miami's Marlins Park. Please exit to the right of the train."

Several families and players rose in unison. Off to the right, we could see one of the five fields, Marlins Park. It was spectacularly groomed. The infield dirt was combed smooth and the electric green grass gleamed.

"Doesn't look like they spare any expense when it comes to watering," I said to Hope. "That field looks like I could putt golf balls on it."

"It does look manicured," she agreed. "Hey, why doesn't our yard look like that?"

"Water restrictions. I've considered ripping the grass out and replacing it with artificial turf," I grumped, kiddingly. "But then every kid in the neighborhood would want to play the Super Bowl in our front yard. We'd have to build a roof over it, add seating capacity, restrooms, and concessions. It would just be too expensive."

Hope laughed.

When we'd finished unloading passengers bound for games in the Eastern Division, the train slowly pulled out of the depot and began to steam forward. We chugged along at a comfortable pace. In just under five minutes, we arrived at our next destination. The hairy-legged conductor picked up his microphone and announced our arrival. "Second stop, National League Central Division. St. Louis' Busch Stadium, Milwaukee's Miller Park, Cincinnati's Great American Ball Park, Pittsburgh's PNC Park, and Chicago's Wrigley Field. Please exit to the right of the train."

"That's us," I said. Everyone popped up and we quickly made our way to the exit. Sam turned and threw the conductor a theatrical wave as she stepped off.

"See ya next time!" She shouted at him happily.

The burly conductor waved back at her with a big smile. "Good luck to all of you today!" He blew the whistle and the train steamed off to its final destination in the Western Division.

As we headed toward the complex of fields, Chase and Brazos chatted amiably. I noted that Ryne was still surprisingly quiet. He was either unbelievably focused, or something was bothering him. I chose to believe he had simply put his game face on early and was ready to play.

Four of the five fields in the Central Division facility intersected with one another via a concrete hub that housed a *Press Box* concession stand, restrooms, a large playground, multiple picnic tables, and enough bleachers to comfortably sit roughly a thousand fans at each park. The walkway, playground, and bleacher areas were mercifully covered to ward off the relentless rays of the sun. The only portion of the complex not shielded from the giant burning orb in the bright Texas sky were the fields themselves. However, the players were able to take refuge in dugouts that were recessed into the ground just like in professional stadiums. The player bunkers were also constantly bathed in a cooling spray from a series of misters located on each rooftop. There was even a modified shower stall located in each dugout. It allowed a player to hang his head beneath a nozzle that released a cold stream of water without soaking his uniform. Every possible way to beat the heat of the brutal Texas summer appeared to have been considered, except for the lazy river idea I'd kiddingly suggested to Hope.

The fifth field was bigger than the rest. It was set off from the others and appeared to have been designed to handle only full-sized, regulation games. Even from a distance, it was immediately recognizable from the large red and white marquee that rose into the sky. It said WRIGLEY FIELD, HOME OF CHICAGO CUBS. I pointed it out to Ryne. He broke his concentration for a moment and stared off into the distance. He turned to me with a little smile.

"Looks just like the real thing," he said, simply.

I smiled and nodded. "Yeah it does, doesn't it?"

We made our way to PNC Park. Already, several Intimidator families had arrived. Beyond the right field fence, we could see a few of the new gold jerseys were headed toward a long row of batting cages in the distance. Chase, Brazos, and Ryne followed in that direction while Hope, Sam, and I made our way toward the bleachers.

"Well, hello, Shaun," I heard a gravelly voice say.

Mr. Blyleven was sitting in the first row, just behind the first base dugout where the Intimidators had been assigned. He rose and shook my hand.

"Well, hey there, Mr. Blyleven," I said, only a little surprised he had made the trip.

"Can I talk to you for a minute?" he immediately asked.

"Sure." He seemed in a hurry so I followed him down a few flights of bleachers until we were safely out of earshot from everyone. He didn't waste any time.

"Is Mano going to be here today?"

I shrugged my shoulders. "I have no idea, sir." I treated Mr. Blyleven with tremendous respect. His presence was strong and commanding.

He looked at me with concern in his piercing blue eyes. "Something's not right. The kid wasn't at practice the entire week. He didn't come to The Hitting Wheel on Thursday, either." Once the Intimidators had hit their stride, Mr. Blyleven had begun showing up frequently at our games. He'd even begun coming to practices about halfway through the season. Like the rest of the parents, families, and fans, he'd become absolutely enchanted with the team as the boys began their spectacular rise. "Something's not right," he emphasized, swiping his handle bar mustache. "I've got a bad feeling."

I was aware that Mano had been out, but I'd been busy at work throughout the week and wasn't aware that he'd missed every practice. "Well, hopefully he'll be here today," I said, trying to be positive. "Have you talked to the coaches?"

Mr. Blyleven sniffed. "No, I haven't. I suspect Ramirez knows something, but he hasn't said a word to anybody."

"What makes you think that?" I asked.

"He's been more reserved than usual. That's not like him. The man is a fully inflated, bag of wind most of the time. This last week, he acted like his bag was only half full. Something's definitely going on." With that, Mr. Blyleven abruptly excused himself and climbed back up the stairs.

Hope came down to me after he left. "Is everything all right?" she asked.

"Mr. Blyleven was asking me about Mano."

Hope bit her lower lip and shook her head. "He's not coming."

I looked at her sharply. "How do you know that?"

"I just know, Shaun. The same way I know when Ryne or Samantha is sick before they know it. I just know."

The mystery of Hope's intuition has baffled me consistently throughout our marriage, but I've learned that she's rarely wrong. Suddenly, I was worried.

*　*　*

Ryne

When Coach Ramirez gathered us for his pre-game speech in the dugout, everyone except Miggy was still anxiously looking around, waiting for Mano and his crummy bat bag to appear. Strangely, Miggy had pulled a comb out of his bag and was raking it purposefully through his thick, black hair. I remember thinking *who carries a comb in their bat bag?* When he was finished, he sat his Intimidators cap carefully on top of his head and raked the portions of hair that protruded from the edges a few more times. He stood up, made certain his jersey was neatly tucked, and brushed at a piece of lint on his pants. If the dugout had come equipped with a full length mirror, I figured he probably would have been turning in a circle in front of it, checking how his rear end looked in his pants.

What the heck? I thought. *He's acting like a girl getting ready for a date.*

"Okay boys, take a seat," Coach Ramirez ordered. I pulled my glove out of my bat bag, zipped it shut, and sat down between Chase and Brazos on the bench. "We're facing a good team today, Intimidators. The Blasters are an outfit out of a top notch, Dallas-based select organization. They have one five-star pitcher and two four-star pitchers. We'll no doubt see their five-star guy today for Game One and one of the four-star guys in Game Two. We're going to throw our own five-star guy in Game One, too." He looked down the row at Jimmy.

"You ready, Jimmy?" He asked.

Jimmy didn't say anything. He just nodded.

"Everybody knows we've got Hootie back so we'll move him in at third and slide Sammy over into right field." He glanced toward Sammy who suddenly looked uncomfortable. Hootie was sitting next to him. It had taken two months, but Hootie had healed and looked normal again, only now he was fitted with a brand new pair of thick-rimmed goggles. He didn't need glasses to see, but his doctor had thought it would be a good idea for him to wear the goggles to protect his eye. I thought he looked like he was more ready to swim a few laps than play third base.

The dugout was oddly quiet after Coach Ramirez announced the fielding change. Sammy fidgeted nervously before he finally found the courage to drop the question that all of us needed to have answered.

"What about Mano, Coach?" Sammy asked, softly. Just then, Coach Weaver appeared at the entrance to the dugout.

"They're ready for Miggy, Coach," he said. Miggy hopped onto his feet and hustled toward the exit like he had just been waiting to be summoned.

134

"Great. Thanks," Coach Ramirez said, ignoring Sammy's question. "Can you finish up here for me?"

"Sure," Coach Weaver answered.

Coach Ramirez and Miggy left immediately. We all heard Coach Ramirez ask someone outside the dugout, "So, where are we at?"

"We're set up down here by the bullpen in right field, Coach," a strange voice replied. Wee Willie was sitting on the far end of the bench, closest to the bleachers. He stood up and peered down the right field line. "What are they doing down there?"

"Sit back down please, Willie," Coach Weaver directed.

"What are those white umbrellas for?" Wee Willie probed further.

Everyone jumped off the bench and moved toward the dugout fence. Down the right field line, we could all see a pair of odd looking umbrellas standing on either side of three tall chairs. There were a couple of guys walking around with earphones. One was positioning a television camera while the other one fiddled with the position of the umbrellas. Standing off to the side was a very pretty woman holding a microphone loosely at her side. She was talking casually to a tall man. He was dressed in a sharp suit, tie and a Baseball World cap.

"It's Kelly Duerson!" Brazos gasped.

"You mean that lady on ESPN?" Curtis asked.

"We saw her when we were coming in!" Chase said. "Wait a minute," he said, as we watched Coach Ramirez and Miggy head down the right field line. *"Is she going to interview Miggy?"*

Coach Weaver tried to herd us all back to the bench. "Sit down, Intimidators," he commanded sternly. We all reluctantly obeyed, catching a last look at Coach Ramirez as he walked with his arm around Miggy's shoulders towards Kelly Duerson and the tall man in the fancy suit and Baseball World cap.

"Is ESPN really going to interview Miggy, Dad?" Curtis pressed as we sat back down.

Coach Weaver nodded. He didn't appear to be too excited about what was happening in right field. He spoke flatly, without emotion. "Coach Ramirez and Miggy are going to be interviewed for a story on ESPN. I think it's about our new playoff format. It's no big deal, boys."

I'm no expert at judging when people aren't telling the truth, but Coach Weaver looked to me like the guy in the movies who gets questioned by the cops. The cops can just tell by the way he's acting that he knows more than what he's telling them.

"So Miggy gets to be on ESPN. There's a surprise," Chase muttered sarcastically under his breath. All of Miggy's primping in the dugout suddenly made sense. I nudged Chase with my elbow. "Look over there." Two guys were putting another television camera on the roof of the Blasters' dugout. I could see another one being lifted into place in the bed of a shiny pick-up truck in centerfield. Chase's eyes became huge.

"NO WAY!!" Brazos suddenly belted. He had seen the cameras too and said out loud what Chase and I were thinking. "Is our game gonna be on TV, Coach?!!"

The dugout began to buzz excitedly. Coach Weaver looked flustered. "Listen, boys. There is a lot of interest in Baseball World around the country," he said, once again trying to make us think that the television crew was no big deal. "Now with Major League Baseball bringing the new amusement and water park here, it's getting a lot of attention. They're going to be breaking ground on the new facility on Monday, so ESPN will be hanging around this weekend looking for some interesting stories. There's a big ceremony planned for the ground-breaking and ESPN will televise that, but they aren't actually televising any of the games."

Just as Coach Weaver said this, we could hear another camera crew began to bang around on the roof above our heads. Apparently our dugout was getting an ESPN camera, too.

"I guess Miggy is one of those stories?" Jimmy asked, suspiciously.

Coach Weaver looked like a kid caught with his hand in the cookie jar. "There are lots of great stories out here, Jimmy. They'll have cameras all over Baseball World."

"Yeah, but they're talking to Miggy."

"Yes," Coach Weaver answered. "They are talking to Miggy." I thought he suddenly looked embarrassed. "Did you see that tall man wearing the suit and the baseball cap? He's one of the owners of Baseball World. Anyway, he'd heard that Miggy was a great shortstop and so he asked Coach Ramirez if he would be willing to do an interview before the game."

Jimmy was unimpressed. "They should be interviewing Mano," he insisted.

Coach Weaver turned toward him. He began to explain. "Jimmy, you know that sometimes a certain player will get attention because..."

Just then Wee Willie's mom stuck her head around the corner of the dugout. "Excuse me," she said, interrupting Coach Weaver. Coach smiled at her politely.

"Yes?"

"I'm so sorry to interrupt you, Coach Weaver, but there's a man up here that wants to talk to you about the pre-game ceremony?"

"Oh, right. They mentioned something about that to me." He turned back to us. "Boys, let's start warming up. Stay off the infield. You can go out to centerfield and begin your stretching. I'll be back in a minute."

Wee Willie immediately jumped up and looked down the right field line. "Miggy and Coach Ramirez are sitting in those chairs under the umbrellas with Kelly Duerson," he reported.

Jimmy stood up. "Who cares?" he said, sounding angry. He picked up his glove and then dropped it back on the bench. He turned to all of us and sarcastically finished Coach Weaver's sentence for him. "You know, Jimmy. Sometimes a certain player will get attention, *just because his father is the head coach!*"

"Knock it off, Jimmy," Hootie warned him. "We don't need that garbage right now."

"Leave him alone, Hootie," Brazos jumped in, defending Jimmy. "We've been seeing it all season long. I'm sick of it, too. No matter how good any of us do, especially Mano, all we hear about is Miggy."

"Where is Mano?" Jimmy suddenly demanded. "He should be the one down there talking to ESPN! Not Miggy!" He looked over at me. "Haven't you heard from him, Ryne?" All eyes turned toward me.

"No," I answered quickly, thankful that the way he asked the question still allowed me to be honest. My promise to Sam was starting to get heavy. I never dreamed I would have had to carry it this far. *Why didn't Coach Ramirez or Coach Weaver just tell us Mano had gone back to Hawai'i?* I wondered.

Hootie stood up. He adjusted his goggles and slipped on his cap. "C'mon, guys. You heard Coach. Let's hit the field and stretch."

We grabbed our hats and followed him out of the dugout. Immediately all eyes went to the "big stage" in right field by the bullpen. Kelly Duerson was leaning forward in her chair, chatting away with Coach Ramirez. The bright television lights were on. Miggy was sitting with his hands on his knees listening to them. Kelly said something to him and she and Coach Ramirez laughed. Miggy smiled like he was embarrassed and shrugged his shoulders.

"This stinks," Jimmy snorted.

"Yeah, it does," Sammy agreed with his brother.

"Shut up, guys," Hootie said to both of them. "Let's go." Together, we broke into a slow jog toward centerfield. No one from ESPN looked in our direction, but that was hardly a surprise. It was clear to all of us that their cameras weren't there for our team, anyway.

They were there for Miggy.

12

Shaun

The opening ceremony prior to Game One between the Intimidators and the Blasters was well done. Both teams were introduced and as each player jogged from the dugout to meet his teammates along the first and third base lines, he was greeted by one of two men wearing vintage Pittsburgh Pirate uniforms.

One player wore number 33 to represent the great Honus Wagner who was one of the first five players inducted into the Baseball Hall of Fame in 1936, and is generally considered the best shortstop to ever play baseball. His picture also graces the rarest and most valuable baseball card in the world. A collector paid $2.7 million for a mint edition of the treasured artifact in 2007.

The second player wore number 21 to honor Roberto Clemente, whom many consider to be the greatest player in Pirates' history. Roberto Clemente was not just a great player - he was also a great person. He died tragically in a plane crash in 1972 while trying to deliver emergency supplies to earthquake victims in Nicaragua. He was inducted into the Baseball Hall of Fame in 1973.

As the Intimidators stood along the third base line in front of their dugout in their new gold and black jerseys, they actually looked like a mini version of the modern day Pirates. Even Brazos, with his long hair streaming out of the back of his cap, could have passed for a younger model of Andrew McCutchen, the 2013 National League MVP, before McCutchen sheared the long locks he sported during his MVP campaign.

"They look so handsome!" Hope exclaimed.

I had to agree.

Once the introductions were completed, the public address announcer directed everyone's attention to the flags between left and centerfield. Players and coaches from both teams turned to face them and removed their caps as a recording of the Star Spangled Banner began to play. I began to get goose bumps and I squeezed Hope's hand.

"This feels like a real major league game!" I whispered excitedly in her ear.

When we had finished singing, the fans let out a loud cheer as the boys returned to their dugouts. We sat down in our seats and waited for them to take the field.

"You want some, Dad?" Samantha asked me. She held up the straw to the frozen concoction I had purchased for her at the *Press Box*. It swirled into an inviting bright rainbow that was practically irresistible. I pursed my lips and Sam inserted the straw between them. I took a short sip and a melody of sweet, icy citrus flavors squirted onto my tongue.

"Oh, wow," I breathed. "That is really good." I took another longer draught and then Sam, sensing I was about to become a larger drain on her drink than she'd intended, quickly pulled the straw away. My lips chased longingly after it.

"Wha... hey!" I whined.

"If you like it that much Dad, you need to get your own!" She scolded, wrinkling her tiny brow. I turned my puppy dog eyes to Hope who had her lips pressed to her own straw. "Don't come begging over here, Buster. I told you to get one," she tormented me.

A darkly tanned hand slipped a large package of sunflower seeds between us. "Here, Shaun. Have some sunflower seeds and quit mooching sweets off the girls," Mr. Blyleven said in his gruff voice.

"Oh. Thanks, Mr. Blyleven." I didn't know he had taken a seat behind us. I took the bag and poured myself a fistful.

Mr. Blyleven had his long white hair stuffed beneath his Intimidators cap. He wore a brilliantly gold polo, pressed black shorts, and a pair of sandals. A huge wad of sunflower seeds was tucked into one cheek. He looked like a wealthy chipmunk on vacation. He anxiously gnawed a seed and ejected its shell expertly into a growing pile at his feet. "So, is Ryne ready to go?"

"I think so," I replied, confidently. "He was really quiet on the ride in this morning. That usually means he's getting into game-ready mode."

Hope shifted in her seat. "Or it means he's got something on his mind," she offered, alternatively.

"Something botherin' him?" Mr. Blyleven inquired.

Hope sipped at her drink. "Something's on his mind, but I'm not sure it's baseball," she said, mysteriously.

* * *

Dear Ryne,

I wanted to let you know that I won't be able to come to the games this weekend. My grandmother is in the hospital in Colorado and we are going to see her and stay with my cousins for a few days. We will be leaving on Friday and won't be back until next Tuesday. It's a long time to be away, but at least we're flying. I guess it will be nice to get away from the heat for a little while. Sometimes I just get so tired of sweating, don't you? Ha!

I have a secret to tell you. Did you know that I used to think baseball was kind of boring? It's true! But I have had SO much fun coming to your games this summer!! Did you like the Intimidators jerseys that Katie and I bought? I was thinking about putting your number on the back of mine. Is that stupid? Anyway, I don't know if you will miss me while I'm gone, but I feel like I am going to miss seeing you a lot.

If you want to write me back, you can give a letter to Chase and he can give it to Katie. I hope you will↳

Well... I guess I will see you when I get back↳

Madison

P.S. Don't forget to WIN↳↳

Go Intimidators↳

* * *

Ryne

As we took the field, I couldn't help but look up into the stands. For the first time since our very first game of the season, I knew Madison wouldn't be there. I did see Katie, though. She was sitting with her parents, sipping one of those giant frozen drinks. It looked like everybody in the stadium had one of those monster Baseball World souvenir cups in their hands. Mom and Sam had one, too. They were sitting a few rows behind our dugout with Dad. I could see he was talking to Mr. Blyleven who was listening intently to something Dad was telling him while massaging his handlebar mustache.

When we had returned to our dugout after the National Anthem, one of the men in the Cooperstown Pirates uniforms had followed us. The player who wore #33 followed the Blasters while #21 came to our dugout. He wore a white sleeveless jersey with a black, three-quarter shirt beneath it. His black Pirates cap was casually pushed back on his head.

"Which one of you is playing right field today?" he asked, cheerily.

We all looked at Sammy. Sammy reluctantly raised his hand.

"Do you know who Roberto Clemente is, young man?"

Sammy shook his head nervously.

"Roberto Clemente was the greatest right fielder to EVER play baseball," he informed Sammy. "He won twelve gold gloves during his career and had the strongest arm anyone has ever seen. He also won the batting title four different times and was once voted the Most Valuable Player in the National League." He flashed a toothy smile.

"He sounds like Mano," Jimmy piped in.

"Who's Mano?" the man dressed like Roberto Clemente asked.

"He's our right fielder," Sammy said.

"But I thought you were playing right field?" The man dressed like Clemente looked confused.

"He is playing right field today," Coach Weaver interjected. "One of our other players couldn't make it."

There, I thought. *It's official. Now Coach Weaver will tell us the truth.*

"Well, I'm sorry to hear that," Clemente's stand-in said. "But young man, I want you to know that the spirit of Roberto Clemente is in every true right fielder. You remember that when you play today and give this game your very best, okay?"

Sammy nodded. He looked absolutely lost.

"Good luck, Intimidators!" Clemente's stand-in waved to us and left.

"Okay, Intimidators," Coach Weaver immediately ordered. "You know your positions. Let's take the field."

Everyone stood up, except Jimmy. He raised his hand urgently, like he was in school and had an important question.

"Yes, Jimmy. What is it?"

"Where is Mano, Coach?" He demanded.

We all stopped and looked at Coach Weaver. Miggy and Coach Ramirez had left the dugout. They had been summoned over to the fence, probably for a last minute kiss from the ESPN camera.

Coach Weaver looked down at the ground, then he looked up at us. "I really don't know, boys."

I stared at him. I'd thought earlier he looked like he knew more than he was telling us. Now the look on his face was honest.

I believed him. I think he really didn't know where Mano was.

*   *   *

I'm usually pretty good about remembering everything that happens during our games. Sometimes, I lie in bed at night and I can almost replay that day's entire game in my head. It's like I'm watching it on a television in my mind. But I don't remember too much about our first playoff game against the Blasters. Now that I look back on it, I guess it's probably because there was only one thing to remember about that game. Funny thing is, it's the one thing I wished I could forget.

I do remember a few of the other things that happened, too. I remember the first two hits the Blasters had went right to Hootie at third base. Neither one of them was hit very hard, but both of them rolled right under his glove. From second base, it looked like there was about two feet of daylight between his black Mizuno infielder's model and the perfectly groomed infield dirt. It was the first of four fielding errors he would make. He was obviously not ready to play third base after his long layoff. Sammy wasn't ready to move to right field, either.

I remember the Blasters hit three balls that went all the way to the right field fence. One was a fly ball that Sammy just misplayed and allowed to go over his head. The second one was a hard hit grounder that went under his glove as he charged it. The third one was a ball that the hitter roped. It found the gap between Wee Willie and our replacement right fielder. Sammy was close to it and dove to try and make one of the great plays Mano had made for us on so many occasions during the regular season. Only this time the ball popped over Sammy's outstretched glove and continued hopping happily along toward the fence.

To make matters worse, Jimmy had a complete meltdown on the mound. He walked five guys, struck out only two, and gave up hit after hit. Coach Ramirez finally pulled him and put Brazos in to throw the inning before our final at-bat. Brazos wasn't bad, but it didn't matter at that point anyway. Their five-star pitcher had his good stuff and it was 13-2 when we came up for the last time.

That was when the one thing I wished I could forget happened.

I have to admit that up to that point, Miggy had played pretty well. I have to give him credit. The ESPN cameras that were watching his every move didn't seem to faze him. He didn't make a single error at shortstop and actually made two awesome throws to nip runners at first base. He didn't do anything spectacular at the plate (none of us did), but he did manage to get a single and a walk in his first two trips.

It was his third time at-bat that I wished I could forget.

There were already two outs when Miggy stepped in. Their manager had decided to pull their five-star starter in the top of the inning because of the big lead. Their new pitcher got Wee Willie to pop out to first base and Curtis to hit a weak grounder to second, but then he became wild and plunked Brazos on the arm with his first pitch and walked Chase on four straight bad ones. So there were two on with two outs when he finally managed to throw another strike, and Miggy hit it for a home run.

It was nothing special. When the ball left his bat, it looked like it was going to just be a long fly out to end the game, but the wind had picked up unexpectedly in the previous inning and it gave the ball an extra boost. It just kept carrying and carrying, until finally it carried just over the right centerfield fence, and became a Top 10 highlight on Sports Center that night. But it wasn't Miggy's new star power with ESPN that got his cheap home run on the Top 10 list.

It was the little kid who caught it.

He came blazing out of a group of families who were sitting on the grassy berm area beyond the outfield fence. He was a squirt, shorter than Samantha, but he was quick, and he had a huge, gray colored glove that looked like a stingray stuck to his hand.

As the ball dove down toward the grass, he dropped onto both of his knees and slid underneath it. The stingray flopped open and the ball disappeared into its mouth. It was an incredible catch, but even more amazing because the little runt who nabbed it was only seven years old.

Of course, it was exactly the sort of "story" Coach Weaver had told us ESPN had come to find that day at Baseball World. Our game ended when Hootie, who was the next batter, finished his horrible day by striking out for the third time. We lost, 13-5. In fact, we played so badly that we probably deserved a spot on ESPN's Not Top 10 list. But of course, it didn't matter. ESPN hadn't come to see us. Their camera in the bed of the shiny pickup in centerfield captured the perfect story of Miggy's three run homer and the squirt's fantastic catch. It became one of two big stories that day from Baseball World.

The other exciting news was weather related. The interesting wind that had boosted Miggy's fly out the park eventually brought with it dark, puffy clouds. In those shadowy clouds were some spectacular bolts of lightning. Play was initially suspended for over two hours and then was finally cancelled altogether when one of the bolts hit a light standard over in the American League side of Baseball World. Minute Maid Park, the home of the Houston Astros, was the unlucky recipient of the thunderbolt. ESPN even managed to catch the lightning strike on camera and played it on Sports Center after the clip of Miggy's homerun and the squirt's amazing grab. Shortly after the bolt struck, a siren went off followed by a public address that Baseball World would be immediately closing. All games, including the second game of our series against the Blasters, were cancelled and re-scheduled for Sunday.

I guess that was probably the only good thing that happened to us the whole stinking day.

* * *

It was Dad who came up with the idea of calling my treehouse the 'Fortress of Solitude'. He named it after the place where Superman sometimes goes to get away from the world. He said that even Superman needs a secret hideaway where he can go to relax and just think.

When we returned home later that night after the game, I told him that I wanted to spend the night outside in my fortress again. I had never stayed the night in it without friends, but it wasn't because I was afraid or anything. I had just never asked because I didn't think Mom would approve of me staying outside the house alone.

I didn't want to talk to anyone about the game. I didn't want Mom or Dad to try and make me feel better about it, either. I just wanted to be by myself. So I probably shouldn't have turned on the television, and I definitely shouldn't have turned it on ESPN.

Miggy's home run actually was number one on the Top Ten list for the day. I could hardly believe it. The clip showed him digging in the box and adjusting his Intimidators' black batting helmet as the ESPN announcer dramatically introduced the video.

"And here we are at *Number One*! It's from the Central Texas Youth Playoffs at Baseball World in Texas. Miguel Ramirez of the Intimidators digs in with two on in the bottom of the fifth inning as he faces Blaster's reliever Brandon Seaver."

The clip showed the Blaster's pitcher winding up.

"Seaver gets this fast ball just a little up in the zone…"

I watched as the pitch came in on Miggy. It looked a lot slower on television that it did in real life.

"And Miggy says…SEE YA! This one is gone for a mighty three run shot to right center!"

It didn't look all that mighty. In fact, as I watched the centerfielder drift back to follow it, I think he thought he was going to catch it. He even put his glove up, but it just kept going, and going. The announcer continued excitedly.

"But watch what happens here. Just beyond the outfield fence…"

While everything else seemed slower than normal, the little kid appeared even faster than I'd remembered. He shot out of the group of families on the grassy berm in centerfield like a water bug. He hit his knees and slid, that big gray stingray on his hand yawned open, and the ball dropped out of the sky, directly into the center of the pocket. He immediately popped up and held the glove high above his head.

"Little seven-year old Michael Rivers comes up with an AMAZING GRAB! HO!! Let's see that again!"

The announcer sounded like he was truly amazed. Even though I'd seen the catch live, it was even more impressive the second time. For the replay, ESPN slowed the video down. I watched the kid slide in slow motion. "Would you look at this kid?" The announcer raved. "Seven years old and he's already patrolling centerfield like he's Willie Mays!"

But that wasn't the end. ESPN had video taken after the game of Miggy and the Rivers kid. Miggy and the little munchkin stood side by side while Miggy signed his homerun ball. They both looked into the camera and smiled like it was Christmas Day.

"Nice day at the park, right, Michael? Make a great catch, make number one on the ESPN Top Ten list, and walk away with an autograph from a future major leaguer to boot. Hold onto that ball, little guy," the announcer encouraged. "You may just be holding the first autograph from a future Triple Crown winner!"

I rolled my eyes, but the ESPN announcer still wasn't finished.

"You can see an interview with young superstar Miguel Ramirez tomorrow on ESPN as we begin our coverage of the ground-breaking ceremony for Major League Baseball's new theme park at Baseball World in Texas." The screen flashed an image of a new Baseball World logo next to a smiling photo of the Commissioner of Baseball. "This is a huge day for youth baseball families around the country and you won't want to miss it." I clicked off the television and collapsed on the bed. I laid there for a long time, staring at the ceiling as a meteor shower of thoughts flew through my brain.

We'd stunk on Saturday. *How could we have played so horrible after winning sixteen straight games?* I wondered. Was it because Mano hadn't been there? And why hadn't Coach Ramirez just told us that he had gone back to Hawai'i, instead of leaving us hanging? Probably because he didn't care, I figured. Actually, he probably didn't care if we won or lost in the playoffs, as long as Miggy did well.

An image of Madison suddenly flashed through my mind, too. I thought of her blonde hair in a ponytail sticking out of the back of her Intimidators cap. I thought about her new Intimidators jersey. I also thought about how it would look with my number on the back.

I thought about her letter. I rolled off the bed and reached between the mattress and the box springs and pulled it out. When I did, I caught a glimpse of the ball Alfonso had told Sam to give me. It was sitting on the nightstand between the beds. I'd thought it looked like the head of a giant, dead lizard when Sam had given it to me. I still did. It was ugly. It was all covered in that dried, green gunk.

I stood up and sat on the edge of the bed. I sat Madison's letter down and picked up Mano's first home run ball. When I did, I started thinking about the differences between the screaming bullet he'd slapped over the crummy fence in our second regular season game and the bomb Miggy had lobbed just over the perfectly built outfield wall at Baseball World in our first playoff game.

First, I thought about the two kids who'd come up with the balls after they'd been hit. Like the Rivers kid, Miggy's little brother Alfonso was just seven years old, too. Only he hadn't made an amazing catch that had landed him on ESPN' Top Ten list. Instead, he'd had to somehow figure out a way to secretly fish the ball out of the middle of a gross, slime covered pond. Why had he done it? I knew why. *Because he'd wanted it*, just as badly as the fast little kid with the stingray glove, and just as badly as he'd wanted the ball from the top of the concession stand Mano had hit in our first game. I guess if you really thought about it, Alfonso's determination to capture Mano's first official home run ball was even more impressive than the amazing catch that little runt had made to nab Miggy's big fly.

Then I thought about the situation when Mano and Miggy had hit their home runs. Which hit had been more important? Mano had hit his three run blast in our final at-bat to tie our second game of the season, and he hit it off a kid who had been throwing some crazy, scary heat. After that incredible bomb, our team had gone on a sixteen game winning streak. Miggy's three run home run had also happened in our final at-bat, but his blow had been pretty meaningless. The other coach had put in a kid to mop up at the end of a game where the score was 13 – 2, and Miggy had hit one out that had made the score 13 – 5. And I couldn't get over the fact that Miggy's home run would have been just a fly out if not for the stupid wind.

Still, Miggy's home run had ended up in a cute kid's glove on national television. We'd be able to watch it on YouTube until the end of time. Mano's home run had ended up buried in a swamp. That just didn't seem right.

I suddenly remembered Jimmy's words at the water park. *Mano is our village chief, not Miggy.* He had been right. After the game we'd just played, it was obvious. We were without our chief.

I squeezed the baseball in my hand. *We need you tomorrow*, I thought. *We really need you, Mano.*

I looked down at the split seams of the ball. I thought of Mano's bat, that old wooden stick that looked like it belonged in a museum. How strong was he that he had crushed a baseball hard enough to split the seams not just once, but twice?

I also thought about the scar on his back. I remembered the look in his dark eyes that night in my fortress as he told us his incredible story. The tiger shark had, for a moment, held him in its jaws. It had begun to crush him. Then, for some unexplained reason, it had decided to let him go. What was it Mano had said?

He niuhi ʻai holopapa o ka moku. The niuhi shark devours all on the island, but it hadn't devoured him. I wondered why?

I looked again at Mano's home run ball in my hand. Suddenly, I had an idea.

I slipped Madison's letter back into its secret place. I needed to write her back, but it would have to wait. I jumped off the bed, opened the door to my fortress and quietly crept over the bridge to Samantha's place. Mom had given her an arts and crafts set that Sam kept

153

underneath a small table in her fortress. I knew she wouldn't mind if I borrowed it. I quickly found it and then made my way back across the bridge. I was just about to close my door when Mom and Dad stepped out onto the back patio.

"Hey, Ryne?" Mom called.

"Yes, ma'am?" I stuck my head out of the door. She and Dad were holding hands. For some strange reason, that made me feel good.

"Are you okay?"

"Sure, I'm fine," I answered.

"She's worried that Big Foot may wander up tonight and sneak into the bunk next to you," Dad joked. Mom elbowed him.

I laughed. "If he does, I'll try and get a picture."

Dad walked over to the bottom of the staircase. "Here," he said, motioning to me. I stepped out and he tossed something up to me. It was his cell phone.

"Text Mom if you need anything tonight, okay?" he said. "Extra blanket, pair of socks, some beef jerky for Big Foot..."

I made a face. Dad laughed. "Seriously. Just let us know if you need anything, okay?"

"Sure, Dad." I looked over at Mom. She had her arms crossed like she was cold, but I knew she wasn't cold. She was concerned. "I'll be fine, Mom," I said, trying to ease her mind.

"Oh, I know you will, punkin," she assured me.

"Really, Mom?" I said, rolling my eyes. She had been calling me punkin since I was two. I had been working on her to retire my little kid's nickname, but sometimes she still liked to use it.

"I love you, Ryne," she said, smiling. "Good night."

"Love you, too," I answered. "Good night. Night, Dad."

"Sleep tight, son," Dad said. They both waved up at me and went back inside.

I shut the door. Then I got down to work.

*   *   *

The X-Acto knife in the kit was unused. I figured Sam probably wasn't allowed to touch it yet anyway, unless Mom was around to help her.

I used it to carefully cut through the seams of Mano's home run ball. I began on the row that was already split and worked my way around the horseshoe shape the laces made until all of them were cut. After that, it was sort of like peeling an orange. The leather came off into two figure-eight pieces and left behind the tightly wound string that surrounded the cushioned cork at its center.

I had watched an internet video once about how baseballs are made. It was interesting. I remembered there was a cushioned cork at center of the ball beneath miles of tightly spooled yarn. It was about the size of a cherry. I began searching for it by unwinding all of those layers of stringy wool that guarded the center. It seemed to take forever, but after about thirty minutes of unwinding and unwinding, I finally got down to that rubberized pill.

When I'd finished stripping off the last bit of yarn, I pitched aside the pile of loose spaghetti that was left behind and held the tiny sphere in my palm. It was like holding a tiny heart in my hand. Carefully, like a surgeon, I used the X-Acto knife to make an incision all the way around the rubber coating. Then I slowly peeled it back to reveal the cork inside.

Beneath my bed, there was a flat sheet of particle board. Dad had intended to use it to mount a dart board on the wall, but I'd changed my mind and had covered the space where the dart board was supposed to go with more pennants. I pulled it out now and used it as a table top. I placed the two leather pieces and the cork "heart" on top of it. Then I used the X-Acto knife to cut small square pieces out of the leather. I used the first one as a pattern for the rest so they would all be exactly the same size. There was just enough leather for eight squares. When I was finished, I used the knife to pick small chunks out of the cork. I placed a single piece on each of the leather squares. Then I pulled some glue out of Sam's kit.

I picked up one of the leather squares and folded it from corner to corner until it made a triangle with the chunk of cork "heart" inside. I opened the triangle up again and drew a thin line with the glue around the edges. I pressed the triangle back to together and squeezed it tightly for a few minutes. The glue was really good and it held quickly. When I was satisfied with the first one, I finished the rest, making them all exactly the same.

As they dried, I picked up the first one and examined my work. It looked pretty good. I was almost done.

Inside the kit, there was a sleeve of permanent markers with various tip sizes and colors. I picked out a red one with super fine tip. I carefully drew imitation red laces along the edges of the triangle where I'd glued it so that it looked like it had been stitched together. Then I picked one of the black markers.

I laid the triangle flat and wrote one word on the leather in neat, exact letters. I turned it over and wrote a number on the other side. I repeated the same process for the others.

When I finally finished, I looked at my watch. It was 1:54 am. I had been so busy I had lost all track of time. Strangely, while I had been working I hadn't felt tired. As soon as I realized how late it was, a huge yawn started up and continued rolling out of me until it made my eyes water. I was pretty whipped.

I gathered up all of the small triangles. I slid my "surgical table," Sam's "operating kit," and the remains from the dissected ball underneath the bed. Then I lay down and closed my eyes.

I think I was asleep in about two seconds.

13

Ryne

Game Two had been re-scheduled for two o'clock on Sunday afternoon. If we won, Game Three would immediately follow.

We were back at PNC Park on the National League side of Baseball World and everything was pretty much exactly the same as it had been on Saturday. It was still stinkin' hot, and there were still lots of people probably getting brain freezes from slurping frozen drinks out of those giant Baseball World cups. The ESPN cameras were in place on top of the dugouts. The one in the bed of the shiny pickup truck parked beyond centerfield, the one that had captured Miggy's home run and that little kid's amazing catch, was still there, too. The only difference I could tell was that Kelly Duerson was nowhere in sight today. Instead, there was a sharply dressed guy wearing an ESPN blazer and an earpiece in the bleachers. He was walking around with a microphone, while another guy wearing cargo shorts and a red ESPN polo trailed him with a camera. We could see them as we warmed up in the outfield, moving among the small knots of our fans in the stands. They would stop occasionally and talk before moving onto the next set of people.

"Hey Chase, are they interviewing your mom and dad?" Wee Willie asked. The sharply dressed guy had a small notepad in his hand and was taking notes. Every now and then, he would turn and point in our direction.

"I don't think so," Chase answered. "He's been talking to everyone up there. It looks like he's trying to match all of us up with our parents."

"There she is!" Brazos bellowed. He stopped his warm-up tosses with Chase in mid-throwing motion. "Over there!"

Kelly Duerson had appeared. She was standing behind our dugout, talking with Coach Ramirez. She had her dark, brunette hair pulled up in a bun on top of her head. She was wearing white jeans and a red ESPN polo like the cameraman. The only difference was she looked about a million times better than he did.

Coach Ramirez pointed beyond the outfield toward the batting cages. Kelly nodded and started in that direction. Another cameraman appeared and began to tag along behind her.

"Miggy!" Coach Ramirez thundered across the field. "Get your bat and helmet and meet us at the cages!!"

Miggy was laid out in the grass, one of his knees tucked beneath him as he stretched out his legs. When he heard his dad, he popped immediately to his feet and sprinted toward the dugout without saying a word to any of us.

"Well, there goes our hero," Jimmy muttered.

"Are they going to interview him again?" Curtis asked.

"Looks like it," Hootie answered. He sounded ticked off. "They're probably going to video his swing while Coach Weaver throws him batting practice." We could see that Coach Weaver was headed toward the cages, too. It seemed that even Hootie, who was always trying to keep a lid on anything negative that might affect our team, was beginning to get irritated with all of the hoopla surrounding Miggy.

Jimmy said, "I don't think Coach Ramirez even cares if we win this game."

"Why do you think that?" Wee Willie asked.

"Because, all he cares about is getting Miggy on Sports Center."

"Did you see the Top Ten list last night?" Sammy jumped in.

"Yeah," everyone except me groaned together.

"Didn't you see it, Ryne?" Chase asked.

"I saw it," I answered.

"What did you think? It looked like a long fly to the second baseman to me, until that hurricane wind decided to blow it out," Jimmy said, sarcastically. "That little kid made an unbelievable catch, though."

I shrugged.

Jimmy threw a warm-up toss to Wee Willie. "We stunk like a fresh dog turd yesterday, guys. Forget Miggy. If we're going to win today, we need Mano."

Everyone, including Hootie, nodded in agreement.

"What in the heck happened to him yesterday?" Chase demanded. "I mean, he didn't just drop off the team, did he? Something bad has got to be wrong. Where is he?"

"Guys, let's go to the dugout," I said. I'd decided it was time to tell them what I knew, no matter what I had promised Samantha.

No one said anything. They just dropped in behind me as I began to jog toward our bunker. We had moved to the third base foxhole after being in the first base dugout on Saturday. When we were inside, everyone except me sat down on the bench. Every eye looked up at me expectantly.

"You know what happened to Mano, don't you, Ryne?" Hootie pressed.

"Actually, I don't know what happened to him," I said, honestly. "But I think I know where he is."

Hootie held his hands out. "Then where is he?"

"I think he had to go back home."

"*To Hawai'i?*" Jimmy almost screamed.

I nodded.

"Why would he go back to Hawai'i?" Sammy asked.

I shrugged my shoulders. "I don't know guys."

"Wait a minute," Hootie said. "Who told you this, Ryne?"

I shook my head. "I can't say."

He eyed me suspiciously. "If that's true, then why hasn't anyone else said anything about it?"

"That's what I keep trying to figure out," I answered him, again honestly.

"At least when Jacob quit, Coach told us," Wee Willie remembered from the night at The Hitting Wheel when Coach Ramirez told us that Jacob Dickey had decided he didn't want to play anymore.

"Guys, I don't think Mano quit," I offered. "I think he had to go back to Hawai'i because his dad probably made him."

I could tell that Hootie knew that I wasn't telling them everything, but he didn't push me.

"Well, I guess that's that," Chase said. He sounded defeated.

"I guess so," Wee Willie echoed. Everyone hung their heads.

"Hang on, guys," I began. Suddenly, it seemed like everyone was ready to just give up. "Look, everybody remembers our second game of the year, right?"

"Of course. We tied against that team with the weird name." Curtis confirmed. "It was the game where Mano blasted his amazing home run into the middle of that sludgy pond out past centerfield."

"And we didn't lose again after that until yesterday," Wee Willie pitched in.

"Exactly!" I said, excitedly. "I think there's a reason we didn't lose again."

"Of course, there's a reason." Hootie looked at me like I was an idiot. "Mano began tearing up the league!"

"Yeah," Everyone chimed in agreement. Except me.

"I don't think it was just because Mano began tearing up the league," I argued. "We all started playing better after that game, but I think it even started before that game. Remember the sleepover at my house? I think something changed when Mano told us what happened to him the day he went spear fishing in Hawai'i."

Jimmy, who had been quiet, suddenly spoke up. "He's right, guys," he realized. "Something clicked for us that night when Mano told us about his shark attack. I know it did for me. Shoot, after that, the more I hung around Mano, the better I played. It's like he gives off some sort of amazing energy."

"Like magic?" Wee Willie asked.

"No, don't be ridiculous," Jimmy groused. "It's like...heck, I don't know." He threw up his hands. "I can't even describe it."

"I can't either," Sammy joined in with his brother. "But I know what you're talking about. I was standing next to him once in the on deck circle during a game and I swear, I could feel it. It felt so good, it made me think I could do anything. I went up to the plate and cracked a double on the first pitch."

"That's the energy given off by a niuhi warrior." Everyone turned to look at Brazos. He was sitting calmly at the end of the bench. He had taken his hat off. He pushed his long hair back.

"What do you mean, Brazos?" I asked, encouraging him.

"Well, it's not magic," he said, directly to Wee Willie. "Mano carries the nature of the niuhi shark inside of him. When we're around him, we feel it. You can't quite describe it, but you know there's something about him that is totally awesome. If you look in his eyes, you can see it, too. His eyes look like a shark's eyes. They're full of power. You can see in them that he's always ready to strike."

"How do you know all of this stuff?" Hootie asked, skeptically.

"He got it from *Shark Week*," Chase answered for Brazos. "We saw it on *Jaws of the Tiger* last night. The guy on that show basically said the same things Mano told us about the niuhi warriors and the village chiefs. It's all true."

"It is," I verified. "The guy told a story about a famous Hawai'ian king and his teacher who was a niuhi warrior. The teacher even had to fight a shark. His student was King Kamehameha. He's the king who eventually conquered all of the Hawai'ian Islands."

"Wow," Wee Willie said in a low voice.

"Look. I don't know for sure what all of this means," Brazos admitted. "But we all agree, don't we? Mano has been the real leader of our team ever since he hit that home run."

"Yeah, without a doubt. Mano has been our village chief," Jimmy insisted.

"So what do we do now?" Wee Willie asked. "Mano's gone."

"Maybe he isn't completely gone," I ventured.

"What do you mean?" Hootie asked. He was looking at me, hopefully.

"I've been thinking, guys. Even if Mano isn't with us right now, it doesn't mean he can't be with us," I said.

"What?" Curtis was puzzled. "That doesn't make any sense."

I walked over and picked up my bat bag. It had a small pocket at the top to keep gum, eye black, sunglasses, and other stuff. I unzipped it and pulled out the eight small triangles I'd made and held them in my open hand as everyone gathered around me.

"What are those?" Wee Willie asked, curiously.

"They look like paper footballs," Chase offered.

"They're talismans," I said.

"What's a talisman?" Hootie asked.

"Ooh, I know!" Curtis jumped in excitedly. "I have one. My grandmother gave it to me for Christmas." He reached under his collar and pulled out a thin silver chain. A fish symbol hung at the end of it.

"That's a talisman?" Sammy said.

"There are all sorts of talismans," I explained.

"There's a game called the *Talisman*," Jimmy added. "Our dad plays it on his computer. It's like an adventure where you have to find the talisman-thing, whatever it is. He said it used to be a board game when he was a kid and they made it into a video game. He loves it."

"How do you know about talismans?" Hootie asked me.

"I had to do some research once for a history lesson on Presidential debates," I explained. "I found out that the second President Bush carried a talisman in his pocket during his debates. Whenever it was his turn to speak, he would put his hand in his pocket and hold it."

Hootie looked mystified. "Why?"

"It gave him confidence," I said.

"What was it?" Sammy probed.

"It was a cross someone had given him," I answered. "I thought it was pretty cool and interesting, so I did some research on talismans. There are all different kinds of them, but they are all made for pretty much the same reason. They're supposed to attract power from whatever they're made to symbolize. The person who makes them is supposed to create a symbol that will attract that power."

Wee Willie pointed to the small pile of triangles in my hand. "Did you make these?"

I nodded. "I stayed up late last night in my Fortress and made them."

"What are they supposed to be?" Sammy asked.

I smiled. "They're shark fins."

Chase grinned. "That's pretty cool, Ryne."

"Why are they dirty?" Wee Willie wanted to know. "They look all green and brown."

"Because I made them out of a baseball."

"A baseball is white," Wee Willie argued.

I looked up at the faces of my teammates. "Unless it's been sitting in a nasty pond for a while."

Brazos shot a look at me. "That's the ball that Mano hit into the pond?"

I nodded.

"How did you get it?" Curtis asked.

"I can't tell you right now," I said, trying not to sound mysterious. "Maybe later."

Chase pointed to the talismans. "What's written on them?"

I picked one up with my other hand. "On this side, I wrote NIUHI. On the other," I said, flipping the talisman over, "I put Mano's jersey number, #9." I turned it so everyone could see. "Each one of them also has a small piece from the core of the baseball inside of it, too. I drew stitches around the edge of it so it would look like it had been laced together, just like a baseball. Here." I handed the first one to Chase and then I went around the circle and gave one to Jimmy, Sammy, Wee Willie, Hootie, Brazos, and Curtis. I kept the last one for myself.

"So it's sort of like a piece of the heart of the ball is in each one," Chase said, getting it immediately. "Too cool, Ryne."

I smiled at him. "Yes. I figured that to be a true talisman and attract the power of a niuhi, each of them needed to carry the heart of the baseball Mano had hit inside."

Hootie stared at his uncertainly. "What are we supposed to do with them? I mean, do we carry them in our back pockets?"

I was stumped. I hadn't considered that.

Brazos removed his hat. "I'm going to keep it in here," he said, tucking the tiny fin into the front lining of his Intimidators cap. "That way the energy will be as close as possible to my brain." He placed the cap on his head. Immediately, everyone else followed suit.

Every team I have ever played on has huddled and stacked our hands, and the coaches have always led us in the ritual. They pull us together before games and pass out last minute instructions while we stand packed together in a tight knot. Between innings they meet us on the foul line as we return to the dugout and give us a short pep talk before we bat, and we stack our hands again. When our at-bat is over and it's time to go back into the field, we huddle once more with our hands in a log pile while we receive another set of instructions as the pitcher and catcher warm up.

We always break on a short cheer, too. Usually they are corny, *rah, rah* war cries that we are supposed to scream so the other team can hear us. Sometimes we just bark our team name loud enough to hopefully get their attention, and maybe scare the heck out of them, but the coaches are always the ones to bring us together. It's their huddle.

Not ours.

This time, there were no coaches. There was no one to lead.

"Okay," I said, dropping my hand into the middle of our huddle. Chase and Brazos instantly placed theirs on top of mine, and everyone else joined us. No one moved. Our hands remained locked together at the center of our group. I'd never given any sort of pep talk, but I felt like I was supposed to say something. I didn't want to say anything fancy. I just wanted to say something that was true. "Our season isn't supposed to end today," I finally managed, as I looked around the circle. "Honestly, I don't think it will."

Everyone was quiet. I reached up with my free hand and pulled my hat low.

"I'm going to wear my hat low today, guys," I added. I thought they might have thought I was being too dramatic, but for some reason pulling my cap lower made me feel different, almost like Mano was really with us. No one said a word about it being stupid. Instead, they just reached up and pulled their caps lower, too.

I bobbed my head once. "Mano isn't here, but I think his niuhi power just might be with us, anyway." Around the circle, every head bobbed. I didn't have anything else to say.

Hootie looked up at me. "*Niuhi*," he said, seriously. Around the huddle, everyone responded immediately, almost like we were at church and they were saying amen together after finishing a prayer. "*Niuhi*," they all answered with one voice.

167

"Let's go," I said. We skipped the corny cheer and broke from our huddle.

* * *

Shaun

"Did that ESPN announcer talk to you yet?" Jennifer Girardi asked as she sat down next to Hope in the bleachers.

"No," Hope answered. "But we've been over at the *Press Box* getting treats. Samantha and I are trying to convince Shaun to install one of those frozen drink machines in our kitchen. I think we're addicted." She took a sip from her giant cup and bumped me playfully with her shoulder.

"Well, he wants to talk to everyone on the team," Jennifer informed us. "He's trying to match uniform numbers, player names, and their parents. I think they're planning on interviewing some of us during the game," she said, breathlessly.

"See, Mom," Sam cheeped around the straw of her own tall cylinder of frozen delight. "I told you we were going to be worldly famous."

"I'm a little surprised to see them back here today," I said. "I really thought they would choose to focus on one of the other fields."

Jennifer looked at me like I was crazy. "Are you kidding? Did you see Miggy's home run on Sports Center last night?"

I smiled and rolled my eyes. "Yep. I saw it. Number one on the Top Ten."

"Of course, it probably doesn't hurt that Coach Ramirez knows one of the owners of Baseball World, too" she added, slyly.

168

Hope and I both raised our eyebrows. "Really?" Hope said for both of us.

Jennifer bounced her head excitedly. "I think they went to college together. He's some sort of commercial real estate guru or something now. Anyway, he's got gobs of money and he's one of the four big investors. He's the guy you see walking around in the nice suit and the Baseball World cap."

I had seen the man she was talking about on Saturday. He had been constantly huddled with someone from ESPN and a few other important looking figures. I'd thought he must have been melting inside of his suit. The heat index had reached 110 degrees before a crazy wind had blown through the facility bringing with it the clouds and lightning that had eventually resulted in the cancellation of our second game.

"So I guess that's why ESPN was interviewing Miggy yesterday before the game?" I concluded.

Jennifer slipped her bug eye sunglasses from the top of her head back over her eyes. "I would imagine so," she said, smirking. "We all know it pays to have friends in high places." She looked up and saw Nancy Weaver, Curtis' mother, and waved. "Excuse me. I need to go see if Nancy got the photos I sent her yesterday. We're putting together a scrapbook for the season!" She hopped up and scurried over to Coach Weaver's wife.

"Well, that explains a lot," Hope said to me, under her breath after she'd left.

"It sure does," I agreed. "No wonder Miggy's getting all of the special attention."

"It's a shame..." Hope began. She trailed off.

"...that Mano isn't here," I said, finishing her thought for her. Knowing what each other is thinking is one of those weird benefits of being married for a long time and really being connected.

She looked at me. "I may not know a lot about baseball, but I know this much. That boy is truly special."

"I've never seen anyone like him, and I've been playing and watching baseball my whole life," I said. "But it's not just the way he plays. There is something mysterious, something really deep about him."

"I know what you mean," Hope said. "He has a presence. I think the other boys know it, too."

I shook my head. "They definitely played differently yesterday without him. They looked lost."

"Oh, look! There's Alfonso!" Sam suddenly piped in. "Hey, Alfonso!!" She waved at Miggy's little brother excitedly.

Alfonso waved back. He said something to his mother who looked up at us and waved. She nodded to Alfonso who began running up the stairs toward us.

"My mom said I can sit with you, if it's okay?" he said to Hope.

"Of course!" Hope responded. Alfonso sat down next to Samantha. "You're not going to be the bat boy for the team today?"

"No, not today."

"Why not, Alfonso?" I asked. He had served as the bat boy for every single Intimidators game during the season. He looked up at me with his soft brown eyes and shrugged his narrow shoulders.

"Miggy is getting on my nerves," he said, shocking me with his honesty.

I laughed a little. "Oh, really? Well sometimes brothers can get on each other's nerves," I commiserated. "Sometimes my older brother used to drive me absolutely crazy when we were kids."

"Did your brother think he was the greatest baseball player on earth, too?" Alfonso asked.

"Well, no," I answered. "He was pretty proud of his hair, though. He used to spend hours every day combing it. I think he thought he was going to be a super model."

Alfonso spit out a short burst of air. "Yeah, Miggy started doing that last Saturday when he found out he was going to be on television. I don't think he's stopped combing it since."

"Huh," I heard Hope say. "He knew a week ago he was going to be on television?" She looked at me over the kid's heads.

"That is an awful long time to spend combing your hair," I said, returning her look.

"It's annoying me," Alfonso complained. "He even combed it between innings yesterday. Can you believe that?"

"You want some fruit snacks?" Samantha asked her friend.

"Sure! Thanks!" Alfonso opened his small hand and Sam poured him a few of the rubbery treats from the opened pouch in her lap.

Hope smiled at them. She looked at me again over their tiny heads. I wondered if our minds were still in sync and she was thinking what I was thinking. It was strange that Miggy had known for a week that he would be interviewed by ESPN.

Coach Ramirez hadn't said a word about it to anyone.

* * *

Ryne

Coach Ramirez had purchased a copy of the *Central Texas Youth League Scouting Service* for pitchers. It tracked all of the pitchers who had thrown in the summer league for players aged nine through sixteen. Each pitcher was given stars for walks, hits, earned runs, innings pitched, and overall arm strength. A pitcher could earn anywhere from one to five stars in each category. His overall star rating was the average across all five categories.

The Blasters' four star pitcher in Game Two was a lefty. The scouting report had given him three fours and two threes. It was an overall rating of 3.6 stars, but the report had rounded the average up to four stars. Coach Ramirez was interested primarily in the threes. He pointed those numbers out to us right before the game.

"From the scouting report, it looks like he tends to get a little wild and walk a few, boys," he told us as we sat in the dugout right before the game began. "His arm strength is listed as average. So be patient at the plate today and take what he gives you."

Every one of us paid attention and nodded as Coach Ramirez reviewed the report. Each of us went to the plate prepared to push the Blasters' pitcher as deep into the count as we could. That is, everyone except Miggy.

In the first inning, Wee Willie followed the scouting report exactly. He took all five pitches the Blasters' pitcher threw and led off with a walk. Then he stole second base.

Sammy batted second. He got the bunt sign from Coach Ramirez and laid one down perfectly in front of the plate. It moved Wee Willie to third as the catcher made the throw to get Sammy at first for the out.

Brazos was next and he worked the count to three balls and two strikes. The Blasters' pitcher threw one that was close and even though it was low, Brazos had to swing to protect the plate. He hit a weak grounder back to the mound. The pitcher looked Wee Willie back to third base before throwing Curtis out at first for the second out.

Then it was Miggy's turn to bat.

He swung at the first pitch. It was a high, semi-fast ball that was well out of the strike zone and he whiffed it badly. The second pitch was in almost the exact same spot and Miggy's hack at it looked like an instant replay. He stepped out of the batter's box and looked down the line at his dad.

Coach Ramirez pushed both of his big hands toward the ground. He mouthed 'Calm down' and Miggy nodded. He stepped back into the box.

The pitcher was no dummy. He threw the third one even higher than the previous two. The catcher had to stand up out of his stance to reach it but Miggy tomahawked at the pitch anyway, like he was trying to swat a June bug as it flew past. He was done after three pitches and Wee Willie was left stranded at third. Surprisingly, Coach Ramirez didn't even yell. He didn't look mad, either. He just clapped for Miggy as he headed back to the dugout.

Normally, I would have been astonished that Coach Ramirez hadn't erupted at Miggy for completely disregarding his instructions to us, but the rules just didn't seem to apply to our shortstop anymore, especially now that the ESPN cameras were rolling with the hope of catching another bomb off his bat. Strangely, I wasn't even mad about it.

It doesn't matter what Miggy does or doesn't do today, I thought. I had a weirdly confident feeling. I was convinced we were not going to lose the game.

* * *

When Curtis finished his warm-up tosses, he turned and looked at me as I fielded Chase's throw down to second. I flipped the ball to him and he nodded his head once, pulling his cap lower over his eyes. I gave mine an extra tug downward toward my nose, too.

Curtis didn't waste any time. The scouting report had awarded him 3.4 stars, but his rating had been rounded down to an even three stars.

He had received an average rating for arm strength, too. If the Blasters coach had purchased a copy of the report like Coach Ramirez, I would have been willing to bet he probably asked for his money back after the game.

Curtis threw harder than any of us had ever seen him throw. Chase's glove made a satisfying smack after each fastball. Pitch after pitch sawed off the bat of the Blasters' hitters. They had a well-balanced line-up with four left-handed hitters and five right-handed hitters, too, but it didn't matter because Curtis threw every pitch on the batter's hands, regardless of the side of the plate he occupied. If the hitter didn't whiff, he hit a weak ground ball to the infield that we quickly gobbled up for an out. A few of them hit crummy pop ups that never made it past the infield dirt.

In fact, through four innings the Blasters managed only two base runners, both of them resulting from sad little bloopers. One looped just over Brazos' head and dropped dead on the first base chalk like a dehydrated orange. The other wafted right to Miggy at shortstop where it somehow slipped through his glove like a wisp of smoke for an error.

But neither runner ended up crossing the plate. So we started the bottom of the fifth inning with time expired and a 3-0 lead. It was the Blasters' last chance.

Their first hitter of the fifth finally managed to hit a pitch off the meat of the bat. He lifted it to short centerfield. Wee Willie charged hard and slid on his knees underneath it to make a really nifty grab for the first out. I smiled, thinking of the play the little kid had made outside the centerfield fence to snag Miggy's homerun on Saturday. It was the first play our outfield had needed to make the whole day. Curtis had pitched that good, but I could tell he was getting tired. When Wee Willie threw the ball into me at second base, I whirled to peg it back to him on the mound. I could see his cheeks were bright red and rivers of sweat were running down his temples.

He placed the ball in his glove, took it off and wedged it under his arm. He slowly removed his hat and swiped the three-quarter jersey on his right arm across his forehead to towel away the perspiration. He paused.

I watched as he reached inside his cap and pulled out the small talisman. He looked at me as he rubbed it gently between his fingers for a moment. He placed it back in the band and slipped his cap on, pulling it even lower until his eyes nearly disappeared. He took a deep breath, turned around and marched slowly back on top of the hill.

The next Blasters' hitter was a thick kid. He wasn't fat, just big. He looked like a football player squeezed into a Blasters uniform that was one size too small. He hit the first pitch that Curtis threw solidly to shortstop.

The ball didn't do anything fancy. It didn't take a weird bounce or skip like a flat rock across a pond when it hit the dirt. It just went right under Miggy's glove.

The next hitter was a left hander who had struck out twice already. He looked at the first pitch that Curtis threw as the thick kid at first base immediately took off to steal second. He was faster than he looked but Chase made a good throw. Miggy covered the bag, while I slid in behind second base, in case the ball got away.

The ball hit Miggy's glove in plenty of time. He went to make the tag, but the ball fell out.

He just dropped it.

The next pitch was a good strike but the batter was ready. He lined it over my head into right center field. The thick kid barreled around third like a running back headed for the end zone. Sammy cut the ball off in right field. That's when I realized the runner was rounding first and churning hard for second. I was the cutoff man so I ducked low and let the ball pass over me for the play at second base where Miggy was covering the bag.

It bounced once, but it was on the third base side of second instead of the first base side. Miggy reached for it but the ball hit his glove and trickled out into left field. The runner immediately jumped up and sprinted to third as Jimmy hustled in from left to corral the ball.

This time Miggy lost it. He took off his glove and slammed it to the ground. "THROW THE STUPID BALL TO THE BAG!!" He screamed at Sammy. "COME ON!!"

I saw Coach Ramirez move to the top step of the dugout, but he didn't call time and come onto the field. He just stood there while Miggy raved.

"PICK IT UP, GUYS!!" He screamed at all of us. "I CAN'T DO IT ALL BY MYSELF!"

Jimmy tossed the ball past him to Curtis. Curtis stood there for a moment, staring at our suddenly crazed shortstop. Miggy glared back and then dismissed him with a wave of his hand.

"Get up there and get this guy out, Curtis!" He demanded. "This is embarrassing! Finish this stupid thing off!!" He put his glove back on and punched his fist into the pocket furiously.

In the dugout, Coach Ramirez touched his nose and then his ear, the signal for Chase to visit the mound. Chase took off his mask and jogged out to Curtis. As soon as he reached the hill, Chase motioned for me to come over. I quickly ran in.

"Miggy is going to blow this blasted game!" Chase spit at me.

"No, he's not," I said, calmly. I turned to our pitcher. His face was drenched in sweat. "Forget the guy at third. Just get the batter, Curtis."

Curtis blew out a long sigh. His lips were dry and cracked. I was worried he might faint.

I made a fist. "*Niuhi*," I said to him.

He grimaced. "*Niuhi*," he answered, unconvincingly.

Chase looked at me. He was angry.

"Forget Miggy," I told him. "*Forget him!*"

Chase nodded, but his face was as unconvincing as Curtis' answer. He slipped his mask on and jogged back to the plate.

But Curtis was hurting worse than I'd thought. He sailed the next pitch over Chase's head. It went to the backstop and the runner at third sprinted home.

It was 3-2, and there was still only one out.

The umpire threw another ball out to Curtis. He caught it in front of the mound and then turned and practically dragged himself back up the hill. His shoulders drooped as he stood on the rubber and waited for the sign from Chase. He went into a sluggish wind up and puffed out a batting practice fast ball.

The Blasters' hitter was their centerfielder. He was fast like Wee Willie, only he was much taller and leaner. His long arms whipped around like two bungee cords and his bat followed, catching the weak pitch perfectly in the bat's sweet spot. The ball rocketed off his stick down the third base line.

Hootie reacted like a pro. He took one step and dove. The ball ripped into the pocket of his glove as he somersaulted over the foul line. Immediately, he jumped to his feet and held his glove high above his head.

The field umpire raised his fist.

"*Out!*"

In the stands, the ESPN reporter rapidly scanned his notes, looking for Hootie's parents. He and his cameraman quickly made a beeline for Hootie's dad who was sitting high in the bleachers. When Hootie had made the catch, he'd stood up and roared like a lion. "*AWESOME PLAY, ROBERT!*"

I don't know if Hootie heard him or not. He simply got up and threw the ball back to Curtis. I saw him pull his Intimidators cap even lower over his eyes. That's when Brazos screamed our new war cry across the infield for the very first time.

"*NIUHI!!*" He yelled, pointing at Hootie. Hootie made a fist and gave it a short pump. He stepped back into his spot at third without any further celebration. He was totally focused.

I shot Brazos a quick glance. He looked over at me and grinned. He pulled his cap lower, too.

We were one out away.

The next hitter was another one of their lefties. He had dropped that flat orange over Brazos onto the chalk down the first base line earlier in the game. He'd had a quick enough bat to get completely around on that pitch, but had popped it up. Now with our pitcher completely gassed, I figured that if he got a fat one over the plate, there was little doubt that he would drive it.

Curtis took his time. Every pitch he made was taking longer and longer. His windup was slower and slower. He began by tossing him two balls in pretty much the same spot, both low and away in the strike zone, but the kid refused to swing at either of them.

A walk would put the tying run on base and that was the last thing we wanted. I watched as Chase looked over into the dugout and got the sign from Coach Weaver. He set his glove over the heart of the plate and waited while Curtis did the only thing he had enough strength left to do—throw another batting practice fast ball right down the middle.

The kid nailed it.

The ball shot past the mound on its way to centerfield. Curtis made a weak stab with his glove, but he was too beat to get his body into a good fielding position. It passed him easily.

I had been cheating up the middle just a little bit and so I got a good jump on the ball as it bounced, once in front of the mound and then again behind it. On its third hop, it hit the infield dirt and scooted, just to the first base side of the bag at second.

I didn't have time to think about anything. I took a couple of quick steps and dove. The ball hit my glove solidly and I felt the pocket automatically close, trapping it inside.

The runner was quick. Plus, since he had started his sprint down the first base line from the left side of the plate, I knew he would be faster than a right handed hitter to the bag. There wasn't time to get to my feet. So I rose on my knees and pivoted, whipping my arm around at the same time. When the ball left my hand, it had everything on it that I could give.

Brazos has always been stretchy. His older sister is a gymnast and his mom used to be one, too. She pushes him to do straddle splits with his sister for fifteen minutes every day to improve his flexibility. I used to think it was ridiculous, but it was about to pay off.

He had already hustled toward first base and was in position. He put his right foot on the bag, turned toward me and pushed his left leg out. It just kept stretching and stretching, kind of like that guy in the Fantastic Four who stretches like he's made of Silly Putty. His glove came up and he pushed it toward me too, straining to reach with it as far as he could.

The ball snapped into the leather. It was just an instant before the final Blasters hitter of the game hit the bag with his foot. The field umpire saw it perfectly, but he heard it perfectly, too. The leather snap came first, *before* the sound of the runner's foot hitting the bag. I watched as he snatched dramatically at the air with his fist.

"HE'S OUT!"

I fell on my back. I looked up into the bright blue sky and closed my eyes.

It was over.

Game Two was ours.

14

Ryne

"Those were two pretty awesome fielding plays to end the game, Coach!" Kelly Duerson exclaimed into the microphone she was holding in her hand. She and Coach Ramirez were standing on the field, just outside of our dugout. It was the closest any of us other than Miggy had been to her. She had undone the bun on the top of her head and let dark brown hair down. It splashed onto her red ESPN polo and rolled over her shoulders. She was wearing a huge smile that was highlighted by the red lipstick she had chosen to match her polo.

Coach Ramirez pushed his hat up dramatically on his forehead. "Great plays, Kelly," he admitted. "Absolutely, but that's the way these boys have played the whole season. As a coach, my job is to set the bar higher for them every day. They don't always clear it, but today they got it done."

Kelly moved the microphone back from Coach toward her. "So you've got a rubber game coming up in about fifty-five minutes. It's hot enough out here right now that you could probably fry bacon on your dugout roof. How do you keep these boys from wilting in this heat?"

Coach Ramirez made a tough face. "We'll pump some fluids into them, apply some cool towels, and keep them in the shade. They'll be ready to go."

Kelly flicked the mike back toward her cherry lips once more and smiled. "Thanks, Coach."

They both waited until the cameraman gave them a sign that the short interview was over. Someone above us immediately called out instructions to Kelly and she nodded and swiftly moved toward the stands above us. Coach Ramirez stepped down onto the first step of the dugout. He pointed a stern finger at us.

"Bathroom break, refreshments and then everybody back here in thirty minutes. If you need something to eat, get it. Remember, no sodas. Drink water." He looked over at Miggy who had a sour look on his face. "C'mon, Miguel. I need you up top."

Miggy looked at his dad and grunted. He stood up and obediently followed him into the stands above us. After they left, Coach Weaver stepped into the dugout. He had a warm, fatherly smile on his face.

"You played like the Intimidators I know today," he began. He looked over at Hootie. "That was a major league stab at third, Hootie," he praised. Hootie didn't exactly light up at the compliment. He still had his hat low over his eyes.

"Ryne," he said, turning to me. "That was just about the best backhanded scoop I've seen at second base…." He paused, thinking. "Well, in a really long time. Brazos, when you can stretch like that and make plays for your team at first base, people notice. And by people, I mean pro scouts," he emphasized. "In fact, I hope those blasted ESPN cameras caught both of those plays, boys. They should definitely make their Top Ten list tonight!"

I glanced quickly over at Brazos and then looked back at Coach Weaver. We both nodded at him, but neither of us gave off even a hint of excitement.

Coach Weaver turned to Curtis. Our Game 2 winner had a cold towel wrapped around his neck. He was sitting bent over with his elbows on his knees. He looked absolutely drained. "Curtis...," he hesitated, almost like he was choking up. "J...just great," he finally managed. "I've never seen you throw so hard. I know you were tired that last inning, son." He made a fist and pumped it. "But you dug deep. I'm proud of you."

Curtis turned his head sideways to look at his father. He bobbed his head once. He didn't smile. He didn't speak, either.

Coach Weaver was quiet. He could tell something was different about the mood in our dugout. He didn't say a word about it. I'm pretty sure he didn't want to interfere with whatever zone he thought we were in. He just clapped his hands together once and said, "You heard Coach Ramirez, Intimidators. You've got thirty minutes."

*   *   *

Between games, the operators of the *Press Box* opened a special 'Players Only' line so that we could grab a snack quickly and head back to the field. All of us stood in it together, except for Miggy who was still off somewhere with Coach Ramirez. Chase and I were the last two in line.

"So, I guess Miggy is off to another interview?" Chase speculated to me.

"Probably," I answered. "But really, who cares?"

"Those plays you guys made were great," he said, punching me in the arm.

"Yes, they were," a familiar gravelly voice agreed. It was Mr. Blyleven. He had walked up behind us. "Both of those plays were just outstanding!"

I smiled, even though I was a little embarrassed. "Thank you, Mr. Blyleven."

Mr. Blyleven walked to the front of the line. He handed one of the *Press Box* employees his bank card. "This is on me," he said. "Just hurry them through. They've got to get back to the field."

"Thank you, Mr. Blyleven!" Wee Willie shouted. He was at the front of the line and added a second hot dog to his order.

"My pleasure, boys. You're playing like a major league team right now. Keep it up!" Mr. Blyleven was fired up. He playfully snatched Wee Willie's cap off his head and gave his buzz cut a good rub. When he did, the small shark fin inside his hat fell out of the lining and onto the ground. Mr. Blyleven bent over and picked it up.

"What's this?" he said.

Wee Willie looked back at me. "Ryne made it. He made one for all of us."

Mr. Blyleven examined the fin closely. "What is it? Some sort of good luck charm?"

"It's a talisman," Jimmy answered.

"A talisman?" Mr. Blyleven repeated. "I'm surprised you boys even know what a talisman is." He flipped the fin on its side. "What's this word written on it?" He struggled to pronounce it. "*Ni-yoo-he?*"

"Ni-you-hi," Brazos corrected.

"What's that mean?" he asked, curiously.

Everyone turned to me. I hesitated.

"It's a Hawai'ian word," I answered. "It's a type of shark."

Mr. Blyleven suddenly looked at me. "This has something do with Mano, I'm guessing."

184

I nodded. "Yes, sir."

"His Number 9 is on it, too," Mr. Blyleven mumbled thoughtfully as he turned the fin over. He rubbed the talisman between his fingers as he continued to study it. "It feels like leather. What did you make this out of Ryne?"

"It's from a baseball."

His eyes lit up. "One of Mano's home run balls?"

"Yes, sir. The first one he hit."

Mr. Blyleven looked up and down the line at all of us. He had a faraway look on his face. "Where is that boy?" he asked. He looked at me. I couldn't lie.

"I think he went back home, Mr. Blyleven."

"That's what I thought." He sighed heavily. "I just want to know why it's been such a big, blasted secret."

Wee Willie, Sammy, and Curtis walked past us with their hot dogs and bottles of Gatorade. "Hey, Sparkplug. I'll bring this over to you in the dugout in just a minute, okay?" Mr. Blyleven said to Wee Willie.

"Uh, sure," Wee Willie replied, hesitantly. "I just need it back before we play, okay?"

Mr. Blyleven gave him a huge smile. "It's got some really good magic in it, huh?"

Wee Willie shook his head. "It's not magic. It's got the heart of baseball in it, though," he answered. He, Sammy and Curtis headed back toward our dugout.

Mr. Blyleven turned to me. His face was so bright he looked about twenty years younger. "Did he just say it has the heart of baseball in it?"

185

"I actually put a small piece of the center of the baseball that Mano hit inside each one of them," I explained. "I read that to attract power, a talisman has to be made in a special way."

"That's pretty doggone special, Ryne," Mr. Blyleven agreed. He held the tiny fin by one of its tips. He was looking at it like he was holding a diamond ring. "Everybody has one inside their hat, huh?"

"Yes, sir. That was Brazos' idea. He thought it was a good idea for us to keep them as close to our minds as possible. You know, to help us focus."

Mr. Blyleven smiled. "Mano really had an impact on all of you, didn't he?"

"He's a niuhi warrior," Brazos stated.

"He's our village chief," Jimmy said.

Mr. Blyleven looked up from the talisman in his hand at both of them. He turned to me. "When this game is over," he said, motioning with his head in the direction of the field, "I'd like to talk to you, okay?"

"Sure, Mr. Blyleven."

"When the celebration's over," he added.

"Celebration?" I said, a little confused.

"Yeah," Mr. Blyleven said. His face was set in stone. "The celebration you guys will be having on the field when you win this game and move on to the semi-finals."

* * *

The ESPN reporter had been sitting about ten rows above us talking to Hootie's dad when Ryne went horizontal at second base and made his incredible grab. Hope and I both jumped to our feet as he rifled a perfect throw from his knees to Brazos at first. We watched dumbfounded as Brazos suddenly turned into a Slinky and strained to reach the ball a step ahead of the runner. When the ball hit his glove and we saw the umpire begin to raise his fist, we both erupted.

Hope squealed. She sounded exactly like Samantha when she's running through the house with a friend, only the ear-splitting pitch was somehow even higher. "*YEEEEEEEEAAAAAA! RYNE!!*"

I raised both my arms in the air. "UNBELIEVABLE!!" I screamed. "NICE STRETCH, BRAZOS. WAY TO GO, RYNE!"

Samantha and Alfonso bounded up and down between us like a couple of rubber balls. Sam grabbed my leg while Alfonso gave Hope a high five.

"They did it, Daddy!" Samantha yelled up at me. "They did it!"

The stands on the first base side of PNC Park roared for several minutes as the Intimidators met the Blasters at the center of the diamond for their post-game handshake. I felt Mr. Blyleven's hand clamp down on my shoulder. Even though he's in his eighties, his grip is still strong. I turned around and he shook my hand.

"Amazing!!" he said, his blue eyes flashing. "Absolutely amazing!! That's a heck of second baseman you have there!"

I grinned broadly at him. "He gets it from his mom!" I laughed, pointing at Hope.

That's when I saw the ESPN reporter who had been talking to Hootie's dad pointing someone in our direction. A few rows down, another cameraman began making his way toward us. Behind him was a tall brunette wearing a red polo and snug-fitting, white jeans. It was Kelly Duerson.

I got Hope's attention. "I think they're coming to talk to us!" I said, gesturing toward the approaching crew. Hope turned to look and as she did, I quickly raked my fingers through my hair. Before I could finish, Hope turned back around and caught me.

"Oh, stop it!" She barked, jokingly.

"What?" I tried to look innocent.

"You act like you're about to meet Miss America!"

"That's ridiculous," I protested. "I'm already married to Miss America."

"Good answer!" Hope laughed.

But before Kelly could reach us, another man standing near the dugout shouted up to her. She stopped and looked down. He waved her back toward the field. Immediately, she complied and began moving away from us. I felt my face fall.

"Aaahh, man. What the heck?"

"Oh, I'm so sorry, honey," Hope began, laughing. "It looks like she's been re-directed!!" I pouted as Kelly Duerson made her way onto the field.

Suddenly, Chase's mother bounced down the stairs toward us. She threw her arms around Hope as she squealed. "THAT WAS AMAZING!!"

"I KNOW!!" Hope squealed back.

"We're going to take the younger ones over to playground and feed them before the second game," she announced. She looked down at Alfonso and Samantha. "Are you two hungry?"

"I'm starving!" Alfonso promptly replied.

"Can I have a hot dog?" Samantha inquired.

"Anything you want, Sugar!" Jennifer bubbled. "Come on!"

Alfonso and Samantha followed her down the stairs like a couple of puppies. Hope picked up her purse and stepped in behind them. She turned around to me.

"Are you coming?"

"I'll be there in a second, honey," I said. "I think I'll get a picture of the scoreboard for the scrapbook and maybe a few post-game shots with my new camera."

Hope blew me a kiss and practically skipped down the stairs after the kids. She was elated by the victory and Ryne's game-ending heroism at second base.

I reached under my seat and pulled out the camera I'd purchased at the end of the regular season. It was a nifty little Nikon with a great long range lens. Ryne had been with me when I'd bought it. He had gently reminded me to get one that was idiot-proof and I had complied. My failings with electronic gadgets are legendary in our family and even though it hurt my pride to admit it, I needed the simplest point-and-shoot I could find.

The long range lens enabled me to get a professional quality close up of the scoreboard. I clicked three or four times, just testing out my new toy, and then turned the lens toward the field. I snapped a few random shots of the players milling around the dugout before they all disappeared inside. I caught a close-up of Coach Ramirez. He was being interviewed by Kelly Duerson. Apparently, he was the reason she had been diverted from interviewing us at the last minute.

Oh well, I thought. *He is the head coach.* I figured my destiny probably didn't include being, as Samantha had termed it, "worldly famous", anyway.

The lens on my new camera was good; so good that I almost felt like a super spy with it. I kept it trained on Coach Ramirez as he moved over to the dugout step. I could see him talking. Soon, Miggy popped out and they headed off together. I casually followed them as they walked up a short flight of stairs into the stands. They were greeted by two men, one of whom I now knew was a principal investor in Baseball World and a college buddy of Coach Ramirez. Once again, he was oddly dressed for the blazing heat in a dress suit and a Baseball World cap.

The other man had his back to me. He was a muscular figure dressed more appropriately in a snug fitting t-shirt and coach's shorts. He wore a dark purple baseball cap with something written on the back. I adjusted the camera lens and it zoomed in even closer so I could see the block letters clearly.

It read Lone Star Elite Baseball.

I put my camera down. I was starting to feel like I was snooping.

Coach Ramirez shook hands with both men. He put his arm around Miggy and introduced him to the muscular man. Miggy shook his hand and then they all four walked up the stairs and onto the landing area above the stands. I watched them until they disappeared from view.

I had an odd feeling. Hope would have called it intuition, but I've always told her that intuition is a woman's territory. Men don't have intuition. We might have indigestion, but not intuition.

But like indigestion, what we have is in our stomachs. It's a gut feeling.

I had a gut feeling that something was up. And the feeling wasn't good.

* * *

When Coach Ramirez reappeared about fifteen minutes before game time and told Chase to get his gear on and head to the bullpen, I knew something was up. Jimmy hadn't thrown too many pitches on Saturday, so he could start again, but Curtis was probably done for the day. We all knew that Brazos was available if we needed him, but that wasn't likely. We needed the win and Jimmy was our guy. However, when Coach Ramirez only asked for Chase, an alarm went off in my head.

Coach Weaver stepped into the dugout. He had his head down. He was staring at the line-up card in his hand like he was mad at it.

"A few changes, boys," he announced, refusing to look up at us. "Hootie will move over to short. Jimmy, you'll play third. Curtis, you'll be in left."

"Are you serious, Dad?" Curtis asked. He sounded completely shocked.

I turned and looked at Hootie. He was sitting straight up. He shook his head. "I'm playing shortstop?"

"Yes," Coach Weaver confirmed. He still didn't look up.

"But coach, I haven't played shortstop since I was nine!"

"Where is Miggy?" Jimmy almost shouted.

Coach Weaver finally looked up at us. "He's in the bullpen."

I felt my mouth open, but nothing came out.

"Go warm-up, Intimidators," Coach Weaver said. He was trying to be cool but I could tell he was about to boil over. Miggy had pitched twice the entire season and he hadn't made it through a complete inning either time. His control was absolutely horrible. Plus, because of that decision, we had just been forced to change the entire left half of our defense. You didn't need to be a coach to see that was probably not a smart plan going into a winner-take-all game.

"But coach, shouldn't I start..." Jimmy began.

Coach Weaver cut him off. "Probably, but I don't make those calls. Hit the field, boys. Now. Game starts in fifteen. By the way," he added. "We lost the coin flip. We bat first." He turned and practically sprinted away from us.

After he'd left, Jimmy stood up and slammed his glove into the dugout floor. "I've had it with this junk!" He yelled. "Why in the heck would he start Miggy? Miggy hasn't started a game the entire year!"

"It's probably because ESPN is here," Sammy offered.

"That doesn't make any sense," Hootie argued. "Why would Coach Ramirez want Miggy to look bad on television?"

"He couldn't look any worse than he did that last inning," Curtis joined in. "Can you believe the way he acted after that ball bounced off his glove and went into left field? What was that, his third error in a row?"

"It doesn't matter," I said, quietly.

Everyone turned to me. "Why not?" Wee Willie asked.

"Because no matter what Coach Ramirez or Miggy does or doesn't do, there is no way we are going to lose this game."

Brazos stood up and walked over to me. "I'm with you, Ryne." He took off his hat and all of his long, springy hair jumped out. He pulled his talisman from the band of his hat and turned around to face the team.

"We aren't going to lose," he said, holding the tiny fin in his closed fist. "In fact, we're going to win big."

Jimmy snatched his hat off his head and took out his talisman. He closed his fist tightly around it and held his hand up in the air like he was ready to punch somebody in the face with it. "Nothing will get by me at third," he promised.

Hootie stood up. He took his cap off and fished out his own shark fin from the brim. He made a fist around it and held it in front of him. He ground his teeth together. "Let's tear the cover off the ball," he snarled.

Everyone took off their caps and found their talismans. We held them in our fists and came together, joining our tightly closed knuckles in our traditional pile.

All eyes turned to me. I felt something deep inside. The bats that were usually there before a big game were long gone. In their place was a different feeling. It was sure and strong.

"Let's get on them early," I said, grinding my teeth. Everyone pushed their fists together. I thought my voice sounded older, and maybe even a little tougher. "*Niuhi*," I finished.

Before Game One, the answer that had come back from the team had sounded like a united "amen" in church after a prayer. This time, the answer sounded much different. It was like the low, threatening growl from a ticked off Doberman.

"*Ni-u-hi*," the team answered.

15

Shaun

The car ride home was quiet.

I looked in my rear view mirror. Samantha was slumped over in her car seat, softly snoring. As we'd pulled out of the parking lot of Baseball World, she'd asked Hope every parent's favorite car travel question: *Mom, how long before we get home?* Hope had promised her no more than an hour and a half. She had then turned in her seat to offer Samantha a cold bottle of water from a small cooler between her legs, but Sam's head was already bobbing. In under a minute, she'd fallen fast asleep.

In the last row of the Suburban, Ryne sat upright with his head lolling against the headrest. The cool air conditioning, the gentle roll of the car across the highway, and the last rays of the Sunday sun streaming through the glass had combined to put him to sleep shortly after our trip home began, too. He wasn't moving.

"They're both exhausted," I said to Hope as we cruised at a comfortable speed along the interstate. "That was a long day in this heat."

Hope didn't respond. I looked over at her.

"Are you asleep too, honey?" I asked, playfully.

Hope stirred from her thoughts. "I'm sorry. What did you say, Shaun?"

"The kids are wiped out," I repeated. "It looks like you are, too."

Hope wiggled in her seat. "I'm just drained," she sighed. "And I feel like an emotional mess."

"Yeah," I agreed. "I'm a little out of it, too."

She turned and looked at Ryne. "He played his heart out today, didn't he?"

I looked up at our peacefully sleeping son in the mirror. "He gave it everything he had," I concurred.

Hope turned and looked at me. "You're still shocked, aren't you?"

I shook my head. "Well, yeah. I didn't think that first inning would ever end! Fourteen runs? Are you kidding me?"

Ryne stirred in the backseat. He groaned softly.

"Miggy didn't pitch well," Hope said, not unkindly.

"That's an understatement," I snorted.

"I don't remember him pitching the whole season before today. Did he?"

"He pitched twice," I stated. "He wasn't very good either time."

"Then why do you think they pitched him today?"

"I'm sure 'they' didn't make the decision. Coach Weaver wouldn't have supported it. It had to be Ramirez's call all the way," I speculated.

Hope sighed again. "It must be hard to coach your own son."

I made a face. "Sure, of course it's hard. That's not the problem here. The problem is the shameless promotion of your own son at the expense of the team."

"Do you mean the ESPN thing?" Hope asked.

"Well, that's part of it," I said. "I'm sure ESPN was looking for a good story this weekend to promote Baseball World and Ramirez had the inside track because his old college buddy is one of the investors. They wanted to profile a kid, so he got them to profile Miggy. That doesn't bother me."

"Then what does?"

I grimaced. "I saw Ramirez and Miggy talking to a guy who looked like a coach before Game Three. He had a hat on that had Lone Star Elite Baseball on the back of it."

Hope looked puzzled. "So? What's Lone Star Elite Baseball?"

"I'm not sure," I said. "But I'll bet it's some high level youth baseball outfit."

"*And?*" Hope rolled her hand trying to get me to make my point.

"That coach was down sitting behind home plate with a radar gun in the first inning while Miggy was pitching."

The light went on for Hope. "Coach Ramirez decided to pitch Miggy so that coach could see him?"

"Bingo!" I said.

"But if Miggy hadn't pitched all season…I mean, it doesn't make any sense. He wouldn't have wanted him to look bad in front of that coach, would he?"

"I'm sure they weren't looking at how well he pitched," I speculated again. "I noticed that he didn't stay very long. He was probably just trying to get an idea of his arm strength. He left after the fifth batter.

Miggy had already thrown enough fastballs by then for the coach to get his number on the radar gun."

Hope was silent for a moment. I could tell that the reality of what I'd just said bothered her. "That isn't right," she whispered, as if she was afraid the kids might hear her in their sleep.

"No, it isn't," I whispered back. "But today was really no different than what's been going on the whole season. Heck, Ramirez kept Miggy in the clean-up spot in the batting order for every game even after it became clear to anyone and everyone watching the games that Mano could have probably batted clean-up for the New York Yankees!" I shook my head. "But everything was on the line today. I guess I thought Ramirez would have put the team first, even if it was just this one time. Clearly, I was wrong."

We both heard Ryne stir again in the backseat. I checked the mirror. He repositioned his head and mumbled. I could tell he was in a deep sleep.

*   *   *

Ryne

I am floating.

The ocean that surrounds me is the most beautiful blue I have ever seen and it is perfectly clear, too. I can see beneath my feet forever. I keep putting my face in the water, but even though I can see everything, I still can't see the bottom.

I know that I am not a strong swimmer. That's why it doesn't make any sense that I am so far away from the shore in this incredibly deep water without a life jacket, but I can see the beach in the distance. The sand is white and fluffy, like an endless stretch of high clouds crawling across the sky on a bright, sunny day.

Someone is standing on the sand. They're waving in my direction.

I start to swim toward the beach. Surprisingly, my stroke is much stronger than I thought. As I pull easily through the water, I keep my head up, which is odd. Whenever I swim in a pool, my face is usually down in the water and my head turns from side to side so that I can take an occasional breath. For some reason, I am afraid to look away from the figure on the shoreline. I am worried that if I turn away, whoever it is that is waving to me will disappear.

I cover half the distance between us quickly. I still have a long way to go, but now I can see that whoever is standing on the sand waving to me is now pointing for me to look over to my left.

Suddenly, I am afraid. I don't want to look.

So I start swimming again. Only now, I don't seem to be making any progress. My feet, which had been moving like propellers, now feel incredibly heavy. I keep telling them to go, but they won't.

I stop. I float. The figure is still pointing to my left, and I still don't want to look.

But I do.

There's a fin knifing through the water. It's huge. It's coming straight toward me.

There is no place for me to go. I'm trapped.

I see something floating next to me. I have no idea where it came from, but it looks like a piece of a ship? I scramble up on top of it and sit up immediately, wondering if it will keep me safe. Quickly, I turn around to locate the shark. In the time it has taken me to climb aboard the broken piece from the mysterious vessel, the fin has disappeared.

Panicked, I look up toward the shore. Thankfully, the figure that has been waving to me is still there. Amazingly, even though the person is still very far away, I can tell who it is.

It's Madison.

She's wearing her Intimidators cap and her blonde ponytail is hanging from the back. It begins to bounce as she runs along the beach waving to me.

Hurry! I hear her say, urging me on. C'mon! Hurry!!

I begin to paddle with my arms. Surprisingly, I move very fast. In just a few seconds, I am right next to the beach. I should be able to put my feet on the bottom and walk the rest of the way. Just to be sure, I put my face in the water. Even though the water is crystal clear, I still can't see the bottom! The beach is just feet away from me, but it's like a cliff hanging over the water.

Madison is standing on the edge of the sand. She reaches her hand out to me, but we're still too far apart. I lie down on my belly and push my arm toward her, stretching my fingers to reach hers which strain back to reach mine.

We are close...so close.

I push my face down. It helps my shoulder extend an extra inch. I can feel our fingertips touching. With my face in the water I can no longer see Madison, but I can see what's below me. Something slips past my view in a flash, so fast that I only catch a glimpse of an enormous tail fin.

Suddenly, I feel pressure on my back. It's dull pain, not sharp like Mano had said it was. I feel like I am rolling, being lifted up. My head rises as my hand is pulled away from Madison's. Only now, it's no longer Madison's hand that is beyond my reach.

It's Mano's.

I can see his deep, caramel skin and his brilliantly white teeth, but it's his eyes that I make the biggest impression on me. They are dark and mysterious. He begins speaking to me.

Niuhi, he says. Niuhi!!

I am lifted higher. The sun is blazing in the sky. The water rolls off of my body in rivers. My arms and legs are limp. Soon the shark will take me under and it will all be over.

Niuhi! I hear Mano say to me again in his smooth accent. Niuhi!!

I feel my body slip into the water. It's not as bad as I thought. There is no pain, now. The pressure on my back gradually releases. My arms and legs slip free. My body begins to gently float away into the ocean.

As I look up into the bright blue sky above, the sun suddenly blinks out.

It's over. Everything goes black.

I am exhausted. I close my eyes.

And I sleep.

* * *

Shaun

Ryne was heavier than I thought. It had been years since I'd had to carry him in from the car because he'd fallen asleep, but he was in such a deep slumber that I couldn't bear to wake him.

I laid him down on his bed and gently pulled my arms from beneath his back. His entire body was limp.

He had immediately taken off his shoes in the car after the game, but I wondered briefly if I should even attempt to peel the dirty black and gold uniform from his body. Hope tapped my shoulder. I turned to her and she shook her head.

He's fine, she mouthed to me. She walked across the room and turned off the light. When she did, Ryne moaned softly.

I placed my hand gently on his chest. I reached up and slipped his Intimidators cap from his head. His face was peaceful.

Twenty-one to seven, I whispered over him. I smiled as I placed the cap on his bedpost. He breathed in and out, softly.

As I watched him, I thought again about Game 3. I thought about Miggy and his horrible day as a pitcher. Of course, when your team scores fourteen runs for you before you even step foot on the mound, I guess it didn't really matter how badly you pitched, did it? The Intimidators had opened the game by bombing four different pitchers in the first inning as they'd batted through their line-up twice. It had been an amazing hitting display.

The semi-finals were a week away. The Intimidators had earned their spot in them, for sure.

Sleep tight, son, I whispered. *I'm proud of you.*

Then I slipped quietly out of the room.

* * *

Ryne

The next morning at the breakfast table, I was still tired. I had slept until nine-thirty, which was pretty unusual for me, even for the summer. Usually, I'm awake by seven-thirty and hardly ever later than eight because I just can't adjust to waking up late once school gets out.

Mom had made biscuits and cream gravy for me for breakfast. It's my favorite, so even though I was still pretty bushed, I attacked my plate. As usual, Samantha skipped the man food and instead picked a bowl of Lucky Charms, while Mom spooned a few bites from a fresh grapefruit half into her mouth. Dad had already left for work, long before either Sam or I had managed to make it downstairs. The three of us were sitting at the kitchen table when Mom's cell phone suddenly began playing Taylor Swift's *Shake it Off.* It was her ringtone. She picked up the phone and looked at the number. "It's Chase's mom," she said.

I took another bite of biscuit. I noticed that after Mom said "Hi, Jennifer" she didn't speak again for a while. She just listened. After a few moments I heard her say, "Really. Hmmm." She looked over at me and continued to listen. I saw her lips tighten.

"What time are we supposed to be there?" she finally asked.

Over her shoulder, I could see the television in the living room. It was already on ESPN. The Baseball World announcement and ceremony with the Commissioner of Major League Baseball was an hour away. Their special coverage was scheduled to begin at the bottom of the hour. I figured that sometime during those thirty minutes they would probably show the interview and other stuff they had done with Miggy.

"Okay, well thanks for calling to tell me, Jennifer. We'll plan on being there tonight." Mom set her cell phone down on the table.

"What's up?" I asked, taking another big bite.

"I'm not sure," she said, thoughtfully. "But Mrs. Girardi was asked by Coach Weaver to put together a players and parents meeting tonight at 7:00. We're going to meet at the Pizza Hut over by the practice field."

"After practice, I guess," I said. Sometimes we practiced at 5:30, sometimes we started later at 7:00.

Mom shook her head. "Actually, Jennifer said he cancelled practice."

"Really?" I was surprised. "That's weird. Maybe they're going to give us a day off to rest?"

"Maybe..." Mom trailed off. She looked unsure.

"I could use a day off," I said. "I'm a little sore and tired, anyway."

"I know you are, punkin." She stopped, catching herself. "I mean, I know, Ryne." She gave me a smile. "Oh, by the way, Mrs. Girardi said to tell you congratulations!"

"For what?" I asked, but I already knew what she meant.

Mom smirked. "Really? You're going to pretend like you haven't already watched it a dozen times this morning in your room?"

I was suddenly embarrassed.

"Yeah, I watched it," I admitted. I looked down at my plate. "So, what did Dad say about it?" I knew he probably hadn't gone to sleep until he'd seen the Top Ten on Sunday's late night Sports Center. Of course, I also already knew what he thought. He'd left a note about it on my pillow practically screaming at me to check out the recording on TiVo whenever I woke up.

Mom smiled proudly. "Oh, he was pretty pleased. He's already locked it so that it can never be erased. I suspect he's probably uploaded it to his Facebook page by now and tweeted it out to the whole world, too."

I grinned. "It is pretty cool," I said, trying my best to sound modest. ESPN had combined both of the plays that Hootie and I had made in Game Two into the number five ranking on Sunday's list of top plays. At first, it had been strange to see myself on television. It was like I was watching someone else make that diving play at second. After I'd rewound it for about the tenth time, it began to sink in that it really was me.

"I told you we were going to be worldly famous," Sam reminded us around a big bite of Lucky Charms.

Mom just shook her head and snorted. "Your father is right. You probably will work for People Magazine someday, young lady."

I took my last bite of biscuit and chewed it hurriedly. I still needed to write a letter back to Madison before she got back on Tuesday and I wanted to get started. Plus, I couldn't help but wonder if somehow she might have seen me on ESPN, too. I secretly hoped that Katie had texted her about it.

The doorbell rang.

Mom got up to answer it. She disappeared down the hallway. In a few moments I could hear her exclaim in her cheery voice, "Well, hi there, Mr. Blyleven!"

His graveled voice immediately came back, "Oh dadgummit, Hope. Would you just call me Bart? You make me feel like I'm a hundred and eighty-two instead of just eighty-two."

I heard Mom laugh. I hopped up from my chair. I'd completely forgotten about my brief talk with Mr. Blyleven after our game had ended. "Tell Mom I'll be right back," I said to Sam. She didn't say a word. She just nodded and kept crunching her Lucky Charms.

I sprinted up the back staircase that leads from our kitchen to the upstairs. I could hear Mom and Mr. Blyleven's voices echoing through the house as I ran. In my room, I pulled my bat bag from beneath my bed. I fished around in the small zippered compartment and pulled out the talismans I had collected after our game had ended. When I had counted all eight, I closed them in my fist and hustled back down.

They were in the kitchen. "Where did your brother go?" Mom was asking Sam, just as I bounced back down the stairs.

"Hey there, Ryne," Mr. Blyleven said, his face breaking into a big smile. He had his long white hair tied in a ponytail. His handlebar mustache was perfectly styled, as usual. He gave it a quick stroke. "Are you still fired up after that game yesterday?"

"A little," I said, grinning.

He barked. "A little? Holy cow! I bet I didn't sleep a wink last night!"

"Did you see Ryne on ESPN, Mr. Blyleven?" Sam piped in.

Mr. Blyleven slapped his hands together as he turned to Samantha. "Of course I saw him, young lady! That was a Gold Glove play your brother made. It was amazing!" He looked up at me, his blue eyes twinkling. "But I still can't decide what was more incredible, Ryne. Your play, Hootie's play, or that fourteen-run first inning you guys put up to start the last game!"

I just shrugged my shoulders and smiled.

Mr. Blyleven continued bubbling over. "There wasn't a ball that was hit in that inning that wasn't just peppered. I don't think I've ever seen an inning of baseball in my life where every hitter in the lineup hit that ball that hard. Every single ball was hit right on the nose!" He stopped for a moment to correct himself. "Well, I mean every ball except for the two that Miggy popped up. Every other ball was hit right on the nose!"

"It was something special, Ryne," Mom added, excitedly. "Your father could not stop talking about it last night after we got home. He was still going on and on until well after midnight. That's when I finally gave up on him ever shutting up and fell asleep!"

"Can we visit for a moment, Ryne?" Mr. Blyleven asked. "You know, about that little matter we discussed yesterday?"

Mom looked back and forth between us. "It sounds like you gentlemen need some privacy," she said. "Come on, Sam. Let's go upstairs for a minute. I need to introduce you to the business end of a vacuum cleaner, anyway. The floor in your room looks like the bottom of a bird cage."

Sam hopped up from the table and carried her bowl to the sink. Then she and Mom passed me on their way up the stairs. Mom whispered a good manners reminder in my ear as she slipped by.

I stepped down into the kitchen and immediately did what she'd reminded me to do.

"Would you like some juice or something, Mr. Blyleven?" I asked.

"Nah, I don't have time right now, Ryne. Be sure and tell your mom I said thanks for asking." He winked at me. "Let's sit for a quick second."

We pulled out our chairs at the kitchen table and sat down.

"So, were you able to collect all of them after the game yesterday?"

I opened my hand and showed him the talismans. "Yes, sir."

He looked at me, seriously. "Are you sure you're okay if I take them for a while?"

I hesitated. "I think so…"

Mr. Blyleven smiled warmly. "I promise you, Ryne. I won't let anything happen to them. I know how important they are to you and the team."

He opened his hand to me.

"There are only eight of them," I said. I was going to tell him that I hadn't made one for Miggy. Mr. Blyleven looked at me with his sparkling blue eyes and I could tell he already knew that.

"I understand," he said.

"What are you going to do with them, Mr. Blyleven?" I asked.

"It's a surprise, Ryne," he said. "But I'm positive you and your teammates are going to like it."

I felt like I needed to tell him that the talismans were kind of a secret. "You know… our parents…well, they don't know about these. It's kind of…uh, well…just for us," I said.

"And we'll be keeping it that way," he said. "I completely understand. It's a team thing."

"Yes, sir." I was relieved that he understood. "Did you play baseball, Mr. Blyleven?" I suddenly asked.

"Of course, I did! Back about a hundred years or so ago, I was a pitcher."

"Were you any good?"

"Oh, I could hold my own. I gave up my fair share of runs, too," he chuckled. He suddenly looked thoughtful, like he was remembering something from a time long ago.

"Did you ever see anyone who was as good as Mano?" I asked.

Mr. Blyleven sat quietly for a moment. "No," he said, instantly. "No, I can't say that I have, Ryne. I've never seen anyone—at any age—who could play ball like Mano." He jiggled the talismans in his hand. "That's why I know how important these are to you and the team." He closed his fist around them and held it up to me.

"The heart of baseball," he said, grinning.

I grinned back. "Yes, sir. The heart of baseball."

We bumped our fists lightly together, and he left.

16

Ryne

There were two rows of long tables set up for us when we arrived at Pizza Hut. It was just like Thanksgiving. There was one table for the parents and another one for the kids. Hootie, Chase, Jimmy, Sammy, Wee Willie, Brazos and I sat clumped together at one end of the kid's table. Wee Willie had bought a small rubber ball from one of the machines at the front of the restaurant for a quarter and we were taking turns trying to bounce it off the table into a plastic cup while we waited.

It was a few minutes after seven when Curtis and his parents walked in. Curtis' younger brother Colton went down and sat at the other end of the table with the rest of the brothers and sisters. Katie was down there, too. Her eyes had barely left her cell phone since she'd sat down and her fingers were constantly tapping at the small screen.

"Hey, Curtis," Hootie said as Curtis joined our end of the table.

"Hey," Curtis returned. "What are you guys doing?"

"We're playing mini-basketball," Wee Willie answered. "I just invented it."

"How do you play?" Curtis asked.

Wee Willie pointed to two sugar packets on the table. "If you can bounce it in from behind this one you get two points." He pointed to the other which was further away. "From behind this one is three points."

"Cool," Curtis said. "I want to play. Who's winning?"

"Brazos," Wee Willie said. "He's got three points."

Curtis laughed. "Just three points? Who's in second?"

"Everybody else. We've all got zero," Chase summarized for him. "We stink."

Coach Weaver and his wife walked over to the parents table. Chase's mom immediately hopped up and went over to him. He whispered something in her ear and she nodded. She clapped her hands together to get everyone's attention.

"Okay, we're going to get started. I've already ordered the pizzas and they should be coming out in just a minute. Before we eat, Coach Weaver has a few words he would like to say."

Coach Weaver stood up at the head of the table. He looked uncomfortable. He took a deep breath and adjusted his Intimidators cap. Just as he was about to speak, two waiters swooped in from the kitchen with the first large pizzas. They came straight to our table and all of us let out a cheer. Coach Weaver smiled and said, "I tell you what. Why don't we eat first? That's probably a better plan, anyway."

"Coach Ramirez and Miggy aren't here yet, either," Brazos' mom pointed out.

Coach Weaver turned his eyes toward the table and quickly sat down. I leaned over and whispered in Chase's ear. "Did your mom say why we were having this meeting instead of practice?"

Chase turned to me. I could tell just by looking at him that he had no clue. "All she said was that Coach Weaver called her and asked her to get everyone together. I don't think he told her what it's about."

We jumped up from our chairs to snag plates from a stack at the center of the table. I grabbed a couple of pieces of pepperoni from one of the steaming pies. As I did, I caught a glance from Katie. She raised her eyebrows at me and did a funny thing with her lips, as if she was asking me a question without saying any words. I was pretty sure I knew what she wanted. I raised my own eyebrows and bobbed my head quickly in response.

She smiled as she picked up a piece of pizza and sat back down. Instead of eating, she immediately picked up her cell phone and began to tap at the screen.

"Did you guys watch the Baseball World special on ESPN today?" Wee Willie asked.

"Yep," Sammy said. Jimmy, who was sitting next to him, rolled his eyes. Hootie just grunted as he stuffed a wedge of pizza into his mouth.

"Did you see the interview with Miggy?" Jimmy smirked.

"I couldn't believe it when Kelly Duerson asked him for an autograph at the end," Chase said. "I'll bet his head is so fat now, he'll have to get a bigger batting helmet."

"I saw the Top Ten, Ryne," Brazos grinned at me. "You and Hootie are famous, too!"

"It's not a big deal," Hootie grumped.

"You were on ESPN!" Brazos shot back.

Hootie waved him away. "Yeah, so? Our phone has been ringing non-stop at home all day. My mom's Facebook and email have been blowing up, too. I've probably talked to every single cousin I have today and a bunch of people I don't even know, and I'm a little sick of it. I just don't get what the big deal is."

"Dude, are you kidding?" Wee Willie exclaimed. "You were on ESPN! Top Ten! *Da da da...da da da!*" He looked over at me. "What about you, Ryne? Has your phone been going crazy all day, too?"

I shrugged my shoulders. "My grandparents called," I said.

Curtis laughed. "That's it?"

"My mom's been on her phone a lot," I added. At first, I thought it had been cool to see myself on television. But, like Hootie, all of the attention was beginning to make me feel uncomfortable. I didn't want anyone to think I was going to start acting like Miggy.

"You guys act like you are a couple of hairy warts," Brazos said.

"We're acting like *what?*" Hootie coughed, almost choking on his pizza.

"Hairy warts!" Brazos emphasized. "My grandmother says whenever somebody does something and doesn't want it to be noticed, they try to hide it, like it's a hairy wart."

"That's kind of gross," I said.

"Pretty disgusting," Jimmy piped in.

"That's why you hide them," Brazos explained.

"Look. I'm not acting like a hairy wart..." Hootie began.

"Oh, you're definitely acting like a hairy wart," Brazos interrupted. "You too, Ryne. Only you're like a smaller, hairy wart. Hootie's a giant one. Put the two of you together, and you could be Hairy Wart and Son of Hairy Wart."

"What's your point, Brazos?" Hootie growled.

Brazos turned serious. "Neither one of you is acting like Miggy, okay? Stop worrying about it."

Hootie grunted. "Thanks, Brazos."

I nodded at our long-haired, wise man. I was glad he had figured out what was really bothering us. "Yeah, thanks."

We went back to gobbling our pizza. After a bit, I got up and went to the bathroom. When I stepped back out into the small hallway, Katie was waiting for me.

"Did you give it to Chase?" she asked, urgently.

I was more than just a little surprised to find her stalking me outside the men's room door. "No. I... I have it," I stammered. I reached for the letter in my pocket. "You're not going to read it, right?"

Katie rolled her eyes at me. "Seriously, Ryne? Of course not." She sounded exasperated.

I looked down at my feet. "So, have you been texting with her while she's been gone?" I asked, nervously.

Katie giggled. "Yes."

"Oh. Okay," I said, not knowing what to say next.

"She saw your play on ESPN," Katie whispered. I looked up at her. She was smiling mischievously.

I felt my face begin to get hot. "Yeah? That's good. Did she say anything about it?"

Katie immediately pulled her cellphone from her hip pocket. She started tapping expertly at the screen, swiping her finger back and forth until she found what she wanted. She handed the phone to me. I read the tiny text through the smudges made by her fingers.

OMG!! Ryne is UNBELIEVABLE! My parents watched it with me and my dad is freaking out!!!

I looked up at her with an embarrassed smile on my face.

"Scroll down!" Katie directed.

I did as she ordered. Katie's reply was first, followed by Madison's.

IKR! Chase said he acted like it was no biggie!

PLZ! TIME!

I looked from the phone to her, my eyebrows scrunched in confusion.

"You don't have a cell phone, do you?" Katie said. She was looking at me like I was a caveman.

"No. I might get one for my birthday," I answered, embarrassed. "PLZ means please, right?"

Katie nodded patiently. "*Uh huh.*" She motioned with her hands for me to continue.

"But I don't know what IKR means. And what did she mean when she said 'time'? Did she have to go?" All I could figure was Madison was trying to call time out in their conversation.

Katie gave me an even bigger eye roll this time. "IKR means, *I Know, Right?*"

"Oh," I grunted.

"And TIME means *Tears in My Eyes.*"

I stared at her, stupidly.

"It made her emotional, Ryne!"

"What did?" I was completely lost.

Katie clapped both of her hands to the sides of her head. She laughed. "Oh, my gosh! You are just like Chase!"

I shrugged my shoulders helplessly. "I don't get...."

"She thinks it's sweet that you are so modest, Ryne! She loves it that you never brag on yourself."

I found that interesting spot on my shoes again. "Really? That's kind of weird," I said.

Katie took her phone back. "Girls like guys who are sweet, Ryne. They like guys who aren't stuck on themselves," she explained.

I scratched the back of my neck. "She's coming home tomorrow, huh?" I asked, trying to sound casual.

Katie's face lit up. "Yes. Her grandmother is okay for now, so they are coming home. She's planning on coming to practice, too."

I smiled. "That's good. I mean...I'm glad. Actually, what I mean is...."

Katie held up her hands to hush me. "I know what you mean," she said, smiling.

"What are you two doing? Playing with Barbies?" Chase suddenly asked. He had somehow managed to sneak up behind us.

"We're just talking," Katie answered.

Chase motioned for us to follow him. "Well, come on. Coach Weaver is ready to talk to everybody."

*   *   *

Shaun

Around the parents' table, the buzz was all about the Baseball World special and the ESPN Top Ten. I had arrived late, but I quickly pulled out my phone and showed my Facebook page to Hope.

"Look at this!" I crowed. "My phone has been exploding all day!"

"Did you manage to get any work done at the office at all?" Hope inquired, teasingly.

"No! I didn't get a single thing done!" I proudly proclaimed. "In fact, I should have just stayed home today and answered all of these messages from my laptop. I've been fat-fingering responses all day from my phone and my fat fingers are tired!"

Hope shook her head with disapproval. "I guess it's a good thing you're the boss," she scolded.

"Ain't it great?" I said, not the least bit bothered by her implied criticism.

"Congratulations, Shaun," Hootie's father said, extending his hand across the table to me.

I smiled so big it seemed my face might crack. "You too, Robert! Junior looked like Brooks Robinson over there at third!"

"Who's that?" Hope instantly asked.

"He was a great third baseman. Played for the Orioles back in the 60's and 70's," Robert Gibson Sr. answered for me. "He was a heckuva fielder."

Hope opened her mouth wide and let out an exaggerated AH. "Are you another walking baseball encyclopedia like my husband, Mr. Gibson?"

Hootie's dad laughed. He's a bear of a man with a wiry beard and forearms made of oak. "I guess I know my baseball history pretty well," he said. "I wished that it had been a subject back in high school. I'm sure I'd have done a lot better in Baseball history than I did in European history."

"You and me both, brother," I heartily agreed. I was on a high. I happily grabbed a piece of pizza from the table's center and took a gigantic bite. I felt Hope's familiar grip on my arm as I did. I turned to her, my jaws chomping merrily away. She looked decidedly less enthusiastic than I did.

"Miggy and Coach Ramirez aren't here," she said into my ear.

I made a quick survey of the room and confirmed that she was correct.

"Okay. So they're probably running late, huh? I'm sure Ramirez had a long day fielding calls from everyone he knows after that interview with Miggy ran on ESPN. Did you see it?" I asked. "It was actually pretty well done. Of course, it made Miggy look like the greatest baseball player since Babe Ruth, but…."

Hope pinched my arm and cut me off in mid-sentence. "I don't think they're coming."

I was surprised. "What makes you think that?"

"Something's going on, Shaun. I can just tell."

At the far end of the table, Coach Weaver stood up. As he did, I noticed Ryne, Katie, and Chase walking in behind him. As they took their seats, I lifted my hand to wave to Ryne but he appeared pre-occupied and didn't see me.

"Intimidators families, if I could have your attention, please," Coach Weaver began. He was wearing a dark coach's polo and his team cap. Around his eyes were two raccoon circles, the typical baseball coach's look resulting from the sun framing the outline of his sunglasses semi-permanently to his face. "First of all, I want to thank you for coming this evening. It's been a long summer season and I'm sure everyone is still exhausted from the weekend."

"We're too happy to be tired, Coach!" Wee Willie's father boomed from the far end of the table. Several of the parents burst into spontaneous applause.

"The boys played great, Coach!" Mike Girardi, Chase's dad echoed. He was sitting next to Jennifer who squeezed his arm excitedly.

Coach Weaver smiled thinly. "Yes. I couldn't agree more. The boys played as well as I could have hoped."

"How about that fourteen run first inning, huh?" Jennifer whooped. Another round of applause and a few whistles from dads swept the room.

I couldn't help myself. I had to join in. "You guys hit like the '27 Yankees yesterday!" I thundered, pointing at the table of players a few feet away. "You were absolutely amazing!"

A few of the players smiled brightly, while others just grinned sheepishly.

Coach Weaver waited until the commotion died down. Finally, all eyes returned to him. He hesitated. He looked down. I felt Hope's hand slowly creep over and lightly grip my leg beneath the table. As usual, she was right. Something was up.

Coach Weaver began again. "I don't know how to say this, so I'm just going to say it." He looked at his wife and then lifted his eyes to the room. His lips were pressed into a thin, hard line. "Coach Ramirez and Miggy have decided to leave the Intimidators."

There was a moment of stunned silence.

"*When?*" Jennifer asked in a low, shocked voice.

"It's effective immediately," Coach Weaver said, bluntly.

Gloria Styles, Jimmy and Sammy's mother, immediately belched in a loud voice, "You have got to be kidding me!"

Instantly, the room began to rumble and rock. Exasperation and anger came to a quick boil.

"This is ridiculous!" I heard someone cry.

"Oh, I'm not surprised," one of the mothers blurted.

"You can't just quit on your team in the middle of the playoffs!" I heard Robert Gibson roar.

In the midst of the growing fervor in the room, I felt Hope's grip on my leg suddenly tighten. I turned to her, my mouth hanging open stupidly. Her eyes were focused intently on the player's table. I looked over and saw that they had formed into a tight knot. It was centered on one player... Ryne.

Coach Weaver held up his hands. "Everyone, please. I know that this is completely unexpected..."

"What a bunch of garbage!" Gloria Styles bellowed.

"Mrs. Styles, please..." Coach Weaver pleaded. Jimmy and Sammy's mother immediately shut off her outburst. She folded her arms across her chest, steam practically shooting from her ears.

"Where did they go?" Mike Girardi demanded.

Coach Weaver's expression pinched even tighter. "Miggy was offered an opportunity to play for a new organization that is forming across the state of Texas. It's called Lone Star Elite."

"What's that? Is it some sort of super select league?" Wee Willie's father snarled.

Coach Weaver nodded. "Actually, from what I understand, it is."

"Holy cow," I mumbled.

Hope shook my leg urgently beneath the table. "What is it, Shaun?"

I leaned over to her ear. "Well, that's who I saw Ramirez and Miggy with at Baseball World yesterday, remember? The guy with the radar gun had Lone Star Elite on the back of his cap. Wow. It sure didn't take them long to move on Miggy," I whispered.

"It's a fantastic opportunity for Coach Ramirez and Miggy and I'll hope you will join me in wishing them the very best," Coach Weaver said to all of us.

Gloria Styles sniffed indignantly. Everyone else sat in reluctant silence. The room grew uncomfortably quiet.

"Hey, Coach?" The young voice came from the player's table. A small hand was raised, like a student in school asking for permission to speak. Ryne stood up from the middle of the tight knot of players at one end.

"Yes, Ryne," Coach Weaver said. He looked embarrassed, as if he had just remembered the players were also in the room.

Ryne spoke in a clear voice. At that moment, I noticed something different about my son. His head was held high, his shoulders were squared. He seemed very confident.

"With Miggy gone, that leaves us with only eight players."

Coach Weaver looked like a deer hypnotized by on coming headlights.

"Yes, Ryne. That is correct," he muttered in response.

The room began to slowly churn once again.

"We don't have anyone to replace him," Ryne said, reminding everyone of the obvious.

Coach Weaver swallowed hard. "No. We don't."

All eyes returned to my son.

"We can't add any new players either, right?"

Coach Weaver slowly nodded while the other dads in the room began to groan. "That's right. Our roster is fixed. You can't add any players at this point in the season - that's the Ringer Rule."

The Ringer Rule had been written to keep teams from adding a player to their roster after a certain point during the regular season, to prevent teams from adding a "ringer" or exceptional player to their roster to boost their chances of winning the state championship.

"So if we can't add a player, then we will have to play with eight," Ryne reiterated.

Suddenly, every parent turned to Coach Weaver. To his credit, Coach Weaver didn't flinch. He just answered Ryne's question. "That's right. We will have to play with eight, and the rules mandate that we will be required to take an out every time the ninth player is due to bat."

Immediately, the parents erupted in a chorus of sighs, groans, and catcalls.

"So what we need is one of our players who is on the roster but isn't playing right now to come back and play with us," Ryne stated clearly, over the parent's grousing.

"Yeah," Robert Gibson interjected. "That's exactly what we need."

That's when the unspoken question that had been on everyone's mind was finally asked. Gloria Styles unfolded her arms and placed both of her hands on the table. She leaned forward.

"Coach Weaver, what happened to Mano?"

Curtis' father took a breath. "I was told that he and his father went back to Hawai'i."

"And who told you that?" Gloria Styles pressed, suspiciously.

"Coach Ramirez." Coach Weaver stood before us with the look of a man who was completely unsure of whether what he was repeating was actually a fact. Gloria Styles picked up on it immediately.

"Well, I think somebody needs to call them and find out if that is true!" She demanded.

The room grumbled in agreement. "I'm sorry, but I don't have any contact information for Mano," Coach Weaver admitted.

"Well," Gloria Styles harrumphed. "I guess we'll never know for sure now, will we?"

The room grew quiet except for some low complaining. Then Ryne spoke up again.

"I think we should call Jacob," he said, decisively.

Wee Willie's father gasped. "That's not quite an upgrade to the team."

Wee Willie stood up. "He can play," he said, defiantly. "And he hustles, too."

I glanced down at Wee Willie's father who suddenly looked ashamed of himself.

"He quit the team, Ryne," Coach Weaver reminded everyone. "I don't think he will want to come back."

Ryne immediately countered, "I'll call him anyway and ask."

"Better yet, Coach" I added. "I'll drive Ryne over to his house and he can talk to him directly."

Ryne turned to me. He nodded and smiled.

Coach Weaver directed his attention at me. He had a doubtful look on his face. "Well, you can certainly try, Mr. Dunston."

The room grew quiet again. Coach Weaver looked out across the sea of our uncertain faces. "We will practice tomorrow night at 7:00. We'll practice hard, and we'll play hard this weekend. I think our boys are committed to that. I know that I am. Thanks for coming and I'll see all of you tomorrow night." With that, chairs began to slide back as everyone prepared to leave.

Hope grabbed my arm before I could stand. She pulled me in close. "Do you think he'll come back to play?"

I shrugged. "All we can do is ask," I replied.

I thought about the comment Wee Willie's father had made, that Jacob was not quite an upgrade to the team. His own son, however, seemed to think differently.

17

Ryne

Jacob Dickey lives on the far side of our town in a subdivision where the houses are pinched together in tight rows. He lives with his mom. His older brother Daniel is in college, but he comes home for the summer. In fact, it was Daniel who answered the door when we arrived. He had headphones stuffed into the holes in his ears and he was all sweaty like he'd been working out.

"Hey there," Dad said to him. "My name is Shaun Dunston and this is my son, Ryne. I had called earlier and spoke to Lisa and she said we could come by?"

Daniel had unplugged one of the earphones from the side of his head. I could hear music screeching from the tiny hole, so he must have been playing it pretty loud. "That's my mom," he said. "Hang on a second."

He turned and yelled back into the house. "MOM – SOMEONE'S HERE TO SEE YOU!"

We stood and waited on the front porch until Jacob's mother came to the door. She was a very tall woman with short, brown hair that she wore in a style tight to the back of her neck.

"You must be Shaun," she said to Dad, pleasantly. She looked at me. "And, of course, I know you, Ryne." Ms. Dickey had come to most of our pre-season practices during Jacob's brief time with the Intimidators. "Won't you come in?"

We stepped inside and followed her into their living room. Daniel came with us, wiping his sweaty face while we walked with a towel. "Would you like something to drink?" she asked. "Maybe some peach tea or raspberry lemonade?"

"Actually, peach tea sounds good," Dad replied. "How about you, Ryne? You want some lemonade?" He gave me a look that meant I was supposed to say yes.

"Yes, I'll have some. Thank you." While we waited, Dad talked to Daniel. He noticed his t-shirt. It was gray with dark splotches of sweat on his chest and spreading from under his arms. In red letters across the front it said STANFORD.

"Do you go to Stanford?" Dad asked.

Daniel wiped away some more sweat from his forehead. "Um, no. Actually, I have a genius friend from high school who goes there," he answered. "She sent me the t-shirt for Christmas last year."

"Oh, tell the truth, Daniel. She's more than just a friend, isn't she?" Jacob's mother called from the kitchen.

Daniel grinned. "Yeah. I guess. We dated our senior year," he confessed to us.

"I see," Dad said, smiling. He noticed a picture of Daniel with a girl on a shelf near the fireplace. He pointed to it. "Is that her?"

Daniel turned around. "Uh huh."

"What's her name?" Dad asked.

"Stacy."

Dad stepped closer to examine the picture. "So she's smart and pretty, huh? You know, I married one of those," he said, looking back at Daniel. "My best friend told me I'd outkicked my coverage."

Daniel looked at him like he didn't understand.

"You know, like punt coverage in football? It's when the punter kicks the ball too far and gives the returner a good chance to run it back," Dad said.

"I don't know too much about football," Daniel replied.

"Oh." Dad curled his lips while he thought. "Hmm. Well, let's just say it was like I'd gone fishing and somehow managed to hook a beautiful marlin when I was just hoping to catch a nice tuna."

Daniel laughed politely.

"That's not a problem for Daniel," Ms. Dickey said as she came back into the room with our glasses. "He's not a bad catch, either. He was accepted to Rice."

We took our drinks and sat down on the couch while Ms. Dickey sat in a big blue chair facing us.

"Really? Wow. Rice is a fantastic school," Dad praised. "They have an outstanding baseball program there, too. Do you ever go to any games?"

Daniel shook his head.

"Actually, Daniel isn't going to Rice just yet," Ms. Dickey answered for him. "We're still trying to put together a financial plan that will get him there."

"Yeah, so I'm hoping to transfer next year," Daniel added.

Dad smiled. "That's great. It really is a good school."

"Daniel, would you go see what Jacob is doing and ask him to come down?" Ms. Dickey asked. "I think he's in his room upstairs."

"Sure." Daniel swiped his face once more with the towel and then disappeared upstairs.

When he left, Ms. Dickey confided to Dad. "I've been divorced for seven years. Rice costs a fortune and the boy's father re-married shortly after we split and started a second family. He really isn't going to be much help."

Dad frowned. "I'm sorry," he offered.

"Don't be. The Good Lord will help us find a way to get him there," Ms. Dickey said, confidently. "But enough with that. You came by to talk about the baseball team?"

"Yes, we did," Dad began. He repositioned his body on the couch toward me. "Actually, it was Ryne's idea to come and visit with Jacob and talk to him about the Intimidators."

Ms. Dickey made a face. "You know, that wasn't a very good experience for Jacob," she said to both of us. She sighed. "That boy has loved baseball since he was five years old. He gets that from his grandmother, my mom. She watches every single Texas Rangers' game on television or she listens on the radio. She drives me crazy sometimes because she schedules everything around the games." She smiled. "My father passed away before Jacob was born, about fifteen years ago. Dad loved baseball too, and Mom just immersed herself in it after he died."

"Baseball is good for the soul," Dad said, sincerely. "My wife and I used to make regular volunteer visits to a nursing home on Sunday afternoons shortly after we got married. I met a nice woman who kept an old transistor radio in her lap as she toured the halls in her wheel chair. She loved to listen to the game, any game. In fact, she swore she preferred listening to the radio to watching on television. She said that when she closed her eyes and just listened, she felt like she was actually sitting in the bleachers." Dad smiled as he remembered. He paused and took a drink from his glass. "But you were talking about Jacob's experience with the Intimidators. It wasn't good?"

226

"No, it wasn't," she stated.

I flinched a little. I remembered how Chase had once said that maybe the only reason Jacob was on the team was to keep the bench from flying away in a high wind.

"I wasn't very fond of the team's coach," she continued. "He wouldn't even give Jacob the time of day."

"Coach Ramirez?" Dad asked.

"Yes." She looked at me as if she was worried I might be mad. "I'm sorry, Ryne. I don't want to say anything bad about your coach."

"It's okay," I said.

"Actually, that's the kind of reason that we're here," Dad explained. "Coach Ramirez is no longer with the Intimidators."

"Really?" Ms. Dickey said. "I'm not surprised. Did the parents finally run him off?"

"Not really. He found a better opportunity for his son and decided to leave the team."

Ms. Dickey raised her eyebrows. "He just left the team?" She turned to me. "Aren't you still playing, Ryne?"

"Yes, ma'am," I answered. "We're in the playoffs."

Ms. Dickey frowned. "Well, even I know it's wrong to quit on your team before the season is finished. I think that was one of the things that bothered Jacob the most about his experience with the Intimidators. He was always worried that his teammates would believe he quit on them." She stopped for a moment, then she asked, "I'm curious. What did Coach Ramirez end up saying to the team about that?"

I looked at Dad, a little bit nervous. "He told us Jacob decided he didn't want to play baseball anymore."

Ms. Dickey blew air from between her lips like she was disgusted. "That sounds about right." She turned to Dad. Her face suddenly changed. She looked angry. "Coach Ramirez called me and said that Jacob wasn't fitting in real well with the team. He said that sometimes that happens; that sometimes personalities just don't click. He recommended that I find another team for him."

"*What?*" Dad said. I could tell he was completely shocked. He turned to me. "Ryne, you said he told the team that Jacob didn't want to play baseball anymore?"

I just nodded.

"Holy cow!" Dad exclaimed. "I'm speechless. I can't believe he would purposefully mislead you like that."

Just then, Jacob came down the stairs. He stopped about half-way when he saw us. I'm pretty average sized for my age, but Jacob is shorter and skinny. His legs were poking out of a pair of green mesh basketball shorts like a couple of toothpicks with knees.

"Oh. Hey, Ryne," he said, like he was surprised to see me. I figured his mother hadn't told him we were coming.

"Jacob, come over here and sit down," Ms. Dickey said to him. Jacob obediently hopped down the second half of the stairs and came over to us. He sat down in a chair that was just like the big blue one his mom was in; only this one was a reddish-brown color I'd only seen before on a horse. "Ryne and Mr. Dunston would like to talk to you," she said.

"Okay," Jacob replied.

Dad seemed like he was a little unsure how we were supposed to start. "Hi Jacob, I'm Ryne's dad," he began, stating the obvious. "We came over today because Ryne wanted to talk to you about the Intimidators."

Jacob didn't say anything. He just looked at my father.

"Ryne, do you want to go ahead?" Dad asked me.

"Sure," I said. "Hey, Jacob." Jacob turned toward me. He didn't smile or anything. "Our team is kind of in trouble. We only have eight players and we were hoping you might want to come back and play with us."

"Why me?" Jacob asked. "Can't you get somebody else?"

"Well, we're in the playoffs now. There's a rule that says you can't have anybody on your team who isn't already on the roster," I said.

"It's called the Ringer Rule," Dad added for Ms. Dickey. "It's designed to keep teams from adding ringer players after a certain date."

"What's a 'ringer' player?" Ms. Dickey asked.

"Somebody who's really good. Not somebody like me," Jacob answered quickly.

"Oh, no. That's not what I meant, Jacob," Dad said. I could tell he was afraid he'd hurt Jacob's feelings. "Ringer is just a term used to describe someone who is brought in specifically to try and give a team an unfair advantage."

"Like I said," Jacob argued. He sounded sort of rude. "Not somebody like me."

"Watch it, mister," Ms. Dickey warned him. She pointed her finger at Jacob. "I won't tolerate that attitude from you toward any adult. I want you to apologize to Mr. Dunston right now."

"Oh, that's okay," Dad said, holding up his hands. I could tell he felt responsible for getting Jacob in trouble.

Ms. Dickey just ignored him. "Jacob. Apologize. Now."

Jacob hung his head a little. "I'm sorry, Mr. Dunston."

Dad looked totally embarrassed. "It's okay, really. What I meant to say is that the 'Ringer Rule' is in place to keep teams from cheating. Even Major League Baseball has certain dates after which you can't add a player to your roster. The rule exists to keep things as fair as possible." Dad turned to me. "I'm sorry for interrupting, Ryne."

"That's all right," I said. I felt bad for Dad. He had just been trying to help, but I could tell that Jacob was still pretty angry about what had happened when he was on our team. "Jacob, we were just at a meeting over at Pizza Hut. Everybody on the team was there and we talked a lot about you. Everyone knows how you hustle. Wee Willie said that when you were with us, nobody worked harder in our drills."

"Wee Willie said that?" Jacob seemed genuinely surprised.

"Yes, he did."

"Huh. I didn't think anybody even noticed."

"We all noticed," I said, honestly. "By the way, I think that you have a really good glove. It's good enough that you could play second base for us."

I felt Dad look at me, but he didn't say anything.

"But isn't second base your position, Ryne?" Jacob asked, like he was surprised.

I nodded. "Yeah. I've played second the whole season, but since we lost Miggy, somebody is going to have to move over to shortstop now."

"You lost Miggy? Did he get hurt?"

"No," I answered. "We just found out tonight that Miggy and Coach Ramirez quit the team."

"Wow," Jacob said. "They quit?" He glanced over at his mother, his eyes wide like he couldn't believe it. He looked back at me. "So now you're going to have to move to shortstop?"

I shrugged my shoulders. "I'm going to talk to Coach Weaver at practice about it."

I could see that Jacob was thinking, hard. He started rubbing his bony knees.

I felt I needed to tell Jacob something important. "Hey, Jacob?"

He looked up at me.

"We're not the same team we were when you were with us at the start of the season. We're different now," I said.

"What do you mean?" Jacob asked.

I looked over at Ms. Dickey, and then at Dad. "It's kind of a team thing," I said. "I can tell you more about it later. I just want you to know that it wouldn't be like it was at the beginning of the season."

Everyone was quiet for a moment.

"Can I think about it for a while?" Jacob asked his mom.

She turned the question over to me. "Can he Ryne? Or do you have to know tonight?"

"That would be okay," I said. "We have practice tomorrow at seven."

"You said there are only eight players on the team now?" Ms. Dickey asked Dad.

"That's right," Dad said. "A complete team is nine."

"So if Jacob doesn't play, what are you going to do?"

Dad explained. "Well, under the rules, they can still play. If they had only seven, they would be forced to forfeit. But you can play with eight. When the Intimidators are in the field, they'll have to play with only two outfielders. When they're batting, they will be given an automatic out whenever they reach the ninth spot in the order."

"Well, it sounds like you really need him to play then," Ms. Dickey said, turning to me.

"Yes, ma'am," I answered honestly. "But…" I stopped.

"But what?" she asked.

What I had to say was important, but I wasn't quite sure how to say it.

"What is it?" Jacob asked, anxiously. He started pulling at a string on his shorts.

I rubbed my hands on my legs. They were sweaty. "The team—all the guy—we just really want you to come back, okay? And it's not just because we need another player," I said, honestly. "We want you to play with us. There's a spot for you, but it isn't just because Miggy is gone and we only have eight players."

I fumbled around, trying to find the words. "We really are different, Jacob. Now with Miggy and Coach Ramirez gone, we'll be even more different." I was frustrated. I couldn't seem to say what I wanted to say, other than we were somehow magically different. What did that even mean? "The spot on the team was already yours," I explained. "So it's kind of just been sitting there, waiting for you to come back. Do you know what I mean?"

"I didn't want to quit, you know," Jacob said, defensively.

"I know," Ms. Dickey interrupted. "I know you didn't want to quit." She turned to us with tears in her eyes. "I didn't tell Jacob the truth. I told him he was going to have to quit the team because I didn't have enough money for him to keep playing."

Jacob looked shocked. "What do you mean?"

"Your mom was put in a terrible position by Coach Ramirez," Dad answered as Ms. Dickey began to sob. "He told your mother that you weren't fitting in on the team."

"Why would he do that?" Jacob said, not understanding.

232

I knew Dad would have a hard time saying the truth because he would be afraid of embarrassing Jacob, so I answered for him. "Probably because he didn't think you were good enough to play with us."

Jacob's face pinched. He looked hurt.

"But he was wrong, Jacob," I quickly added. "You are good enough. Every guy on the team - Hootie, Jimmy, Sammy, Wee Willie, Chase, Brazos, Curtis, and me - we all believe it."

"You should play, Jake," Daniel said from the staircase. It was the first time I'd heard anyone call him Jake. He came over to his mother and placed his hand gently on her shoulder while she continued to cry. She reached up and patted him. "That coach sounds like he was a real dirt bag. If he's gone now? Well, these guys need you," Daniel said, lifting his head toward me. "Plus, it sounds like they really want you on the team."

Jacob's eyes had darkened. He looked confused.

"I promise, Jacob," I said, hoping he would believe me. "Everybody on the team wants you to play with us."

Ms. Dickey wiped at her tears with a couple of fingers. "I tell you what," she said, snuffling a little bit. "Let's sleep on it tonight. Jacob can call you and let you know in the morning. I think that's a good idea, don't you Jacob?"

Jacob watched his mother as she spoke. When he answered her, his voice sounded very small. "It's okay, Mom. You didn't do anything wrong."

Ms. Dickey smiled. Her eyes were shining with tears. "Let's talk about it and you can call Ryne tomorrow, okay?"

Jacob nodded.

"That's all we can ask," Dad said as he stood up. We could both tell it was time for us to go. "We'll get out of your hair and give you some family time to talk. Thank you so much for having us over at the last minute, Lisa. Ryne and I really appreciate your hospitality." He reached over and shook Daniel's hand, and then he walked over and shook Jacob's, too. I followed him, shaking Daniel's hand first. When I got over to Jacob, I held out my fist. He looked up at me and bumped it. "Thanks, Ryne," he said. He even smiled a little.

"Sure, Jacob. I'll talk to you tomorrow."

Ms. Dickey got up and followed us to the door. As we stepped out onto the porch, she reached out and touched my arm. "Ryne, I just want to thank you for coming by today. No matter what Jacob decides, I know that it meant a lot to him." She was struggling not to let anymore tears fall.

"Yes, ma'am," I said. Dad put his hand on my shoulder.

She smiled. "And it meant a lot to me, too," she added.

She and Dad said their goodbyes and we left.

* * *

Shaun

On the ride home, Ryne was quiet. He stared out the window, lost in thought as the world sped by.

"I didn't remember Ms. Dickey until I saw her again," I said, breaking the silence. "I don't think I ever saw her at the practices at the beginning of the season."

Ryne remained motionless as he gazed out the window.

"She really appreciated the way you spoke to Jacob," I continued. "It was a good idea for you to reach out to him."

Ryne stirred. "Why would Coach Ramirez do that to a kid?" he asked.

I exhaled heavily. "Heck, Ryne. I would imagine that what you told Jacob was probably the correct answer. He probably decided he wasn't good enough to be on his team."

"It's not his team," Ryne said, simply. "It's ours."

I smiled at the modest perfection of his statement. It was absolutely true.

"You're right, son, but there probably aren't a lot of coaches out there who see it that way."

Ryne lapsed back into silence for a while. I didn't push the conversation. I figured if he wanted to talk, he would. After a few minutes, he turned away from the window.

"I wonder if he did the same thing to Mano."

I thought about that for a moment. I was still struggling myself with the surprising truth that Lisa Dickey had revealed about how Coach Ramirez had torpedoed her son off the team. Could he have done the same thing to Mano, a player who was probably the most talented kid any of us had ever seen? If he had, was he really so selfishly motivated that he could have potentially torpedoed the Intimidators' chance at a championship?

"I don't know, Ryne, but I'd like to find out."

Ryne looked over at me. "Do you think that maybe you could, Dad? Do you think you could find out if Mano really did go back to Hawai'i?"

"I can try," I said, trying to think of how I could track him down. My mind went back to Coach Weaver's announcement at Pizza Hut. "I can call Ramirez. Honestly, I would kind of like to find out more about this Lone Star Elite outfit they're joining, anyway."

"Why don't you drive over to his house and talk to him?" Ryne asked. He smiled at me.

"Ah, I see what you did there," I said, recognizing that he'd just bounced my own advice to talk to Jake in person right back at me. I grinned and pointed my finger at him. "Good point."

"I guess it's better to have some conversations in person that it is to have them over the phone, huh?" Ryne said.

"It is," I agreed.

"That's why you took me to Jacob's house wasn't it, Dad?"

"I knew the conversation was important for you and that you needed to look Jacob in the eye when you had it," I said. "But honestly Ryne, I never dreamed things would have gone the way they did. I don't know if things would have gone the same way if you'd just called him on the phone."

We turned onto our street. The summer sun was finally giving up on the day and beginning to slip below the horizon.

"Ryne, did you watch the whole special on Baseball World, or did you turn it off after the stuff on Miggy?" I asked.

Ryne shrugged a little. "I actually stopped watching when the Commissioner started speaking," he said. "It was starting to get boring. Why?"

"I think that's probably what everybody did," I said. "Because not one of the parents said anything about the two surprises at the end."

Ryne's eyes widened. "What surprises?"

I whipped into the driveway and shut off the engine. In the backyard, I could see Samantha and one of her friends racing up the steps to her 'Fortress of Solitude'. Hope was following them, taking the staircase at a more leisurely, adult pace. I turned to Ryne.

"When the Commissioner finished speaking, the owners of Baseball World talked about the current playoff series. Your division is one of four different groups from ages eight to fourteen that are playing for a

236

championship against teams from across the state. Each bracket was originally made up of eight teams who qualified based on their regular season performance. It's a new setup that's very different from most tournament formats."

Ryne nodded. "Yeah, I know. I think it's been kind of cool. The three game series feels more like real baseball."

"I agree," I said. "But at the very end of the Baseball World special, one of the owners said that something even better was coming. He promised that it was going to change the world of youth baseball forever."

"What was it?"

"Well, there weren't any specifics. He said that an announcement would be coming soon."

"Huh. Do you think that has anything to do with why Miggy left?"

"Actually, I do," I said. "I found out that Coach Ramirez went to college with one of the Baseball World owners, so I think he has the inside track on whatever the new format is going to be. I'm betting that Lone Star Elite outfit that Coach Weaver mentioned tonight is involved. In fact, I saw Coach Ramirez talking to a Baseball World owner and a guy from Lone Star Elite at the game on Sunday."

Ryne thought about that for a moment. "Do you think they were recruiting Miggy?" He asked.

"I do."

"So what was the second surprise?"

"That one was mysterious, too," I ventured. "But the Commissioner of MLB said that the winner of the twelve year old division would be part of something extraordinary for the Labor Day weekend. They are planning on announcing it after the championship series."

"What do you think it is?" Ryne asked eagerly.

"I have no idea. I'm sure they're purposefully creating a little mystery to generate excitement and keep people following the plans for the theme park. But I think it's got to be part of whatever ongoing promotional campaign they have in mind for Baseball World. That theme park is a huge deal so I imagine they have one heck of an advertising and marketing budget planned to give it the best possible exposure as they move into the construction phase." I could see the wheels turning in Ryne's mind as he wondered what the surprise could be.

In the backyard, Hope stepped back out onto the small porch at the front of Samantha's treehouse. She saw us and waved.

"C'mon. We'd better get inside," I said.

"Hey, Dad?"

I was already half-way out of the car. I stopped and turned back around.

"Thanks for taking me to see Jacob."

I smiled at him. "I'm proud of you, Ryne. I can see your team is looking to you as a leader. It took courage for you to go see him. I imagine it's going to take some more courage to move to shortstop."

"I haven't played shortstop since I was eight," he answered. I could tell he was already a little nervous about the prospect. "But somebody has to step up, and it probably makes more sense to move me than it does to take Hootie off the hot corner."

"I agree," I said. "It'll be a big day at practice tomorrow for a lot of reasons."

"Yeah," Ryne said as he opened his door. He looked at me once more before he stepped out. "I just hope Jacob says yes."

* * *

Dear Madison,

I hope you don't have any trouble reading this. I wrote a letter to my Grandma once and she told me it looked like it had been scratched out by a left-handed chicken, whatever that's supposed to mean. My Grandma is great but she has no problem letting you know when you stink at something. Once she came to one of my games when I didn't get a single hit. She told me after the game that I hit like a left-handed chicken, too.

I hope your Grandma is doing okay. I've never been to Colorado, but that's because my mom doesn't really like snow too much. We used to live in Chicago when I was little. She told me that snow looks great on a Christmas card but it doesn't look so good on the end of a shovel when your feet are freezing inside your shoes like a couple of popsicles. I think she used to have to shovel snow a lot.

Anyway, I'm going to give this letter to Katie so she can give it to you. Oh yeah, one more thing. I did see the Intimidators jersey you bought. It's cool. And it's okay if you want to put my number on the back of it.

Also, I'm really glad you have been coming to our games this season. I hope you can come this weekend since we are going to the semi-finals. I don't know if this will sound stupid, but I think I play a little better when you are in the stands.

I hope I will see you at practice this week.

Talk to you later,

Ryne

*   *   *

Ryne

Coach Weaver gathered us at the pitching mound before practice started. It was about 6:55. I kept checking the parking lot over his shoulder as he talked.

"Gentlemen, I had planned on running a little competition tonight to see who might be able to fill the hole we have at shortstop," he said. "But Ryne came and talked to me a few minutes ago. He has volunteered for the job."

Wee Willie and Brazos reached over and punched my arms with their gloves. The other guys tightened up around me in the huddle and pushed their gloves at me to show their support, too.

Hootie was standing next to Coach Weaver. "Thanks, Ryne," he said, sincerely. He looked relieved.

"Of course, that creates another hole for us," Coach Weaver continued, "which means we'll need to find a new second sacker."

Just then, I saw a white car pull to the curb. The door opened and Jacob popped out with his bat bag. He started running toward the field, his pants flapping against his skinny legs.

"He's here, Coach," I said.

Coach Weaver turned around as Jacob ran into the dugout. He unzipped his bag and pulled out his glove. He tore out of the doorway to the field and began running toward us.

"I told you he hustles," Wee Willie pointed out to all of us.

Curtis and Jimmy stepped back, creating an opening in our huddle as Jacob came toward us. As soon as he arrived, Wee Willie reached out with his glove to welcome him. "Hey, Jacob!"

Jacob smiled. His eyes were bright. He looked really happy. "Hey, Wee Willie."

Immediately, everybody stepped toward him with their gloves raised. One by one, everyone touched their mitt to his. I was last. I had a pretty big smile on my face.

Coach Weaver made a fist and held it out to Jacob. Jacob knocked it with his glove. "Welcome back, Jacob," he said.

Jacob grinned. "Thanks, Coach."

I looked up at Coach Weaver. He had a warm expression on his face. I knew that Dad had called him and told him the whole story. Coach Weaver now knew that Jacob hadn't actually quit our team at the beginning of the summer, but that he'd been forced out by Coach Ramirez.

"Intimidators, I need to say something" he said. "But I'm only going to say it once and then we'll never talk about it again." He looked over at Jacob.

"I want it to be clear to each of you that Jacob Dickey never quit this team. Sometimes in life, things happen that are beyond our control. As kids, you probably know that better than most adults because so much of your life is beyond your control. When these things happen, well…it seems unfair. The reason it seems that way," he paused, jabbing with his finger toward the ground, "is because it usually is unfair. But we can't control what happens to us. It doesn't matter if you're a kid or you're an adult, you can't control your circumstances. Jacob left this team because of something that was beyond his control. Now he's back with us."

Coach Weaver bent down deeper into the huddle and lowered his voice. He looked directly at Jacob. "Jacob, you are here today because your teammates made a decision to do what was right. It was their decision to ask you to come back. And, since I'm the coach of this team now, I just want to say one thing to you and to them. I'm very glad they did." He held out his hand, this time with it open. Jacob took it and they shook.

"Now we've got a practice to run. As I was saying, we have to find ourselves a new second baseman." He looked over at Jacob again, and then gestured toward me. "Ryne seems to think you can soak up some ground balls at second, Jacob. What do you say? Want to run some drills with the infield?"

Jacob nodded. His eyes were serious. "Yes sir, Coach."

"Alright then. Let's break out into groups. Give me Brazos, Jacob, Ryne, and Hootie. The rest of you guys head over to the cage. Mr. Gibson, Hootie's dad, is going to join our team as our new assistant coach. He can pitch and he's a southpaw, so you're going to get some good practice hitting off a lefty. He's waiting for you over there. Now let's get moving. We've got an hour and a half tonight, so let's make the most of it."

We broke from our huddle. After we'd spent about ten minutes warming our arms, we took the infield. Brazos went to first and Hootie went to third, while Jacob and I took our places up the middle. Coach Weaver began by hitting us some straightforward ground balls and having us make the play at first. Hootie and I both scooped our first chances and made our throws. I'd thought it would feel strange to throw from shortstop, but it didn't. I just came up and fired the ball harder than I normally would. Brazos didn't even have to move. The ball smacked solidly into his glove.

When it was time for Jacob to take his first ball at second base, I have to admit that I was nervous for him. Coach Weaver didn't hit him a baby stroller, either. He smacked one hard right at him.

Jacob moved into a solid fielding position. The ball scooted over the edge of the infield grass toward him. He dropped his mitt into the dirt. His head followed the fast moving grounder as it approached his glove.

Then the ball hit something. A pebble, a stick, or maybe a worm who decided to pop his head up at just the right time. I don't know what it was, but the ball jumped up and busted him hard in his bony shoulder before it tried to run away from him into right field.

Jacob hustled after it, snatched the ball with his bare hand before it could reach the outfield grass, turned and fired a neat pistol shot right into the heart of Brazos' glove. There wasn't a runner of course, but in my mind I saw one; and Jacob got him by a step.

The ball had hit him hard, but Jacob never even reached up to rub his shoulder. He just ran immediately back to his spot at second.

"Excellent play on a bad hop, Jake!" Coach Weaver bellowed at him across the field. Hootie and I banged our hands against our gloves and whooped. Brazos pointed at him and pumped his fist. From that moment on, our new second baseman began to go by that shortened, tougher version of his name that I'd heard his brother call him.

He became just plain ol', tough as nails, Jake Dickey.

*　*　*

At the end of practice, I stuffed my glove, my batting helmet, and my bat into my bat bag. I took a long drink of water from my bottle to wash the infield dirt out of my throat. Even though the bottle is insulated, the water gets warm if I don't drink it fast enough. I swished a mouthful around and spit it through the fence.

Chase came up next to me and began packing his catcher's gear into the giant gold bag he carries. It's huge and has wheels on it that look like tractor tires. On the panels and down the back it screams NO ERRORS in big block letters.

"I don't know where Katie and Madison are," he said under his breath to me. "I didn't see them the whole practice."

"Yeah? I wonder where they were." I said, trying to act like I'd just noticed they weren't there. Actually, I had checked the stands every couple of minutes during practice. I hadn't given up on them coming until the very end, but I didn't want Chase to know that.

"Dad always drops me at practice on his way to the gym and Mom takes Katie and they pick up Madison. Then they come and watch, and we take Madison back home after practice is over. That's been the routine the whole summer."

"Where's your mom?" I asked.

Chase shrugged. "I don't know. Neither one of my parents is here."

Coach Weaver walked over to us. The rest of the team was already packed up and headed to their cars. I could see Dad over in the parking lot. He was standing next to our Suburban talking to Hootie's dad.

"Hey guys," Coach Weaver began. "Great practice tonight."

"Thanks, Coach," we both answered together.

"Hey Chase, do you mind if I talk to Ryne a minute?" Coach Weaver asked.

"Sure," Chase answered. He zipped up his giant bag and lifted it off the bench. He rolled it out of the end of the dugout and headed up the hill to wait for his parents.

Coach Weaver and I sat down on the bench.

"So, how do you feel at shortstop?" Coach asked me.

"A little rusty," I said, being honest. "But it didn't feel as weird as I thought it would."

"Well, when you've spent so much time on the right side of the infield, it's got to feel a little different when you switch to the left."

"Yeah. I did feel a little bit like a left-handed chicken." The words came out of my mouth before I even realized it.

"A left-handed chicken?" Coach Weaver repeated, laughing. "Where did you get that from?"

"It's something my Grandma says," I said, laughing too. I'd been thinking about the letter I'd written to Madison throughout practice.

Coach Weaver took off his hat and scratched his head. "Ryne, I just wanted to say thank you for stepping up and making the move to shortstop. I know Hootie didn't want to leave third. Even though I was going to open it up to the team, I felt deep down that it had to be either you or Hootie who would fill the hole. I honestly don't think Hootie wanted the job."

"Nah. Hootie loves third. Everybody knows that," I insisted. "It's his spot."

"Jake looked really good at second tonight," Coach Weaver added, sounding surprised. "He's got a little pop in that arm of his. I didn't remember that from the practices at the beginning of the season. And the kid really does hustle, doesn't he? He ran to every drill."

I smiled. "I'm glad he came back."

I suddenly heard Chase's voice from behind us. "He's over there with Coach Weaver."

I turned around and saw Chase's mother coming down the grassy hill toward the dugout. I could tell by the look on her face something was wrong.

"Hey, Jennifer!" Coach Weaver called out to her in a friendly voice.

Mrs. Girardi barely cracked a smile. "Hi, John," she said. Rarely did any of the parents use Coach Weaver's first name. Coach Weaver picked up on the tension, too.

"Is something wrong?" he asked.

Mrs. Girardi walked into the dugout. She came down to us. "One of Katie's friends received some bad news today."

I felt the bats take off in my stomach. Mrs. Girardi looked right at me.

"Madison McMannis' grandmother passed away."

"Oh. I'm very sorry to hear that," Coach Weaver replied. "Madison is the one who comes to practice all the time with Katie, right?"

"Yes, that's her," Mrs. Girardi answered, still looking at me.

"But I thought Katie said she was doing a lot better?" I asked, feeling the bats swirling in my stomach.

Mrs. Girardi's eyes were wet like she'd been crying a lot. "They thought she was, sweetie," she said to me, like I was a little kid. "So they flew home this morning and then they got a call just a few hours ago that said she had suddenly died. The entire family is just devastated, especially poor Madison. She was very close to her grandmother."

Mrs. Girardi turned back to Coach Weaver. "Madison's mom is a very close friend of mine," she told him as a tear escaped from one of her eyes and began rolling down her cheek. "Katie and I have been over at their house during practice. We were going to pick up Madison and bring her tonight, but they had just received the phone call right before we arrived."

Coach Weaver stood up. "I'm very sorry, Jennifer," he said, sincerely. He reached out and warmly patted Mrs. Girardi's shoulder. More tears fell from her eyes.

"Ryne, the McMannis family is flying back to Denver tomorrow morning," she snuffled, turning back to me. "I left Katie over there tonight to comfort Madison. She and I are going to go with the family tomorrow to Denver. We'll stay for the funeral and then come back. I don't know when that will be yet." She reached into her pocket. "Madison asked me to give this to you," she said. Her hand was trembling as she handed me a small, lemon-colored envelope.

"Oh... uh, thank you," I said, feeling a little embarrassed in front of her and Coach Weaver.

"You might want to call Madison in a day or so," she boldly said to me, wiping at her tears. "You know - just to check on her. I'm sure your mom and dad won't mind."

I nodded nervously. The bats in my stomach were doing barrel rolls.

Coach Weaver looked down at me sympathetically. "Oh, is Madison your girlfriend, Ryne?"

My face immediately began to burn. I couldn't even answer. I just looked up at him and quickly dropped my head, rolling my shoulders.

"Well, I'm sorry, but I have to go," Mrs. Girardi said. "I've got to get Chase home and start packing." She turned and started walking out of the dugout. Coach Weaver followed her saying, "Janice and I will be glad to help with Chase while you're gone, Jennifer. We can help get him to practice. Let us know how we can help."

I heard Mrs. Girardi thank him as they began walking up the hill.

I just sat in the dugout by myself. I held the letter from Madison in my hand. On the front in big, happy purple letters it said,

Ryne

I got up, picked up my bat bag, and walked out of the dugout. I could see Dad in the parking lot, still talking to Mr. Gibson. As I walked toward them, a strange mood came over me. It was weird, but for some reason I couldn't explain, I suddenly felt very...

Alone.

Shaun

When I pulled up in front of Coach Ramirez's house, I rolled down the windows and shut off the engine. I just sat there for a minute considering what I was about to do. The next day, the Intimidators' semi-final series was scheduled to begin. With Jake Dickey's return, our team would field a complete nine-player squad. At practice during the week, I'd noted that every parent had been relieved, even if there was some remaining uncertainty about Jake's playing ability. However, the mystery about Mano's disappearance remained unsolved. Ryne had asked me to try and find out if the team's brightest star had really gone back to Hawai'i, and I had promised him I would try.

Even though it was August—the time of year when grass in Texas will turn to dust unless it is consistently watered—the lawn in front of the Ramirez's two-story home was perfect. It was neatly trimmed like the surface of a well-maintained putting green. As I stepped out of my truck, the lawn had a pleasant, just-been-mowed smell. I walked up a winding sidewalk that was lined with two rows of solar-powered path lights to a massive front door. Through the decorative glass panels, I could see shapes moving around inside. I swallowed hard and rang the doorbell.

Immediately, I could see a smaller shape run rapidly toward me. There was a click and the big, heavy door swung open. Standing in front of me, dressed in a pair of bright red, Spider-man swim trunks, was Alfonso.

"Hi, Mr. Dunston!" he said excitedly, as if he was really happy to see me.

"Hey there, Alfonso!" I returned, trying to match his enthusiasm. Before I could say another word, he peeked around me in the direction of my truck.

"Did you bring Samantha with you?" he asked, hopefully.

"Actually, she's at home with her mom," I regretfully informed him.

"Ah... bummer," he replied, clearly disappointed. "I was just about to go swimming."

"Are your parents here?" I had gambled on showing up without calling first.

Alfonso nodded. "Mom is, but Dad and Miggy are gone."

"Oh," I said, disappointed that I had spun the wheel of fortune and lost. Just then, Ana Ramirez appeared at the end of the long hallway that led from the front door into the interior of the house.

"Who is it, Alfonso?" she asked.

I gave her a friendly wave. "It's me, Shaun Dunston," I answered for him. I added for clarification, "Ryne and Samantha's dad."

"Well, hi there!" Ana said cheerfully as she moved down the long hallway toward us. "It's good to see you." Her voice sounded pleasant, but as she reached the doorway I could see in her face a tinge of uneasiness. "Won't you come in?" she offered.

I hesitated. Since Coach Ramirez wasn't home, I figured there wasn't really any point in staying. However, I didn't want to appear rude.

"Thank you," I answered, stepping inside.

"Alfonso was just about to go swimming and I was going to sit outside and watch him for a bit. We can visit out by the pool, if that's okay with you?"

"Uh, sure," I answered, following her while Alfonso skipped ahead of us down the long hallway. As we walked, I glanced around me. The home was rustic, decorated in the familiar style that was popular in our neighborhood: pine furniture, limestone accents, cowboy portraits, and the mandatory large, metal lone star which insisted on having an entire wall all to itself. As we passed the living room, I saw an impressively-sized Texas state flag pressed into a frame above a large limestone fireplace. A huge pair of longhorns was mounted to the mantle beneath it. Across a landscape of plush leather furniture, I could hear George Strait softly crooning in his familiar country twang about his efforts to get to Amarillo by morning. The Ramirez home said *Texas,* and it said it proudly.

"Your home is beautiful," I mentioned to Ana, as we stepped out the backdoor. "Clearly, Coach Ramirez is one heck of a decorator."

She turned around and laughed at my obvious joke. "That man can barely decorate his own body with clothes. He won't admit it, but I am positive he is color blind. I think that's why he always wears khaki pants. He thinks everything goes with khaki."

"You mean it doesn't?" I said. I looked down at the dark green golf shirt I was wearing. Suddenly I was worried that it didn't match my own khaki pants as well as I'd thought.

Ana smiled mischievously as we sat down at a glass outdoor table next to the pool. "I'll let your wife answer that question for you!"

Alfonso skipped merrily over to the diving board. "Hey, Mr. Dunston, watch this!" He took off, planted his feet solidly at the end of the board and sprung forward, executing a perfect flip into the pool. When he broke the surface of the water, I immediately applauded for him.

251

"Wow! That was impressive, Alfonso!" I exclaimed. "You should think about the Olympics!"

He swam quickly over to the side of the pool, clambered out, and raced back to the board. He made certain I was watching, and then took off again. This time when he hit the end of the board, he bounced high into the air and opened his arms like an eagle's wings. He soared gracefully through the air and brought his thin limbs back together at exactly the right time in a straight line above his head. His narrow body split the water like a knife. I turned back to his mother.

"He's really good!" I complimented her. "I mean, he's really, really good."

Ana nodded. "Alfonso is a natural athlete at just about every sport he's tried, except baseball." She made a face. "Of course, that drives his father crazy."

Alfonso swam the length of the pool after his dive. His stroke was powerful.

"When we adopted Alfonso, I think Miguel thought that he would automatically love the game since he was native to the Dominican Republic." She shook her head. "I guess he thinks every male from the Dominican Republic is born to play baseball."

"Kind of like he thinks everything matches khaki?" I joked.

This time, she didn't laugh. Her eyebrows squeezed together. It was like a sudden storm had come upon her face. "My husband takes baseball too seriously. Much too seriously," she said, sternly. She checked Alfonso. At the far end of the pool he'd found a diving mask and a snorkel. He was busy adjusting the strap to fit his head.

"That's why you came tonight, isn't it?" she said, turning her attention back to me. "You wanted to discuss Miguel's recent poor decisions."

Her blunt honesty caught me off guard. "Actually, I was hoping he might settle the mystery of what happened with Mano."

She suddenly looked uncomfortable.

"Yes. I guess that's where all of this began, isn't it? With that sweet Hawai'ian boy."

I looked at her blankly. I wasn't sure where she was going.

"You know, I was there when he hit his first homerun," she professed, like it was a privilege to have witnessed the feat. "You know, the one that landed on top of the concession stand in the first game?"

"Oh. I remember. But the ump said that one was foul..."

"It wasn't foul," Ana Ramirez interrupted me. Her speech was sharp with conviction. "I saw it. It was most certainly a homerun." She lowered her voice and leaned toward me. "You know Alfonso has that ball," she whispered. "He keeps it in his room in a special place that only he and I know."

I pursed my lips thoughtfully. "He hides it?"

"Oh, yes," she answered, as if I must already know the reason. "If Miguel knew he had it, he would have made him get rid of it."

"That seems a little strange," I opined. "Why would he do that?"

She gave me an exasperated look, as if I hadn't been paying attention. "Miguel takes baseball *much* too seriously," she emphasized, in case I hadn't heard her the first time. "And he has become simply ridiculous about Miggy's baseball future. He is very jealous of protecting his and Miggy's perception that our son is the best."

I suddenly felt as if we were straying into dangerous territory. I had intended to talk directly to Coach Ramirez and simply ask him about Mano. But I couldn't find a way to back out of the conversation with Ana, so I pressed onward.

"Are you saying Coach Ramirez felt threatened by Mano?"

She raised her eyes at me. "Of course! Anyone could see that boy was an amazingly gifted baseball player. Listen," she said, her eyes narrowing. "I don't care if you are watching a world class violinist play a concert, an actor giving an Academy award winning performance in a movie, or an athlete winning an Olympic gold medal - it simply doesn't matter. When you see someone who is head and shoulders above everyone else in their field, you know it."

"He was absolutely amazing to watch," I agreed. "But there was something else about him, too—something truly special. The team really responded to his presence."

I watched Ana become uncomfortable again. Once more, I saw a look come across her face. She appeared almost guilty.

I shifted in my seat as Alfonso explored the pool with his mask and snorkel behind us. "Ana, what happened with Mano? Do you know? Did he really go back to Hawai'i?" I asked.

Coach Ramirez's wife nodded. "Yes, he and his father went back home to Molokai. Mano's father—his name was Kekoa, I believe—called here one night and spoke with Miguel. He told him they must go back to Hawai'i immediately, but Miguel said he didn't say why." She checked on her son again. His head remained submerged as he surveyed the bottom of the pool. "Alfonso was devastated."

"But Miguel and Miggy, not so much?" I ventured.

She shook her head sadly. "No. I believe they were both glad that he was gone, and the competition between Mano and Miggy was over."

"Competition? What do you mean?"

Ana sighed. "It has been awful here for the last few months. After every practice and every game, Miguel ranted and raved at Miggy. He kept pushing him, telling him he wasn't playing well enough, that he expected more from him."

"But the team was playing so well," I reminded her. "They won sixteen games in a row."

"Yes. But that didn't please Miguel. In fact, nothing pleased him this season after Mano joined the team. He was angry all the time. The better that Mano played, the worse things were at home. They stayed that way until he got a phone call from one of his old college friends."

"One of the owners of Baseball World?" I guessed.

She looked at me, surprised. "So you know about that?"

"Jennifer Girardi told me that Coach Ramirez went to school with one of the owners."

Ana looked down at the table in front of her. "I wished he'd never received that phone call."

"Why is that?"

Ana Ramirez looked up at me. She was trembling. "Because that is when Miguel went completely mad." She looked over at Alfonso. He was happily exploring the pool. His mask-covered face was still focused on the pristine bottom, the snorkel cutting through the water above his small head as he searched and searched. When Ana turned back to me, her eyes were glassy with tears.

"To tell you the truth Shaun, I don't know if I can ever forgive my husband for what he has done."

Before I could ask her what she meant, the water thrashed behind us and Alfonso disappeared in a dive toward the bottom of the pool. In seconds, he returned, triumphant. He spit the snorkel out of his mouth and bawled, "I found it!! I found it!!"

Ana and I both hopped from our chairs and moved to the side of the pool to see. Alfonso held the treasure high in the air between his thumb and forefinger.

"What is it?" Ana asked.

Alfonso swam over to us. "Mano gave it to me. It must have fell out of my pocket when I was swimming last night. I thought I had lost it forever!"

He handed a tiny sphere to his mother. She held it up for us both to examine.

"It looks like an old marble," she speculated. She handed it to me. The ball felt solid in my palm. It had a few nicks in its surface.

"Feels like it's made of lead," I said.

"It's called a musky ball!" Alfonso proclaimed proudly. He climbed out of the pool and stood next to us. He pushed his mask up on top of his head. "Mano said it was very special, too. He said he wanted me to have it so I would always remember him. He gave it to me after the last game he played."

"What's a musky ball?" Ana asked me.

"I think he means *musket* ball. That's what it looks like, anyway. I've only seen them in museums."

"Yeah, musket ball," Alfonso confirmed. "That's it. Mano said they used to shoot them in wars out of long guns."

"It's a bullet?" Ana inquired.

I nodded. "I don't know much about the history of muskets, except what I remember from a tour of a Revolutionary War exhibit at the Bob Bullock Museum in Austin," I explained. "They existed for hundreds of years prior to the invention of guns with chambers to hold multiple rounds. A musket ball was hand packed down into the barrel of the gun along with a charge of powder. Then you had to pour some more powder back where the hammer of the weapon was located before it was ready to fire. It worked on the same principles as a cannon. In fact, I think they were even called hand cannons." I looked at Alfonso thinking that if he'd been given this present by Mano after the Intimidators' last regular season game, then Mano must have known then that he was leaving the team. "I wonder where Mano got this. It's a special treasure for him to give to you."

Cool water ran off Alfonso's smooth body and formed a puddle around his feet. He swiped his arm across his nose as he nodded his head in agreement. "I know. Mano said that someday soon I would understand why it was so special."

"Someday soon?" Ana repeated.

Alfonso just shrugged his dark, thin shoulders. "Can I have it back, please?"

I immediately handed it to him. He unzipped a pocket on his Spider-man swim trunks and pulled out a plastic insert designed to hold valuables. He placed the musket ball inside, sealed the pouch, and then placed it back in the pocket and zipped it safely shut, before hopping back into the pool.

"That's interesting," Ana remarked. "I wonder what Mano meant that 'someday soon' Alfonso would understand why that little ball would be considered special."

"I don't know," I said, absently. I was lost in thought. I suddenly remembered the day the Intimidators had played their second game of the season. It was the day Mano had hit his first amazing homerun into the swampy pond beyond centerfield to give the Intimidators a 5-5 tie against *The Phoenix*. I had stopped to take a picture of the scoreboard in centerfield, and I'd seen Mano's father in the parking lot with two men. They had laid something on the hood of the car that from a distance had looked like a map. On the side of their official looking vehicle it had said *Texas A*.... I hadn't given it too much thought at the time. But the musket ball, Mano's comment about how Alfonso would know someday soon understand how special it was, and the sudden return of our star right fielder to Hawai'i, suddenly had the wheels in my head spinning. Was there some sort of connection?

"Ana, I should probably go now," I announced. "Tomorrow is a big day for the Intimidators and I need to help Hope get some things ready." I didn't have a complete answer to the mystery of Mano's sudden disappearance from the team, but at least I now knew that his departure, unlike Jake Dickey's decision to leave the team, apparently had nothing to do with Coach Ramirez.

Ana looked at me with a serious expression. "Before you go, Shaun, I need to tell you something." She drew a deep breath as her eyes filled with tears. "I need to tell you what Miguel has done."

I looked at her uncertainly. I wasn't sure if she needed to tell me, but clearly she wanted to tell me. Her eyes were pleading. I could tell the weight she was carrying was more than she could bear.

I couldn't just leave. We walked back over to the table and sat down. I listened patiently as she unburdened herself and told me exactly what the Intimidators' former coach had done.

* * *

When I arrived at home later that evening, Hope was in the kitchen. She was just finishing the evening dishes. I immediately walked over, kissed her on the cheek, and picked up a towel to dry.

"Something still smells good," I said, sniffing the air.

"It's spaghetti. Your plate is in the oven." She smiled at me. "Don't worry about drying. Go ahead and eat, Buster."

I was starving so I didn't argue. I immediately walked over to the oven and pulled out the plate she'd prepared for me.

"Are the kids already in bed?" I asked.

"I just sent them to their rooms about fifteen minutes ago. They both moaned a little about having to go to bed early again on a Friday night." She dried her hands on a towel and followed me to the table.

"It's going to be scorching hot again tomorrow, so I told them they needed to store up their energy."

I shoved a huge bite of spaghetti in my mouth before I even sat down. A long string plastered itself to my chin and swung like a vine toward my golf shirt, dribbling sauce as it went.

"Oh, Shaun," Hope scolded. "You're as bad as the kids. Sit down before you get it all over the floor." She reached for my plate to hold it so I could slide out my chair.

I turned away from her, guarding my food like a dog. I growled playfully. "Stay back," I warned. "Hungry dogs bite."

She whacked my backside with her open hand and I yelped. "And bad dogs sleep in the garage." She leaned over and kissed my cheek as I laughed.

"I'm sorry, honey! You know how I love your spaghetti," I confessed. "And I'm sooo hungry."

We both sat down. Hope put her elbow on the table and propped her head in her open hand as she watched my jaws open wide to accommodate another shovelful of her finest Italian cuisine. "Impressive," she said, sarcastically praising my stuffing ability. "It's like I'm falling in love with you all over again."

My cheeks puffed out as I chewed. "What can I say?" I mumbled. "I'm irresistible when I eat."

"I'm not quite sure irresistible is the word you're going for there, Buster. What is the word?" She started snapping her fingers. "Oh, yes. Gross. That's it."

I smiled broadly and took an even bigger bite.

"Well, while you gorge yourself like a little piggy, I'll talk. That way you can chew and I won't have to see your food while you talk."

"*Guuf plin,*" I said. The words *good* and *plan* were muffled by the wad of spaghetti in my jowls.

"I bought Ryne a cell phone today," Hope said, stopping me in mid-chomp.

"*Wha...?*"

"Close your mouth. I told you, I don't want to see your food. Really Shaun, you're worse than the kids." She picked up a napkin and tidied the corners of my mouth while she continued. "We'd already talked about getting him one for his birthday next month. I just moved the timetable up a bit."

I looked at her suspiciously. However, I was still too hungry to deviate from my plate.

"I let him use it to call Madison in Colorado this afternoon. I think she needed to hear from him."

I furrowed my brow.

"I really think he needed to talk to her, too."

I wanted to speak, but Hope held up her hand. "Keep eating, Buster. I just realized I've got you right where I want you. This is actually working out well. I've often thought that I needed to tie you up and gag you before I needed to tell you something important. Turns out, it saves time by eliminating all of your '*but, but, but*' butting."

I frowned at her. I continued shoveling and chewing obediently.

"I got a call from Jennifer this morning. She said that Madison has been having a very difficult time with her grandmother's passing. Having Katie there has helped tremendously, but she felt it would really help if Ryne called her before the funeral tomorrow. I also thought that allowing them the ability to text one another might provide her some additional comfort."

I made a face, but didn't say anything. I just lifted my fork and pitched in another load.

"I know you think he's too young to have a girlfriend, Shaun, but we both know that Ryne is very mature for his age. He'll be twelve in less than a month. I remember someone telling me that you had your first girlfriend when you were ten! What was her name again?"

I stopped chewing for a moment, silently bemoaning my wife's private conversations with my mother. I repositioned the food and then, out of the corner of my mouth, I managed to carefully say, without spitting, "*Roxanne.*"

"Oh, yes! My predecessor! Dear, sweet, Roxanne," Hope twittered, sarcastically. "I believe you even exchanged bracelets, didn't you?"

I rolled my eyes. My mother clearly had no shame in telling all of my childhood secrets. I grumbled like an ogre and took another bite.

"But seriously, Shaun. Ryne was very appreciative. Jennifer gave me Madison's number and he programmed it into his new phone. Then he went out to his 'Fortress of Solitude' and called her. Of course, I had to encourage him a little bit because he was so shy about it," Hope confided. "But when he came back in about... oh, fifteen minutes or so later, I'm telling you, he looked better than he has all week."

I finished chewing. I swallowed.

"What does that mean?"

Hope's tone changed. She was very serious. "He's been carrying a lot, Shaun. We both know it. Ever since Mano left, he's taken on a leadership role for his team. Now Miggy and Coach Ramirez have left, too. But look at how he's responded to it! He's played so well! His play the other day was on ESPN for goodness sakes!" She proclaimed proudly. "But it's not just the way he's played that matters. Look at what he's done. He reached out to Jacob Dickey and brought him back to the team. He's stepped up and volunteered to move to

261

shortstop to replace Miggy. It's been a lot for him to handle, but he's handling it."

I held one last bite on my fork. "He has grown up more this summer than I could have imagined," I said, admiringly. "What did you mean when you said 'he looked better than he has all week'?"

Hope reached beneath the table and placed her hand on my knee. "I think Madison having to go back to Colorado for her grandmother's funeral shook him. On top of everything else he's been dealing with, she's suddenly disappeared from his life, too. He won't admit it, but I know he was really looking forward to seeing her at practice on Tuesday. By the time she gets back, it will have been over two weeks since he's seen her. At his age, that's forever and a day."

I chewed my last bite thoughtfully. My heart was slightly troubled at the thought of my son feeling a need for a female other than his mother at the tender age of almost twelve. I was also a little mystified that Hope seemed to have no problem with it. But at the same time, I also realized that, as usual, she was right. Ryne had been dealing with an awful lot in his world.

I swallowed. "I just don't know if I'm ready for a girlfriend," I muttered beneath my breath.

Hope squeezed my knee. "Well, you'd better not be, since you're already married." She smiled teasingly at me.

"He's in bed?" I said, gesturing toward the stairs.

"He's probably not asleep yet," she answered.

I pushed my chair back.

"Aren't you going to tell me what happened with Coach Ramirez?" she asked.

"Let me go tell the kids goodnight first. Then I'll meet you in our room."

Hope couldn't wait. "Is it bad, Shaun?"

I pursed my lips. "Let's just say it's predictable."

I turned and headed up the stairs.

* * *

Ryne

I was jittery on Friday night, more so than was usual before a game. It had been building all week, I guess. With Miggy and Coach Ramirez gone, Coach Weaver had tried to keep everything as normal as possible for the team, making sure we kept our regular practice schedule, including our Thursday night meeting at The Hitting Wheel, but everything felt far from normal for me.

Jake had practiced hard at second base and was looking surprisingly good after not playing the whole season. I was adjusting to shortstop, although I was struggling a bit with my footwork when covering the bag at second. Coach Weaver was right. After spending an entire season on the right side of the field, the switch to the left side did feel a bit awkward. He told me I probably wasn't going to get completely comfortable after just two practices, and to just slow down and relax. Coach Weaver also said I should think less and play more. He reminded me that no matter what, baseball was still a game and it was supposed to be fun. He'd even smiled when he said it. I couldn't remember Coach Ramirez ever saying anything like that to our team.

Still, no matter what Coach said to make me feel better, I felt like I was under a lot of pressure. The two biggest stars on our team were gone. Even if Sammy played well in right field—and I somehow managed to fill in for Miggy at shortstop—I had no idea if it would be enough for us to win. A double-header was scheduled for Saturday, just like for our quarter-finals series. The third game would be played on Sunday, if we split the two games on Saturday. It was without a doubt the biggest baseball weekend of my life, but I didn't know if I was really ready to play.

Mr. Blyleven had come to The Hitting Wheel on Thursday. He had pulled me aside and promised me that the project he was working on with our talismans would be completed in time and he would bring them to Baseball World on Saturday before our first game. I had no idea what he was doing, but I had to trust him. I was a little anxious about getting those talismans back in our hands before the game. With the way I was feeling, I wanted all of the extra help I could get. There was a knock at my door.

"Uh, yeah? I mean, come in."

The door opened. It was Dad.

"Hey, Slugger," he said. He walked over to my bed. I was stretched out with my hands behind my head. "You look more like you're deep in thought, instead of getting ready to go to sleep. Thinking about the games tomorrow?"

"A little bit," I said, sitting up. He rubbed the top of my head and sat down on the side of my bed.

"Are you ready?" he asked.

I smiled weakly. "I suppose so."

"You don't sound so sure."

I just shrugged.

"You okay, Ryne?"

"I'm alright," I said. "Just tired, I guess."

He gave me the look Mom gives me when she knows I'm not feeling well. "Is something troubling you?"

I looked down at the bed. "Do you ever feel alone, Dad?" The words surprised me. I hadn't planned on saying them. They had just jumped out of my mouth.

Dad was quiet for a moment. I looked up at him. His forehead was wrinkled like he was worried. He said, "Yeah. I actually used to feel that way a lot in college. It was hard being away from home that first year." He paused. "But I don't think that's the kind of alone you're talking about, is it?"

"I don't know," I said. It was the truth. I didn't know what I was feeling. I had just been feeling it a lot ever since I'd heard that Madison's grandmother had died.

Dad reached over and placed his hand on my leg and gave it a shake. "You're growing up, Ryne" he said. His eyes were suddenly a little watery. "You're just growing up."

"Why would growing up make me feel alone?" I asked. That didn't make any sense to me.

He smiled sadly. "The more you grow, the more you are bound to experience loss, son. You've been experiencing loss quite a bit over the last few weeks. That can make you feel very alone in the world, but it isn't just loss that makes you feel alone. Responsibility can make you feel that way, too."

I didn't understand. Dad could tell I didn't, just by looking at me.

"When other people look to you to lead them, you begin to realize that a lot is resting on your shoulders. You don't want to let them down, but you worry that you will. That can make you feel alone, too. You feel alone because you think it's all up to you, that if you don't do everything exactly right and things fall apart, it will mean you failed."

I didn't say anything for a while. Dad didn't either. He just sat there, like he was waiting.

"But I didn't start feeling this way until Mrs. Girardi told me that Madison's grandmother had died," I insisted. "Why would that make me feel alone?"

Dad smiled at me patiently. "It's a little complicated. Actually, when you start adding in things you feel for girls, it gets really complicated." He took a deep breath. "Hey, you know how you can have a bad inning in baseball? First, somebody boots an easy ground ball. Then someone else makes a bad throw. The next play, there's a bad hop that's nobody's fault, and a run scores."

I nodded that I understood. Those kinds of innings drove me crazy.

"How does the team usually feel after that inning is over?"

"We're ticked," I said.

"Exactly. Then you come to the plate the next inning, and one of your best hitters who never strikes out, strikes out. Two batters later, you're suddenly back in the field because you went three up and three down. Before you know it, the game's over. You lost. Where did it all start?"

It was obvious to me. "It started with the error on the easy ground ball. Everything went bad after that."

"Did it?" Dad said. "Or did it actually start when the guy who made the error struck out the inning before? Suddenly he's distracted and not fully focused in the field. So he boots an easy ground ball."

"So it started when he struck out?"

"Maybe. Or maybe it started when he got to the field that day and found out he left his batting gloves at home."

"You're making it too complicated, Dad," I said, getting frustrated.

"I don't have to make it complicated, Ryne. Things get that way all by themselves." He repositioned himself on my bed. "The point is this: you might think that you started feeling alone when you heard about Madison's grandmother, but there has been so much else going on in your life recently—Mano leaving, Miggy and Coach Ramirez leaving, the leadership role you've been taking on with your team—that when you heard the bad news, it was enough to finally bring that feeling of loneliness to the surface."

I thought about that for a moment. It actually made sense.

"I heard you got a phone today."

I reached over and picked my new gadget off the nightstand and I handed it to him. "Mom gave it to me."

Dad nodded. He looked the device over. "Nice. You called Madison, huh?"

I looked up at him. For some reason, I didn't feel embarrassed like I normally did when someone mentioned her. "Yeah. Mom thought it would be a good idea."

"Mom is usually right about those kinds of things. Is she doing okay?"

"She's pretty down," I said. "But she seemed really glad that I called. She even laughed once."

"Yeah?"

I snickered a little. "She asked me what it felt like being in the Top Ten on ESPN. I told her that Brazos said me and Hootie were acting like a couple of hairy warts about it."

Dad laughed out loud. "Yeah. I know neither one of you actually likes to be center stage." He slapped my leg and stood up. "Well, I'm glad you called her. Did it make you feel any better?"

I smiled. "Actually, it did."

He looked down at me, grinning. "You like her, huh?"

I shrugged. "Yeah. She's nice."

Dad turned and walked to my door. He turned around. I guess I must have had a funny look on my face because he asked me, "What is it?"

"You want to know something weird," I said. "I sort of feel like I play better whenever Madison's around."

Dad chuckled. "Wow. That's, uh... that's interesting. I don't think I would have ever expected you to say that."

"Why not?" I asked.

Dad shrugged. "That's the way I feel whenever your mom's around. I feel like whatever I'm doing, I somehow do it a little better when she's there." He looked at me from the door and for a moment, I kind of felt like a grownup.

"Hey, Ryne?"

"Yeah, Dad?"

He pointed his finger at me. "Don't grow up too fast, okay? Being a grownup isn't as great as it seems."

I thought I knew what he meant. "Did you talk to Coach Ramirez?"

"No, he wasn't there," he answered. "But I did manage to find out that Mano really did go back to Hawai'i, and it wasn't like the situation with Jake. Coach Ramirez had nothing to do with it."

"So you still don't know why he left?" I asked.

Dad shook his head. "No. I'm sorry."

"That's okay," I said. "Thanks for trying."

Dad opened the door and stepped into the hallway. But before he shut it, he poked his head back inside. "You know, Ryne, sometimes we don't get the answers we want. Other times we do get answers, but we just don't get them when we want them."

I looked at him, a little puzzled.

"Don't ask me why, son. But I just don't think any of us have heard the last of Mano," he said. He gave me a thumbs up. "Sleep tight."

He turned off the lights and shut the door.

I laid there in the dark, thinking. I didn't know what Dad meant, but I hoped he was right. I really hoped there was a chance I might someday see Mano again.

19

Ryne

The crowd at Baseball World was bigger than it had been the first weekend. We were forced to stand in a longer line at the entrance, and the first Press Box concession stand just inside the gate was already packed, even though it was only nine a.m. The amusement park was still two years away from being completed, but I figured a lot of people must have seen the Baseball World special on ESPN and had come to check it out. Everywhere I looked, kids and adults were already slurping rainbow-colored frozen drinks out of their giant Baseball World cups.

We rode the train just like the first weekend, only this time our games were scheduled on the American League side of Baseball World. The giant, airport-style television screen announced that we would be playing at 10:30 a.m. at the Globe Life Park in Arlington, the home of the Texas Rangers. It probably wasn't a coincidence that we drew that particular park, since the team we were facing actually was the Rangers.

The American League West was the last stop for our train. We piled out with several other families from younger teams bound for the other parks in the west. One of the Rangers' players traveled with us. His entire family was huge, and so was he. His uniform looked like it had been issued by the major leagues. He was wearing a red button up jersey, red cap with a white T on the crest, white pants, red socks, and black shoes. He also had thick red hair. When he got off the train, he stood next to me for a moment waiting for his brother to hand him his bat bag. I felt like a t-baller next to him. He was probably six inches taller than me and outweighed me by about eighty pounds or so.

His mom was wearing a red cowboy hat, a white western shirt, red jeans, and red boots. She had poofy hair and smelled strongly of hair spray and perfume. I know because I caught a good whiff when she walked past me. She was also clanging because she had a big cowbell in her hand. Mom got off behind her, rolling her eyes as she looked at me. I almost started to laugh. Samantha pulled on my jersey so I'd bend down to her ear.

"Is that a real cowgirl?" she asked.

"Nah. She's wearing way too much perfume to be a real cowgirl," I told her.

Mom bent over to my ear and whispered sarcastically, "I'm *sooo* looking forward to listening to that cowbell for four hours today."

Dad suddenly butted his head into our small huddle. "Did we make a wrong turn and end up at the rodeo?" We all watched as the Rangers family walked toward the stands, the bell making a single clang with each step she took. "Seriously? She's not going to ring that thing all day is she?" Dad asked. "This is a baseball complex! There aren't any cows here."

"Calm down," Mom said, squeezing his arm. Then she joked, "Maybe if cows start showing up when she rings it, somebody from Baseball World will ask her to stop. I'm sure they don't want fresh cow pies dropped all over their shiny new facility."

Samantha had worked her way into the middle of our huddle. She looked up at all three of us with her tiny face. "Will cows really come if she rings that bell, Mommy?"

"No, Sam. Mom was just kidding," Dad said. "No cows will come. A few goats might show up, though. But don't worry - they don't drop pies; just little chocolate covered raisins."

Samantha made a face. "Yuck, Daddy. You're gross."

"Really? I'm gross? You started the poop jokes, but I'm the one who's gross?" Dad complained to Mom as we started toward the stadium.

As we walked down the stairs behind home plate, I saw Coach Weaver in the outfield. Wee Willie, Curtis, and Sammy were with him. They were in left field moving toward center. I figured Coach was probably discussing how deep he wanted them to play. In the right field corner, I could see several of the Rangers were already stretching. The huge kid with red hair was jogging toward them while his family made their way to the bleachers behind third base, his mom clanging with each step.

I looked over toward the first base dugout and saw Chase. He was unloading his catcher's gear. Sitting in the first row of the stands directly behind the dugout was Mr. Blyleven. He stood up and waved to us immediately.

"Hey, there's Mr. Blyleven," I said, relieved that he'd made it.

We moved down the steps into the stadium toward him.

"Hello there, Dunston family," he said to us, cheerily. "Are you all ready for a big day?"

Dad reached out and shook his hand. "Yes sir, Mr. Blyleven. I know I'm ready."

Mr. Blyleven tipped his cap formally to Mom and Samantha. "Good to see you, ladies. You're both looking lovely this fine Saturday morning."

"Well, thank you, Mr. Blyleven," Mom said, while Samantha squirmed like she was embarrassed by the compliment.

He turned to me, smiling brightly. "How's the new shortstop doing?"

"I'm good," I said. Behind him on top of the dugout was a long cardboard box.

"Hey, Ryne. Do you think that we could speak for a moment, privately?" he asked.

"Sure," I answered. I sat down my bat bag. "I'll be right back," I said to Mom, Dad, and Samantha.

Mr. Blyleven picked up the long box and I followed him up the stairs. When we reached the top, we walked out of the stadium and found an empty picnic table underneath the big sun screens. No one was around it so we went over and sat down.

"So, how are you feeling today?" Mr. Blyleven asked.

"A little nervous, I guess," I said, honestly.

"That's normal," he assured me. "I've always felt that the only players who didn't get jitters before a big game were those who didn't care enough." He smiled and added, "Or they knew they weren't good enough to make a difference in the game, anyway."

I smiled politely.

"But that's not you, Ryne. I know you care and there's definitely no doubt that you make a difference every time you step on that field."

"Thanks, Mr. Blyleven," I said.

"I mean it, son," he continued. "You've got baseball in your blood. I can tell." He reached toward the long cardboard box and slid it over in front of him.

"I finished the little project for you and the team," he began. "You know, Ryne, baseball players have always had their little superstitions. Some refuse to change their socks when they're on a winning streak. Some eat the same exact food before every game. A lot of batters have silly routines they refuse to break before entering the batter's box. Remember when the Boston Red Sox grew those hideous, wooly beards they wore the whole season before they won the World Series?"

I nodded. "Oh, yeah. I remember. Some of those things were nasty."

Mr. Blyleven tugged at his handlebar mustache. "Mustaches, yes. Beards, no. They itch."

We both laughed.

"But all of those little superstitions are an important part of the fabric of the game, son," he insisted.

"Like when players avoid stepping on the foul line when they're walking on or off the field?" I asked.

"Exactly!" Mr. Blyleven agreed. "I actually have a good story about that one. During a game in high school, my coach was coming out of the dugout to visit me on the mound because I was having a pretty rough inning. I wasn't much focused, throwing a lot of balls, and any strike I did throw was getting a good lick put on it. So I was pretty sure he was coming to give me the hook before we got too far behind. I just didn't have my good stuff that day."

"Well, whenever Coach visited the mound during a game, he absolutely refused to step on the foul line. But I guess that day he must have been thinking pretty hard about his next pitching move because he totally forgot about his superstition. At the last minute, just as he saw he was about to step on the line, he swung his foot out of the way, kicked himself in the heel of his other foot, and did a barrel roll onto the grass in front of the entire stadium."

"Holy cow!" I said. "Did everybody laugh?"

"Are you kidding?" he said, rolling his eyes. "Most of the people in the stands thought he'd just had a heart attack. Of course, he immediately popped back up and just kept coming toward me like nothing had happened. When he got to the mound, first thing he said to me was, 'Did you see that?' I said, 'See what?' He looked at me real seriously and didn't say anything for a long time, but I never cracked a smile. He spit on my shoe and said, 'Alright. If you're disciplined enough to keep a straight face after that, then you can throw strikes. You just earned yourself another batter. Don't screw it up.' Then he turned around and went back to the dugout."

I slapped my hand on the table and laughed. "That's hilarious, Mr. Blyleven!"

He laughed enough that he had to wipe a tear from the corner of his eye. "That's baseball, Ryne. I have so many good memories of my teammates and coaches. You know, the best part of that story is that I struck out the next two batters and finished the inning. My coach's little tumble somehow did manage to reset my focus and calmed me down. I actually pitched great after that."

He looked down at the box in front of him and ran his hand along one of the edges. "Yeah, Baseball has it superstitions. I think, because baseball is in your blood, you know that. You *feel* it. That's why you made those talismans for your teammates." He smiled at me and for a moment, it sort of felt like he was my grandfather. "And that's why I had these made for you and the boys."

He opened the box. Inside was a row of hats. Mr. Blyleven reached in and pulled one out and handed it to me. It had a gold crown and a black brim. Matching black piping ran down each of the five seams and divided the crown into neat sections. The six eyelet holes around the crest were also black. On the front, a black letter *I* was embroidered in brushed script. They were sharp and looked as professional as any ball cap in the major leagues.

But it was the top of the hat that caught my attention. Every baseball cap has a button that sits on its peak. It's the place where the seams intersect. Normally, it wasn't something I would have noticed. Except these caps didn't have ordinary buttons. Instead of a normal, round little knob on top of the hat, these caps had small, black shark fins.

My mouth opened wide. "Holy cow, Mr. Blyleven!! These are so cool! Where did you get them?!!"

His smile just got bigger.

"One of my high school teammates owns a company that makes sports apparel for youth, high school, and college baseball teams. When I called and told him what I wanted to do, he asked me to fly out and meet him and his son—who is the CEO now—at their company's factory in Phoenix, Arizona. You know, I actually think it was cooler in the desert that it is here," He said, laughing. "Anyway, his son had already had his people design a prototype of the cap by the time I arrived yesterday. When I approved it, he interrupted his regular production run and made them on the spot. The shark fin buttons are done by hand, so that took a little extra time because he had to make sure they fit the dimensions of what you had done."

I looked at him not understanding.

"What do you mean?"

Mr. Blyleven reached over and touched the tip of the fin. It rose out of the top of the cap, like a shark breaking through the surface of a dark ocean. "Your talismans are inside each fin, Ryne. Take a closer look."

I pulled the cap closer. There was very small, raised stitching that couldn't be seen unless you looked real close because it was the same color as the fin. On one side, was Mano's number. On the other, there were tiny letters that spelled *Niuhi*. I gently squeezed the tip. I could feel there was something inside.

"Your talisman is in there. Each hat has one sown inside of it, except this one," Mr. Blyleven said, touching the last cap in the row. There were nine hats in the box, but only eight talismans. "All of the hats are that flex-fit sizing, small-medium," he said. "None of you has a noggin that's too big yet, so they will all fit perfectly." He looked at me with a grim face. "In other words, it doesn't matter who gets what hat."

I understood what he meant.

"Look, Ryne. I wouldn't want to tell you what to do. This is your team, but if it was me, I think I'd give that last hat to the new boy."

I thought for a moment as I looked at the hat in my hand. "You flew all the way to Arizona just to get these hats for us?" I said. I could hardly believe it.

"John Jackson is my former teammate who owns the company. He was our catcher. We used to call him Stonewall because he was a dang good backstop and, just like the famous Civil War hero, General Stonewall Jackson, he was tougher than cowhide." Mr. Blyleven drummed his fingers on the table. He looked a little sad. "Our high school team used to have reunions, up until about ten years ago. But they just kept getting smaller and smaller. The last one we had only four of us were left. Well, now it's just me and my old battery mate, Stonewall."

I didn't really know what to say. "I'm sorry, Mr. Blyleven."

He gave me that warm, grandfatherly smile again. "Sorry? Are you kidding me, Ryne? I got to go out and spend almost the whole day with Stonewall. Shoot, his son did all the work on the caps! We just parked our tired old backsides and told baseball stories all day. We even played catch a little bit in a tiny grass area next to the parking lot outside the factory." He reached up and rubbed his shoulder like it was sore. "I didn't have my good stuff yesterday, either. I bounced one off the ground and it hit old Stonewall right in the shin. Would you believe he cried like a little girl?"

"Really?" I said, completely fooled.

Mr. Blyleven laughed. "Nah. I'm just kidding. He actually yelled at me like an old man. I think he even invented a new cussword." He stood up. "We could sit here all day shooting ducks, Ryne, but you've got a couple of ballgames to win."

He came around the table as I stood up. I didn't even think about it. I just stepped in to him and wrapped my arms around his chest.

"Thank you, Mr. Blyleven," I said.

He reached up with one of his darkly tanned hands, took my cap off and rubbed my head affectionately. "You're welcome, Ryne." He put the cap back on, picked up the box of new hats and handed it to me. "There's nothing like being on a real team, Ryne. It's been over sixty years since Stonewall and I stepped on a baseball field together. But when I called him about my idea for those hats, he didn't even hesitate. Do you know why?"

"No sir," I answered.

Mr. Blyleven bent closer to me. "Because he and I were *real* teammates, Ryne. We believed in each other. Even though we went on and had different lives in different parts of the country, we remain real teammates to this day. I knew that if I asked him for something like this, he would help me. Real teammates always have each other's back. I would warn you that just being in the same dugout together doesn't necessarily make someone a real teammate, but I think you already know that, don't you?"

"Yes, sir," I said, nodding my head firmly.

He suddenly grabbed my shoulders and held them tightly. "I've been watching you, son. I've been watching you this whole season. You are a real teammate and a real leader too, Ryne. I know Mano was an incredible player and that he inspired all of you to play better than you thought you could, but you've stepped into the hole he left when he disappeared. It's something Miggy didn't do and, frankly, could have never done. He was just too selfish as a player. Unfortunately, I think he gets that from his father."

He turned me around so that I was facing the field. He draped his arm around me. "That diamond out there is a special place, son. I have seen some amazing things happen on it in my lifetime. I expect I'll see a few more before the Good Lord calls me home, too. And I'd like to see some of them today."

He squeezed me and gave me a nudge toward the field. "Go get 'em, Ryne."

"Yes, sir," I said, smiling. "Thank you for these hats, Mr. Blyleven. Thanks a lot!" I turned and started jogging back toward the field. When I got about halfway, I heard him shout from behind me.

"Hey, Ryne!"

I stopped and turned around.

He cupped his hands around his mouth. "Niuhi!" he yelled at me.

I grinned. "Niuhi!" I yelled back.

Then I turned and ran to the field.

*   *   *

When I got back to the dugout, I slid the box under the bench. A few guys—Wee Willie, Sammy, Brazos, and Curtis (who was our starting pitcher)—were in the outfield warming up. Everybody else was at the batting cages. I grabbed my bat and helmet and hustled out beyond the outfield fence down the path toward the row of cages in the distance. I could see Hootie's dad in the first cage. He was throwing batting practice to Hootie who was smoking pitch after pitch right back at his father. Jimmy and Chase were standing outside the cage with Coach Weaver when I jogged up.

"Hey, Ryne," Jimmy said. Chase turned and lifted his head to acknowledge me.

"Sorry I'm a little late, Coach," I said to Coach Weaver. "Mr. Blyleven needed to talk to me."

Coach Weaver was focused on Hootie. "Don't worry about it, Ryne." He interrupted what he was saying to praise Hootie for ripping another rope off his dad in the cage. "That's it, Hootie! You're really firing that back hip. Keep it up!"

He turned his attention to me. "I think everybody is here, except Jake. Did you see him over there?"

I shook my head.

"I think I've figured out why that boy hustles so hard on the field," he said, frowning at his watch. "He's trying to make up for always being the last one dropped off to every practice and game."

Hootie finished off his turn with one last screamer. It struck the metal front of the L-screen shielding his dad hard enough to dent the frame that held the net. Mr. Gibson took off his glove and examined the dent. He picked up a small towel near his feet and wiped at the sweat that was pouring down his face. "Nice work, Hootie," he commented.

"Thanks, Dad," Hootie replied.

"You're really locked in today, Hootie," Jimmy said to our third baseman as he stepped out of the cage.

Coach Weaver agreed. "You'll be in the clean-up spot today, Hootie," he informed him as Hootie bent over to pull his own towel out of his bag. "From the look of that show you just put on in the cage, it looks like you're ready for it, too."

Hootie didn't respond. He just wiped down the handle of his bat with the towel before swiping it across his face.

"Go warm-up," Coach Weaver told him. Hootie grabbed his bag and headed back toward the field as Jimmy stepped into the cage. He got a little way down the path and turned back toward us. "Hey, Ryne. Got a sec?"

I jogged over to him. He looked a little different. His eyes were normally blue. I noted they were a slightly different color. They looked sort of gray - almost like steel.

"Did you bring those talismans with you?" he asked me, quietly.

"I have them," I said, simply. I didn't say anything about the hats.

"Good. Look, after you, Jimmy, and Chase finish hitting, I want us all to meet in the dugout, without the coaches," he said. "I want to tell you guys something. I had a weird dream last night. It was about Mano."

Hootie is the tallest player on our team which means you have to look up to him. Today, he seemed ever taller. His eyes really did look different. The steel-gray color made his black pupils look even darker.

"Okay," I said. I turned and headed back toward the cages.

"Hey, Ryne!"

I turned back around.

"You really have them, right? You didn't leave them at home?"

He seemed awfully worried about the talismans. "No, I have them, Hootie," I said. To reassure him, I added, "They're actually in a real safe place in the dugout."

"Okay," he said. He turned around and began cruising toward the field. As he did, I noticed he was running differently, too. Usually, Hootie sort of lumbered when he ran. Chase thought he loped around like a clumsy, baby giraffe. But as he jogged back toward the field, his legs were moving smoothly. Powerfully.

I don't know why, but that seemed very strange to me.

* * *

The entire team had gathered in our dugout. It was still thirty minutes before game time and everyone was present, except for Jake.

Coach Weaver was worried. "Boys, sit down and stay out of the heat for a bit," he ordered. "I'm going to grab my cell phone from my wife and see if I can reach Ms. Dickey." He left us and headed up into the stands. Hootie's dad, who was exhausted from throwing batting practice in the heat, had headed over to the nearest Press Box concession stand to get a drink. He'd told us he was going to buy one of those frozen rainbow concoctions and put it in a bucket so he could stick his head in it. It was just ten in the morning, but already it was too blasted hot.

Brazos was the last one to walk into the dugout. He flopped down on the bench. "We haven't even started yet and I'm already tired," he complained. He took off his hat and pitched it onto the flat upper portion of the bench behind him. He shook his long hair like a dog, sending perspiration flying in all directions. Some of it rained onto Wee Willie.

"Hey, stop it!" he yelled at Brazos. "You're getting me all wet! And it's not even water. It's your nasty head sweat!"

Brazos snickered. "Relax. Gee. Why are you so torqued?"

Wee Willie glared at him. "I'm not torqued. I just don't want to take a shower in your sweat, okay?"

"Consider it a gift, little dude," Brazos teased.

His joshing only annoyed Wee Willie more. His cheeks were already ripening from the heat. "Stop calling me 'little dude'. It ticks me off," he protested.

"Whatever you say, *little dude*," Brazos replied, sticking him again.

Suddenly, Wee Willie lunged at him. Jimmy was between them and he caught Wee Willie before he could get to our long haired first baseman

"What's the matter with you?" Brazos laughed, which made Wee Willie even madder. Jimmy had to hold onto him like he was wrestling a calf. I'd never seen Wee Willie so upset.

"Knock it off, Brazos!" Hootie demanded. He left his spot on the bench and came down to the center of the action. He helped Jimmy corral Wee Willie.

"What did I do?" Brazos asked, like he was completely innocent.

Hootie scowled at him as Wee Willie continued to struggle. "Tell him you're sorry," he commanded.

Brazos looked up uncertainly. Hootie towered above him. Hootie wasn't exactly threatening him, but he wasn't budging either.

"Tell him," Hootie said again, sternly. He didn't let go of Wee Willie.

Brazos kept his eyes on Hootie. He could tell he was serious. "Geez...sorry, Wee Willie," he finally offered.

Wee Willie finally stopped struggling. Jimmy and Hootie relaxed their grip. He sat down hard on the bench, like he was still upset.

"Hey, Willie?" Wee Willie looked up at Hootie. It was the first time I could recall anyone dropping his nickname from the front of his regular name.

"Yeah?"

"Shake his hand," Hootie ordered.

Wee Willie obediently got up off the bench and took a couple of steps down toward our first baseman. He stuck his hand out and Brazos shook it. "Sorry, dude," Brazos said again, this time more sincerely. He dropped little from in front of dude this time, too.

Wee Willie accepted his apology. "It's alright," he said. "I guess I'm just a little nervous. I'm tired of being hot all the time, too." He went and sat back down. Jimmy sat down next to him. He gave the bill of Wee Willie's hat a friendly swat.

Hootie remained standing. All of us looked up at him from the bench.

"Hey, guys," he began. "I told Ryne that I wanted to tell you about something. I don't know why, but I think it's important." He paused. "I had a dream about Mano."

Everyone suddenly sat up a little straighter on the bench. "You dreamed about Mano?" Wee Willie asked, obviously interested.

"Yeah. We were in a boat together. All of us, except for you, Ryne," he said, looking down at me. "It was a small boat, like one of those that you see people get into when a ship sinks."

"A life boat," Jimmy filled in for him.

"Yeah," Hootie confirmed. "That's it - a life boat."

"Was it like a blow up raft, or was it made out of wood?" Curtis asked.

"It was a wood boat, like one of those from an old movie," Hootie said. "Only it had just one oar for us to row with."

"Who got the oar?" Sammy asked.

"Mano," Hootie answered.

"Mano was with us?" Wee Willie asked. He sounded both surprised and hopeful.

"Yeah, he was sitting in the back of the boat, rowing like crazy. The rest of us were sitting in a row in front of him. And this is one of the weird parts... we were sitting in batting order." He looked at Wee Willie. "You were up front, Wee Willie. Then it was Brazos and Chase. After that, there was an empty seat, and then it was me, Jimmy, Sammy, and Curtis. Jake was in the back, right in front of Mano."

"Where was Ryne?" Chase asked. I was kind of wondering that, too. I felt sort of left out.

"Hang on a second," Hootie said, patiently. "It's a dream, so you know everything doesn't make perfect sense."

"Well, that empty seat sure makes sense," Brazos chimed in. "That's where Miggy was supposed to sit."

Hootie looked down the row at Brazos. "Yeah, I know."

"So what else happened?" Sammy piped up. He'd been really quiet, as usual, but he was sitting on the edge of his seat, like Hootie was telling us a ghost story.

"Well, it was really hot. We were in the middle of the ocean, too. I have no idea where we were going or even how we got in the stupid boat in the first place. But Mano is back there, just rowing like crazy, as if he knows where we're going. So I stood up and I asked him."

"What did he say?" Wee Willie asked.

Hootie looked at him. "He said we were going to Hawai'i."

"*Awesome*," Wee Willie said, breathlessly.

"When I started to sit back down, Mano told me I had to move up one seat because the boat wasn't balanced. I didn't want to. So I sat back down in my seat, or at least I thought I did. Because when I turned back around to look at Mano again, there was a blank seat between me and Jimmy. I turned around again, and Chase was right in front of me." Hootie looked confused. "It was like I sat down in the wrong seat." Hootie's eyes met mine. They still had that new and different gray color to them.

"That's when I saw you, Ryne," he said.

"Where was he?" Chase asked, urgently.

"He was floating in the water, all by himself," Hootie answered. "It looked like he was hanging on to a broken piece of a ship."

My mouth went dry. I had not told anyone about the odd dream that I'd had after our last game the previous week.

"When I turned back to Mano, he was sitting in that blank seat right behind me. He had the oar in his hand and he gave it to me. He pointed at Ryne and said we had to go pick him up. So I took it and turned around and started rowing as hard as I could. But it didn't seem like we were going very fast, and Ryne was starting to get further away. So I turned back around to ask Mano what to do. When I did, he was gone."

"What happened after that?" Sammy could hardly contain himself.

"I looked for Ryne again. He was even farther away, but now I could see a beach. I figured it must have been Hawai'i, so I started rowing toward it as hard as I could. That's when I saw someone standing on the sand."

"Was it Mano?" Curtis asked.

I could hardly breathe.

Hootie shrugged. "Huh uh. Actually, it was a girl. I don't know who she was, but she started running down the beach, waving at Ryne. That's when I woke up."

Everyone was quiet for a moment. Finally Sammy said, "That's a really weird dream."

"It's not weird at all," Brazos disagreed. "It means something." Everybody turned to him.

"Does it?" Hootie practically pleaded.

Brazos leaned back against the bench and put his hands behind his head. "Sure it does. Miggy and Mano have been our power hitters all season. Now they're both gone. Who's going to take their place? You're worried it has to be you."

Hootie frowned a little.

"That's why Mano told you to move to the empty seat to balance the boat," he continued. "But you didn't want to move, did you? When you sat back down, you were in the seat you didn't want to be in."

"The fourth seat," Jimmy filled in.

"The clean-up spot!" Wee Willie exclaimed. "I get it! Because we were all sitting in the boat in our batting order, right?"

Brazos smiled at him. The unusual tension between him and Wee Willie was already gone. "That's right. Hootie didn't want to move into the clean-up spot in the batting order."

"So that's it? You're saying my dream was about me being scared to bat fourth?" Hootie asked. He seemed unhappy with that answer.

"I never said you were scared to bat fourth, Hootie," Brazos replied. "I just don't think you want to."

"That's crazy," Curtis said. "Everybody has always thought that Hootie should bat clean-up for us. Of course he wants to. Right, Hootie?"

Hootie looked down at his feet. He didn't say anything for a while. "I shouldn't be batting clean-up for this team," he confessed. "It should be Mano."

"But in your dream when you turned around, Mano was behind you," Brazos reminded him. "Then he gave you the paddle."

"Yeah, so?" Hootie wasn't following.

"Don't you see?" Brazos asked all of us, as if he was surprised we didn't get it. "Mano came to you in your dream to tell you that you're our clean-up hitter now. When he handed you the paddle, it was like he was handing you a bat."

"How do you know all of this stuff, Brazos?" Curtis asked. He sounded like someone who's been amazed by a magic trick and wants to know how it was done.

Brazos smiled confidently. "You pick stuff up when you read. My mom says reading is better for my brain than video games, so she makes me read a lot. I know that dreams sometimes mean important things. It's like Joseph in the Bible—the guy who had that fancy coat. When that pharaoh had some weird dreams, he got Joseph out of prison just so he could tell him what they meant."

"Wait a minute," Chase said, jumping in. "Are you saying Mano somehow magically came to Hootie in a dream?"

"I don't think its magic," Brazos said, seriously. "Remember, Mano is a niuhi warrior."

"That's ridiculous!" Chase spewed. "Mano doesn't have the power to come to you in a dream, Hootie! You don't really believe that junk, do you?"

"I thought we all did," Brazos answered casually. "Isn't that why we carried those talismans that Ryne made out of the ball that Mano hit into the swamp?"

Jimmy suddenly turned and looked at me. "Hey, Ryne. Where are those at, anyway?" he asked, urgently.

I didn't answer him. Instead, I stood up. I reached under the bench and pulled out the box of hats that Mr. Blyleven had given me. I moved slowly toward Hootie. I felt weirdly disconnected from my body. The whole conversation about the dream had left me feeling strange.

"Guys, I have something for everybody," I said. My voice cracked a little and I had to clear my throat. "It's...*ahem*. Well, it's a present. Mr. Blyleven had them made for us." I opened the box and pulled out the first hat in the row. I handed it to Hootie.

"Wow," Hootie remarked. "These are really nice."

I took out the next hat and handed it to Brazos. I went down the line and handed one to Jimmy, Wee Willie, Sammy, Curtis, and finally, to Chase.

288

"Whoa! What's this?" Wee Willie remarked. He was looking at the small fin that covered the button on top of the hat.

"It's got Mano's number on it," Sammy said, studying one side of the fin.

"And it says NIUHI on the other," Brazos added, without looking. "It's a shark fin!"

Jimmy figured it out immediately. "The talismans are *inside*, aren't they?"

"Mr. Blyleven had them made special, for us," I confirmed.

"Too cool!" Wee Willie exclaimed. He took off his other Intimidators cap and slipped the new one on his head.

Hootie stood next to me with a faraway look on his face. He held the hat in the palms of his hands, admiring it like it was a golden crown.

At that moment, Jake burst around the corner of the dugout. He was sweaty and out of breath, as if he'd been running flat out. "Hey guys!" he wheezed. "Man, sorry I'm late. Mom got lost."

Brazos scooted over and made a place for him. "Sit down. You look like you're about to pass out, dude."

"Thanks," Jake exhaled. He dropped his bat bag on the ground and flopped onto the bench.

"Why are you so out of breath?" Wee Willie asked him.

"I ran... all the way... from the parking lot," Jake wheezed again.

Sammy came down from where he was sitting. "But then you rode on that awesome train here, didn't you?"

Jake gulped some air. "We were waiting for it, but I told Mom I was late and I had to go. So I just ran along the side of tracks until I got here. It wasn't that far." He took a deep breath and then noticed the new caps. "That hat is *awesome*!" he exhaled to Sammy.

I stepped forward. There were two hats left in the box. I reached in and pulled one out and handed it to him. "This one's for you," I said. He immediately flipped off his other cap and put on the new one. He didn't even notice the fin. "Thanks!"

Coach Weaver appeared at the doorway to the dugout. He breathed a sigh of relief when he saw Jake. "Okay, good. I'm glad you're here."

"Sorry I'm late, Coach," Jake apologized.

Coach Weaver smiled patiently. "I just talked to your Mom. She's riding the train down."

"She got lost, Coach. I'm really sorry." He seemed embarrassed.

"Don't worry about it, Jake," he said. "How did you beat her here?"

"He ran!" Sammy answered for him.

"You ran? All the way from the front of the park?" Coach Weaver laughed. "Wow. You really are a little Charlie Hustle, aren't you son?"

"I'm a *what*?" Sammy asked.

None of us knew what Coach was talking about.

"Never mind," Coach Weaver grinned. Then he noticed our new caps, too. "Hey... where did those come from?"

Ryne

"Hey, Ryne? You okay?"

I was looking up into the sun. Jake was above me and his face was blocking a portion of the blazing yellow ball in the sky. He had just pulled the ball from my glove and made a relay throw to home, but it was too late. A run had scored and we trailed again, 8-7.

My brain was fuzzy. I remembered going across the bag at second base. Jake had just made another great play. The ball had been hit between him and Brazos and he'd snagged it just before it reached the outfield grass. He'd spun around like a professional and had thrown a perfect dart to me at second. I'd felt the ball sink into my glove. Then it felt like I ran into a brick wall. The next thing I knew, I was flat on my back looking up into the sky.

"He hit you pretty hard," Jake said. "Just be still. Here comes Coach."

The next thing I knew, Coach Weaver was kneeling next to me. He looked worried and mad, all at the same time.

"Hey, buddy. You okay?" He squeezed my arm.

"Yeah. I'm fine," I replied, even though I didn't feel fine. Mr. Gibson suddenly appeared. He choked out the rest of the sun with his huge body as he stood over all three of us.

"Hey, Ryne," he said in his deep voice. "How ya' doing, son?"

"I'm alright," I said, feeling a little better. They sat me up.

"He's gonna be fine," Mr. Gibson said to Coach Weaver. "I've got him. You go ahead and talk to the ump."

Coach Weaver stood up and went directly to the field umpire who was standing a few feet away. I heard him say in a stern voice, "He can't do that."

The umpire spoke calmly. "The runner was in the baseline, coach. There was no intention to interfere with a thrown ball. He also did not interfere with his ability to catch the ball because the shortstop already had the ball in his glove when they collided."

"He didn't slide!" I heard Coach Weaver say.

"Your shortstop was late to the bag, Coach," the umpire insisted. "He and the runner arrived at the base at the same time. There's no requirement to slide."

"He deliberately ran into him!" Coach Weaver objected again, this time much louder.

"Don't lose your temper, Coach," the umpire warned him. "I don't want to have to run you in a close game like this. In my judgment, he did not deliberately run into him. The contact was incidental. The rule is specific when that happens, no call should be made. Go look it up."

The umpire looked over at me as Mr. Gibson and Jake helped me stand up. "He's had a rough day, Coach. Take some time and get him a drink of water. Make sure he's okay. We know this is an important game. We're in no hurry." He turned and walked away.

The words 'rough day' stung my ears. Even an umpire, who usually never said squat to you about how you were playing, knew that I stunk. Coach Weaver came back over to us. He was still fuming.

"You don't think he has a concussion, do you?" he asked Mr. Gibson.

"Nah. He's fine," Hootie's dad said. "He's just a little sports car that ran into a big truck, and the big truck won." We all looked over at third base where the big truck was now parked. It was the red headed kid we'd followed off the train. He stood with his arms folded. He looked bored.

Hootie poked his head in to check on me. "You alright, Ryne?"

Hootie had been having a heck of a day. We were playing Game Two and he'd hit a triple and two doubles, and he'd made three great plays at third. Jake had two singles and was playing like a major leaguer at second. I was just a dog turd sandwiched between them at shortstop.

"Yeah. I'm fine," I said.

Samantha ran up to our huddle with a bottle of water. I looked up and saw Mom and Dad standing up behind the dugout. Mom had her hands folded together beneath her chin like she was praying. Dad had his own hands stuck down in his pockets. They both look worried.

Coach Weaver patted me on the back and then he and Mr. Gibson headed back to the porch in front of the dugout while Hootie and Jake returned to their position. There was one out in the top of the fifth. There were runners at first and third.

Jimmy had the ball. While the coaches had been deciding whether or not they needed to cart me off on a stretcher, he'd kept his arm loose by throwing to Brazos. He stepped to the back of the mound and looked straight at me.

"Niuhi," he said.

I didn't say it back. I just looked down at the ground and sort of nodded.

"Batter up!" the plate umpire bellowed.

I thought I could feel Jimmy still looking at me, but when I lifted my head he was already back on the mound and ready for the sign from Chase. The Rangers' player at the plate was another one of their whopper-sized kids. He'd hit two balls right at me today already in the first game, and I'd booted them both. The first one had been a sinker that I could have caught before it hit the ground, but I'd lifted my head at the last second to check the runner at first and it had hit the heel of my glove. The second one had been like a couple of the others I'd missed. It had just been a hard hit ground ball that had rocketed under my glove and continued on its way toward left field. I should have had all of them, but I didn't get any of them.

So now I was doing something I hadn't done since I was seven years old. Back then, I'd actually been afraid of the baseball. I was always worried that any ball hit to me would take a bad hop, hit me in the face, and break my nose. Basically, I was afraid of exactly what had happened to Hootie earlier in the season. Every time the batter would step into the box, I'd start thinking.

Please. Please don't hit it to me!

I hadn't done that in years. But now, as the next Ranger's batter had stepped into the box, that stupid, old verse was starting to play in my head again.

Please. Please. Please don't hit it to me!

Jimmy threw a first pitch strike. Then he threw one that traveled low and outside. The count was 1-1, and the verse played again.

Please. Please. Please don't hit it to me!

Jimmy threw a change-up. The Rangers hitter wasn't fooled. He jumped on it and hit a sharp grounder between Hootie and me. I moved slowly toward the ball, but because Hootie had been holding Big Red at third, he got a great jump off the bag as he moved into his fielding position. He cut sharply across the grass in front of me and the ball hopped neatly into his glove. He turned his head quickly toward Big Red, who froze after coming a few steps down the line, and threw a bullet across the diamond to Brazos for the out.

Big Red wasn't fast. He bluffed a bit coming down the third base line, but I'd swung in behind him to cover third base. Brazos immediately moved into the middle of the infield with the ball, and Big Red had to hustle back to third.

Coach Weaver and Mr. Gibson both applauded. Coach Weaver cheered, "Nice play, gentlemen! That's the way you hold the runner, Hootie. Beautifully done!"

Hootie jogged back toward third. He looked directly at me and made a fist. I just drew my lips into a line and nodded at him.

There were two outs. The Rangers had base runners at second and third. Their shortstop, who had played a billion times better than me, stepped into the batter's box. He'd made every fielding chance look easy, plus he'd gotten a hit every time he'd been to the plate, except when Curtis had struck him out in the first game. Another hit would probably bring in two more runs.

Jimmy got the sign from Chase. I felt my stomach tighten.

Please. Please. Please don't hit it to me.

The Rangers' shortstop didn't waste any time. He swung, but I guess he thought Jimmy was going to throw him a fastball. Instead, he got a change-up.

The ball cued off the end of the bat toward Jake. It was a baby stroller, and Jake was playing deep at second because there were two outs. The ball was hit hard enough to get past Jimmy, but not by much. It scooted just beyond his glove as he came off the mound.

Jake was already in a dead run toward it, but the Rangers shortstop was fast. As things turned out, it didn't matter.

Jake grabbed the ball with his bare hand and side-armed a throw into the heart of Brazos glove. The sharp spear beat the Rangers' shortstop by at least five steps.

From the top step of our dugout, I heard Coach Weaver explode. "Great play, Jake!"

It was a great play. By my count, Jake had made about six really good plays during both games. More importantly, he'd made zero bad plays. I, on the other hand, had made exactly zero great plays, and at least seven horrible ones. The only thing that was going right was that old verse I'd been chanting again in my head seemed to be working. No balls were coming to me at shortstop.

* * *

When Hootie stepped up to the plate in the bottom of the inning, there was nobody out. He was the second hitter to bat. Chase had led off with an infield hit on a dribbler down the third base line. It had been an ugly roller off the bottom of his bat that had bumped heavily along the third base foul line until it finally just came to a stop, like a chunk of rock somebody had tossed on the ground. The third baseman had decided to just watch it, hoping it would go foul, but when it had finally stopped rolling, it was still two inches inside the line.

Now Chase was standing at first base.

Normally, I would have expected Coach Weaver to give Chase the steal sign. We needed a run to tie the game, and Chase was pretty doggone fast. But the Rangers' catcher was Big Red. He had an arm that the Navy could have probably mounted on one of its battleships. He'd already thrown out two of our runners in the first game, plus one more in this game. It really wasn't very likely that Coach Weaver would risk having Chase thrown out too, particularly since Hootie had been ripping the cover off the ball.

Hootie dug into the batter's box. As he did, I watched their shortstop creep back toward the grass. Their third baseman took two steps back into a much deeper position at third, and moved a little closer to his right to protect the line, too. Hootie had already drilled three different balls over third into the left field corner. He was on fire at the plate. I think we were all hoping that he would finally just cream one over the left field fence. Their left fielder seemed to be thinking that, too. He had moved all the way back until he was just about ten feet in front of the warning track.

The Rangers' pitcher reached back and threw his first pitch. It sailed high for ball one.

Hootie stepped out of the box. He took a long look at Coach Weaver who went through his series of signs. I was watching Chase at first the whole time. He was standing with both feet on the bag, his hands on his hips, watching Coach Weaver across the field in the third base coach's box. He moved carefully off the bag into his lead. He kept his eyes glued to the pitcher, inching out a little bit at a time, but not too far. In fact, his lead was kind of pitiful. Hootie's dad, who was coaching first now that Coach Weaver had moved to third, was keeping him tight to the bag. He wasn't going to risk having the tying run picked off.

The Rangers' pitcher checked him over his shoulder, saw how sad his lead was, and realized he didn't need to throw over to keep him close. He turned back toward the plate, and lifted his leg. As soon as Chase saw his knee come up, he immediately took off.

I couldn't believe it.

The pitch was high again. Big Red started to come up of out of his crouch so he could snatch the ball and make the throw to easily nail Chase at second, but Hootie made certain the pitch never even reached Big Red's catcher's mitt. He squared around and slid his right hand up the neck of the bat. I heard someone yell, "BUNT!"

The ball plinked off the aluminum and dropped straight to the ground where it began rolling down the third base line. It had more speed than Chase's weak infield hit, but the ball was never close to going foul. Instead, it stayed in the grass and rolled perfectly dead when it was even with the mound.

The pitcher arrived before the third baseman, who probably had to take a bus from his position behind the bag to finally reach it. I think he was as shocked as everyone else. Our clean-up hitter had just laid down a flawless bunt.

Everybody in our dugout went crazy and rushed to the fence. Our fans screamed louder than they had the whole day. The Rangers' coach, who was standing on the porch in front of their dugout, took off his hat and ran his fingers through his hair like he was frustrated. Quickly, he put his cap back on and started clapping hard, encouraging his players. I looked over at Coach Weaver. He wasn't smiling, screaming, or going crazy like everybody else. He was just politely clapping like he was at a pro golf tournament and one of the players had just sunk a short putt that everyone had expected he would make.

Wee Willie scream to Hootie at the top of his lungs, "NIUHI!" Then Sammy joined him. "NIUHI!" At first base, Hootie pumped his fist, pointed at our dugout, and answered them.

"NIUHI!!" he yelled.

Jake was standing with his hands locked into the fence in the dugout cheering with everyone else. I was the only one still sitting on the bench. He turned around to me and said, "Hey, Ryne... why do the guys keep yelling knee high? Does that mean you should hit a pitch that is knee high?"

"Sure," I lied.

Our dugout was rocking as Jimmy left the on deck circle and walked to the plate. When he returned to us a few minutes later after grounding out to first base, the guys gave him a hero's welcome. He had hit an outside pitch to the first baseman and moved Chase and

Hootie up one base each. The tying run was now at third. The go ahead run was at second, and there was one out.

Sammy walked to the plate. But just then, the field umpire lifted his hands high in the air. "Time has expired," he announced. "We will finish the inning." We were the home team.

This was it. It was our last chance.

Curtis moved into the on deck circle. I was in the hole behind him, and I didn't want to bat. I'd already gotten hits in both the first and the second game, but that didn't matter to me now. I had zero confidence, and my play showed it. We had one out and there were two guys who would hit before it would be my turn.

The crowd was standing and cheering as Sammy walked to the plate. I could hear Big Red's mother ringing that blasted cow bell, and I thought of cows showing up to drop their big stinking pies all over Baseball World's bright, shiny facility. But thinking of Mom's joke couldn't even make me smile. Nothing could. I was too worried.

Sammy took two pitches. The first was a ball. The second was a strike.

Between both of them, the crowd shrieked again and I could hear that cow bell banging and clanging. Our whole team was plastered to the fence in front of me, cheering and screaming. I was frozen to the bench.

I couldn't even move.

The noise died down as the Rangers' pitcher got ready to deliver again. The cow bell stopped clanging. The stadium grew eerily quiet. The Rangers' pitcher reached back and threw.

Sammy hit the ball squarely on the nose, but it went right back to the mound. The ball jumped obediently into the pitcher's glove. He took one quick look at Chase, who had frozen at third, and he hummed the ball to their first baseman for the second out of the inning.

Their fans exploded. The cow bell went nuts.

And I had to get up off the bench.

* * *

Curtis had already left the on deck circle by the time I came out of the dugout. I walked over and picked up the heavy donut he'd left behind and slid it over the knob of my bat, but I didn't start swinging it. Instead, I just stood there and watched him walk toward the batter's box. In my mind, a new chant had started up.

Please. Please. Please let Curtis finish it.

Please. Please. Please let Curtis finish it.

Curtis stopped outside the batter's box and took a good, long look at his dad at third base. Coach Weaver went through the signs and Curtis nodded that he understood.

Behind the Rangers' dugout on the first base side, their fans transformed into a red and blue monster between every pitch. The beast slobbered and snarled. The cow bell around its neck clanged louder and louder.

The verse played again inside my head. *Please. Please. Please let Curtis finish it!*

Curtis waited to swing until the third pitch. When he did, he hit a foul ball over the net down the first base side that disappeared into the red and blue monster. The beast quickly gobbled it up and grew quiet for a moment. However, as soon the umpire tossed another ball out to their pitcher, the slobbering and snarling began again. The cow bell jangled loudly, as if it was warning us that the monster was about to break free and attack the field at any moment. Then it grew quiet as the monster waited on their pitcher.

Curtis swung at the next pitch, too. He just nicked the ball and Big Red caught it for strike two. The monster growled and roared its approval.

My palms were sweating. I kept wiping them along the sides of my pants to dry them off, but as soon as I wiped the moisture away, it came right back. It was like my hands were raining.

Curtis stepped out of the batter's box and took another look at Coach. Coach Weaver went through the signs, but there was nothing special in them. There were two outs, and there were two balls and two strikes. Chase was the tying run at third, and Hootie was the winning run at second. Coach Weaver might as well have been flashing Curtis directions to the nearest Chuck E. Cheese for all the good it would do him now. There was only one thing for him to do.

Protect the plate.

The Rangers' pitcher got his sign from Big Red and settled into his stretch. He looked briefly at Chase, and turned toward Curtis. He lifted his leg, kicked, and threw.

The pitch bounced in the dirt, wide of the plate. Big Red had to dive out of his catcher's crouch to stop it. His big chest protector immediately spit the wild pitch back out safely in front of him, like it was a bad tasting berry. Chase had moved a few steps down the line from third, but the Rangers' pitcher had immediately taken off to cover for his mistake and was already closing fast on the plate. Big Red moved faster than I would have ever dreamed he could. In a second, he had scooped up the bitter berry and tossed it to the pitcher who turned and threatened to make Chase eat it. Coach Weaver instantly called our catcher back to him at third as the blue and red monster screamed nastily at him from behind the Rangers dugout.

The count was three balls and two strikes. I knew that I was now just one more bad pitch away from the batter's box. I desperately wanted the pitcher to throw the next pitch right down the middle so that Curtis had to swing.

Please. Please. Please just throw a strike. I thought.

Please. Please. Please just throw a strike!

There were no signs from Coach Weaver this time. He just clapped for Curtis as he looked down the third base line toward him.

"Watch it closely," I heard Coach Weaver preach through the noise. "*Protect the plate.*"

I wanted to scream out, "No, Curtis. Swing! You've got to swing, no matter what!" Instead, I just stood in the on deck circle with my palms raining, feeling ashamed of myself for what I was thinking.

Curtis confidently rotated his bat once with a helicopter whirl, and measured the center of the strike zone with it. I heard Jake yell from behind me, "Yeah! *Knee high*! That's where you want it!" On top of everything else, I now felt like a complete jerk for letting Jake believe everyone on our team had been yelling knee high throughout the game.

The pitcher stared in to get his sign from Big Red. He took a long time, and that made me nervous. Maybe he was going to try and throw another curve ball, which might have been as bad as the one he'd just tried to throw. If he did, Curtis would trot down to first base with a walk, and I would have to bat.

My stomach rolled. My hands rained.

Please. Please. Please, just throw a strike!

The pitcher checked Chase at third. Again, he stared at him longer than he really needed to because Chase wasn't moving. He took a deep breath.

Why was he taking so long? I thought. *Pitch it! Stop messing around and just pitch it already!*

Suddenly, the Rangers' pitcher stepped off the rubber. The plate umpire held up his hands behind Big Red to call time. The Rangers' head coach started walking slowly out toward the mound. Big Red took off his catcher's mask and walked out, too.

Are you kidding? I thought miserably. *He wants to talk to him now? Why? What could he possibly have to say to him right now?*

That's when I noticed the new kid warming up in the Rangers' bullpen down the right field line for the first time. He was tall and skinny with arms as long as a pterodactyl's wings. As the red and blue monster grew quiet, I could hear his catcher's mitt popping solidly with each throw he made. That's when it all became clear to me. The manager was stalling to give Pterodactyl Arms a little more time to get warm. From the bullpen I heard the glove pop again, even louder.

On the mound, the Rangers' coach took his time. The umpire watched them with his hands on his hips. When it became clear that the Rangers' coach was in no hurry, the ump began his slow walk out toward their huddle. He was about half-way there when the manager realized his time was up. He patted his pitcher on the back and turned around and headed back toward the dugout. Big Red said one last thing to his pitcher and put his mask back on and rumbled like a slow moving dump truck toward the plate. The umpire followed him, slipped his own mask back over his broad face, and settled in behind him. It seemed to take forever, but soon everyone was finally back in their place.

I could hardly breathe. If the next pitch was a ball, Curtis would get to walk down to the open base at first. The Rangers' coach would stop the game again, this time to summon Pterodactyl Arms from the bullpen. He would get his warm-up pitches and I would have to stand there and wait even longer for him to finish them, watching him fire missile after missile at Big Red, until it would finally be my turn to step into the box.

And strike out.

Please. Please. Please just.... This time, I couldn't even complete the thought in my head. I was just too nervous.

The Rangers' pitcher went through his routine all over again. He stared down at Big Red, as if he didn't already know what pitch to throw. He checked Chase who was standing with his lead in foul territory in the exact same spot he'd been standing for the last ten minutes. This time, the Rangers' pitcher didn't stare too long. He immediately turned his head toward Curtis, kicked his leg, and fired.

It was a fastball, right down the middle. Curtis did his job. He protected the plate. He swung and made contact. I watched the second baseman turn his shoulder toward the outfield. He hesitated for just a moment, like he was unsure. Then he started up again and began to run into right field.

The ball was looping. It had a funny tail on it too, like it was spinning away from him. The Rangers' right fielder was too deep in the outfield to be of any help. He came running anyway, but he was too late.

The hit fell just over the second baseman's glove. Because of the weird spin, the ball immediately kicked away from him, but he hustled after it, chasing hard while it spun away across the top of the grass. Quickly, he scooped it up.

Chase had already scored. He was standing behind home plate waving his arms like crazy at Hootie who was coming hard around third. Coach Weaver was waving too, pointing toward home and repeating, "*Go, go, go, go, go, go, go, go...*"

The blue and red monster was gnashing its teeth and Hootie was running right into its mouth. The cow bell clanged angrily at him, but Hootie didn't slow down. He wasn't running like a clumsy baby giraffe, either. His legs were churning and his feet were spitting up chunks of grass behind him as he powered out of his wide turn at third and sprinted for home.

Big Red was in good position, just in front of the plate, waiting for the throw. The Rangers' second baseman whipped around and threw the ball home. He threw it hard and on a straight line, but he threw it high.

The ball sailed well over Big Red's head. He knew it was impossible to reach, so he didn't even bother to try and jump. Behind him, Hootie was already into his slide. Even if the throw had been perfect, I thought he would probably still have beaten the tag. He jetted smoothly across the plate like he was on a slip n' slide. Immediately, he popped up and jumped on top of Chase. When he did, the red and blue monster instantly died, but the gold and black one behind me roared to life.

I felt the entire dugout pass by me like a tornado. One by one, they began to leap, piling on top of Hootie and Chase. Mr. Gibson ran down the first base line toward them. He was carrying Curtis with him like a rag doll. After Curtis the Hero had reached first base, Mr. Gibson had whisked him skyward and thrown him over one of his huge shoulders. Then he'd taken off toward home with Curtis laughing the whole way. When they reached the pile, Mr. Gibson tossed him gently onto it, like he was pitching another log into a roaring bonfire. For a second, I thought he was going to jump on top too, because he was so excited, but I guess he thought he might crush everybody. He took off his cap and hurled it into the pile instead before he began to jump up and down like a little kid.

Coach Weaver came down from third base in a slow jog. He was clapping modestly the whole way, just watching the crazy scene the way parents sometimes do when their kids tear into their presents on Christmas morning. His smile was big and he looked really happy. Everyone did. I even saw the umpire smile a little. Of course the Rangers, their coaches, and their fans weren't smiling, but neither was I.

My feet had somehow directed me closer to the pile, but I didn't jump on. Instead, I hung well back. My hands came up and clapped, but they felt like wooden puppet hands. There were strings that made them come together, whether I wanted them to or not. So I just stood there, watched, and awkwardly clapped. I wasn't real excited. In fact, I felt more relieved, and I was embarrassed that I felt that way.

Suddenly, there was a hand on my shoulder. I turned.

It was Mr. Blyleven.

I don't know when he had come onto the field. His eyes were bright, but he had an odd look on his face, like he knew a secret. He reached up toward the top of my cap. I could feel him touch the shark fin button with his fingers. He squeezed it, then he brought his hand back down and rested it on my shoulder.

We both watched as the pile of my teammates began to break up. Curtis took off in a dead run toward the pitcher's mound as the entire team chased him. Hootie caught him first and dragged him back to the ground while Curtis laughed hysterically. The pile up started all over again as Wee Willie, Jake, Brazos, and the rest of the team caught him and began diving on top of each other.

I was sure Mr. Blyleven was going to push me to follow them, but he didn't. Instead, I felt his grip on my shoulder tighten. He bent slightly and spoke directly into my ear. He only said one word.

"*Sacrifice.*"

I didn't know what he meant. At that moment, I really didn't even want to try and figure it out. So I just nodded. We both stood there and watched my teammates laugh and roll across the ground. We'd won Game Two. Oh... I guess I forgot to mention one other thing. We'd also won Game One, 10-6, too. So even though I'd done practically nothing to help the team, we'd done it. *We'd really done it.*

We were actually going to the Baseball World 12U championship series.

Epilogue to Part II

Dear Ryne,

I am writing this fast so Mrs. Girardi can give it to you after practice.

I have been crying for two hours! I just can't stop! This is the worst thing that has ever happened to me! I just don't know what to do. I want somebody to tell me it's just a dream, but I know it's not.

I have your letter. Katie gave it to me. Oh, Ryne! At first, I just thought it was so sweet. Then when you wrote what your Grandma said about you being a left-handed chicken, my heart stopped!

For my whole life, my grandma has always called me her little left-footed goose! When I was six, I used to fall down all the time when I was in dance class. My feet would just get tangled up. I couldn't help it! Once when she was visiting, she came to my class and I must have fallen down about ten times! The last time I fell down I started crying. She came over and picked me up and hugged me and told me I was her cute little left-footed goose. She has called me that ever since!

I have to go pack now. I just found out that Katie and her mom are going with us to Colorado. I am glad Katie will be with me so I won't feel so alone.

I am so sorry I am going to miss your baseball games, Ryne. I am going to take my Intimidators shirt with me and wear it EVERY day while we are gone!

I will miss you so much!

Madison

* * *

I looked at my phone. There were messages—maybe fifteen or so—from Madison. There were another five from Katie, too. I also had one missed phone call. It was from Madison. My phone said I had a voice mail, but I hadn't checked it because I was in a bad mood.

I didn't want to talk to anybody.

I looked at the last message from Katie. She was really mad. I could tell because the message came in giant, angry letters.

WHY AREN'T YOU ANSWERING MADISON? SHE'S WORRIED ABOUT YOU!!

I had switched my phone to vibrate, but even the vibration was beginning to make me crazy, so I just turned it off and put it in the drawer beside my bed.

I was outside, in my fortress. Mom had said I could spend the night if I wanted. This time, it had been Dad who had to be convinced to let me stay by myself, probably because he wanted to encourage me after I'd played so poorly. When I'd asked to sleep outside, he'd actually said no, but then Mom had outvoted him, two to one. I have never really understood how that works exactly, but Mom always seems to get an extra vote when she needs it. I think she understood that I just needed to be alone for a while…to think.

I laid down on my back and stared up at the ceiling. I had put most of the minor league pennants there because the major league flags were already covering up the walls. There was one right in the middle of all of them that held my attention. The pennant was for one of the San Diego Padres' minor league teams, the Lake Elsinore Storm.

The team flag was black. Along the bottom, in fancy white script letters it said *The Storm*. On top of the letters were two eerie red eyes and a swooping gray brow. It's the pennant I'd liked the best when I'd opened the box and began unpacking them. I'd thought it looked kind of mysterious, so I'd asked Dad to put it in the very center of the ceiling. Mom had thought I was crazy. She said she certainly wouldn't want those eyes staring at her all night while she was trying to sleep, but it hadn't bothered me. Sometimes, I would come out and just lie on the bed and stare back at those two red eyes. It was like I was playing a game of chicken with them, to see who would blink first. I'd stare at them forever, until my eyes began to sting and burn. Then, when I couldn't take it any longer and it felt like my sockets were about to burst, I'd close my eyes. After a while, I could see the image of those two red and white halos in the darkness, like they were burned into the back of my eyelids. They would just float there, staring back at me.

It was quiet in my fortress. I stared at the Storm pennant. I refused to blink. Soon, my eyes began to sting; then they began to burn. I wasn't about to back down. It was stupid, and probably even a little crazy, but I wanted to win. I wanted to make those mysterious eyes on my ceiling blink.

The burning got worse, but I told myself I could take it. I just needed to push on a little longer. I could do it. *I really can win this time*, I thought. I kept staring. I didn't blink, even though the burning was maddening. I imagined my eyes were bleeding tears of fire. That made me feel tougher.

It didn't matter. My eyes finally closed, all by themselves. I was angry. I'd lost, again.

I squeezed my eyelids tightly shut. Slowly, the burning began to fade. It didn't take very long for the Storm eyes to appear this time. They were branded onto the black screen in front of me. They were brighter than normal. Much brighter. They floated there in the blackness, glaring back at me like always. Then—to my surprise—*they actually did blink.*

Suddenly, the white around them grew whiter. The red began to transform and the color drained away from them until there was nothing left but black. The swooping brow faded away, too. In its place, the brim of a baseball cap appeared.

The new eyes stared at me. I hadn't seen them in a while, but I recognized them immediately.

They were Mano's.

The rest of his face soon began to appear, too. It was very light at first, but gradually it became darker and clearer. I don't know what happened, but suddenly it was like I was transported to some place far away. I was standing on a beach. There were huge palm trees everywhere. Mano was there too, but he was further down the sand from me. I could see him waving for me to follow him. Suddenly, he took off in a full run.

I started to run too, but Mano was faster. The sand felt heavy and my feet kept sinking into it, deeper and deeper. I watched him cut up away from the water toward the fringe of the trees. He stopped and waved to me again. I kept thinking he would wait for me to catch up, but the distance between us never changed.

I ran up the beach toward the trees after him. Instantly, I became worried because I was barefooted and I was afraid I might step on something, like a snake. I looked down at the ground, but it was clear. There was a narrow, sandy path that led deep into the jungle. Up ahead, I could see Mano's brown back. He wasn't wearing a shirt, just the board shorts he'd had on when he came to our very first practice. He was still running, just not as fast.

I ran faster. It was easier on the sandy path. The ground felt firmer beneath my feet and it seemed as if I was catching up a little bit.

Then Mano suddenly disappeared.

I came to a place on the path where it rose into a small hill. I figured that he was probably on the other side. I quickly ran up it. When I got to the top, I stopped dead in my tracks. There, in the middle of the tropical forest, was the opening to a cave. It was very dark inside, and Mano was nowhere in sight. I walked closer to the entrance. I couldn't see a thing. I kept looking, expecting that I would see him appear any moment from the darkness. I heard a voice whisper clearly into my ear.

"*Niuhi.*"

I could see two eyes again. They were coming toward me, out of the darkness of the cave, but I realized they weren't Mano's eyes. These were bigger. Much bigger. Beneath them was a row of gleaming white, razor sharp teeth. I felt water all around me. I wasn't in the jungle anymore. I was in the ocean, but the cave was still there in front of me.

And so was the shark. It came out of the darkness, straight for me. It had been waiting inside the cave. It had been waiting to devour me.

He niuhi 'ai holopapa o ka moku.

The niuhi shark that devours all on the island.

There was nowhere to go. I couldn't escape. There was nothing to do but close my eyes and wait for it to take me.

I heard a voice. It was Mano. He whispered harshly, *"Don't be afraid!"*

Afraid? Was he kidding? Of course, I was afraid! I was going to die!

Another voice whispered to me, again. *"Don't be afraid."*

This time, it wasn't Mano's voice, however. This voice was softer; gentler. I opened my eyes.

The shark was gone. The cave was gone, too. I wasn't in the jungle anymore. I was back on the beach. Standing there, just a few feet away, was Madison. She had her back to me. Her blonde hair was tied back into a ponytail. She was wearing her Intimidators jersey. On the back of it was my number.

She turned around.

"Don't be afraid," she said to me. She smiled.

Suddenly, I wasn't afraid anymore. I walked over to her. She reached her hand out to me, then she just disappeared. Everything went dark.

The eyes were there in front of me once more. They were white and red, covered by the swooping gray brow. Beneath them it said, The Storm. I stared at the pennant. I blinked. *Just another crazy dream*, I thought.

I rolled over and stared at the wall next to the bed. The championship series was one long week away. I wondered who we would play. I wondered about the surprises Major League Baseball had for the winner.

But more than anything, I wondered about Mano and sharks, and if somehow I really had captured some mystical power inside the talismans. Wouldn't that explain why everyone but me had played so fantastic in the semi-finals?

I picked up the TV remote and pressed the power button. The screen immediately came to life. The channel was set to ESPN, as usual. There was a baseball player on the screen, but he wasn't in color. It was old black and white footage, taken a long time ago, I figured.

He stood alone, swinging a bat. His face was tense. I thought he looked familiar, but I couldn't remember who he was. The sound on the television was muted, so I pressed a button on the remote. As soon as I did, I heard an announcer say, "Joltin' Joe DiMaggio. The owner of the greatest record in baseball history."

Almost instantly, the screen went dark and a commercial began. I hit the rewind button on my remote and froze the playback when it reached the image of the player swinging the bat. His tense face didn't look into the camera. Instead, he stared out to where I imagined the infield was probably located. I determined he was probably watching a pitcher warming on the mound, carefully planning his attack.

Joe DiMaggio. Joltin' Joe DiMaggio.

I suddenly remembered being at The Hitting Wheel, watching Mano smash one screamer after another back into the center of the wheel. I remembered Mr. Blyleven staring at him.

Joltin' Joe. That's what Mr. Blyleven had said that day.

Joltin' Joe.

I stared at the screen, realizing that Joltin' Joe DiMaggio was who Mr. Blyleven had been referring to as he watched Mano in the cage. I hit the play button again and the announcer's voice came to life.

Joltin' Joe DiMaggio. The owner of the greatest record in baseball history, he said again.

I knew the record. It was one of the most important records in the history of baseball. But what I didn't know was just how strangely important that record would become in my life in another week.

I rewound one more time and froze the playback. I stared at the stern face of Joltin' Joe. Something about him seemed so...familiar. The feeling reminded me of a sensation I'd had once at Dad's family reunion. One of his cousins had seemed so familiar to me, even though we'd never met. There had been something about his face, something that made me think we'd met already. I'd told Dad about it and he'd said it was probably because we were related and something deep inside of me, something sort of primitive, was recognizing my own family blood.

Joltin' Joe, I thought. *Gee. It sure would be nice if you were my family blood.*

I clicked off the television. The room was quiet. Somewhere outside, a dog barked a few times. It stopped, and then it was quiet again.

Quiet enough for me to fall back to sleep.

The BallShark Select Baseball Series continues in

BallShark

Voodoo Rising

The unique fusion of baseball, mystery and adventure continues in *Voodoo Rising*, the second installment in the BallShark Select Baseball Series. Ryne Dunston and his Intimidator teammates find themselves face to face with a superior elite youth organization that mercilessly destroys opponents. The Lone Star Elite Voodoo is on the fast track to national stardom, eager to claim the inaugural Baseball World title and claim for themselves the secret prize promised to the winner by Major League Baseball. How can the Intimidators hope to compete with such a high-powered club without their star player?

Seeking to solve the mystery surrounding the disappearance of the Intimidators' amazing right fielder, Ryne's father has set out on a quest. Guided by an unusual intuition and a strange series of coincidences, Shaun Dunston pursues the truth behind the mysterious young man and his elusive father. But as the peculiar twists of fate continue to lead him forward, Shaun finds himself challenged by a curious psychological theory. Can it explain the odd happenings surrounding the Intimidators' summer baseball season and the unusual convergence of events involving Ryne and Major League Baseball history?

About the Author

Randy Floyd has coached youth baseball, football, and basketball for nearly twenty years. He is the former president of Georgetown Youth Baseball in Georgetown, Texas and is the founder and CEO for BallShark. He divides his time between his home in Texas and BallShark headquarters in Florida.

Acknowledgments

Every author owes debts that he simply can't repay. I owe an impossibly large one to my editor, Heather Bonham, who listened for hours to my vision for the BallShark Select Baseball Series even though she knows not a whit about youth baseball. Her enduring patience with me brought the manuscript to life and I am extremely grateful to her.

Works of fiction necessarily embody an author's experiences and although all characters in BallShark are fictitious, there are bits and pieces of actual players that I have coached, parents that I have known, and major leaguers whom I've admired sewn into each personification. If you recognize yourself among any of the BallShark characters that you enjoy, I can assure you that my only intention was to salute you. If you see yourself in any of the characters who represent the often disappointing side of youth baseball, don't worry. I didn't base them on you, but on members of the opposing teams we played.

Finally, I owe the greatest of debts to my family who has given up immeasurable time with me while I gave time to coach, teach, and serve in the most rewarding arena I have known, youth baseball. BallShark will always be a labor of love and writing about the game is something I am simply compelled to do. Thank you for allowing me the time to do it.

55520848R00186

Made in the USA
Middletown, DE
16 July 2019